THE LOST FLEET

VICTORIOUS

THE LOST FLEET

VICTORIOUS

JACK CAMPBELL

TITAN BOOKS

The Lost Fleet: Victorious
ISBN: 9780857681355

Published by
Titan Books
A division of Titan Publishing Group Ltd
144 Southwark St
London
SE1 0UP

First edition: April 2011
10 9 8 7 6 5 4

Planet courtesy of NASA/JPL Caltech; low key portrait of scary looking man © dundanim/shutterstock; 3d alien UFO space ship © Alperium/shutterstock

Visit our website: **www.titanbooks.com**

What did you think of this book? We love to hear from our readers. Please email us at: readerfeedback@titanemail.com, or write to us at the above address.

To receive advance information, news, competitions, and exclusive Titan offers online, please register as a member by clicking the 'sign up' button on our website: www.titanbooks.com

A CIP catalogue record for this title is available from the British Library.

Printed and bound in Great Britain by CPI Group UK Ltd.

To Paul Parsons, a man of great enthusiasms, a great mind, and a great heart, all of which he shared in abundance with the many who will miss him.

For S., as always.

THE ALLIANCE FLEET

CAPTAIN JOHN GEARY, COMMANDING

As reorganized at Varandal Star System prior to offensive actions against the Syndic star system.

Second Battleship Division

Gallant
Indomitable
Glorious
Magnificent

Third Battleship Division

Paladin (Capt Midea) (lost at Lakota)
Orion (Capt Numos)
Majestic (Capt Faresa) (lost at Lakota II)
Conqueror (Capt Casia)
Dreadnaught (Capt Geary)
Dependable

Fourth Battleship Division

Warrior (Capt Kerestes) (lost at Lakota II)
Triumph (lost at Vidha)
Vengeance
Revenge

Fifth Battleship Division

Fearless
Resolution
Redoubtable
Warspite

Seventh Battleship Division (Reconstituted)	Eighth Battleship Division
Indefatigable (lost at Lakota)	Relentless
Audacious (lost at Lakota)	Reprisal (Capt Hiyen)
Defiant (Capt Mosko) (lost at Lakota)	Superb
Sustain	Splendid
Encroach	
Resound	

Tenth Battleship Division	First Scout Battleship Division (Disestablished)
Colossus (Capt Armus)	Arrogant (lost at Kaliban)
Amazon	Exemplar (CDR Vendig) (lost at Heraldo)
Spartan	Braveheart (lost at Cavalos)
Guardian	

First Battle Cruiser Division (Reconstituted)

Courageous (Capt Duellos) (lost at Heradao)
Intrepid (lost at Heradao)
Renown (lost at Lakota)
Formidable
Brilliant (Capt Caligo)
Inspire (Capt Kila)
Implacable (CDR Neeson)

Second Battle Cruiser Division

Leviathan (Capt Tulev)
Dragon
Steadfast
Valiant

Fourth Battle Cruiser Division

Dauntless (flagship) (Capt Desjani)
Daring (Capt Vitali)
Terrible (lost at Ilion)
Victorious
Intemperate

Fifth Battle Cruiser Division (Reconstituted)

Invincible (lost at Ilion)
Repulse (lost in Syndic home system)
Furious (Capt Cresida) (lost at Varandal)
Adroit (Capt Kattnig)
Auspice
Assert
Agile
Ascendant

Sixth Battle Cruiser Division

Seventh Battle Cruiser Division (Disestablished)

Polaris (lost at Vidha)
Vanguard (lost at Vidha)
Illustrious (Capt Badaya)
Incredible (Capt Parr)
Invincible (new construction)

Opportune (lost at Cavalos)

Third Fast Fleet Auxiliaries Division

Titan (CDR Lommand)
Tanuki (Capt Smyth)
Witch (Capt Tyrosian)
Jinn
Alchemist
Goblin (lost at Heradao)

Thirty-seven heavy cruisers in seven divisions (Thirty-seven when Geary first assumed command, minus sixteen lost in battle, plus nine reinforcements at Varandal)

First Heavy Cruiser Division
Third Heavy Cruiser Division
Fourth Heavy Cruiser Division
Fifth Heavy Cruiser Division
Eighth Heavy Cruiser Division
Tenth Heavy Cruiser Division

Minus

Invidious (lost at Kaliban)

Cuirass (lost at Sutrah)

Crest, War-Coat, Ram and **Citadel** (lost at Vidha)

Basinet and **Sallet** (lost at Lakota)

Utap, Vambrace, and **Fascine** (lost at Lakota II)

Armet and **Gusoku** (lost at Cavalos)

Tortoise, Breech, Kurtani, Tarian, and **Nodowa**
  (lost at Heradao)

Lorica (lost at Padronis)

Kaidate and **Quillion** (lost at Varandal)

**Fifty-two light cruisers in ten squadrons (Sixty-two
when Geary first assumed command, minus twenty-
two lost in battle, plus twelve reinforcements at
Varandal)**

First Light Cruiser Squadron
Second Light Cruiser Squadron
Third Light Cruiser Squadron
Fifth Light Cruiser Squadron
Sixth Light Cruiser Squadron
Eighth Light Cruiser Squadron
Ninth Light Cruiser Squadron
Tenth Light Cruiser Squadron
Eleventh Light Cruiser Squadron
Fourteenth Light Cruiser Squadron

Minus

Swift (lost at Kaliban)

Pommel, Sling, Bolo, and **Staff** (lost at Vidha)

Spur, Damascene, and **Swept-Guard** (lost at Lakota)

Brigandine, Carte, and **Ote** (lost at Lakota II)

Kote and **Cercle** (lost at Cavalos)

Kissaki, Crest, Trunnion, Inquarto, Intagliata, and **Septime** (lost at Heradao)

Estocade, Disarm, and **Cavalier** (lost at Varandal)

One hundred fifty destroyers in eighteen squadrons (one hundred eighty-three when Geary first assumed command, minus forty-seven lost in battle, plus fourteen reinforcements at Varandal)

First Destroyer Squadron

Second Destroyer Squadron

Third Destroyer Squadron

Fourth Destroyer Squadron

Sixth Destroyer Squadron

Seventh Destroyer Squadron

Ninth Destroyer Squadron

Tenth Destroyer Squadron

Twelfth Destroyer Squadron

Fourteenth Destroyer Squadron

Sixteenth Destroyer Squadron

Seventeenth Destroyer Squadron

Twentieth Destroyer Squadron

Twenty-first Destroyer Squadron

Twenty-third Destroyer Squadron
Twenty-seventh Destroyer Squadron
Twenty-eighth Destroyer Squadron
Thirty-second Destroyer Squadron

Minus
Dagger and **Venom** (lost at Kaliban)
Anelace, Baselard, and **Mace** (lost at Sutrah)
**Celt, Akhu, Sickle, Leaf, Bolt, Sabot, Flint, Needle, Dart,
Sting, Limpet,** and **Cudgel** (lost at Vidha)
Falcata (lost at Ilion)
War-Hammer, Prasa, Talwar, and **Xiphos** (lost at
Lakota)
War-Hammer, Prasa, Talwar, and **Xiphos** (lost at Lakota)
Armlet, Flanconade, Kukri, Hastarii, Petard, and
Spiculum (lost at Lakota II)
Flail, Ndziga, Tabar, Cestus, and **Balta** (lost at Cavalos)
**Barb, Yatagan, Lunge, Arabas, Kururi, Shail, Chamber,
Bayonet,** and **Tomahawk** (lost at Heradao)
Serpentine, Basilisk, Bowie, Guidon, and **Sten** (lost at
Varandal)

Second Fleet Marine Force -
Major General Carabali commanding (acting)

1,420 Marines divided into detachments on battle cruisers
and battleships

1

He had faced death many times and would cheerfully do so again rather than attend this briefing.

"You're not going to face a firing squad," Captain Tanya Desjani reminded him. "You're going to brief the Alliance grand council."

Captain John Geary turned his head slightly to look directly at Captain Desjani, commanding officer of Geary's flagship, the battle cruiser *Dauntless*. "Remind me again of the difference."

"The politicians aren't supposed to be carrying weapons, and they're more afraid of you than you are of them. Relax. If they see you this tense, they'll believe you really are planning a coup." Desjani made a face. "You should know that they're accompanied by Admiral Otropa."

"Admiral Otropa?" Geary had literally been out of the loop for a century, so his knowledge of current officers was limited to those in the ships of the fleet itself.

Desjani nodded, somehow investing the simple gesture with

disdain that obviously wasn't aimed at Geary.

"Military aide to the grand council. Don't worry about the grand council trying to hand command of the fleet to him. No one would accept Otropa the Anvil as fleet commander in place of you."

Geary looked back at his reflection, feeling nervous and uncomfortable in his dress uniform. He had never enjoyed briefings, and a hundred years ago he would never have imagined that he would be called upon personally to brief the grand council. "The Anvil? That sounds like a strong nickname."

"He's called the Anvil because he's been beaten so often," Desjani explained. "With his political talents far exceeding his military skills, Otropa finally figured out that the position of military aide to the grand council was risk-free."

Geary almost choked as he tried to swallow a laugh. "I guess there are worse nicknames than Black Jack."

"Many worse ones." Out of the corner of his eye, Geary saw Desjani cock her head to one side questioningly. "You've never told me how you picked up the Black Jack name or why you don't like it. Like every schoolkid in the Alliance, I learned the official story in your biographies, but that story doesn't explain your feelings about the nickname."

He glanced her way. "What's the official story?" Since being awakened from survival sleep in a lost and damaged escape pod, he'd made an effort to avoid reading the authorized accounts of his supposed heroic nature.

"That you never got a red deficiency or failure mark in evaluations of yourself or any units under your command," Desjani explained. "Your marks were always 'meets or exceeds expectations' black, hence Black Jack."

"Ancestors preserve us." Geary tried to keep from breaking into laughter. "Anyone who really looked at my records would know that wasn't true."

"So what is the truth?"

"I should have at least one secret from you."

"As long as it's a personal secret. The captain of your flagship needs to know all of your professional secrets." She paused before speaking again. "This meeting with the grand council. Have you told me everything? Are you going to do as you told me?"

"Yes, and yes." He turned to face her fully, letting his worries show. As commander of the fleet, Geary had been forced to project confidence publicly no matter how bad things got. Desjani was one of the few people to whom he could reveal his qualms. "It'll be a tightrope act. I need to convince them of what we have to do, convince them to order me to do it, and not make them think I'm taking over the government."

Desjani nodded, seeming not the least bit concerned herself. "You'll do fine, sir. I'll go make sure everything is ready at the shuttle dock for your flight to Ambaru station while you straighten up your uniform." She saluted with careful precision, then pivoted and left.

Geary kept his eyes on the hatch to his stateroom after it had shut behind Desjani. He'd have the perfect professional relationship with Tanya Desjani except for the fact that he'd done the incredibly unprofessional thing of falling in love with her. Not that he'd ever openly said that, or ever would. Not while she was his subordinate. It didn't help that she apparently felt the same way about him, even though neither of them could openly speak of it or act on it in any way. That should have felt like a small problem in a universe a century removed from his own, where the Alliance believed him to be a mythical hero returned from the dead, where an unwinnable war had been raging for that entire century between the Alliance and the Syndicate Worlds, and where the worn-out citizens of the Alliance were so disgusted with their own political leaders that they would have welcomed him declaring himself dictator. Sometimes, though, that "small" personal problem felt like the hardest thing to endure.

He focused back on his reflection, not able to spot any imperfections in his uniform but knowing that Desjani wouldn't have dropped that broad hint about straightening up if she hadn't seen something. Scowling, Geary moved a few things a fraction of a millimeter, his eyes going to the multipointed Alliance Star hanging just beneath his collar. He didn't like wearing the medal awarded him after his supposed death in a last-stand battle a century ago, not feeling that he had really earned such an honor, but regulations demanded that an officer in dress uniform wear "all insignia, decorations, awards, ribbons, and medals to which that officer is entitled." He couldn't afford to pick and choose which regulations to follow because he knew that he had the power to do just that, and if he started, he had no idea where it might end.

As he began to leave, his comm alert sounded. Geary slapped the acknowledgment and saw the image of Captain Badaya appear, smiling confidently and apparently standing before Geary even though Badaya was physically still located aboard his own ship. "Good morning, Captain." Badaya beamed.

"Thanks. I was just about to leave to meet with the grand council."
He had to handle Badaya carefully. Although Badaya technically
was simply commanding officer of the battle cruiser *Illustrious*, he
also led the faction of the fleet that would, without a second thought,
back Geary as military dictator. Since that faction made up almost
the entire fleet now, Geary had to ensure they didn't launch such
a coup. Since assuming command of the fleet, he had gone from
worrying about mutiny against himself to worrying about mutiny
against the Alliance itself in his name.

Badaya nodded, his smile getting harder. "Some of the captains
wanted to move some battleships over near Ambaru station just to
remind the grand council who's really in charge, but I told them
that wasn't how you were playing it."

"Exactly," Geary agreed, trying not to sound too relieved. "We
have to maintain the image that the grand council is still in charge."
That was the cover story he was using with Badaya anyway. If the
grand council ordered Geary to do something the fleet knew Geary
wouldn't have chosen to do, Geary would feel obligated to follow
those orders or resign, and all hell would probably break loose.

"Rione will help you handle them," Badaya noted with a
dismissive gesture. "You've got her in your pocket, and she'll keep
the other politicians in line. Since you say time is tight, I'd better
let you go, sir." With a final parting grin and a salute, Badaya's
image vanished.

Geary shook his head, wondering what Madam Co-President of
the Callas Republic and Senator of the Alliance Victoria Rione
would do if she heard Badaya saying Rione was in Geary's pocket.
Nothing good, that was certain.

He walked through the passageways of *Dauntless* toward the shuttle dock, returning enthusiastic salutes from the crew members he passed. *Dauntless* had been his flagship since he'd assumed command of the fleet in the Syndic home star system, the Alliance fleet trapped deep inside enemy territory and apparently doomed. Against all odds, he'd brought most of those ships home, and their crews believed he could do anything. Even win a war their parents and grandparents had also fought. He did his best to look outwardly calm and confident despite his own internal turmoil.

But Geary couldn't help frowning slightly as he finally reached the shuttle dock. Desjani and Rione were both there, standing close together and apparently speaking softly to each other, their expressions impassive. Since the two women usually exchanged words only under the direst necessity and often had seemed ready to go at it with knives, pistols, hell lances, and any other available weapon, Geary couldn't help wondering why they were getting along all of a sudden.

Desjani stepped toward him as he approached, while Rione went through the hatch into the dock. "The shuttle and your escort are ready," Desjani reported. She frowned slightly as she examined him, reaching to make tiny adjustments to some of his ribbons. "The fleet will be standing by."

"Tanya, I'm counting on you, Duellos, and Tulev to keep things from going nova. Badaya should be working with you to keep anyone in the fleet from overreacting and causing a disaster, but you three also need to make sure Badaya doesn't overreact."

She nodded calmly. "Of course, sir. But you do realize that none of us will be able to hold things back if the grand council overreacts." Stepping closer, Desjani lowered her voice and rested one hand on his forearm, a rare gesture, which emphasized her words. "Listen to her. This is her battlefield, her weapons."

"Rione?" He had never expected to hear Desjani urging him to pay attention to Rione's advice.

"Yes." Stepping back again, Desjani saluted, only her eyes betraying her worries. "Good luck, sir."

He returned the salute and walked into the dock. Nearby, the bulk of a fleet shuttle loomed, an entire platoon of Marines forming an honor guard on either side of its loading ramp.

An entire platoon of Marines in full battle armor, with complete weapons loadout.

Before he could say anything, a Marine major stepped forward and saluted. "I'm assigned to command your honor guard, Captain Geary. We'll accompany you to the meeting with the grand council."

"Why are your troops in battle armor?" Geary asked.

The major didn't hesitate at all. "Varandal Star System remains in Attack Imminent alert status, sir. Regulations require my troops to be at maximum combat readiness when participating in official movements under such an alert status."

How convenient. Geary glanced toward Rione, who didn't seem the least bit surprised at the combat footing of the Marines. Desjani had obviously been in on this, too. But then Colonel Carabali, the fleet's Marine commander, must have approved of the decision as well. Despite his own misgivings at arriving to speak to his political superiors with a combat-ready force at his back, Geary decided that trying to override the collective judgment of Desjani, Rione, and

Carabali wasn't likely to be wise. "Very well. Thank you, Major."

The Marines raised their weapons to present arms as Geary walked up the ramp, Rione beside him, bringing his arm up in a salute acknowledging the honors being rendered him. At times like this, when he seemed to have been saluting constantly for an hour, even he wondered at the wisdom of having reintroduced that gesture of respect into the fleet.

He and Rione went through to the small VIP cabin just aft of the pilots' cockpit, the Marines filing in behind them to take seats in the shuttle's main compartment. Geary strapped in, gazing at the display panel before him, where a remote image showed stars glittering against the endless night of space. It might have been a window, if anyone had been crazy enough to put a physical window in the hull of a ship or a shuttle.

"Nervous?" Rione asked.

"Can't you tell?"

"Not really. You're doing a good job."

"Thanks. What were you and Desjani plotting about when I got to the shuttle dock?"

"Just some girl talk," Rione said airily, waving a negligent hand. "War, the fate of humanity, the nature of the universe. That sort of thing."

"Did you reach any conclusions I should know about?"

She gave him a cool look, then smiled with apparently genuine reassurance. "We think you'll do fine as long as you are yourself. Both of us have your back. Feel better?"

"Much better, thank you." Status lights revealed the shuttle's ramp rising and sealing, the inner dock doors closing, the outer doors opening, then the shuttle rose, pivoted in place with jaunty smoothness, and tore out into space. Geary felt himself grinning. Autopilots could drive a shuttle technically as well as any human, and better in many cases, but only humans could put a real sense of style into their piloting. On his display, the shape of *Dauntless* dwindled rapidly as the shuttle accelerated. "This is the first time I've been off *Dauntless*," he suddenly realized.

"Since your survival pod was picked up, you mean," Rione corrected.

"Yeah." His former home and former acquaintances were gone, vanished into a past a century old. *Dauntless* had become his home, her crew his family. It felt odd to leave them.

The journey seemed very brief, the huge shapes of Ambaru space station's exterior structures looming near as the shuttle slid gently toward its assigned dock. Moments later, the shuttle grounded. Geary watched until the status lights indicated that the dock was pressurized, then took a deep breath, stood up, straightened his uniform yet again, and nodded to Rione. "Let's go." Rione nodded back at him, something about her feeling both familiar and yet out of place. Geary realized that Rione was exhibiting the same manner Desjani showed when combat loomed. Like Desjani facing Syndic warships, Rione seemed in her element at that instant, ready to do battle in her own way.

The dock was much larger than the one on *Dauntless*, but the first thing that Geary registered was that his Marine honor guard had deployed around the ramp in a circular formation, facing outward, their weapons in ready positions rather than at present arms and their armor sealed. Raising his gaze, Geary saw that on three sides of the shuttle dock the bulkheads were lined with what seemed to be an entire company of ground forces, all of them armed but none of them armored, the ground troops staring nervously at the Marines.

So Rione had been right. She'd warned him that the grand council might try to arrest him immediately and isolate him from the fleet, in the belief that he would want to become a dictator. Feeling a tight coldness inside at the insult to his honor, Geary stalked down the ramp to where a familiar shape waited. He'd never actually met Admiral Timbale, but he had received several messages from the man, every one begging off any conversation and completely deferring to Geary.

He stopped in front of Timbale and saluted, holding the gesture as Timbale stared back in momentary confusion. Then a light of understanding appeared in Timbale's eyes, and he hastily sketched a crude return salute. "C-captain Geary. W-welcome aboard Ambaru station."

"Thank you, sir." Geary's flat words echoed in the otherwise-silent dock.

Rione came up beside him. "Admiral, I suggest you disperse your honor guard now that they have greeted Captain Geary."

Timbale stared back at her, then at the Marines, a drop of sweat running down one side of his face. "I..."

"Perhaps if you contacted grand council chair Senator Navarro, he would modify whatever your original orders were?" Rione suggested.

"Yes." Backpedaling with ill-concealed relief, Timbale muttered into his comm unit, waited, then muttered again. Forcing a smile, the admiral nodded to Rione, then turned toward the ground forces arrayed along the bulk-heads. "Colonel, return your troops to their quarters." The ground-forces officer stepped forward, her mouth open in apparent protest. "Just do it, Colonel!" Timbale snapped.

The ground-forces soldiers pivoted in response to their orders and filed out, more than one of them casting awed glances toward Geary before they left. He wondered what would have happened if he had simply given orders directly to those soldiers. Would they have done what Black Jack ordered? The thought brought a tight sense of worry as the reality of what he could do, of what he might cause to happen if he didn't handle things right, came home to him clearly.

When the last ground-forces soldier had left, Geary looked to his Marine major. Now what? Bring his escort with him? Bring some of them? What reason did he have to believe that more ground-forces troops wouldn't appear and try to arrest him again as soon as he left the dock? Prudence dictated taking at least some of the Marines with him.

Which would also mean walking into the presence of the grand council with armed and armored Marines at his back. To anyone watching or hearing, such an action would scream two things: an imminent coup and a fundamental distrust on Geary's part of the Alliance's political leaders. The impact of those things could destroy everything he hoped to achieve and trigger the coup he feared.

But if he was arrested, the fleet would act, no matter his expressed wishes.

Rione was watching him, apparently relaxed. She wouldn't tell him what to do now, not with so many others watching and listening, but her attitude conveyed a message. Confidence. Calm.

Taking a deep breath, Geary nodded to the Marine commander. "Stay here. Stand easy. I don't know how long we'll be."

"Sir?" The Marine major gestured to his troops. "We can send a squad—"

"No." Geary looked around, trying to act like a man with nothing on his conscience and no reason to fear his superiors. "We're on friendly territory, Major. We're among friends. Citizens of the Alliance need not fear their government or each other." He didn't know who was listening, but whoever it was should understand what that meant.

The major saluted. "Yes, sir."

Timbale had his eyes on Geary, too, puzzlement there along with concern. "Could you inform me as to your intentions, Captain?" the admiral asked quietly.

"I've been ordered to report to the grand council, sir. I intend to follow orders." Would Timbale recognize the greater significance of that last statement?

Rione gestured toward the interior of the station. "We shouldn't keep the grand council waiting, Admiral."

Admiral Timbale looked from her to Geary, then seemed to reach a decision. "Just a moment, please." He stepped to one side, speaking rapidly into his comm unit, waiting, then speaking again in angry tones. Finally satisfied, he turned back to Geary. "There shouldn't be any more hindrances to your reaching the grand council, Captain. Please accompany me."

Geary allowed Rione to fall in beside Timbale, then walked behind them as the group left the hangar. Most of his nerves had vanished, a cold fury at the grand council's assumption that he would act dishonorably driving away any doubts. Following Timbale, he and Rione walked through a maze of passages and spaces. Like many orbital stations, Ambaru had grown by adding successive layers. Unsurprisingly, the grand council had chosen a meeting room in the innermost and therefore most secure part of the station.

As Geary entered the room, he saw that one wall was given over to a very large virtual window into space, as if the room were on the outer edges of the station. Floating over the large conference table was a star display, while off to the other side a miniature representation of the fleet and other ships in Varandal Star System hovered. Behind the table sat seven men and women in civilian clothes, while to one side of them a ground-forces general and an admiral stood uncomfortably.

Geary had held many conferences since assuming command of the fleet, but this one was different. Unlike in the fleet conference room on *Dauntless*, everyone present was actually, physically there rather than most attending through virtual meeting software. More importantly, this time Geary wasn't the senior officer present. He hadn't realized how used to that status he'd become in the months since assuming command of the fleet as it teetered on the edge of destruction. But Geary realized that perhaps the most disturbing difference here was that Captain Tanya Desjani wasn't present. He'd grown very used to her presence, her support, and her advice at critical meetings.

Geary marched to a point opposite the center of the table and saluted. "Captain John Geary, acting commander of the Alliance

Fleet, reporting," he announced with rigid formality.

A tall, lean civilian in the center of the council nodded and made a vague gesture. "Thank you, Captain Geary."

"Who," another male politician demanded, "appointed you acting fleet commander, Captain?"

Geary kept his gaze on the bulkhead as he answered. "Admiral Bloch appointed me to the position in the Syndicate Worlds' home star system immediately prior to his leaving the fleet to conduct negotiations on the Syndic flagship, sir. When he died, I retained the position based on my seniority within the fleet."

"You already knew that," a short, stout female politician muttered to her colleague.

The man who'd first spoken gestured the others to silence, then glared as two began to talk anyway. "The council chair is speaking," he snapped. After staring down some defiant looks from the other politicians, the man gazed steadily at Geary for a long moment before talking again. "Why are you here, Captain?"

"To present my report on recent operations while the fleet was under my command and out of contact with Alliance authorities," Geary recited, "and to provide recommendations for future operations."

"Recommendations?" The tall civilian leaned back, his eyes searching Geary, then they shifted suddenly to Rione. "Madam Co-President, on your oath to the Alliance, does he mean that?"

"He does."

The ground-forces general spoke abruptly. "He's separated from those treasonous Marines, Senator Navarro. We can arrest him now. Get him off this station and out of Varandal before anyone——"

"No." Senator Navarro shook his head. "I was at best ambivalent about what was presented as a simple security precaution. Now having met this man, I am certain it would have been a mistake."

"This is a decision for the entire council to make," a thin woman broke in.

"I agree with Senator Navarro," the stout woman replied, drawing some startled looks, which told Geary she didn't customarily support Navarro.

Another male council member shook his head belligerently. "He boarded this station with a Marine assault force—"

"A wise precaution, wasn't it?" the stout woman shot back.

"We can stop this now!" the general insisted. "Stop him in his tracks!"

Senator Navarro's hand struck the table with a blow hard enough to echo around the room, bringing momentary silence. Navarro gave hard looks around the table, then fastened his gaze on the general. "Stop *what*, General Firgani? Tell me, why would Captain Geary have left those Marines at the shuttle dock if he intended acting against us here and now?" The general glowered silently at Geary, while Navarro fixed another look on him as well. "Captain Geary, I think we've barely avoided a very serious mistake. The Alliance has never arrested its citizens for crimes they haven't yet committed, especially not when they have given no signs of intent to commit such crimes, and especially not citizens who have done such a service to the Alliance as you have. My apologies, Captain." Navarro rose and bowed slightly toward Geary, as the general's glower deepened, and some of the other council members displayed annoyance.

"Thank you, sir," Geary replied, some of his anger dissipating at the courteous treatment from Navarro. "I was dismayed to have my honor called into question."

The other male senator who had challenged Geary made a barely audible noise of derision, but Navarro ignored him, turning to the general and the admiral beside him. "Captain Geary will present his report to the council now. General Firgani, Admiral Otropa, Admiral Timbale, please monitor the situation in Varandal Star System while we are closeted in here with Captain Geary and Senator Rione."

The three officers started to leave, with varying degrees of success in hiding their disappointment at the abrupt dismissal, but Geary spoke up. He had no reason to think kindly of General Firgani or to respect whatever opinions Admiral Otropa might generate, but Admiral Timbale had never crossed him, in fact had helped ensure that the fleet's ships got everything they needed, and had apparently ensured that Geary could reach this room without being arrested. "Sir, if I may so request, I would appreciate Admiral Timbale's presence while I make my report. As an operational fleet officer who observed the engagement with the Syndicate Worlds' flotilla in this star system, he might be able to add to some aspects of my reporting."

Navarro raised one eyebrow but gestured to the startled Timbale to remain. "All right, Captain Geary."

Admiral Otropa stared wide-eyed from Timbale to Geary to Navarro. "I should not be excluded from this meeting if officers junior to me are present."

Some of the council began to speak, but Navarro cut them off with a sharp voice and a weary expression. "Certainly, Admiral.

30

Stay. General," he added, as Firgani appeared ready to press his own claim to be present, "since you are concerned about the security of the council, you should personally keep an eye on events outside. Thank you."

"But, Senator—" Firgani began.

"Thank you."

Firgani flushed slightly, then marched out of the room. Admiral Timbale edged slightly away from Admiral Otropa, then both officers stood silently as Navarro turned back to Geary and spoke with renewed control. "Captain, we're all familiar with the outlines of your report, but we understand that there's a lot more to be told. Please do so."

Geary reached to the display controls on the table and plugged in his comm unit, not trusting to the security of any wireless link even here. The star field vanished, replaced by images burned into his memory, a sphere of battered Alliance ships behind a wall of less badly damaged warships, both formations facing a curved Syndic arrangement of warships with overwhelming superiority in numbers. The situation in the Syndic home star system at the point he assumed command of what was left of the Alliance fleet after it had fought its way through the initial Syndic ambush. Geary's memories of the time after he had been awakened and leading up to that crisis were dimmed behind the barriers of post-traumatic stress that he had been battling, trying to adjust to learning that he had been frozen in survival sleep for a century. But everything came into focus after that, driven by the demands placed on him once he assumed command. Taking a deep breath to calm himself, Geary began reciting his report.

He faltered at one point. "I directed the fleet to withdraw toward the jump exit for Corvus Star System. During that withdrawal, the battle cruiser *Repulse* sacrificed herself to keep the leading Syndic elements from catching and destroying other Alliance warships before they could jump." *Repulse*, commanded by his grandnephew Michael Geary, a man older than he was, bitter from a lifetime growing up in the shadow of the legendary Black Jack Geary.

The heavyset woman broke in. "Do you know if Commander Michael Geary survived the loss of his ship?"

"No, ma'am, I do not."

She nodded with exaggerated sympathy, but another senator spoke in demanding tones. "You brought back the Syndic hypernet key provided by the Syndic traitor?"

"Yes, sir," Geary confirmed, wondering why the question was posed in an accusing manner.

"Why didn't you use it again? Why didn't you get the fleet home quickly that way?" the senator pressed.

"Because the Syndics could easily reinforce star systems with hypernet gates along our path," Geary explained in what he hoped were patient tones. "We knew we had to get that key safely back to Alliance space, but getting it back meant avoiding Syndic hypernet gates. We did attempt to use it at Sancere, but the Syndics fired upon their own hypernet gate and caused it to collapse before we could."

"It's useless, then." The senator looked around belligerently, as if challenging anyone to contradict him.

"No," Geary said in what he hoped was a firm but respectful tone. "It's critically important. The key has been analyzed and duplicates are being manufactured though I've been informed that will take some time. The original has been returned to *Dauntless*, where it will continue to offer us the huge benefit of being able to use the enemy's own hypernet. The only way the Syndics could negate that advantage is by collapsing their entire hypernet, which would itself give the Alliance a tremendous economic and military advantage. There are other issues that I will address—"

"I want to know *now*—" the senator began.

Navarro broke in as well, his own voice sharp. "We will allow Captain Geary to make his report, then any questions it raises will be dealt with."

"But these reports about hypernet gate collapses—"

"We will address that after the report," Navarro insisted. The other man looked around as if seeking support, but apparently saw none and subsided, with a sulky glare at Navarro.

Geary continued, the display shifting to show the Alliance fleet's passage through Corvus Star System, then onward to star system after star system, battle after battle, Geary dryly reciting declining fuel-cell reserves and food supplies and desperate engagements against the Syndic attempts to trap the Alliance fleet once more.

Admiral Otropa, clearly unused to standing quietly while another officer was in the spotlight, listened with obviously growing impatience until he took advantage of a pause in Geary's narrative to interrupt. "Members of the grand council, I do not believe Captain Geary is accurately depicting the course of these battles."

Everyone turned to Otropa with varying expressions, but only Rione spoke. "Indeed, Admiral? Are you arguing that the logs of Alliance warships and the reports of their commanding officers have been falsified to that extent?" she asked in a deceptively mild tone.

"Yes!" Otropa nodded vigorously. "Our ancestors knew the secret of winning, all-out attack, with every captain competing to see who could display the most valor and strike the enemy first and hardest. These victories we're being told about violate those principles! They cannot be true, not if we honor our ancestors."

Geary stared at Otropa in disbelief, only slowly becoming aware that everyone else was watching him, waiting for his response to the admiral, who looked back at Geary with a smug expression. "Admiral," Geary began slowly, "my own honor has been called into question by the charges you have just made without any evidence to support them. You have also questioned the honor of every officer and sailor in the fleet. I have never suggested that they lack valor, that they ever failed to press the enemy to the utmost. The ships and crews lost during our long journey home are a testament stronger than any words I could say to the courage of our personnel."

"I'm not—" Otropa began.

"I'm not finished, Admiral." Geary had been dealing with recalcitrant officers long enough while in command of the fleet not to want to suffer Otropa gladly, superior rank or not. For a moment, he was seeing Numos blunder at Kaliban, Falco leading ships to their deaths at Vidha, Midea charging *Paladin* blindly into destruction at Lakota, and all his patience with fools had fled. "Our ancestors fought with wisdom as well as courage. I know. I was there. They made their battles and their sacrifices count. I had the honor to command the ships in our current fleet and the men and women of their crews, and I had the honor to show them how our ancestors truly fought. In battle the competition is against the enemy, not against each other. Within the teamwork of a well-trained and disciplined fleet, there is abundant room for individual courage and competitiveness, but not at the cost of our duty to the people and worlds we protect."

Otropa frowned, seeming to be searching for a reply. Beside him, Admiral Timbale didn't show any signs of being interested in coming to his assistance, instead gazing off into a corner of the room as if disassociating himself from his fellow admiral.

The stout woman chuckled. "Do you have any proof for your assertions that the fleet records displayed here have been falsified?" she asked Otropa mockingly.

"No, Madam Senator," the admiral got out in a strangled voice. "But these results, to claim to have destroyed so many enemy ships while losing so few of our own—"

"Then perhaps we should allow Captain Geary to continue his presentation while you go in search of such evidence," she suggested.

Otropa reddened, but Senator Navarro nodded and jerked his chin toward the door.

After Otropa had left, Geary waited an uncomfortable moment, then continued, finally adding the highly classified portions of his presentation, what was known and reasonably conjectured to be known about the alien race beyond Syndic space. The expressions of the civilian politicians betrayed first disbelief, then growing worry. When Geary explained how the aliens had tried to ensure the Alliance fleet's destruction at Lakota Star System, one of the other women shook her head. "If there were any other explanation,

Captain, I wouldn't spend five seconds believing this."

Geary twisted his mouth. "Believe me, ma'am, if there were any other explanation, we would have jumped on it just as quickly as you would have."

When he explained the alien worms in the navigational and communications systems on the Alliance warships, Timbale's jaw dropped, and Senator Navarro lurched forward. "You found these worms? Our own ships have been sending their positions to these... whatever they are?"

"We haven't figured out how they work," Geary added. "We did come up with a means to scrub them from our systems in the fleet, but we have to assume that other Alliance ships and installations are riddled with similar worms. The Syndics', too."

"I wonder why none of us knew this before now?" the thin man asked in a bland way that made Navarro's expression tighten slightly.

"We weren't looking," Rione answered. "None of us were looking. Not for something like that, which is so much more advanced than anything we or the Syndics have."

"Maybe not," the thin woman replied. "Though the reasons we weren't looking doubtless varied."

The stout woman laughed. "Is that a comment on the intellects or the morals of your fellow council members, Suva?"

Navarro managed to get the group quiet again, his displeasure more and more obvious. "Please continue, Captain Geary."

Everyone flinched when Geary replayed the destruction of Lakota Star System after Syndic warships guarding its hypernet gate destroyed that gate. "We were lucky here. As I described in my earlier reports, experts have stated that the potential level of energy discharge from a collapsing hypernet gate ranges up to nova scale." The politicians cringed some more. "We believe that the aliens have the capability to cause spontaneous collapses of hypernet gates anywhere in Alliance or Syndicate Worlds' space. That seems the only explanation for what happened at Kalixa."

Timbale nodded rapidly. "We managed to shove a scout through to Kalixa. It just got back. The star system has been totally devastated."

Senator Navarro, who had one hand over his eyes, slowly lowered it. "Then you weren't really concerned about spontaneous collapses as the message broadcast by the fleet when it arrived at Varandal said. You were worried that these aliens would start causing collapses of hypernet gates."

"Yes, sir. As they did at Kalixa. I thought it best not to broadcast that information, however."

The thin woman shook her head. "You caused enough panic with what you did send to everyone. Those images from Lakota scared the hell out of everybody."

Rione answered. "It was judged important to motivate everyone to get safe-fail systems on their hypernet gates as soon as possible."

"You certainly achieved that," Navarro agreed. He blew out a long breath. "Just before this meeting, I was informed that the hypernet gate at Petit Star System has collapsed. It took them a little while to jump a ship to the next star system with a hypernet gate and get word here. Thanks to the safe-fail system they had finished installing twelve hours prior to that, the resulting energy discharge was only on the level of a midrange solar flare."

Admiral Timbale glanced at Geary. "We've built a lot of shipyards at Petit in the last fifty years. Aside from being heavily populated, it's important to the Alliance war effort. If what I saw of Kalixa had happened at Petit, it would have been a horrible tragedy and a horrible blow to our defenses."

"Do all Alliance star systems with hypernet gates have safe-fail systems installed?" Rione asked.

"They should," Navarro replied. "We haven't had time to get confirmation back from all planets, but even the gate at Sol Star System should have a safe-fail in place now, and that's at the farthest extent of the Alliance hypernet."

A short male senator bared his teeth. "We've got the war-winning weapon at last! We have these safe-collapse systems, and the Syndics don't! We can destroy their gates and wipe out their star systems and—"

"Are you insane?" the thin female senator named Suva interrupted. "You saw what one gate did at Lakota."

"But it could win the war," the heavyset female senator agreed reluctantly.

Geary could see them wavering, just as he and his most trusted officers and Rione had guessed. Presented with an inhuman weapon that offered a means to end the century-long war, the leaders of the Alliance were seriously considering setting off novas in human-occupied star systems. But before he could say anything, Rione spoke. "No, it can't. The Syndics also know their gates can collapse, and they certainly already have similar safe-collapse systems installed on them."

"Certainly?" another senator asked Rione.

"Yes," Rione replied flatly. "We know the Syndics have them."

"I feel compelled to add," Geary said, "that I would resign my commission rather than carry out orders to collapse hypernet gates with a goal of wiping out human-occupied star systems."

Navarro shook his head. "Resign your commission? You wouldn't simply refuse the order?"

"Refusal of a lawful order is not an option under Alliance fleet regulations, sir. I would remind you as well, sir, that destroying a hypernet gate requires warships close by firing upon its tethers. Destruction of those warships is a certainty."

"A suicide mission," Navarro commented.

"But look at what could be gained!" another senator insisted. "The people and the armed forces of the Alliance expect us to make the hard decisions necessary to win this war! If that means trying to use the Syndic hypernet gates as weapons at the cost of the Alliance warships sent on such missions—"

"They expect us to use some wisdom when we make decisions about spending their lives," Navarro countered. "You may consider it hard to decide to send people to their deaths, but I'm fairly confident that it's a lot harder on those who do the dying."

"We need to win! Some of us may not *want* victory—"

"There are no grounds for making charges like that against any member of the council!" another senator countered.

"No *proof* perhaps—" another senator chimed in.

"I wonder"—Navarro's voice cut across the debate—"if the Alliance wouldn't be better off if those Marines had followed Captain Geary in here." In the shocked silence that followed, Navarro fixed each senator in turn with a hard look. "We could win by wiping out human-occupied star systems? At what cost? At what cost to our own humanity?" The senators stared at each other, none seeming to have a ready answer to that. Finally, Senator Navarro shrugged. "It seems the option of using the hypernet gates as weapons no longer exists for anyone, so there's no need for such a decision or argument. Personally, I thank my ancestors I don't have to make that decision, and I thank the living stars that the threat to us has been contained."

Navarro paused, his eyes once again on Geary. "It occurs to me that the knowledge of the threat posed by the gates, and how to use them as weapons, would have been an unstoppable advantage to anyone seeking to gain control of the Alliance government or to exploit the hysteria that collapsing gates within Alliance space would have caused. Instead, you gave us that knowledge."

"It never occurred to him to do otherwise," Rione remarked. "He requires politicians to point out such options, but fortunately he disregards such possibilities."

"Fortunate, indeed," Navarro agreed dryly. "I'll need to give thanks to my ancestors tonight. You could have held on to that Syndic hypernet key as well, since it offers such a great advantage to any Alliance force. You could have made yourself indispensable, Captain."

Geary wondered how much of his reaction showed. "The last thing I want is to be indispensable, sir."

"Some people seek it as a guarantee of job security, Captain Geary. Continue with your report, please."

There wasn't much left by that point. Geary ran through the last engagements, finally bringing his account up to the battle at

Varandal, when his fleet made it home. "You're certain the Syndics planned to collapse the hypernet gate here in revenge for the gate collapse at Kalixa?" the heavyset woman demanded.

"That's our best estimate, Madam Senator, and is consistent with Syndic actions during that period. I wish to add that the valiant defense of Varandal by the Alliance personnel and warships here prior to and after our arrival may well have made all the difference in foiling the Syndic plan."

Navarro turned to Admiral Timbale. "What did the prisoners from the Syndics' ships destroyed here tell us about this? They're from that reserve flotilla, aren't they?"

Timbale pressed his lips together as he formulated his answer. "Most didn't appear to know anything, or why they had been stationed along that border so far from the Alliance. There seem to have been widespread rumors of a mysterious enemy, but no certain knowledge among most Syndic personnel. Under interrogation, a few of the most senior prisoners revealed that they did intend collapsing the hypernet gate here to wipe out this star system in retaliation for Kalixa. They also betrayed awareness of an intelligent nonhuman species on the far side of Syndic space from the Alliance. We were able to confirm that had been their mission, to defend against that species. But they don't seem to know any specifics about these aliens, nothing that we can get them to say or trick out of them, anyway."

"But they confirmed such a race exists?" another senator asked.

"Yes, Senator, they did. That is, their brain patterns betrayed that in response to our questioning."

"And that this race is hostile?"

Timbale hesitated. "The Syndic prisoners wouldn't say anything, but they were clearly worried about these aliens." He glanced at Geary with a tight smile. "The fact that the Syndics kept a powerful naval force tied up so far from the Alliance is to me strong evidence that the Syndics don't trust the aliens."

Senator Suva shook her head. "Why haven't previous prisoner interrogations revealed the existence of this race? We've captured the occasional Syndic CEO before."

Rione answered. "Nobody was asking those questions. Why would they? We didn't know of any reasons to inquire about a possible intelligent nonhuman species on the far side of Syndicate Worlds' space."

"But you figured it out," Navarro commented, looking at Geary.

"Not on my own, sir," Geary denied. "We also ended up having access to Syndic records and territory that Alliance personnel haven't seen. It was a combination of events."

Navarro seemed suddenly older. "You believe the aliens may have provoked the war between the Alliance and the Syndicate Worlds?"

"We consider it a reasonable possibility. It fits what we know and explains some things that otherwise don't make sense."

Another senator spoke with so much bitterness that Geary could almost feel it. "Even if true, that wouldn't relieve the Syndics of responsibility for this war, for all the pain and suffering we've endured."

"I'm not arguing that it would, Senator," Geary replied. "The Syndic leaders made their decision. However, if the aliens did trick them into attacking us, it would be another clear indication that the aliens already regard us as a threat to be dealt with. It would also be consistent with the use of the hypernet technology as a means of fooling not just the Syndics but all of humanity into seeding our star systems with unimaginably powerful mines."

"Experts on the hypernet have been consulted?" Navarro asked. "They agree with the theory that the hypernet is alien technology deliberately leaked to both human sides in this war, and that the hypernet gate at Kalixa could not have spontaneously collapsed?"

"Yes, sir. That is, I've spoken with the experts within the fleet. I have not consulted with outside experts pending authorization to do so, given the sensitivity of the matter." Geary looked down for a moment. "Unfortunately, the fleet's best expert on the hypernet, Captain Cresida, died in the battle here at Varandal when her ship, the battle cruiser *Furious*, was destroyed."

"Jaylen's dead?" a previously silent senator blurted. "I hadn't heard. Oh, damn. I know her family. But you say she was promoted to captain before then?"

Geary nodded. "A field promotion. There are a number of such actions I took, which I am hereby formally submitting to my superiors for their approval and confirmation. I hope the government will consider them favorably. There were also a number of disciplinary actions taken and charges referred for courts-martial, which I regret to report but hope will be validated."

The members of the grand council stared back at Geary for a moment with a variety of expressions. Then Navarro laughed softly as he called up the document from Geary's report. "I'm sorry, Captain Geary, but sometimes your phrasing seems... well, antiquated. But in a good way, I hasten to add. Why do you think your superiors need to confirm field appointments and promotions?"

Geary stared back at the senator. "I just assumed things still worked that way."

"The fleet has a bit more autonomy now," Navarro commented dryly. "Let me see what you have here. You ask that we confirm certain field promotions, such as that of Commander Cresida to captain. I can't see any problem there. You recommend that Colonel Carabali be promoted to general in light of her performance while under your command. We shall certainly give that careful consideration."

Senator Suva interrupted again. "Marines in full combat gear confronted Alliance troops and prevented them from carrying out their orders! To just what, or who, is this Colonel Carabali loyal?"

"The Alliance," Geary stated firmly.

"That can mean many things these days," the heavyset woman noted sourly.

"Yes," Senator Navarro agreed wearily. He paused, rereading the list of Geary's recommendations. "Numos. Falco. I met Falco once, a long time ago. Kila. She's out of our hands now. May the living stars judge her as she deserves." Then Navarro looked at Geary once more. "I keep looking for something, and it's not here."

"What's that, sir?" Geary asked, alarmed that he might have overlooked something important.

"There's nothing about *you*, Captain Geary."

Geary frowned, baffled by the statement. "I don't understand, sir."

"You're not asking for anything for you, Captain. Promotion, awards, nothing."

"That wouldn't be appropriate," Geary objected.

Some of the politicians laughed. Admiral Timbale looked embarrassed.

Navarro smiled briefly, then any trace of humor vanished. "You've done astounding things, Captain Geary. Those things, plus the mythic reputation of Black Jack Geary, which our own government has worked so hard to cultivate, make you very, very powerful. What do you want, Captain?"

2

The tension inside the room suddenly intensified. Geary chose his words carefully, knowing he had to get meaning and intent across and knowing he couldn't afford any misinterpretations. "My recommendations are presented in detail in my report, but in brief I request that I be permitted to remain in command of the fleet, sir, and I request that the government and my military superiors favorably consider the plan of action I have submitted."

"Request. You surely know that you could demand such things."

"No, sir, I could not," Geary objected.

"Don't play games with us, Captain," Senator Suva declared with a glower. "We both know what you could do with a snap of your fingers."

"Madam Senator, I acknowledge that I might have the power to make demands, but I cannot do so. I have taken an oath to the Alliance, and I will not break that oath. I am subject to your orders and authority."

The heavyset woman narrowed her eyes at Geary, her face grim. "You're giving us your fate, Captain, and leaving the fate of the Alliance up to a group of people whom you have surely seen are less capable than they should be given our responsibilities."

He hadn't expected any senators to argue in favor of a coup. Geary managed to hide his reaction, then spoke calmly. "I gave my fate up a long time ago, Madam Senator. I swore to follow lawful orders, and I will do so. Or I will resign my commission if I cannot in good conscience follow those orders."

Rione finally spoke again, her voice quiet but firm. "He means it. He's not posing. I had the same suspicions you all do, that Black Jack would turn out to be an eager dictator-to-be, using his military role to supplant political authority." Her gaze rested briefly on the stout woman and another senator, almost but not quite implying that those two might have had not suspicions but hopes. "However, I got close enough to Captain Geary to ensure that he's genuine. Put him in an interrogation room, and you'd see no deception at all. Captain Geary is untainted by a century of war, my fellow senators. He still believes in the things our ancestors held dear. He still believes in all of *you*."

Some of the senators looked away, as if embarrassed, but Navarro fixed his gaze on her. "We have reports that you got very close indeed to Captain Geary, Madam Co-President. Is your assessment in any way biased by that?"

"A physical relationship," Rione acknowledged casually. "For a brief time." The ease dropped, and Rione sat straight, her voice becoming formal again. "Some of the information the fleet acquired in Syndic space indicates my husband was captured alive

47

by the Syndics. He may still live. My loyalties are to the Alliance and to him."

Another senator was shaking his head. "You slept with another man when your husband might still be alive? There are no words for the dishonor—"

Rione's face flushed red in a very unusual display of anger, but Geary spoke first. "She didn't know he might still be alive," he said. "Not then. Co-President Rione is a woman of honor."

"Whereas you, Senator Gizelle"—Rione's low voice cut into the silence following Geary's words—"wouldn't know honor if it wrapped both hands around your neck and squeezed until your head popped."

Navarro stood and slammed his hand down again, cutting off any more argument. "That's enough. Just answer the question, Senator Rione. Is your judgment impartial?"

"Yes." Rione shook her head, looking around, apparently already in control of herself again. "Everyone here knows what Captain Geary could be doing right now. What he could have already done. He could be in Unity Star System right now with warships at his back, the entire senate under arrest, and the population of the Alliance would be *cheering* him. And do you have any idea how long it took him to realize that could happen? The thought didn't even belong in his universe. It still doesn't. But there are people who would act allegedly in his name, and we need to keep them from starting something no one might be able to stop. So please avoid any more nonsense like trying to arrest Captain Geary. He's not going to use his power against the Alliance."

"I want to believe that," Navarro replied. "I don't know if I dare believe it, though."

"Let me show you something, then." Rione downloaded a file, activated it, and Geary saw an image of himself on the bridge of *Dauntless*. He wondered how Rione had managed to access *Dauntless*'s log and where this recording had been made, then heard what was being said and knew. This showed his words and actions at the point where he finally grasped that personnel of the Alliance fleet were planning to murder prisoners of war as if it were a routine operation.

When the clip ended, Rione gestured to Geary. "That happened at Corvus, soon after he assumed command. Do you think he was acting? He wasn't. That was our ancestors speaking, fellow senators, through this man."

"I need to have a talk with mine," Navarro muttered, his eyes lowered for a moment, then looked at Geary once more. "Summarize your recommended actions, Captain Geary. Since you won't be bringing the fleet to Unity to shove our sorry butts into jail, where do you want to take it?"

He had never imagined personally briefing the grand council, but that would have seemed more likely than getting a question from the chair of the grand council formed in those words. Geary brought up the star display again. "I have two proposed courses of action. First, I believe it's critical that we follow up on the damage done to the Syndic fleet in recent engagements. Given time, the Syndics can rebuild their forces, but if we strike quickly, we may force them to agree to a halt to the conflict." The display shifted, centering on one star, and Geary didn't imagine the sighs that came from the other side of the table.

"The Syndic home star system?" the heavyset woman asked in

disbelief. "Isn't that where you came in, Captain Geary? A trap from which you barely extracted the fleet?"

"Yes, ma'am, but the situation has changed. The Syndic fleet has been decimated. Some warships escaped from here when we beat off their attack, but even with those and whatever new-construction warships the Syndics have fielded, we should still have good odds." Geary indicated the star. "We managed to bring the Syndic hypernet key home safely, and now we can use that same key to take our fleet quickly back to the Syndic home star system, clear out the defenders, and demand meaningful negotiations from the Syndic leadership. It offers us the advantage we need to strike quickly and deeply into the heart of Syndic space."

"And if the Syndic leaders don't agree to meaningful negotiations?" Navarro asked, resting his chin on a fist formed from both hands.

"Then, sir, we use deep-penetrating munitions to bring about a change of Syndic leadership." He'd seen plenty of evidence that the Syndic leaders were willing to sacrifice large numbers of their people while themselves remaining safe, but he wouldn't give those leaders that opportunity this time.

"What terms would we demand?" Senator Suva asked.

Rione answered. "That's for the council to decide, but my advice is this, to consider how little we would gain from demands made on the Syndics versus the costs of this war continuing. I suggest that we offer the Syndics a halt to hostilities with a return to conditions prior to the war, including a full exchange of living prisoners and information regarding all prisoners over the course of the war."

"All of our sacrifices would be in vain?" the heavyset woman shouted.

"As would all of the Syndics' sacrifices," Navarro observed. "You make an excellent point, Senator Rione, and you know as well as we the state of the Alliance right now." Some of the other senators started to speak, but Navarro waved them to silence. "We'll privately debate and discuss your proposal, Captain Geary, as well as Co-President Rione's suggestion. What's the second item?"

Geary swung his arm to indicate the far side of Syndic space. "That if possible we deal with whatever is out there. We have no idea how powerful they are, how much territory they span, what their capabilities are. We do have strong evidence that their technology is superior to ours in some areas, including faster-than-light communications systems. They've also held the Syndics in place and pushed them out of a few star systems, and from what we know of the Syndics, that wouldn't have come easily. But they've been meddling with humanity, they tricked us into setting up nova-scale bombs in all of our most important star systems, they deliberately destroyed at least one human-occupied star system at Kalixa, and according to what you told me, they tried to do it again at Petit. They need to understand that intervening in human affairs and attacks on humanity must cease."

A long silence followed, then one male senator closed his eyes and spoke hollowly. "We need to start another war?"

"No, sir. That's the last thing I want. But there's a good chance that a war may already be under way without our knowledge. We need to stop that war, too, or at least manage a cease-fire."

Rione pointed to the star display. "The Syndics kept that reserve flotilla on their far border from us to deter the aliens. Now that reserve flotilla is gone, much of it destroyed, the rest probably being gathered for a final defense of the Syndic home star system. What will the aliens do when presented with easy pickings?"

"Who cares?" the heavyset woman grumbled. "They're Syndics."

"They're humans, Senator Costa," Rione replied. "And every star system taken from them lessens the strength of humanity and increases the strength of these aliens."

Senator Suva laughed. "You want us to go from enemies of the Syndics to allies? Defending them?"

"It's about defending us," Rione corrected. "We can't assume another intelligent species will treat us differently than they do the Syndics just because among humans we regard ourselves as different."

Senator Navarro's eyes had remained fixed on the region of space where the alien territory adjoined that of the Syndics. "If there truly is another intelligent species out there..."

"There may be many," Rione finished. "And right now the Syndics lie between us and the regions where those species may be."

Admiral Timbale drew a sudden, excited breath. "If we're involved with defending that border, then we'll have access to what's beyond!"

"Exactly," Geary agreed. "And with the Syndics on the ropes, they may be forced to agree to just that. At the very least, if we can bring about an end to the current war with the Syndics, we might then be able to take some ships to that area and see what else we can learn, perhaps even establish independent contact with these beings."

Navarro nodded. "An intriguing possibility. All right, Captain Geary. You saved the Alliance fleet and the Alliance itself, you practically wiped out the Syndic fleet and established conditions favorable for forcing an end to the war, you've both discovered and neutralized a threat to all humanity, and you've established the real likelihood that a nonhuman intelligent species exists. Is there anything else?"

"Not at the moment, sir."

"Thank you, Captain Geary. If you, Senator Rione, and Admiral Timbale would please leave us, we'll discuss your report and recommendations."

"Some of the rest of us still have questions," a senator broke in.

"We'll discuss those in private as well," Navarro stated, staring down the other man.

Geary waited a moment to be certain he should go, then saluted again, pivoted, waited while Rione and Timbale left, then walked out behind them. As the door sealed in his wake, Admiral Timbale stepped close. "Thanks, Captain Geary. Being in there meant a great deal to me. I hated the idea of being lumped in with the Anvil."

Geary nodded back. "We're fleet, sir."

"Damn right."

"Speaking of which..." Timbale turned to Rione. "Madam Co-President, with your permission I'm going to go check on what Otropa and Firgani are doing."

"Thank you, Admiral."

As Timbale walked quickly down the passageway, Geary took a long breath, blowing it out slowly, then glanced at Rione. "I assume we're being monitored here."

She took a look at her bracelet, tapping a couple of the jewels. "They're trying to, but they're not getting through my jamming.

I've had a chance to upgrade my systems since we got back, so they're state-of-the-art again."

One more little trick in Rione's arsenal of which Geary hadn't been aware. "But now they know that you're wearing that capability."

"Every politician carries around some security gear. The minor ones have enough to keep someone from overhearing the odd conversation about bribes or vote-trading or whatever. The more important politicians have more extensive setups." She shook her head. "They would have been shocked if I wasn't jamming them, and certain that whatever I was letting them hear and see was an act. Don't worry."

"I'll try not to. I thought things went okay in there."

"Possibly."

"That one senator, Costa, seemed supportive."

Rione breathed a short laugh. "Yes and no. Costa thinks she is supportive of the military, but she would have voted to order suicide missions to collapse Syndic hypernet gates. You could see that as well as I. And I have no doubt that she would have welcomed a military coup. Not for personal gain, but out of misplaced patriotism. You can't trust her to do what's really best." She glanced toward the ceiling. "My equipment says there are some cameras up there, but my jamming gear is fogging their views so they can't read our lips. Anyway, you can't count on Costa, but she can be useful if properly guided."

"Not many of the council appeared openly hostile," Geary said.

"'Openly' is the key word. Gizelle doesn't like you, but that's a badge of honor in my book. He's the sort who would welcome a coup as a chance to make loads of money and gain more power."

Rione smiled wryly at Geary. "He's doubtless a bit upset that you're standing at the gate preventing that. I never did find out what deals Gizelle made with Admiral Bloch, but Gizelle did work hard behind the scenes to get Bloch's plan approved, and we both know what Bloch's ambitions were."

Geary rubbed his eyes. "What about Senator Navarro? What did those digs at him mean?"

"They mean he's suspected of making covert deals with the Syndics. He's from Abassas Star System, near the border, and surrounding Alliance star systems have been hit multiple times by the Syndics. Abassas hasn't been hit since Navarro was elected to the grand council."

At the least, that didn't look good. "Do you think he's dealing with the enemy?"

Rione looked away for a moment, thinking. "I've never heard any proven charges of corruption against Navarro. That is, of course his enemies spread charges of corruption, but he's never been caught at it. I'd know even if it had been covered up. Aside from the curious lack of Syndic attacks on his home star system, there's no evidence of treason or any lesser crimes." She paused. "I think he's as honest as any of us these days, and I think he's trying to do his best for the Alliance. But he's had to compromise in many ways to hold things together. That's the difference between good military commanders and good politicians, John Geary. You've shown me that a good military commander spends the lives of their people reluctantly and with regret, but does spend them when necessary. The good politician does the same thing with principles. There aren't any fine burials for sacrificed principles, though."

"Are you saying he's like you?"

"In many ways."

"Then, despite the lack of attacks on Abassas, we can trust him."

Rione gave him an exasperated look. "I wouldn't advise you to trust me in everything. But, yes, I believe he's going to endorse whatever course of action seems to him to be truly best for the Alliance. You saw that his ability to keep the council under control is hampered by the suspicions against him, though."

Something else had been bothering him, and now Geary asked it. "Is that why Navarro let the council approve Admiral Bloch's plan given the odds against it and the chances that Bloch would try to ride success into a dictatorship?"

"The chair of the grand council rotates." Rione shrugged. "When Bloch's plan was approved, Costa was chair. Navarro argued against approving Bloch's plan, but because of the doubts about him, those arguments didn't prevail. A traitor wouldn't want a war-winning plan approved, would he?"

"I see. Of course, neither would a prudent and loyal individual given the risks posed by Bloch's plan." He looked toward the sealed door. "Why wouldn't you tell me anything about those politicians before I gave my report?"

"Because I wanted you at your apolitical military best, Captain Geary." Rione sighed. "If you'd been briefed on their personalities, you might have reacted to them on a personal level. You might have come across as political yourself. This way, you were totally professional, completely detached, a paragon of a military officer who wasn't even thinking about politics but just how to do his job." She laughed derisively. "You probably couldn't tell how much that rattled them. They were expecting another politician, though one wearing a uniform, and when you betrayed nothing of that, they had no idea how to get a handle on you. At one point I could tell Navarro realized that you weren't acting, that you were exactly what he was seeing and hearing, and at that point I really started to hope we could succeed here." Her mood suddenly shifting again, Rione turned a sardonic look on him. "It's a good thing I'm in your pocket, isn't it?"

He paused in the act of replying, then settled for a mild statement. "I didn't realize you were monitoring all of my communications."

"I'm not," she assured him. "I'm trying to monitor all of Badaya's. Getting through your security screens is very difficult thanks to the diligent efforts of *Dauntless*'s commanding officer, but in that particular case I came in through Badaya's transmission. Don't worry, I won't hurt the man unless he becomes a loose cannon. Right now all of his illusions are useful to us."

That sounded wrong in any number of ways. "I'm not deceiving him for personal gain. Neither are you."

"Don't think you know everything about me, Captain Geary." Rione smiled coldly. "Trust no one any more than you have to."

Instead of arguing, he just nodded. Rione remained a riddle, but as far as he could tell, she also remained an ally. He also had no doubt that Desjani, Duellos, and Tulev were keeping a close eye on her for any signs of betrayal.

The wait dragged. Geary could only stand stiffly while Rione leaned against the opposite wall, her eyes distant. Not the first time, Geary wished he could tell what she was thinking.

Timbale eventually returned, shaking his head. "General Firgani was planning an operation to take out your Marine 'honor guard.' I finally convinced him of the stupidity of that by contrasting his available assets with the massed weaponry of the fleet, and demonstrating that it would be impossible to overcome a platoon of armored Marines in an outer-shell compartment like that without the entire star system spotting the fireworks. Even Firgani isn't dumb enough to start a battle that one-sided."

"And Admiral Otropa?" Rione asked.

"He had a lot of questions about what had gone on after he was asked to leave." Timbale made no effort to hide his glee. "He wanted me to give him a full report. I told him I was needed back here." The admiral's demeanor had changed dramatically, with Timbale now acting as if he were firmly on Geary's team instead of being terrified of what Geary might do next. "There's no hidden game here, is there? I can't see the point of one, but my ancestors know I wouldn't have seen half of what you did in Syndic space."

Geary shook his head. "No hidden game, sir."

"That's a relief. I don't mind telling you that." Timbale looked older for a moment. "A lot of us knew what Bloch intended. Plenty of other officers were jockeying for similar moves."

"What would you have done had Bloch returned victorious?" Rione asked.

The admiral took a deep breath. "I shouldn't even answer that, but Captain Geary obviously trusts you. To be perfectly honest, I don't know what I would have done. Truly. A lot of us didn't. We were as despairing as the rest, didn't trust the government, knew how frayed the entire Alliance was becoming, didn't know what else to do. But a coup... Have you heard of the quantum cat,

Madam Co-President? The one where you have to look in the box to tell whether it's alive or dead, and the universe doesn't actually decide one way or the other until you look? It was like that. If Bloch had come back, a lot of us would have been opening that box to see what our hearts told us. Only then could we have seen the answer. I'll never know that answer now, to my relief and to my shame. As that one senator said, it used to be a lot easier to know what loyalty to the Alliance meant. But maybe it wasn't easier, and maybe now it's not really all that complicated. Maybe the answer never changed, just the questions we were asking."

Rione seemed impressed by Timbale's candor. "What about when Captain Geary brought the fleet back? You had no similar internal uncertainty?"

"At that point? The fleet believed lost, the Syndics running amuck in this star system, our few defenders barely hanging on, then the fleet appears and swoops down like angels of vengeance on the Syndics, and transmissions tell us that Black Jack is back, that he's saved the fleet, and now he's saving us." Timbale laughed softly. "At that moment, Black Jack was a god."

"That's not—" Geary began.

"It's how you were seen," Rione said. "I told you it would be that way."

"Exactly," Timbale agreed. "Black Jack didn't need me. It didn't matter what I did. If I got in the way, I'd be run over, that's all. I admit I was worried, for myself and for the Alliance, so I kept my distance and watched Captain Geary's actions, but I'm not fool enough to think he needed my support or would be stopped by my opposition." He turned a still-puzzled look on Geary. "When you told me at the shuttle dock that you were here to follow orders, I doubted my sanity for a moment. How could you have said that? But you were leaving all of the Marines behind, so you were either sincere or crazy. I decided to hope for sincerity, since if you were crazy, we were all doomed anyway."

Timbale checked his comm unit as it beeped urgently. "The grand council is ready for us."

Rione straightened up, rolled her shoulders lightly, and flexed her hands as if preparing for hand-to-hand combat, then led the way back into the room, where the senators of the grand council sat silently awaiting them.

Senator Navarro spoke first as Geary came to a halt before the table. "Captain Geary, are you promising victory in this war?"

He hesitated, then shook his head. "No, sir. I am reasonably confident that forces under my command can overcome any Syndic defenses."

"You don't call that victory?" Costa asked.

"I can achieve a military victory," Geary stated. "You're asking me about victory in the war. I don't know how you define that."

"But Senator Rione has suggested a peace that denies the Alliance any gains from this war!"

"Yes, Madam Senator. It also denies the Syndics any gains."

Rione came up to the table and leaned forward, tapping her finger on the surface for emphasis. "Survival is victory. Neither we nor the Syndics can prevail if we keep trying to destroy the other. But both the Syndicate Worlds and the Alliance can be torn apart from within. I've seen reports of the demonstrations and riots on worlds of the Alliance when it was believed that the fleet was truly lost. If Captain Geary had not brought it home, which outcome would you all be praying for? You might have been forced to accept whatever terms the Syndics dictated."

"He did bring the fleet home," a male senator insisted.

"Yes. The living stars gave us a gift. Do we accept it with humility, or do we demand they give us more? Who here will go to their ancestors and ask that they pass on a message of ingratitude and greed?"

Geary could tell that Rione's latest shot had gone home, but once again Senator Navarro halted the threatened outbursts from more than one member of the council. "The bottom line is this," Navarro said. "The apparent strength of the Alliance is deceptive despite Captain Geary's successes against the Syndics. We can't take an indefinite continuation of the bloodshed, destruction, and costs associated with a war we didn't begin."

Navarro raised a finger toward the star display once again floating above the table. "The reports the fleet brought back from within Syndic space show how badly stressed they are as well. Senator Rione is right. We've been given a chance to offer the Syndic leadership a deal they cannot claim will weaken them but which will also offer them no advantage to show for the war they began. We will have successfully defended the Alliance, punished aggression with terrible losses inflicted on the Syndics over the last century, and will finally be able to halt the human and economic costs of the war to the Alliance. That is how I define victory at this point, and that is how a majority of the council feels as well. Now, we have already voted, and I see no reason for debate further even though we all wanted to hear Captain Geary's answer to the question about victory. Captain Geary, this council was desperate enough earlier to approve Admiral Bloch's plan, and as I'm sure you're aware, that admiral was not your equal. Conditions have changed, we have a commander we can trust, and the council therefore gives its approval for your proposed plan to attack the Syndics. Needless to say, you'll remain in command of the fleet to carry out that plan."

Geary felt a weight come off of him. "Thank you, sir."

"What about the aliens?" Rione asked.

"That is difficult," Navarro murmured. "We need to know so much more." He met Geary's eyes. "Without Syndic consent, getting to that area may be too risky, but we'll leave it up to you based on whatever conditions prevail. If you can end the war and get Syndic agreement to send Alliance warships to that border region, then you have the council's agreement in advance. We'll be counting on you to avoid fighting unless it's unavoidable, to discover all you can about these beings without provoking negative responses, and if you must fight them, to keep hostilities to the bare minimum necessary to counter future aggression against humanity."

Senator Costa rolled her eyes derisively.

Geary understood the gesture, since those orders required him to do a great many contradictory things. But perhaps he could use that to gain some flexibility where it was needed. "Yes, sir. Then you approve of my plans?"

"Our guidance to this man is vague and meaningless," Senator Gizelle mumbled loud enough for everyone to hear. Costa rolled her eyes again.

"It's been debated and voted on," Navarro said. "I will not tie the hands of a trusted emissary with detailed instructions when we know so little of what will be faced, and Captain Geary *has* earned our trust. Nonetheless, Captain, because of the significance of negotiations with both the Syndic leadership and this alien race, we will insist that more political representatives of the Alliance accompany your fleet this time." He looked at Rione. "Apparently the presence of Co-President Rione wasn't too disruptive."

The fleet would undoubtedly have expressed different opinions on the matter, but Geary nodded. "We were able to accommodate her presence, sir."

Rione spoke up with unusual diffidence. "In view of the working relationships I have established within the fleet, and the continued presence of warships from the Callas Republic and the Rift Federation within the fleet, I request that I be allowed to be one of those accompanying the fleet this time as well."

Gizelle opened his mouth but shut it when Navarro gave him a warning look. "Thank you, Madam Co-President," Navarro said. "That request can probably be accommodated. I'm certain your working relationships are of great value. We'll decide who the other political representatives will be and communicate that to you, Captain Geary. When will the fleet leave Varandal?"

"I want to strike the Syndics again as soon as possible, but there's been a tremendous amount of battle damage to deal with, and supplies of every kind on every ship were nearly exhausted. I need one more week, sir, minimum, to get the worst damage to my warships repaired and every ship fully loaded out with supplies."

"How do your crews feel about that?" another senator demanded.

"They've only been home a few weeks. Will we have morale problems? Mutiny?"

Rione's laughter rang through the room. "I'm sorry, my fellow senator. It's just... I suggest you talk to members of the ships' crews."

"You don't think morale will be a problem?" Costa asked.

"As long as Black Jack is in command? They'd dive into a black hole if he told them to do it, and they'd be cheering him all the way to the event horizon."

Navarro nodded. "Our own reports show the same. Captain Geary, there's one more matter we must address now. Please wait outside this room while the council speaks with Senator Rione and Admiral Timbale."

Now what? Geary waited in the passageway, alone this time and acutely aware that without Rione's jammers nearby he was probably being monitored by the best full-spectrum surveillance gear the Alliance possessed. Even though he had nothing relating to his duty to the Alliance on his conscience, it was still surprisingly hard to look innocent when there were so many surveillance devices trained on him.

Senator Navarro, Co-President Rione, and Admiral Timbale came out of the conference room, and Geary stiffened to attention. "Please relax," Navarro said. "The council had to decide on something else, and we've done so though it took some arguing." He glanced at Rione. "You inspire some impressive loyalty, Captain Geary, but more importantly, your actions confirm what we needed to know." Navarro looked down at something in his right hand. "As should be obvious, we can't have a captain negotiating and acting on behalf of the Alliance government. Not for something this big. And the fleet requires a senior officer in command. We also know that you may need to reach critically important decisions without the time to consult with higher authority. You need the authority yourself to, if necessary, negotiate and bind the Alliance to agreements."

Geary watched Navarro with a growing sense of unease. "Sir, I thought that Co-President Rione and other senators would accompany the fleet as representatives of the government."

"Yes, they will," Navarro agreed. "But your rank should reflect your position and responsibilities. That's how Admiral Timbale expressed it. Therefore, please accept these on behalf of the grand council of the Alliance." He held out his right hand.

Geary looked down at Navarro's palm, at the golden, stylized supernovas there. It took him a moment to realize what he was seeing. "Sir, there must be some mistake."

The senator frowned down at his palm. "Aren't these the insignia for the Admiral of the Alliance Fleet?"

Fleet admiral. Not just admiral. Fleet admiral. The highest rank possible. The uneasiness had grown into disbelief and denial. "Yes, sir, but——"

"Then there's no mistake. The grand council knows you need this authority, and it is the judgment of the majority of the council that you can be trusted with this rank. You and I both know that you already have more power than is embodied in this rank."

"Sir," Geary protested, "no one has ever held the rank of Admiral of the Alliance Fleet."

"Not until now," Rione agreed with a half smile.

"But, sir, I..."

Navarro laughed with evident relief and looked at Rione. "You were right! You really don't want this rank, do you?" he asked Geary. "Do you know how many admirals have pleaded for this rank for themselves since the war began? But *you* want to turn it down."

Geary tried again. "Sir, I am not qualified for such a rank."

"Not qualified? Read your own record, man. Independent command under the most difficult circumstances, and you succeeded where no one else could have." Navarro glanced at Admiral Timbale this time, who nodded back at the senator. "You didn't do what you could have done, Captain Geary, but we assume there will be attempts to force that issue. Giving you this rank should satisfy those who want to see you with more formal power and help defuse the threat to the government."

Timbale nodded again, firmly. "I believe you are correct, sir. The fleet's personnel will see this as a recognition of their concerns and needs."

"Thank you, Admiral. So, Fleet Admiral Geary, are you going to take these from me?"

Given the significance of the issues Navarro had brought up, Geary felt guilty that the primary thing filling his mind was not that he felt deeply inadequate for the position. His main worry was, in fact, a purely personal thing.

Rione was watching him and spoke evenly. "What do we need to do to get you to accept this rank, Captain Geary?" He looked at her, knowing that she knew about his greatest concern and wondering if even Rione could cruelly taunt him because she knew that. But her next words showed a different reason for her question. "Perhaps if it wasn't permanent?"

He latched onto that like a drifting sailor thrown a lifeline. "Yes. A temporary appointment to that rank."

"'Temporary'?" Navarro asked in astonishment. "How long do you envision that being?"

"Until... the end of the war. When the war ends, when I bring the fleet back with its missions accomplished, I will relinquish the temporary rank, relinquish command of the fleet, and revert to my permanent rank of captain."

Admiral Timbale stared at him. "You do realize that to the rest of us anything based on the end of the war is permanent."

"Not to me, Admiral." Geary gave Navarro a pleading look. "Can I put that condition on accepting the rank? Formal conditions? A promise from the government?"

Navarro thought, then made a why-not gesture. "Certainly. I'll have it entered in the official record. When the war ends, and when you return the fleet to Alliance space, you will immediately revert to the permanent rank of captain and will also relinquish command of the fleet at that time."

Geary had a moment's hesitation, wondering why Navarro had given in so easily. In his experience, people had not been willing to let Black Jack Geary walk away from the things for which they needed him. But he couldn't refuse the government's orders when it had already agreed to conditions he hadn't had any right to demand. "Very well, sir."

Navarro held out his hand again. "Then take the insignia, Captain. Excuse me, take the insignia, Fleet Admiral."

Geary let the gold supernovas drop into his hand, then just stared at them.

Rione stepped closer and folded his hand around them. "Let your captain help you put them on," she murmured. "It'll make her happy. This wasn't my idea, but once it was raised, I argued strongly in its favor."

Navarro smiled at Geary. "Good luck, Fleet Admiral. It's a very odd thing. I've gotten used to being regarded as a low form of life who cannot be trusted to act in the best interests of the Alliance. Now I find myself hoping I won't let you down because you really do believe that I'm more than that."

Another mental weight fell from Geary as his shuttle accelerated away from Ambaru station, the Marines relaxing in the back. If not for the insignia in his fist, he would have felt light-headed, but the gold supernovas anchored him as firmly as if they had the gravitational pull of real stars.

"Sir?" the pilot called back. "*Dauntless* is requesting routine passenger ID and status. Are you still... uh..."

Geary realized that he and Rione hadn't told anything to anyone yet. "My apologies. Yes, I'm still the fleet commander."

"Thank the——! I mean, thank you, sir!"

"She's going to tell the entire star system," Rione murmured.

"I'm sure an official announcement will be made soon anyway," Geary replied with a shrug.

"That's not all they'll be announcing, *Captain* Geary." She leaned back, eyes closed, apparently relaxing.

The comforting hull of *Dauntless* eventually loomed close, then all around as the shuttle docked with an extra twist and spin as if the craft itself were exuberant. Geary led the way off again, smiling as he saw Desjani waiting at the bottom of the ramp. She nodded to him, smiling back briefly, then Rione came into sight, and Desjani's mouth twisted slightly as Geary saluted the sideboys drawn up to render honors to the returning commander of the fleet.

"Here you are," Rione announced, when they reached the end of the ramp. "John Geary, returned safe and sound, not a scratch on him."

Desjani kept her eyes on Geary. "You're to remain in command of the fleet? For how long?"

"Until my mission is done," he replied.

She knew what that meant, and Desjani's eyes lit up. "Welcome back aboard, sir. When do we leave?"

Geary saw Rione heading off in another direction as he and Desjani walked toward his stateroom. "At least another week for repair work, resupply, and reinforcements."

"Those will all be welcome." Desjani flicked a glance in the direction Rione had gone. "Did she have to come back here? Isn't there some planet or asteroid or penal colony that urgently needs her presence?"

"She's probably going with us again, Tanya." Geary tried not to smile as Desjani winced. "There'll be some other senators, too. I don't know who yet."

"I think I'd rather have Syndics aboard. Don't they trust you?"

"Yes, they do." He hesitated, finding himself unable to tell Desjani about the promotion yet. "The grand council approved both proposals. We're going after the Syndics, then, if circumstances permit, we're going to have a talk with some aliens."

"Excellent." She turned a triumphant look on him. "I never

doubted you. I knew you'd succeed."

"We haven't succeeded in either assignment so far."

"I won't let you down. Neither will the fleet, and you've never let us down." She smiled again as they reached his stateroom. "I expect you'll want to rest a bit. When you're ready, I'd be grateful for a fuller briefing."

"Sure." He held out his free hand as Desjani started to go. "There's one more thing. Something I have to show you."

Desjani frowned but followed him inside the stateroom.

Once the hatch sealed, he finally opened his hand and held it out to her.

She looked down, then a smile slowly grew, and Desjani looked up. "Congratulations, Fleet Admiral Geary."

An instant later her smile vanished. "Is it effective already?"

"The new rank? Yes."

Desjani glowered at him in sudden anger. "You didn't inform us before you arrived! My ship didn't render proper honors to a fleet admiral! How could you make *my* ship look bad?"

"I guess I wasn't—"

"No, you weren't." Desjani pulled out her comm pad. "Bridge, formally notify the rest of the fleet that Captain Geary has returned to *Dauntless* and has been promoted to Admiral of the Fleet."

Geary could hear the bridge watch-stander's startled response. "Admiral of the Fleet?"

"Did I stutter, Lieutenant?"

"No, Captain! I'll notify the fleet immediately!"

Desjani transferred her frown back to Geary. "Why haven't you put on your insignia?"

"I—"

"A fleet admiral can't be out of uniform." She reached to remove Geary's captain insignia, then plucked the gold supernovas from his palm and began attaching them to his uniform. "You cannot be so casual, Fleet Admiral Geary."

"Tanya—"

"Wait." She finished putting on the insignia, stepped back and studied his appearance carefully, then nodded with satisfaction. Straightening to attention, Desjani saluted with strict formality. "May I be the first to render my congratulations, Fleet Admiral."

Geary returned the salute. "Tanya—"

"You deserve it. If anyone has ever deserved this promotion, it's you."

"I didn't ask for it."

"Do you think I didn't know that? I'm incredibly happy for you."

"Tanya, after the war ends—"

Her professional veneer cracked for a moment. "I understand what this means."

"It's not—"

"You had to accept the rank for the good of the Alliance. Any personal concerns that might exist can't—"

"Tanya!" He gave her an angry look, determined to finally finish a sentence. "It's temporary! I told them I'd only accept the rank if it was temporary! When the war ends, I revert to the rank of captain!" She stared at him, wordless for several moments. "Tanya?"

"Why?" Desjani finally asked.

"You know why."

"No, I don't." She seemed dazed. "Fleet Admiral, to cast that aside—"

"I had the best possible reason," Geary insisted. "Someday I hope to honorably relinquish command of this fleet, but as an admiral I could never have a personal relationship with a captain, regardless of whether or not she was under my command."

"I would never—"

"I made a promise."

"A promise drawn from you under duress?" Desjani almost shouted. "And you think I'd hold you to that?"

He felt his own temper rising again. "What makes you think I need to be held to it?"

"I didn't mean to offend your honor—"

"This has nothing to do with my honor!"

"Then you're an idiot!"

He stared at Desjani, who seemed shocked that those words had come from her own mouth. "What are you saying?"

"I don't know." She swallowed, shaking her head. "I do know that for you to give up something so important—"

"I *know* what's important, Tanya."

She stepped back. "Maybe it's a sign. Maybe we're being told this is wrong. We know it's wrong. Against regulations, against honor—"

"We've done and said *nothing* against either regulations or honor."

Desjani's eyes bored into his. "We have in our hearts." Her jaw tightened. "No one is that important. No one could demand such a sacrifice from another and be comfortable with it." She straightened to attention once more. "By your leave, sir. The crew will want to stage a formal ceremony for your promotion. I hope that will be acceptable."

He nodded, feeling immensely tired. "Yes, Captain Desjani. Thank you."

She left, and he sank into the nearest seat, his dress uniform rumpling.

Compared to trying to deal with Alliance politicians, crushing the Syndics should be a piece of cake, and compared to trying to understand Captain Tanya Desjani, figuring out what the aliens wanted should be easy.

3

Admiral Timbale's image saluted awkwardly. To Geary's surprise, even such a senior officer seemed to take pleasure in the gesture of respect Geary had reintroduced into the fleet. "We can't provide you with as many fast fleet auxiliaries as we'd like for a mission this deep into enemy territory. Bloch started out with ten, which was almost all we had then. You inherited four, and how you managed to get three of them back here in one piece I'll never know. You'll retain *Titan*, *Witch*, and *Jinn*. *Tanuki* and *Alchemist* have been ordered to Varandal and should be here soon. You'll have them both."

"Five is better than three. Thank you, sir." He checked his own data, seeing that *Tanuki* was the same class as *Titan*, while *Alchemist* was a sister ship to the smaller *Witch* and *Jinn*.

"We'll give you what additional firepower we can," Timbale continued. "There are five new-construction battle cruisers on the way, all part of the new *Adroit* class."

"I'm sure they'll come in handy." Geary read the names. *Adroit*,

74

Auspice, *Assert*, *Agile*, and *Ascendant*. Brand-new ships, brand-new crews, probably only a smattering of veterans among them. He constantly had to remind himself that losses in the war had become so routinely awful that veteran crews were a rare exception. Or had been. He had kept most of his ships and their crews alive to apply their experience to future engagements.

"You'll also get a new *Invincible*," Timbale added. "She was just finishing trials when you got back and confirmed the loss of the old *Invincible*, so her temporary name was made permanent."

The irony of having a new *Invincible* to replace an older, destroyed *Invincible* didn't escape Geary. He didn't comment on it outwardly, but Timbale must have seen something.

The admiral gave a crooked smile. "You may not be aware that *Invincible* is regarded as a bad-luck name in the fleet. Ships named *Invincible* tend to get destroyed quickly. No one knows why. The sailors blame it on the name being a too-proud challenge to the living stars."

"But we keep naming ships *Invincible* anyway?"

"I think the fleet bureaucracy is determined to eventually disprove the curse no matter how many *Invincibles* we lose in the process," Timbale suggested dryly.

Geary made a face. "Before the fight at Grendel, there was talk about naming ships after planets or people."

"It still comes up occasionally. Every time it gets shot down because no one can agree on a formula for choosing which planets and people get the honors. Too damn much hate and discontent get raised over that issue, so we always fall back on naming battleships and battle cruisers after qualities and attributes, which everyone

75

can pretend we all agree on." Timbale shrugged. "So the five *Adroits* and the latest *Invincible* plus *Intemperate* and *Insistent* are your new battle cruisers. Then there are the battleships," Timbale concluded. "You've already got *Dreadnaught* and *Dependable*. *Resound*, *Sustain*, and *Encroach* are on their way. Besides those major combatants, you'll have a total of twelve new heavy cruisers, ten more light cruisers, and nineteen destroyers." The admiral gave Geary an apologetic look. "The grand council wants to keep a lot of destroyers here to act as scouts and couriers."

"That's all right. I'm grateful for everything being added to the fleet," Geary assured him.

"Is there anything else? Anything at all?"

Geary studied his fleet status display, then shrugged. "Nothing I can ask for in good conscience. The Alliance is giving me an awful lot of what it has left."

Admiral Timbale nodded. "I only wish we had more repair capability here." He hesitated. "Fleet Admiral Geary, there's been something I've been meaning to say. When you arrived in this star system, you could've squashed me. You could've been arrogant, and you could've walked all over me in front of the universe. But you didn't. You treated me with all the courtesy and respect your superior officer could have asked for. That's why I am happy to serve under you now. Thank you."

The praise made Geary uncomfortable, as did the naming of his still-new rank, but he just smiled back at the other officer. "That was only my duty, Admiral Timbale."

"You had a choice," Timbale disagreed. "When does the fleet leave?"

"Two more days if those additional ships are here by then."

"They should be."

After Timbale's image had vanished, Geary turned back to his fleet status display. A tremendous amount of repair work had been done, with the extensive facilities at Varandal working around the clock, but there had also been a tremendous amount of damage to the fleet's ships.

Still, the battle cruiser *Incredible* had lived up to her name, somehow getting back into shape for combat despite the awful damage suffered in battles on the way home. *Inspire*, under the command of Captain Duellos, had also returned to full combat capability, even though not all of the repairs would have passed fleet inspections, and Duellos reported that much of *Inspire*'s crew remained slightly shell-shocked from what had become of their former command officer. It was one thing for a captain to die in battle and another thing entirely to lose a captain because of treason.

Other battleships and battle cruisers had either regained almost full capability, or enough to accompany the fleet once again. Given enough resources, any ship could be patched together again as long as it hadn't been blown to pieces, and Varandal and the surrounding star systems had poured everything they had into the repair effort.

Geary frowned as his eye rested on the name of *Orion*. That battleship's performance had been nothing but disappointing while she was commanded by Captain Numos and ever since as well. His plans to break up her crew and recrew the ship had been stymied by all the problems that would have created in reassigning so many fleet personnel while everyone was scrambling to get their ships back into shape.

He wondered what the captains of the new ships would be like, how much retraining they might need to fight with the rest of the fleet's ships. Following that line of thought, he brought up data on the new battle cruisers, wondering what the *Adroit* class was like. Scanning the information, Geary felt like punching the virtual display. Under the guise of producing a new class of ships, the Alliance had reduced their size and capabilities as well as their cost. The *Adroit*-class ships were shorter and massed less than *Dauntless* and her sister ships, they carried fewer hell lances in fewer batteries, and fewer specter missiles, grapeshot, and mines. At least their propulsion capability seemed to match the older battle cruisers'.

Unhappily reading over the differences in the new ships, Geary had a deeper understanding of why the fleet was so unhappy with the government. Even though he knew how badly stressed the Alliance was by the cost and resources demanded by the war, he still felt angry at the diminished capability of the *Adroit*-class ships.

But he had learned by now that he had to fight with what was available. Five more battle cruisers of lesser capability were still five more battle cruisers.

Geary looked up as the alert on his stateroom hatch sounded. "Come in."

The hatch almost flew open, and Tanya Desjani stormed in, a thundercloud on her forehead.

Leaping to his feet, Geary stood as she slammed the hatch shut and stalked to stand directly in front of him. "What's the matter?"

"That woman! That politician! She brought a Syndic aboard this ship without notifying me!"

Geary felt a familiar headache beginning. "Why did Rione bring a Syndic aboard this ship?"

"She didn't deign to inform me!" Desjani was as angry as he'd ever seen her, incensed at the disregard of her prerogatives as commanding officer of *Dauntless*. "I respectfully request, Fleet Admiral Geary, that you intervene in this matter since the senator is not under my command!"

He had a million things he needed to be doing at that moment. Given the bad blood between them, he could guess why Rione had failed to tell Desjani, but why had Rione also not told him? Geary was reaching to call her when his hatch alert chimed again. "Come in."

Co-President Rione entered, appearing oblivious to Desjani's glower. "Oh, good, you're both here. I wanted to inform the captain that there was a last-minute high-priority prisoner diversion. My apologies for not getting that information to you sooner."

Desjani spoke with obviously forced control. "Madam Co-President, I am supposed to be informed and give my approval before any prisoners are transferred on or off this ship."

"It was, as I said, last-minute. I had to make a snap decision to keep the Syndic from being sent on to the prison ship taking the others to the camp at Tartarus."

Breaking in before Desjani could erupt again, Geary spoke to Rione. "What's so special about this Syndic?"

"He wants to talk to you."

Geary glared at Rione. "There's a billion somebodies who want to talk to me. What's so special about *this* Syndic?"

She gazed back dispassionately. "He's the CEO who was the

second in command of the Syndic reserve flotilla, captured by us after his ship was destroyed in the battle here."

"He is?" Geary's anger drained as he considered that. "Why does he want to talk to me?"

Rione leaned back against the nearest bulkhead, crossing her arms. "He says he wants to make a deal."

"A deal." His limited experience with Syndic CEOs had left Geary with a bad taste in his mouth, but on the other hand, there were a couple of them who had acted honorably.

Desjani, whose opinions of Syndics and their trustworthiness rarely rose higher than the tiniest possible increment above absolute zero, kept her glower. "What kind of deal?"

"Isn't it obvious?" Rione asked. "As a high-ranking officer in the reserve flotilla, he probably knows as much about the aliens as any Syndic outside their Executive Council. He wants to trade that knowledge for something."

Geary gave Rione a skeptical look. "What's he like?"

"I don't know enough to give you an assessment."

"But you think I should talk to him."

Rione rolled her eyes. "Yes, Black Jack. Talk to the man."

"Fleet Admiral Geary," Desjani said in a tight voice, "I recommend caution in dealing with an enemy who has nothing to lose."

Without waiting for Geary's reply, Rione nodded seriously to Desjani. "I concur. Would you agree to accompany us to the interrogation, Captain?"

Desjani shot a suspicious glance at Rione over her courteous words, but nodded. "Thank you."

Geary paused to grab some painkiller for his headache, then headed for the hatch. "Let's go."

The Syndic had been taken to the interrogation rooms in the intelligence section, rooms whose systems could remotely monitor everything going on inside and outside any person seated within. Geary took a moment to review what was known of the Syndic CEO. Name—Jason Boyens. Rank—Third-Level CEO. Last-known assignment— second in command in a flotilla. Except for the name, it told him nothing new at all. "All right. Let's get this over with." Geary glanced over at Desjani and saw her face still set with barely controlled anger. "What?"

"I'm just recalling the last Syndic turncoat who offered us a deal, sir," she answered in a harsh voice. "He had a Syndic hypernet key we could use to reach the Syndic home star system."

"Oh." That sounded stupid as well as inadequate. "Wasn't that guy ever questioned in an interrogation room?" He'd never felt any desire to learn more about the events that had led to the fleet's near destruction.

Rione answered, her own gaze fixed on the readouts. "He was. Either he was incredibly gifted at deceptive answers so subtly rendered that we couldn't see the truth, or he was himself duped by the Syndics and didn't realize the role he was playing for them."

"Whatever happened to him? I've assumed the ship he was on was destroyed in the Syndic ambush."

Rione didn't answer, but her eyes flicked meaningfully toward Desjani.

Desjani's own expression took on a stony cast. "He was aboard *Dauntless*, sir."

"Then what—?" He choked off the question, knowing what the answer had to be. The fleet he'd assumed command of hadn't had any compunction about killing prisoners of war. It wasn't hard to figure out what had happened to a Syndic who had double-crossed that fleet once it became clear that his offer had actually been a trap.

But Desjani answered anyway. "He was executed on the spot per orders from Admiral Bloch," she said in a toneless voice. "The spot in question being three meters behind and one-half meter to the left of the fleet commander's seat on the bridge."

It took Geary a moment to get it. "He was sitting in the observer's seat?" He couldn't help looking at Rione, who had customarily used that same seat ever since Geary had assumed command, but she seemed both unsurprised and unmoved by the news.

"We burned the seat cushions," Desjani added. "The bloodstains would've come out, but nobody wanted to use them again." She paused at whatever she saw in Geary's eyes. "No, sir. I was busy trying to fight my ship through the ambush. The execution was carried out by the Marine guarding the traitor."

He looked away for a moment. "It was a lawful order. I couldn't have blamed you if you had carried it out." It wasn't hard to remember the shell-shocked expressions of the crew after the Syndic ambush, how badly they'd been stressed by the sudden loss of so many of their sister ships in the fleet. None of them would have hesitated for a moment to take revenge on an individual in great part responsible for that. "We won't let this Syndic do the same."

"We can't trust him," Desjani repeated.

"I have no intention of trusting him." Desjani seemed slightly mollified by Geary's words, so he turned and walked into the interrogation room while Desjani and Rione remained behind, along with the intelligence personnel, to watch the monitors.

CEO Boyens stood up when Geary entered the room. He looked nervous, which was understandable. One leg was still in a light flex cast, revealing battle injuries that hadn't quite healed. The CEO hesitated at the sight of Geary's insignia. "Admiral Geary?"

"Yes." Geary kept his voice hard. "What's the deal you want?"

The Syndic took a deep breath before speaking again. "I have information you need. In exchange for it, I want your agreement to defend human space against the aliens."

He took a moment to absorb that. "You're the first Syndic to openly admit they exist, and you want us to commit to protecting the Syndicate Worlds from them?"

"Yes."

He's telling the truth so far, Lieutenant Iger's voice whispered to Geary through the comm link.

On the heels of Iger came Rione's voice. *How much does he really know?*

That was a good question. Geary frowned at the Syndic CEO. "How do I know that you know all that much?"

Boyens smiled crookedly. "I've been second in command of the reserve flotilla for ten years. I know as much as our Executive Council told anyone and as much as I could personally observe."

Ten years? Desjani's voice demanded.

Geary understood her question. "That's a very long time for anyone to serve in any assignment. Why were you there that long?"

This time Boyens shrugged. "I was exiled to that assignment, for want of a better word. I'm an engineer by training, and I'd established a promising start-up company. A much-bigger corporation wanted our business, and the CEOs running that corporation had the ears of the CEOs running the Syndicate Worlds. My company got taken from me. Instead of being smart and lying low while I worked my way up the CEO ladder until I could exact revenge in a few decades, I made a fuss over it, citing the Syndicate Worlds' laws that had been ignored. Before I knew it, I'd been ordered to a position in the reserve flotilla." The CEO shrugged again. "An assignment out on a border far from any chance for advancement. I couldn't even tell anyone why I was really there since officially the reserve flotilla only existed as a backup against the Alliance. I also couldn't get transferred out, thanks to the people I'd ticked off earlier."

It all reads out as truthful, Iger advised.

Geary sat down and leaned back slightly, eyeing Boyens. "And now you want the Alliance fleet to help you get revenge against those people?"

The CEO shook his head. "No. That's not what this is about. Those people are part of a ruling group that has driven the Syndicate Worlds into this war and fumbled its execution time and again. I don't expect you to believe me when I say this, but I'm also motivated by a desire to protect my own home from the corruption and idiocy of the people who've been leading the Syndicate Worlds."

"Do you consider yourself a patriot, then?" Geary asked.

Boyens flinched. "I don't know. I do know that thanks to the decisions of the Syndicate Worlds' leaders, and thanks to the victories you've won, we're wide open to attack by not only the Alliance but also the aliens. I know how they act as well as any human does. That's not very well, and no one really understands how they think, but I'm very worried."

"Which 'they' do you mean?" Geary asked. "The aliens or the leaders of the Syndicate Worlds?"

The CEO flashed an anxious smile. "Both. I'd bet my life that right now the CEOs on the Executive Council are gathering in the home star system every remaining warship in the Syndicate Worlds' mobile forces."

Geary snorted. "You are betting your life."

"That's what I figured."

As CEOs went, this one seemed both candid and shrewd. As Geary paused to think, rubbing his chin, Rione's voice whispered to him again. *He's reading out as honest in his statements. He's also worried, but that could be because of fears for personal safety rather than fears for the people of the Syndicate Worlds.*

Give us more readings, sir, Iger urged. *Ask him about the aliens.*

"I need to know more about what you're offering," Geary stated. "Tell me something about these aliens."

Boyens hesitated. "The things I know are my bargaining chips. If I tell you enough, you might not need to make a deal."

"CEO Boyens," Geary said coldly, "I won't make a trade no matter what information you have unless I know that what you're proposing is in the best interests of the Alliance and humanity as a whole. So I suggest you start trying to convince me."

The CEO watched Geary for several seconds, then nodded.

"That matches what we've seen of your behavior. What do you want to know?"

"What do the aliens look like?" That maybe wasn't the most important thing, but it was a question he had been wondering about for some time.

"I don't know. As far as I can tell, no one does." Boyens smiled crookedly at Geary's reaction. "It's true. If any human has ever personally encountered the aliens, they haven't reported back on it. We have had ships vanish in the border regions, and long ago on exploration trips beyond the border. Maybe their crews are prisoners, maybe they're dead. But none of them have come back."

"Haven't the Syndics talked to the aliens?"

"Comm links. Negotiations are pretty rare, but I've observed two of them." Boyens spread his hands in a frustrated gesture. "I'm not talking virtual meetings, just viewing the other side on a screen. But what they show us are obviously human avatars, fake images of humans against fake backgrounds."

How does he know they're fake? Iger asked. Digital signals wouldn't carry any means of knowing whether the content was real or altered.

"Fake?" Geary asked in turn. "What makes you certain that they're fake?"

"They're realistic enough to fool someone at first, but after a little while you start picking up on tiny inconsistencies and behaviors that feel *wrong*. It's like... suppose you were pretending to be a cat. You could probably get good enough at it to fool other humans. But real cats would still know the difference."

He believes that's the truth, Iger assured Geary.

For his part, Geary locked his eyes on Boyens'. "Humans vary a great deal. How do you *know* they're not really human?"

This time Boyens startled Geary by laughing, but the laughter held a sharp edge instead of humor. "If you ever see them, you'll know. I've talked to people from different cultures. I know how points of view can vary. But there's something about the aliens that goes beyond that, no matter how hard they try to hide it. Tru—" He laughed again, through clenched teeth. "I was about to say 'trust me.' But that's not going to happen, is it?"

"No. Tell me what these aliens want. You must have some idea."

The CEO frowned. "Only in general terms. From the records I've been able to access, and that's too damned few since anything regarding the aliens is classified and compartmentalized as much as possible, after first contact it seemed that all the aliens wanted was for us not to push into their territory. In the next couple of decades they seemed to want to push into *our* territory, but very cautiously. About seventy years ago they stopped that, and aside from occasional tests of our defenses, they've been quiet. No one knows why, because whoever has talked to them gets the clear impression they want some of the star systems occupied by the Syndicate Worlds. But there hadn't even been a feint within the last five or six months before we were ordered to leave that border and attack the Alliance."

That didn't tell Geary any more than he had already guessed. "What do their ships look like?"

"We don't know. They've got some kind of stealth gear that's a million light-years better than ours. You see nothing on sensors but a big blur on which our best gear can't make out any details." Boyens glared at Geary, plainly expecting this statement to be challenged.

"We've tried everything we can think of to get a decent look at one of their ships. Decades ago, some volunteers in stealth suits were vectored toward some alien ships that had entered a Syndicate Worlds' star system for negotiations. We hoped they would get close enough to get inside the alien stealth bubble, if that's what it is, and get a real look at things, but they all died before they saw anything."

"The Syndics have never destroyed an alien ship and had wreckage to examine?" Geary demanded.

"No." The Syndic CEO stared at the deck.

He's holding something back, Lieutenant Iger reported.

"Have you ever fought them?" Geary asked Boyens.

"No."

That answer surprised Geary, so he waited for Iger to report that it was a lie, but no such statement came. He was still thinking about his next question when Rione spoke. *Ask him if the Syndics have ever fought the aliens. Not him personally. The Syndics.*

The deception was obvious once Rione pointed it out. Geary set his jaw angrily as he eyed the Syndic. "Have the *Syndics* ever fought the aliens?"

Boyens's own jaw clenched for a moment, then he nodded. "Decades ago."

"What happened?"

"I wasn't there."

Evasion, Iger announced.

"Do you know what happened?" The Syndic stood silently, and Geary got up. "You want us to trust you when you're obviously withholding critical information? Why shouldn't I leave the Syndic border area to its own devices?"

The Syndic flushed with what seemed to be a mix of anger and embarrassment. "They always seem one step ahead of us. I was briefed on one program that should have worked. We jumped ships into star systems only a light-year or so from alien-occupied star systems, then launched asteroids hollowed out to hold sensors at the alien star systems. Even at the speeds we launched them, they would have taken decades to reach their targets, but they should've looked like nothing but high-velocity rocks since all of their sensors were passive and their power systems were so heavily shielded. It didn't work. Sensors tracking the trajectories of the rocks spotted their destruction short of the alien star systems."

Interesting, Rione's voice noted unemotionally, *but also a diversion. He's still avoiding talking about what happened when the Syndics fought these aliens.*

Geary rubbed his chin as he thought about ways to get this Syndic to say more about the alien sensors and combat capabilities. "I assume the Syndicate Worlds has also tried crewed missions into alien-occupied star systems."

"Right. None came back. We never heard anything from any of them."

"What about the star systems you've abandoned to them? Did you try leaving anything on those that could report back?"

Boyens stared at Geary. "How did you—? Yes, we've abandoned some star systems to maintain peace on the border, and yes, sensors were left behind. We hid automated courier ships in the star systems to pick up what those sensors saw, then jump out with the information. None of those ships ever reported in. It's like the damned aliens know everything we're doing the moment we do it.

Before we do it, even."

"Is that what happened when the Syndics fought them?" Geary pressed.

The Syndic CEO seemed to spend a long moment deciding what to say, then he met Geary's eyes. "Yes. And on those occasions when our warships could acquire targets and fire on them, the shots had no effect. Hell lances were absorbed with no indications of damage, grapeshot simply vanished against the alien screens, and our missiles were all destroyed short of their targets."

Geary smiled thinly. "Why didn't you want us to know that?"

"Because I wanted you to fight them. I was afraid if I told you, then you'd decide not to confront the aliens and leave the Syndicate Worlds to deal with the threat."

"You think we can do what your warships couldn't?"

Boyens's face reddened. "Don't toy with me. You've annihilated Syndic flotillas time and again, including flotillas that substantially outnumbered your own forces. I don't know how. But you obviously have a major advantage over us."

Rione's voice came again, sounding amused this time. *I wonder if he realizes that he's looking at that advantage as he speaks.*

Unable to give Rione an annoyed look, Geary stayed focused on the Syndic. "What else can you tell us?"

The CEO hesitated, then spoke roughly. "Not a lot. Most of what I have to offer is experience. Experience dealing with senior CEOs and the aliens. I can help. I just want you to help hold off the aliens."

"Why?"

Boyens sighed, then spread his hands helplessly. "I helped

defend them for ten years. I got to know them. I... feel responsible for them."

"You say that like you should be apologizing for caring about them," Geary challenged.

Boyens didn't answer, looking away, then faced Geary again. "Mobile-forces CEOs, any mobile-forces officers and personnel, are discouraged from developing any personal ties with local populations... because it might lead to their hesitating when they have to take necessary internal-security actions."

"Internal-security actions. Such as bombarding your own planets?"

"Yes."

"How the hell does any human being agree to do that?" Geary demanded.

Once again, the CEO was silent for a while. "To keep everyone safe. I know how that sounds. Threaten to kill your own people to keep them safe. But it maintains order. It keeps us strong enough to face external threats. It's about what's best for the majority of the people. We can't let small groups jeopardize the security of everyone else."

Apparently the aliens weren't the only beings with thought patterns hard to understand. Geary was trying to decide what else to ask, whether or not to order Boyens transferred off *Dauntless* again, when Rione spoke. *Ask him about Senator Navarro, about the lack of attacks on Abassas.*

Why did Rione want to know that? But maybe the answer would provide an important insight. "One more thing, CEO Boyens, and I'll tell you frankly that if I don't like the answer, you'll be off this ship. Why hasn't Abassas Star System been attacked for a while?"

Boyens looked perplexed. "Abassas? Is that near Syndicate Worlds' space?"

"Yes. It's the home star system of the current chair of the Alliance grand council."

The Syndic CEO appeared puzzled a moment longer, then suddenly laughed. "You're falling for that? Seriously? It's the oldest trick in the book."

"What is?" Geary demanded.

"Avoiding attacking property belonging to an enemy leader. It makes the enemy wonder what kind of deal that leader might have cut. I don't have personal knowledge of Abassas, but that's a common strategy for sowing dissension in the enemy ranks." Boyens stopped laughing and spread his hands. "I don't know if you like that answer or not, but that's the only answer I know."

Geary nodded abruptly. "Thank you. You'll be taken to the brig on this ship while your offer is evaluated." He turned and left, trying to resist the urge to yell at the Syndic.

Halting in the observation room, Geary took in the displays. "What do you think?" he asked everyone there.

Rione answered first, her own eyes on the readouts. "He didn't register as deceptive in his request for aid, though there were other places where he was clearly shading the truth and being certain to phrase his answers carefully."

Lieutenant Iger nodded. "That matches my assessment, sir. The request for aid appears to be sincere. He didn't tell us anything that was a lie. That doesn't mean that he didn't hold back other things, though. Things that might be important."

Desjani, her eyes narrowed in thought, was gazing not at the Syndic or the displays, but into the distance. "They're not acting like they're more powerful than we are."

It took Geary a moment to realize what she was referring to. "The aliens?"

"Yes." She turned her head to focus on him. "Concealing your strength, capabilities, and dispositions are all usually good tactics in battle, but there are still times when it's a good idea to let the other side know that you have overwhelming superiority. Instead, they're hiding their capabilities."

Rione was watching Desjani and nodded in agreement. "That's so. Especially in negotiations."

"But," Desjani continued, "it's also useful to make the enemy think that you're stronger than you actually are. To keep him guessing. It's a very good tactic to employ when you're actually weaker than the enemy."

Everyone stood silently for a few moments while they thought about that. "How do we know," Geary finally said, "that they're thinking like we would? Maybe to them, all of this mystery is just normal."

"Even hiding the shapes of their ships?" Desjani shook her head. "If what that Syndic said is true, then these aliens have devoted a huge amount of effort to keep humans from learning anything about them. Maybe they are privacy freaks who hide themselves under every possible disguise and cover, but if this were a human foe, I would ask myself what they are so concerned with hiding."

Lieutenant Iger spoke deferentially. "Captain, that's from a human perspective. On Earth and many other planets, the dominant life-forms use physical displays to overawe opponents, trying to make themselves look bigger than they are. Humans do it, too, to some extent. But there are life-forms that use very different approaches, such as lurking hidden until their prey comes close enough, then striking before the victim can react."

Rione made a disgusted noise. "You'd think the Syndics could have learned a little more in a century of contact. This CEO *is* holding back information." She suddenly seemed to think of something. "How long ago did the Alliance and the Syndicate Worlds 'discover' the hypernet technology and begin creating their own hypernets?"

Desjani tapped her data unit, then read the answer. "The first segments of the hypernets on both sides were activated sixty-nine years ago."

Rione's lip curled in anger. "The CEO claimed the aliens were fairly active until about seventy years ago and have been mostly quiet since then. Those bastards spent a few decades learning more about humanity, then sent in the hypernet technology and since that time have been sitting back and waiting for us to annihilate ourselves."

"Why the probing attacks during that time?" Geary wondered.

"To make sure our sensors and weapons hadn't changed in any major ways," Desjani suggested.

"That's plausible," Iger agreed.

There were still far too many questions, and the Syndic CEO seemed to have far too few answers. "Is he worth keeping on this ship?" Geary asked.

"I'd recommend it," Rione said. "I believe his answer regarding the lack of attacks on Abassas. It registered true, and strikes me as a very effective tactic. I may have to use it myself sometime."

"I'd recommend keeping him as well, sir," Iger added. "He could have more information, and he told us that he knew the people in the border star systems, the ones in charge out there. We might need those contacts."

Desjani looked unhappy, then slowly nodded. "We need every advantage we can get when we know so little about these aliens. And if he tries to betray us, I want him within easy reach of an Alliance Marine with a loaded weapon."

Two and a half days later, Geary ordered the fleet into motion. He watched the swarm of warships come together into the single large formation he'd ordered for this part of the transit. Except for the flaring main propulsion units at their sterns, the warships resembled sharks of various sizes, a bit shorter and chunkier than any shark in the case of the battleships, but otherwise the comparison came easily. Fins carrying sensors, weapons, and shield generators projected from the curved surfaces of the hulls, which were designed to deflect hits. The fast, lean, and small sharks that were destroyers darted swiftly to their assigned positions relative to *Dauntless*, the larger light cruisers moving among them with almost as much agility. The heavy cruisers swung through space with calm authority, their greater armor, weaponry, and bulk reflecting their primary mission as killers of other escorts.

The battleships moved like the monsters they were, huge, bristling with weapons, slower, and almost clumsy because of their massive size, yet as near to indestructible as anything humanity put into space. Around them came the battle cruisers, about the same size as the battleships and well armed, but leaner and faster, having traded protection for more ability to accelerate and maneuver.

Near the center of the formation were the so-called fast fleet auxiliaries. "Fast" only in the minds of whoever had given them the name, the auxiliaries were neither rounded nor sharklike. Instead, their blocky lines resembled what they were, mammoth self-propelled manufacturing facilities that carried their own raw materials to fashion replacements for needed repairs as well as new fuel cells, missiles, grapeshot, and mines to replace those used by the warships. In combat, they were a constant worry, unable to maneuver as well as the warships or protect themselves very well, but without the resupply and repair capability on those auxiliaries, Geary could never have brought the fleet back through Syndic space. He hoped he wouldn't need them as badly this time.

The images of the new *Adroit*-class battle cruisers held his gaze for a moment, and he had to avoid frowning at his display in displeasure. There was no telling what anyone watching him might think the frown was about, and he knew from long experience that everyone watched the most senior officers to judge their current attitudes and emotions. It was one of the first survival tactics any reasonably smart junior officer learned.

But he wasn't unhappy at anyone in the fleet or the actions of any of the warships. His displeasure sprang from having used the fleet's software to conduct a virtual tour of *Adroit* herself several hours ago. Geary had long ago resigned himself to the fact that the warships in this future weren't finely honed structures built to endure for decades. Instead, they were all built quickly, with few frills and many a rough edge. A century of war had resulted in warships whose short expected life span didn't justify craftsmanship.

But the *Adroit* class had taken that to a new and lower level, worse than he had realized just from reviewing the official statistics about the new battle cruisers. As Geary's avatar had toured the ship, he had been forced to ever greater efforts to avoid revealing how appalled he was by construction shortcuts and design compromises that had saved time and money at the cost of creating significant weaknesses in the *Adroit* and her sister ships. He could tell from Captain Kattnig's explanations and occasional apologies about equipment that *Adroit*'s commanding officer was well aware of her shortcomings, and any veterans among her crew surely knew as well. But it would have served no purpose for him to emphasize and openly fixate on the design problems. Geary had been on the receiving end of that before, stuck with equipment he knew wasn't all it should be, then forced to endure failing grades and harsh criticisms aimed at him and his personnel from inspection teams that seemed to think crews were supposed to miraculously overcome the accumulated failures of the design, procurement, and testing processes.

So he took care to hide his reaction because *Adroit*'s crew could too easily have assumed that his disapproval was about them. Nothing could have been further from the truth than that. The crew was eager to prove themselves, disappointed at having missed the desperate voyage home that the rest of the fleet had endured, determined to shine in the eyes of Black Jack Geary. Captain Kattnig knew Captain Tulev. "We were enlisted men serving together on the *Determined*, and both received our field commissions after a battle at Hattera." Kattnig's eyes had gone wistful for a moment. "That was a lot of ships, a lot of battles ago. Tulev and I are still here, though."

"I'm glad to have both of you under my command," Geary replied. "I understand *Adroit* was only commissioned two months ago."

"About that, yes, sir. But we're ready," Kattnig insisted. "We can keep up with the fleet."

"I've no doubt of it." Geary had spoken clearly enough for nearby crew members to hear. "*Adroit* feels like a veteran ship. I know you'll fight well."

Captain Kattnig nodded, his expression tense. "We will, sir. None of us could be with you on the long return to Alliance space, and we all regret that."

The absurdity of regretting missing out on the desperate retreat made Geary smile, but he managed to make the smile an understanding one. He didn't have any trouble grasping why people wanted to be with their comrades at such times. "We could have used you, but you're with us now."

"I understand Captain Tulev did well," Kattnig added in a lower voice. "He excelled."

"He did. Captain Tulev is both reliable and capable. I was very glad to have him along."

"That's good to hear. Captain Tulev and I were commissioned together."

"Yes, so you told me."

"Did I? My apologies, Admiral." Captain Kattnig glanced around, as if studying his own ship. "They say you'll end the war. This may be the last campaign."

"If the living stars grant us that blessing, this will be the last campaign of the war," Geary agreed.

"Yes. A good thing." Kattnig sounded slightly uncertain, though. "I couldn't be with the fleet, you know. My last ship, *Paragon*, had been badly damaged in the fighting at Valdisia, so we were undergoing major repairs at T'shima."

"I see."

"Then *Paragon* was rushed into action to defend the Alliance when the fleet was... unable to be accounted for. We were so badly shot up defending Beowulf that the ship was written off."

"It must have been a valiant action," Geary said, wondering why Kattnig seemed to be trying to justify his absence from the fleet when it first attacked the Syndic home star system.

"It was, sir. It was." Kattnig's voice sank to a whisper, his eyes staring into the distance, then he focused back on Geary. "I demanded another ship. To... to be with the fleet this time."

Geary spoke quietly and firmly. "The defense of the Alliance while the fleet was gone was a critical task. Otherwise, we would have returned to find ruin and defeat. You performed well."

"Thank you, sir. You will see how well my ship can perform," Kattnig promised.

Geary had done what he could to keep morale on *Adroit* high, but his inspection had provided too many proofs that her crew could fight better than the ship they had been given. Necessary redundancies in critical systems had been reduced past the safe minimums, weapons capabilities were hindered by cost-cutting in the lines supplying power to the hell lances and in the missile magazines, which carried fewer specters than even their limited size could have managed if properly laid out. Sensors lacked redundancies and capabilities as well, the *Adroit* class having been designed to be dependent on the sensors being employed by other ships. All well and good in a fleet engagement, but an *Adroit*-class ship on her own would be significantly handicapped by that feature. He couldn't even send an *Adroit* out in company with only escorts, since the capabilities of cruisers and destroyers couldn't completely compensate for the shortfalls of the sensors on the new battle cruisers.

The design of the *Adroit*-class warships had once again driven home to him just how bad things were, just how much the economies and industrial base of the combatants had been strained by a century of warfare beyond even the abilities of interstellar civilizations to sustain. If he didn't succeed in bringing an end to this war, everything would continue to deteriorate, an accelerating spiral toward collapse, as if the war were a black hole sucking in humanity and everything humanity had created among the stars. He could now understand the desperation that had led Desjani to demand his promise to stick to the mission she believed he had been assigned by the living stars themselves. He could understand the hope with which people looked to him. He wondered how much all of them understood the strain their hopes put on him.

Desjani did. He felt certain of that. She understood well enough that she had as much as offered to surrender her honor to him if he asked that of her, if Geary said he needed that. His reaction to that offer, a refusal to do such a thing to her, had given him the strength to keep going. Humanity's civilizations might be crumbling, but as long as people like Desjani kept fighting and believing, there was hope the fall could be arrested.

So Geary sat in the fleet command seat on *Dauntless*'s bridge as the fleet's warships settled into their assigned positions, then the entire fleet began accelerating toward the jump point for the Syndic-controlled star system of Atalia, hundreds of warships moving as one.

He became aware that Desjani was watching him, unaware of his own inner thoughts. At least, he hoped she was unaware of them. At times, Desjani had shown an unsettling ability to seem to be reading his mind. "What?"

"They're a fine sight, aren't they, sir?" she asked. "I never saw them maneuver like this. We were always sloppier before. What counted was getting to grips with the enemy, not looking good in formation. We didn't realize that there was a connection between those two things."

"They look very good. They *are* very good. But they won't all be coming home," Geary noted in a quiet voice.

"No. It's been a century since they all came home, Fleet Admiral Geary. Perhaps you'll finally change that."

"If I do, I won't have done it alone, Captain Desjani."

The fleet headed out, every eye in Varandal Star System on its progress.

"Our first stop will be Atalia," Geary confirmed to the officers watching him. "We'll assume battle formation before jump even though we don't expect to encounter significant opposition at Atalia. If the Syndics want a fight there, though, we'll give it to them." The fleet conference room seemed to be huge just then, with a very long table occupied by the virtual presences of every commanding officer of every ship in the fleet. In addition to the fleet officers, newly promoted Marine General Carabali was present, along with Co-President Rione and two grand council representatives, the stout Senator Costa and a male senator named Sakai, who'd spoken little when Geary met with the council.

Most of the fleet officers were doing their best to ignore the presence of the two new politicians but were treating Rione with marginal courtesy since it was known that Geary trusted her. The officers of the ships from the Callas Republic and the Rim Federation had always regarded Rione as their politician and defended her, but even they had been happy that they had never had to choose between her and Geary.

Where Captain Cresida should have been, one of the new battle-cruiser captains sat. A replacement, and yet not a replacement. But at least the stolid, reliable presences of Captains Duellos and Tulev were there, and Desjani was physically present.

"In order to ensure security for our plans, I'll give further orders at Atalia," Geary continued. "I'm not happy keeping you in the dark until then, but it's critical to keep our plans secret. Are there any questions?"

Most of the officers looked disappointed but nodded in acceptance. However, the newer commanders, those who had joined the fleet at Varandal, looked around with confused expressions. Geary knew what they were expecting, to have him lay out a plan that he would try to convince the fleet's officers to support, using political maneuvering to build up enough support until the fleet commander called for a vote among the fleet captains sanctioning the plan. He'd done away with that procedure as fast as he could, though for a long time fleet conferences had been painfully contentious.

"Fleet Admiral Geary"—Captain Olisa of the battle cruiser *Ascendant* sounded torn between respect and challenge—"fleet officers are accustomed to receiving more information about proposed plans at this point."

Geary gave Olisa a polite but firm look in return. "My plans aren't proposed, Captain. They've been made. I'll let you know more when I can."

"But we need to discuss—"

Tulev broke in, speaking dispassionately. "Fleet Admiral Geary is open to suggestions and comment, Isvan. I assure you he will listen, but he does not do things as you are accustomed. He follows the path of our ancestors."

"Our ancestors?" Olisa grimaced, but nodded. "I had heard things were different. It takes some getting used to, though."

"I understand," Geary replied. "I had a number of things to get used to as well."

"Can you confirm our mission, Fleet Admiral Geary?" Captain Armus of the *Colossus* asked. "Are we indeed aiming to force an end to the war?"

Geary weighed his response. Armus had been difficult at times and was by no stretch an inspired officer, but he was also brave enough and followed orders. At the moment he was, in addition, being respectful and proper, which deserved the same treatment in return. Geary finally nodded. "That's correct. We intend backing the Syndics into a corner and keeping them there until they agree to halt the fighting. Not just a cease-fire. An end to the war."

Captain Badaya, who had seemed smug and contented since Geary's promotion, nodded back as if sharing a secret with Geary. "Using *your* plan, Fleet Admiral Geary."

"Yes. You'll all get much more detail on it at Atalia, I promise."

As the officers' images vanished, Geary saw that the two new political observers remained as if expecting something. "Yes, Senators?"

Costa gave Geary a quick smile. "You can brief us now that the others have left."

Desjani seemed to be literally biting her lip to keep from saying something. Geary searched for the correct and diplomatic response.

But Rione turned to Costa with a reassuring smile. "I'll bring them up to date, Fleet Admiral Geary."

She would? Geary hadn't confided his exact plans to Rione. Had she broken his security? But then on the side of her face away from the other senators Rione dropped a slow wink to Geary. "All right," Geary said. "Captain Desjani?"

He left hastily with Desjani, wondering what Rione would tell the others to keep them happy. "I wonder if there's any way to freeze those two out of the meeting software?"

"At least you have that politician to handle them," Desjani grumbled. "May my ancestors forgive me, but I'm actually grateful for the moment that she's on board."

"You'll get over it."

"And very quickly, too," Desjani agreed. "Will you be on the bridge for the jump to Atalia?"

"Of course." Geary paused. "There's a lot riding on this. There's somewhere I should go before then."

"I'm on my way there, too." They walked into the depths of

Dauntless, to the most protected part of the ship, where the rooms set aside for religious purposes rested. Desjani bade him farewell at the door to one room, her eyes searching his for a moment before the privacy door closed.

He sat down on the traditional wooden bench in his own room. He wondered for the first time from which world the wood had come. So many worlds had trees or similar vegetation, and humanity had brought many plants with them on their long march through the vastness of space. Geary lighted the single candle, then sat watching the flame for a while. It was hard to put his many emotions into words, but finally he spoke softly. "I'm not asking for success for me, but for all of those who are counting on me. Please help me end this, and if my fate is to die on this mission, please see Tanya Desjani safely to her home again."

Half an hour later he was on the bridge of *Dauntless* along with Desjani as the fleet, divided into three subformations and arrayed for battle, jumped for Atalia.

4

Four days later, the Alliance fleet flashed back into normal space at the jump point on the fringes of the Syndicate Worlds–controlled Atalia Star System.

"What the hell?" was Geary's first response as the fleet's sensors updated the situation.

No mines blocked their exit from the jump point, no powerful flotilla of warships waited nearby or cruised in distant orbit about the star Atalia, but only four light-minutes distant a large gaggle of Syndic merchant ships hung at rest relative to the jump point as if they were awaiting the Alliance warships.

Desjani, frowning in disbelief, turned to bark out orders to the bridge watch-standers. "Find out everything you can about those merchant ships."

"Captain," the operations watch-stander reported, "every one of those merchant ships has smaller craft hanging on them, up to twenty on the larger ones."

"Mother ships." Geary waited impatiently for more detailed reports from the sensors' examination of the enemy craft. "Carrying what?"

"Those things are too big to be missiles," Desjani commented. Then her eyes widened in recognition. "Damn. They're—"

"Syndic fast attack craft," the operations watch-stander reported triumphantly.

"They're sending FACs against us?" Desjani seemed almost horrified, but not as if she feared the news. "Against this many warships in open space?"

"FACs?" Geary hastily read as a description popped up on his display, and understanding came. "They look like they're pretty much the same as the SRACs a hundred years ago."

"SRACs?" Desjani asked.

"Short-range attack craft. Those were only intended for operations very close to planets or other major space objects because of their limited range and capabilities."

"Then they're effectively the same thing," Desjani confirmed. "Out here, unable to dart into atmosphere or behind a planet, they're going to have problems."

Problems indeed. Geary hurriedly studied the capabilities of the FACs. At point one light speed, the Alliance fleet only required forty minutes to cover four light-minutes of distance. Ten minutes had already passed, and he had to assume that the FACs would launch as soon as possible, then would speed toward the Alliance ships, further reducing the time until contact.

Like the SRACs he had known, these FACs were small, carrying only one or two human crew members. In addition to a single hell-lance particle-beam projector with a slow recharge time, some models carried a single missile, while others had a couple of single-shot grapeshot launchers. Their armor was nonexistent, and their small power plants could support only weak shields. "Who the hell sent them on this suicide mission?"

"They must all be volunteers," Desjani offered.

Alerts sounded as the fleet's sensors spotted the FACs starting to launch from the improvised merchant mother ships three minutes ago. Looked at only in terms of numbers, the swarm of small craft seemed impressive.

Rione obviously thought so. "Can we handle this?"

"Easily," Desjani muttered.

Geary nodded in agreement.

"But they're smaller, faster, and more maneuverable," Rione insisted.

"Smaller, yes," Geary replied. "Faster and more maneuverable, no. Whoever came up with this plan must be primarily a planetary defense officer, who thought because FACs look sort of like atmospheric craft compared to space warships, that the physics would work the same as aircraft versus seagoing ships on planets with atmospheres and oceans. But those FACs aren't operating in a much-less-dense medium than our ships, they're operating in exactly the same medium, so it's all about mass-to-thrust ratios. The FACs are small, but that means they've got small propulsion systems and small power plants. They're certainly more maneuverable than battleships, but our destroyers have bigger propulsion units and better mass-to-thrust ratios." On his display, the FACs had finished scrambling from the merchant ships and were accelerating toward the Alliance fleet.

Desjani shook her head, looking disgusted. "Any of those small craft that somehow survived this attack could never get home. They don't have the fuel or life-support endurance. I hope the Syndic commander responsible for this is on one of those merchants."

"He or she is probably a dozen light-years away," Geary said. "How stealthy are these FACs?"

"Some capability, but they're out here in the middle of nowhere, accelerating, and we watched them launched. The combat systems will have no trouble tracking them even after they— And there they went. Stealth systems on the FACs have gone active, and we've still got solid tracks on all of them."

"Okay." Geary spent a few more seconds watching the horde of FACs heading to intercept the Alliance fleet, then scrolled through some of the formations he had worked out before this and loaded into the maneuvering systems. After checking to confirm the time required for a message to reach the most distant unit in the current Alliance formation, he tapped his comm controls. "All units in the Alliance fleet, this is—" He'd almost said Captain Geary, but caught himself. "Admiral Geary. Execute Formation November at time four seven."

Desjani glanced at him, pulled up the formation on her own display, then nodded. "It will do. But you should slow the formation a little to ensure as many kills on the FACs as possible."

"Thanks. Do you think point zero eight light speed will be slow enough?"

After repeating the question to her combat-systems watch-stander and waiting for a swift answer, Desjani nodded again. "Yes, sir."

Rione spoke with resignation. "If they're doomed, do we have to destroy them and risk casualties of our own?"

"Yes," Geary replied. "We can't swing far enough to one side to evade missiles fired by that mass of FACs, which means the units on that flank would run risks of being hit by missiles on high-deflection run-ins, which are a lot harder to hit with defensive fire than low-deflection runs. I'd be particularly worried about some of the missiles targeting the auxiliaries as we went past the FACs."

At time four seven, the current Alliance formation dissolved, the squadrons and divisions of warships proceeding to new stations relative to *Dauntless*. Geary waited until the fleet had formed into five rectangles, the broad sides facing in the directions of the fleet's movement, the largest rectangle in the center, the four smaller rectangles only a short distance off each corner of the large one. To Geary's aggravation, two of the new battle cruisers, one of the new battleships, and several smaller combatants ended up pushing far forward of their assigned stations. "*Adroit, Assert, Insistent, Dungeon, Pavise, Demicontres, Halda, Tschekan*, assume your ordered stations immediately."

Unlike at Corvus and engagements soon after that, the bulk of the fleet held formation firmly, acting as a powerful example reinforcing Geary's commands. Leaving only one eye to watch the errant warships, Geary put most of his attention on the movements of the fleet and the oncoming mass of FACs, which seemed to fill space ahead of the fleet. "All units in the Alliance fleet, brake velocity to point zero eight light speed at time zero nine, then brake to point zero four at time one two, then accelerate to point zero six light speed at time one five."

"None of our ships can actually change velocity that fast," Desjani noted.

"I know. But this will keep their velocity changing so much just prior to contact that the FACs' targeting systems will be screwed up trying to estimate the time to fire their hell lances and grapeshot. I wouldn't try it against other major warships because our formations are going to get disrupted by that many velocity changes on top of each other, but against the FACs, this tactic is supposed to work." At least, that was what the official guidance against SRACs had said a century ago.

One more command to pass. "All units in the Alliance fleet, turn up zero three five degrees at time two four." That would bring the fleet through the mob of FACs, then turn it upward to pass well above the merchant shipping.

"We'll miss the merchants," Desjani complained, then she gave him a knowing glance. "They're too attractive. Too easy a target. They're not trying to run even though they've finished launching the small craft."

"Right. Are they just easy targets, or are they bait?" Geary shook his head. "I don't trust anything about those merchant ships."

The fleet began its braking maneuver, thrusters pushing the bows of the warships up and over so that their main propulsion units faced forward, followed by the propulsion units kicking in to slow the ships as fast as momentum, the power of the propulsion units, and the ships' inertial dampers would allow. After the two braking maneuvers, and just prior to contact with the FACs, the warships would pivot again to reaccelerate, swinging their bows forward once more to meet the Syndic attack with their heaviest armor and firepower.

"Still coming straight at us," Desjani commented.

Something about her casual, confident tone worried Geary. He tapped his controls again. "All units in the Alliance fleet, these FACs have only one punch, but that can be a powerful punch. Don't underestimate them until they've been killed. All units conduct on-station evasive maneuvers immediately prior to contact with the FACs." On-station told his ships not to veer too far from their assigned positions but allowed them to make the small changes in vectors that could further throw off attempts by the enemy fire-control systems to predict their future positions well enough to score hits during the fraction-of-a-second-long engagement envelopes.

More alerts sounded as the first FACs began firing missiles. Only one missile per FAC, and only perhaps half of the FACs carrying missiles, but that added up quickly when there were that many small craft coming at the fleet. "All ships, weapons free. Engage the missiles, then the fast attack craft."

At short range, with the opposing forces closing swiftly, there wasn't time for the enemy missiles to engage in their own evasive actions. Hell lances blazed from the Alliance warships, filling space with directed high-energy particle beams, which at close range punched through armor as if it were paper. Syndic missiles exploded prematurely or came apart under the hail of fire, then the surviving missiles began running into patterns of grapeshot. The clusters of metal ball bearings tore into oncoming missiles, each metal ball that struck a target vaporizing from the force of the impact. Struck by the shotgun blasts of massed grapeshot batteries, the remainder of the enemy missiles were blown apart as the Alliance fleet rushed into contact with the fast attack craft.

The sheer numbers of the attack craft could have made up for their frail defenses and limited armament, concentrating their individually weak firepower to hit larger ships again and again, but not under these conditions, not when facing a fleet of larger warships in formations in which the already greatly superior firepower of the warships overlapped and reinforced each other. FACs were supposed to engage small numbers of isolated warships, ideally one or two. Given the right conditions, near a planet or other base where the small craft could linger stealthily and silently while awaiting the approach of the enemy, enough FACs could even take down a battleship operating on its own, though probably while suffering serious losses as well.

These weren't the right conditions.

Alliance destroyers were in their element against this kind of enemy, rampaging through the smaller, weaker FACs like hawks among a flock of sparrows, hell lances stabbing out as fast as they could fire to smash through the flimsy protection of the much smaller spacecraft. Light cruisers moved almost as nimbly among the destroyers, their heavier armaments taking out several small attack craft with each volley. Coming right behind the lighter escorts were the heavy cruisers, not so fast and maneuverable, but better protected and far outgunning the FACs. Against the Alliance warships, the FACs tried to focus their fire on single ships enough to overcome shields and armor, but with so many targets coming so fast, not enough hits could be scored on any one ship in time to make a difference.

The Alliance fleet formation merged with the swarm of fast attack craft at a combined velocity of almost point zero five light speed, the cloud of FACs evaporating as it merged with the warships like a flock of gnats running head-on into a massive land vehicle. Syndic small attack craft blew apart or spun away uncontrolled, with dead systems and crew. Due to sheer numbers, some of the small craft penetrated past the Alliance escorts, only to be instantly torn to pieces by the firepower of the battleships and battle cruisers.

The moment of contact and destruction of the horde of FACs happened almost too quickly for it to register on human senses, then the Alliance fleet was through the enemy and following Geary's command to turn sharply upward, "up" being defined by humans as the direction above the plane of the star system, just as "down" was beneath the plane of the star system. Geary studied his fleet status display anxiously, aware that collisions with FACs or a lucky barrage of hits could have done significant damage to or even destroyed one of his escorts. The status reports were still updating, showing weakened shields and occasional hits on destroyers or light cruisers, when something else caught his attention. "*Dungeon*, return to formation immediately! Alter your track to avoid those merchant ships!"

Unlike the rest of the fleet, the lone heavy cruiser had continued onward instead of altering her course upward, and was now heading straight into the mass of Syndic merchant ships waiting silently along the path the fleet would have taken. Geary waited as seconds passed, having flashbacks to the senseless loss of a cruiser and three destroyers to a minefield at Sutrah.

Dungeon's reply finally came, her captain sounding baffled. "We're going to let these Syndic ships escape?"

"It's a trap!" Geary called back immediately. "Use your head! They're not trying to run, and there are no escape pods leaving those merchants! They had no crews embarked, just the pilots of those FACs, and they're probably rigged as booby traps. Get your ship clear *now*!"

Seconds later, *Dungeon* finally began pulling up, her course vectors altering oh-so-slowly toward the rest of the fleet, while momentum still carried her closer to the merchants.

Desjani was watching the heavy cruiser's progress silently, her face an emotionless mask, doubtless also remembering Sutrah.

"Ten seconds to closest-point-of-approach for Dungeon to the nearest merchant ships," the operations watch reported.

"They're lighting off their propulsion systems," Desjani said an instant later. The merchants' propulsion systems had kicked in, thrusters pushing the clumsy vessels up, aiming to try to intercept the Alliance fleet, which would pass over them. "They all lit off at about the same time. It must be automated controls with all the merchant ships slaved together. No bunch of civilians could have managed that coordinated an action."

"Even if a bunch of civilians were willing to charge at this fleet," Geary agreed, his eyes on the seconds counting down for *Dungeon* to clear the merchant ships.

Given the light-seconds separating the rest of the fleet from *Dungeon* and the merchant ships, they saw the explosions three seconds after they'd taken place. "The two merchant ships closest to *Dungeon*'s track have suffered core overloads," the operations watch reported. "Assess that *Dungeon* will be within the outer limits of the danger area and may sustain damage."

"They thought they could use your own trick against you?" Desjani complained.

"Maybe they thought someone else might be in command, or else that Admiral Geary had grown complacent," Rione replied.

Whatever the reason, the Syndics had modified the improvised ship minefield Geary had used at Lakota. "That's not a bad idea," he commented, "putting their ships under automated controls to close on their targets if the targets aren't coming to them. We need to keep an eye out for that kind of tactic happening again."

"Even the Syndics wouldn't throw away functioning warships that way," Desjani said. "But from now on, I am going to be inclined to shoot first if any merchant ship tries to get close." She frowned at her display. "Lieutenant Yuon," Desjani called to one of the watch-standers, "those Syndic core overloads seemed much more powerful than they should have been. Find out how much the Syndics have boosted the power of those explosions and get an estimate of how they did it." She gave Geary a warning look. "If we get within hell-lance range, we might be close enough for those things to damage some of our ships."

"Concur. Let's not take chances." He had developed a hesitation to use specter missiles as the fleet's supply dwindled during the long retreat home, but the fleet's missile magazines had been topped off at Varandal, and missiles were clearly what was called for here. Still, merchants only had shields good enough to block radiation, no armor, no defenses, and these merchant ships were lumbering along easily predictable, smooth vectors aimed at trying to intercept the Alliance warships. It was the work of a couple of seconds to ask the fleet combat systems to assign one missile each from enough warships to engage each merchant ship with the single specter, which would be all that was needed to destroy it. But before Geary could tap the execute command, a delighted laugh from Desjani drew his attention.

"The Syndics packed the formation too tight," she explained. "It would have been more effective if we'd run straight into them, but as it is..." Desjani laughed again and waved at her display.

The two merchant ships that had destroyed themselves with core overloads had been close enough to some of the other merchant ships for the blast effects to trigger core overloads in the other ships as well. As those merchant ships blew, they took out more of their neighbors, whose own core overloads set off even more destruction in the ships close to them.

An expanding wave of destruction was unfurling through the mass of Syndic merchant ships as the Syndic minefield obliterated itself in a flurry of fratricide. "I guess we can save our missiles," Geary commented, then his satisfaction at watching the self-elimination of the Syndic booby trap vanished as *Dungeon* staggered out of the edges of the zone of destruction created by the core overloads of the first two Syndic merchant ships. Geary bit back a curse as he saw automated damage status reports coming in from *Dungeon*. By the time *Dungeon* had become aware of the explosions, it was too late to react, and the heavy cruiser had taken the brunt of the blasts on one side of her stern. Geary hit his comm controls harder than he had to. "*Dungeon*, I need a full damage report and estimated time of repair to your damaged propulsion units as soon as possible." Switching circuits, he made a call to *Tanuki*.

Captain Smyth, who at Varandal had assumed command of

the auxiliaries division from a visibly relieved Captain Tyrosian, answered several seconds later. "Yes, Admiral?"

"I need your assessment and repair estimate for the damage to *Dungeon*," Geary explained. "Initial reports indicate the damage to most of her propulsion units is too severe for *Dungeon* to fix herself. If that's the case, I want to know how long it would take to get enough of her propulsion units back online so she can keep up with the fleet."

"Certainly," Captain Smyth answered cheerily. "I'll get back to you."

"Casual attitude, even for an engineer," Desjani commented.

"True," Geary agreed. "But he seems ready and willing to follow orders. Tyrosian did an okay job as division commander, but she never enjoyed it and seemed overwhelmed at times."

"That's putting it mildly."

"Captain?" Lieutenant Yuon reported. "The core overloads were about fifty percent stronger than merchant-ship core overloads should have generated. Analysis indicates the Syndics packed the merchant cargo containers with explosives and accelerants of various kinds."

"They wanted to get us while we thought we were outside the danger area," Desjani commented. "That won't be a problem now." She smiled as the Syndic merchant ships at the far edges of the improvised minefield blew themselves apart as the wave of destruction reached them, leaving only an expanding field of debris where the large group of merchant ships had once been. "Lovely, isn't it? The only thing better than blowing away Syndic warships is watching Syndic ships blowing away each other."

Geary just smiled back at her briefly, then focused on the rest of the situation. The Alliance warships were well clear of the debris field and opening the distance. *Dungeon* was far too close to the danger area but should be able to avoid being caught again. Now that he'd dealt with the Syndic forces near the jump exit, he could take the time to evaluate other Syndic defenses in Atalia.

There wasn't much else. As a front-line star system, Atalia had been fought over repeatedly for the last century, defenses in fixed orbits cratered or blown apart as fast as they could be constructed. Since the last time the Alliance fleet was there, a short while ago, the Syndics had thrown together a variety of fixed defenses like rail guns mounted on moons, asteroids, and a new orbital fort. In addition, a few Syndic Hunter-Killers, roughly similar to but smaller than Alliance destroyers, hung around the two other jump points Atalia boasted. One jump point led back to Padronis, a white dwarf star with nothing to commend it, and the other to the ruined star system of Kalixa. In about four more hours, once the Syndic HuKs saw the light announcing the arrival of the Alliance fleet, one of them would undoubtedly jump out to carry the news of the Alliance fleet's movements to other star systems. Maybe two HuKs would jump if the Syndics had tried to rebuild anything at Kalixa.

Aside from the HuKs, there was only a single light cruiser orbiting one of the planets in the inner system. No surprise there. With the Syndics so short of warships, they had probably pulled back just about everything left to defend their home star system. The FACs had been a defense of desperation.

Geary told the combat system to come up with a plan for bombarding the fixed defenses with kinetic projectiles, "rocks" in fleet parlance, then, when the solution popped up a moment later, punched approve and watched as dozens of his warships began spitting out chunks of solid metal that would strike their targets with tremendous amounts of energy gained by their speed. Nothing in a fixed orbit could possibly avoid getting hit, but for his warships, dodging any shots fired by the rail guns at the fleet across light-hours of distance wouldn't be hard at all. Still, Geary didn't want to have to worry about dealing with that as the fleet cut across the outer reaches of the star system, nor did he want those rail guns targeting *Dungeon* with barrages while the heavy cruiser was trying to make repairs.

Dungeon still hadn't called when Captain Smyth's image reappeared. "Quite a mess," Smyth announced in the same cheerful tones. "*Dungeon* should have ducked! That cruiser can't fix herself. Two main propulsion units are totally blown. *Tanuki* or *Titan* can do the job, but it will take an estimated four days. Until then, that cruiser is going to be limping along."

Meaning the fleet would have to limp along with it. Geary took only a moment to consider his options, knowing that slowing the fleet down that much in enemy territory wouldn't be wise. "Thank you, Captain."

"Anytime!"

"I wonder how he reacts to really bad news," Desjani said.

"Probably the same. More stuff needs fixed, so he's happy," Geary speculated.

"You can't ask for a better attitude from an engineer. Speaking of engineers and attitudes, did Captain Gundel ever finish that study you assigned him to keep him out of your hair?"

"No, he didn't. I left him in Varandal, still working away on it."

Desjani shook her head. "How long do you think it will take him to realize that since the fleet made it back to Varandal, there is no more need for a study on logistical requirements for getting back to Varandal?"

"I don't think Captain Gundel is deterred by minor issues like whether or not a report has any purpose. In any case, the point of that report was just to keep him occupied with something harmless, so it's still fulfilling its function." There wasn't any sense in putting off what he had to do next. He called *Dungeon*.

The cruiser's captain stared out of the virtual window floating before Geary's display. "Sir, we're still evaluating the damage."

"My readouts and an evaluation from the engineers on the auxiliaries indicate repairs will take four days and require major external support," Geary replied. "Is that consistent with your evaluations so far?"

Dungeon's commanding officer nodded even though he clearly didn't want to. "Yes, sir."

"The fleet can't slow down enough to accompany you that long," Geary stated bluntly. "*Dungeon* will have to return to Varandal and get repairs there. You can report on the results of our action here in Atalia."

Now the cruiser's captain simply seemed horrified. "Please, sir. It's not about me. The crew deserves to accompany the fleet on this historic mission. *Dungeon* can keep up, sir."

"No, she can't. I don't like doing this, Commander, but your own actions created this situation. I'm just grateful that *Dungeon* wasn't destroyed by that improvised minefield. I give you credit for reacting, belatedly, to my orders to steer clear of it. If not for that obedience to my orders, you'd be relieved of command. But you did follow orders, although too late to keep your ship from being damaged. I won't imperil every other ship in the fleet and our mission by spending four extra days crawling through this star system while *Dungeon* gets repaired. I regret that *Dungeon* won't accompany the fleet, and my report will state that *Dungeon*'s return to Varandal in no way reflects adversely upon her officers and crew, but I have no choice here. Detach and return to Varandal at best speed for repairs, Commander."

"Yes, sir." Looking as pale as a ghost, Dungeon's captain saluted awkwardly.

Geary sat slumped for a moment afterward, glaring at his display.

"He was lucky," Desjani finally commented.

"I know. So were we. How desperate must the Syndics be to have rigged that kind of defense here?"

"Very desperate." The thought seemed to bring further joy to Desjani.

Rione finally spoke again. "Did any of the Syndics on those small craft survive?"

Desjani grimaced at the query, then looked a question at one of the watch-standers.

"Probably not, Madam Co-President," that lieutenant answered. "The FACs are so small that any hit is likely to hit the crew, too. There's no survival pod, just the FAC itself and the suits of the one or two personnel in the crew. Survival time with the FAC's systems knocked out is... uh... estimated at half an hour to an hour."

"Then there's no sense in asking *Dungeon* to search for survivors and take them prisoner?" Rione asked.

Without speaking directly to Rione, Desjani answered this time. "They were on a suicide mission. They knew it. If any still survive long enough for *Dungeon* to get close, they might well trigger further explosions on the wrecks of their craft or by using explosives attached to themselves."

Seeing Rione's unhappiness, Geary called Lieutenant Iger, relaying Desjani's assessment. "Do you concur?"

Iger spoke to some of the other intelligence personnel, then nodded. "Yes, sir. Whoever was crewing those FACs under these conditions had to be fanatics ready to die for their cause. Unless one of them is dead or unconscious, I wouldn't get close." He paused in thought. "But even then their bodies might be rigged with proximity fuses activated by a dead-man mechanism. I wouldn't risk it, sir."

One more reminder, as if Geary needed any, of how ugly this war had become over the course of a century. "Sorry, Madam Co-President."

"I understand." She stood up. "I'm going to go back to my stateroom and pretend I was there during this entire time. Senators Costa and Sakai are not aware that politicians are permitted on the bridge during such periods, and I'd rather they not learn differently."

As Rione left, Desjani gave her a suspicious glance. "Why is she being nice?"

Geary followed her gaze. "I have no idea."

"Does she know your plans?"

"Not in detail." He could have added "not like you," but decided that would be overkill.

Desjani smiled grimly. "Good. When does everybody find out?"

"A day and a half, just a few hours before we jump out of here."

"Good," she repeated. "*Dungeon* will have hobbled back to the jump point and left for Varandal by then, so no last-minute messages to her can compromise your plans."

"Right." He said it as if he'd already thought of that, but Desjani's grin told Geary he hadn't gotten any better at lying.

The fleet had been in the Atalia Star System for just over twelve hours when the transmission came in from the primary inhabited world. Seven individuals stood behind a broad desk, one of them speaking earnestly. "From the senior Syndicate Worlds' CEOs in Atalia Star System to Captain Geary. We have voted to secede from the Syndicate Worlds and establish an independent star system. We wish to offer the formal surrender of Atalia to the Alliance on the condition that you personally guarantee the safety of everyone in it from further attack or reprisal."

Geary leaned back in a chair in his stateroom, staring at the screen, then forwarded it within *Dauntless*. "Madam Co-President, I need you to look at this message."

Less than ten minutes later, his hatch announced Rione's arrival. She carried an air of triumph mingled with worry as she entered. "Surrender. Do you know the last time a Syndic star system surrendered to the Alliance?"

"No."

"It's never happened. They can be conquered and subdued with great effort, and individual groupings of forces or cities might surrender under pressure, but not an entire star system." Rione sat down, her eyes hooded. "There's no sign of revolution within this star system?"

"No. It doesn't seem to be happening like it did at Heradao. Fleet sensors and the intelligence section haven't picked up internal fighting or any problems with the Syndic command and control net."

Rione's eyes went toward the star display in Geary's stateroom. "We killed the backbone of the loyalist forces at the jump exit. All the ones who would have died rather than surrender. They did, and now what remains is far less eager to fight hopeless battles."

That made sense but still left a big question. "How the hell do I accept the surrender of a star system? I don't have a fraction of the Marines and other ground forces we'd need to occupy just a few critical places."

She gave him a rueful look. "You might also ask how you intend protecting this star system from Syndic retaliation. I assume you're not interested in leaving a substantial portion of your fleet behind."

"No." Geary paced, trying to figure out how to respond. "*Dungeon* hasn't jumped yet. I checked her position, and we should have time to get a message to her before she leaves for Varandal. *Dungeon* can carry the message, and the Alliance can push some other units in here to handle any light warships the Syndics might still have in this region."

"Atalia has been pounded to hell for the last century. It's not exactly a prize for the Alliance." Rione shrugged and stood up. "But we're not annexing it. I'll prepare a message for *Dungeon* to carry to the grand council, suggesting we offer limited protection but avoid promising any more than that. The Alliance can't afford

JACK CAMPBELL

to take on the responsibility of fixing up Syndic star systems as well as our own. Make certain that you specify in your message to *Dungeon* that you've promised on your own honor that the people in Atalia won't be bombarded again unless in response to attacks on Alliance units in this star system."

He set to work crafting his replies as Rione left. At one point an alert announced the arrival of the Alliance kinetic bombardment launched twelve hours ago at some of the distant targets at which it had been aimed. There wasn't any halting the onward progress of that bombardment, since the Alliance couldn't stop the rocks any more than the Syndics could.

One other thing bothered him, though. Atalia hadn't surrendered to the Alliance. It had surrendered to him.

Captain Duellos—the man, not his virtual image—leaned back and glanced around Geary's stateroom. "I always expect a place to seem different when I'm there in person no matter how realistic my virtual visits were supposed to be. Too many people use filters that show a virtual visitor a false image of grandeur or whatever other spotless illusion they prefer to their own reality."

"So, is this different?" Geary asked, dropping into the seat opposite.

"Not that I can tell." Duellos shrugged. "I didn't expect differently. To me you've always seemed uncomfortable with illusions."

Most visits among the fleet's ships were virtual ones, but while physical visits were unusual, they weren't totally unheard of. With no enemy threat still present, Duellos had taken a shuttle to see an old acquaintance who was now commanding officer of one of the new battle cruisers, then swung his shuttle by *Dauntless* on the way back to *Inspire*. "How's your friend on *Agile*?" Geary asked.

"He's fine, though a bit worried about everything he's hearing about these radical new ways of fighting that Black Jack Geary is employing. I reassured him that they are honorable, effective, and learnable, as he saw when we arrived at Atalia. He wanted to see me in person to pass on a memento from a mutual friend of ours who died in battle a little while back and wanted me to have something of his to remind me of... our times together." Duellos sat silent for a moment, then looked directly at Geary. "I keep expecting to get a message from Jaylen Cresida with the latest on her researches or some tactic she wanted to talk about."

"I know how you feel. It's hard to look at the fleet and not see *Furious* there."

"But... we go on." Duellos blew out a long breath, then nodded at the star display. "We go, to be specific, back to the Syndic home star system."

"That's the plan," Geary agreed.

"Aren't you curious as to how I knew it was the plan?"

Geary made a face, waving toward his desk. "According to reports from Lieutenant Iger, the intelligence officer assigned to *Dauntless*, everybody in Varandal Star System, military and civilian, seemed to know that before we left. I had to brief various parties on the plan and get their approval, you know."

"And somehow the plan got leaked," Duellos remarked with obviously feigned surprise. "Where are we really going?"

"To the Syndic home star system."

He frowned and leaned forward, searching Geary's face. "Are you trying to make them think that because everybody knows we are going there we couldn't possibly be really going there? Manipulating the mind of the enemy is an inexact and often failed art."

"So I've heard." Geary sighed as well. "I didn't want it to leak, but I suspect the Syndics knew we'd be aiming for there anyway. It's the only objective that makes sense, the one place the Syndics can't afford to lose, and the Syndic leaders can't abandon their home star system without suffering a massive hit to the morale of the Syndicate Worlds."

"That's true of our leaders," Duellos agreed. "Is it true of theirs as well?"

"As near as we can tell. The Syndicate Worlds are very close to falling apart as it is. A little piece just broke off here at Atalia. Having their leaders run would shatter everything that's left."

Duellos was studying the star display again. "The only way to get there fast is by using the Syndic hypernet, which means barging in the front door again. I hate to recall how many mines we encountered outside that hypernet gate."

"My plan takes that into account," Geary confided. "We have to go to the Syndic home star system in order to strike a decisive blow, but there's more than one way to get there fast. I've done my best to let only the fewest possible people in on it, then not use comm systems unless I have to, but when we're about to jump out of here, I'll brief the fleet on it just as I promised."

"I understand your hesitation to use even the ultrasecure comm systems. I'm sure you guessed that's why I came by in person." Duellos gave Geary a sidelong glance. "You're talking to Tanya? She's in on the planning?"

"Yes."

"Excellent."

Geary smiled. "Why would you think I wouldn't have her in on the planning?"

Duellos was studying his fingernails. "Personal reasons."

"They're not getting in the way."

"She asked me to talk to you," Duellos continued in relaxed tones. "Tanya, that is. 'Beat some sense into him,' she said."

"What'd I do this time?" Geary asked.

"Something about the rank of fleet admiral being temporary." Duellos raised both eyebrows at Geary. "You do have the grand gesture down. Most men regard that giving-up-everything-for-their-love thing as a theoretical exercise and don't actually intend ever doing it."

Geary laughed. "Roberto, I'm not qualified to hold that rank." He held up a hand to forestall Duellos's reply. "I can command this fleet. But fleet admiral is a lot more than that. I lack the necessary experience in diplomacy, logistics, planning, and lots of other things."

"I must respectfully disagree, Admiral." Duellos dropped all hint of humor. "In all seriousness, is that what you wish? Is that what's best?"

He looked back at Duellos, letting some of his own emotional strain show. "I think I've given a great deal, I think I've done a great deal. There'll always be more that's needed. I know that, and I've stopped deluding myself that I can walk away from it. I won't abandon those who depend on me. I've never done that. But how long can I keep going if I don't... don't look to what I need as well? Our ships were running out of fuel cells at Varandal, Roberto. Sometimes I feel like that, like my power core has reached exhaustion and needs to shut down. And then I talk to Tanya, and I can keep going."

Duellos nodded, his expression thoughtful. "Have you told that to her?"

"I can't! Not that way. You know that. It's improper, it's unprofessional, and it would place her in a dishonorable position. I respect her too much to do that."

"Respect?" Duellos quirked a questioning eyebrow at Geary. "Or some other emotion you can't say out loud?"

"Both," Geary admitted. "But I won't compromise her honor."

"And she refuses to compromise yours." Duellos shook his head. "You're waiting until you are both captains again? And you've relinquished command of the fleet, so she's no longer in your chain of command, and you can legally and honorably have a relationship?"

"Right." Geary made an angry gesture. "Which would be impossible if I remained an admiral. Hence the temporary rank, and I will not bend on that. The Alliance government agreed that I would revert to captain and give up command of the fleet when the war is over, and I've returned the fleet to Alliance space."

Duellos nodded once more. "So Tanya told me. Did the government promise not to promote you again immediately and just as quickly reappoint you to command of the fleet?"

Geary stared at Duellos, feeling a sudden weight in his gut. "No."

"Then you'd better plan for that."

No wonder Senator Navarro had given in so easily. No wonder

the officers in the fleet had such low opinions of politicians. At least this confirmed for him that his talk to Badaya about how politicians would easily manipulate officers had indeed been true and not just a tactic to convince Badaya not to force a military coup. Small comfort that was at the moment, though. "But, how do I... ?"

Duellos stood up, smiling wryly. "Move fast, outwit the enemy, strike in ways they don't expect." His smile faded. "You'll need to be certain that Tanya feels the same."

"How the hell do I do that when we can't talk about it?"

"I haven't any idea." Duellos shook his head. "Tanya sent me here to talk about your career, not about your relationship with her. I can't honorably act as an intermediary on that issue. You know that."

"Yes, I do. No one can. We'd be asking them to take dishonorable actions, to assist in breaking regulations. The only people we could ask would be those we trust the most, and wouldn't that be one hell of a way to repay that trust?" Geary faced the star display as if an answer might be read there among the stars. "I'll figure out something."

"Just remember that Tanya is going to be making her own plans. They may not coincide with yours."

"Why not?"

Duellos took a moment, apparently deciding whether or not to answer. "You'll have to ask her."

"I *can't*."

"No. Sorry." Duellos moved to leave, then paused. "I'll tell her you're firm in your decision on the rank issue. She won't be happy."

"Great. Right now that makes two of us."

Duellos followed Geary's gaze. "You're looking at *Dreadnaught*."

"Yeah. I still haven't heard anything from Jane Geary except required professional reports."

"That I can try to help with. There's nothing dishonorable about seeking to discuss personal matters with a close relative. I'll speak with her," Duellos promised.

"Thanks." Geary stood, looking closely at Duellos. "I'm glad to finally meet you in person. Just in case." They'd be going into battle again, and in the tiny fractions of a second in which warships clashed on their firing runs, chance played a big part in who lived and who died.

"Yes. Just in case. I'll go pay my respects to Captain Desjani and report the failure of my mission."

Despite it all, Geary found himself smiling after Duellos had left.

There were smiles all around the conference table. Every commanding officer was happy about the one-sided slaughter of the Syndic fast attack craft and had already heard that Atalia had surrendered to Geary. The only unhappy face would have belonged to the captain of *Dungeon*, and that cruiser had jumped for Varandal twenty hours ago.

For the first time since he had assumed command of the fleet, Geary felt a need to tamp down the high spirits. "We've won minor victories here, but the big fight is yet to come. Some of the Syndic forces that attacked Varandal escaped, and they'll have picked up reinforcements. We need to finish off that force."

He called up the star display, knowing that this was the moment they had all been anticipating. "We'll jump from here to Kalixa.

The hypernet gate there was destroyed, but from Kalixa we can make a jump to Indras." His hand traced the planned path of the fleet deeper into Syndic space. "Assuming the Syndic hypernet gate at Indras has been fitted with a Cresida safe-fail system, we'll approach that gate and use the Syndic hypernet key aboard *Dauntless* to allow the fleet to enter the Syndic hypernet and head for Parnosa." The path on the display shot across space, ending at a distant star.

A moment's silence was broken by Commander Neeson of *Implacable* asking the question Geary could see on every face. "Parnosa? Why Parnosa?"

"Because none of us trust the Syndics, and recent history warns us against entering the Syndic home star system through the front door represented by the hypernet gate there." The reference to the Syndic ambush that had inflicted horrible losses on this same fleet didn't need any elaboration. "So we're going to come at them from an unexpected direction. From Parnosa, we'll jump to Zevos, and from Zevos to the Syndic home star system."

A moment's silence followed while everyone absorbed that, then Captain Jane Geary spoke for the first time at one of these conferences. "Zevos is not within jump range of the Syndic home star system."

"Yes, it is," Captain Duellos responded in a thoughtful voice. "Not within official range, but when this fleet jumped to Sancere, Captain Geary showed us how to get extra range from the jump drives. The distance from Zevos to the Syndic home star system is less than we jumped then."

"Exactly," Geary agreed. "Whatever surprise the Syndics may

have prepared for us won't be targeted at anything jumping from Zevos. We'll arrive at a jump point the Syndics regard as useless because they think there are no stars close enough for it to be used."

Neeson's smile was back. "So the Syndics won't have anything there waiting for us. We'll take their ambush at the hypernet gate in the rear this time."

Captain Armus was frowning, though. "What if the Syndic defenders just bolt through that hypernet gate instead of fighting us? We'll be giving them an easy escape."

Rione normally remained silent in these meetings, but now she spoke up. "They can't afford to run because the Syndic leadership can't afford to run. The defenders have to stand and try to win because if the Syndic Executive Council flees their home star system, their remaining veneer of authority will vanish, and most of the Syndicate Worlds' other star systems will follow the lead of places like Atalia and Heradao. We know this, and they know this. They must fight."

Armus and some of the other captains had frowned more deeply at Rione interjecting herself into the meeting, but as she finished, the frowns eased. "That's good, then," Armus conceded. "Fleet intelligence supports that assessment?" he asked Geary.

"It does." Naturally, the fleet's officers wouldn't take a politician's word for anything. "This plan isn't set in stone, because if the gate at Indras is also gone or hasn't yet been fitted with a safe-fail device, we won't be able to use it. If that happens, we'll keep jumping deeper into Syndic territory until we find a gate we can use."

Dependable's captain gestured for attention. "Admiral, the Syndics may not have installed those systems on any of their gates. I know this fleet rode out shock waves from gate collapses at Sancere and Lakota. Why can't we attempt to use a gate even if it lacks a safe-fail system?"

Geary could tell the suggestion didn't have support from any of the officers who'd been present at Lakota, but the question was an understandable one from someone who hadn't been there. "We're going to Kalixa next. I think once you see what's left of that star system, you'll have your answer to that. Are there any other questions?"

Captain Kattnig of the *Adroit* stood. "I wish to volunteer the battle cruisers of the Fifth Battle Cruiser Division for the vanguard of any future action against the Syndics."

The other commanding officers exchanged glances, some approving, some disapproving, many simply of understanding at the request. Geary took a moment to answer. "Captain, the fleet's formation in action will be dependent on the situation we encounter. I assure you that every ship in the fleet will play an important role in any engagement."

Kattnig nodded respectfully. "This is understood, Admiral, but my battle cruisers have not had the opportunity to prove themselves under your command and are eager to do just that."

"I will keep that in mind, Captain." The request was in keeping with the offensive mind-set of the fleet, so there wasn't any sense in outright denying it. Kattnig sat down again, and Geary studied the other officers. "I have just one thing more, then." He had been thinking about how to say this and hoped he had the talk down right. Desjani waited with a confident expression. He'd tried the speech out on her, and she had suggested only small changes.

"When I first gained command of this fleet," he began speaking, "our situation was desperate. We fought desperately, as those who had nothing to lose. As we fought our way closer and closer to home, our emotions became the desperation of hope, the willingness to risk everything so we could return to our homes and loved ones. Now things have changed. We're no longer desperate. But we must fight now to avoid complacency, to avoid the belief that the hard fighting is over, and painless victory is certain. We won easily at the jump exit into Atalia. But had we been unworried then, had we not shown the wariness of combat veterans, then this fleet would have plowed straight into that mass of merchant ships, and many of our own ships wouldn't have come out again after those Syndic ships sprung their trap."

He paused, letting the point sink in. "I don't know what the next trap might be, but we need to be alert for it. We have to fight as hard and as desperately as we did on the way home because everyone in the Alliance believes we can end this war. We can't let them down, so we must be brave, wary, wise, and strong. Just as we were before."

Another pause, everyone listening, most nodding. Rione mimed clapping her hands in approval. "Thank you," Geary ended. "We're going to the Syndic home star system, and we're going to finish this. That is all."

They cheered then, rising to salute. The images of most of the virtual participants vanished rapidly, leaving only the virtual presences of Senators Costa and Sakai, Rione, and the real presence of Tanya Desjani with Geary. Costa was watching Geary with a surprised and wary look she was trying to conceal. Senator

Sakai nodded politely to Geary. "A fine speech," he said softly. "This is your true plan you presented?"

"Yes. I wouldn't mislead my commanders. If I lose their trust... Well, I assume you're aware of what almost happened to the heavy cruiser Dungeon soon after we arrived in this star system. They need to know they can count on me."

"Once the Syndic defenders in their home star system are eliminated," Sakai continued, "Senator Costa, Co-President Rione, and I will take the lead on negotiations."

Rione flicked one finger in a way that told Geary not to debate the issue at this time. "Certainly, Senator."

After the images of Costa and Sakai disappeared, Rione laughed. "Did you see Costa?"

"Yeah. What was bothering her?"

"She's just realized that she may have been underestimating the competition. That's you. Costa believed that she could outmaneuver any military officer, but now she has her doubts." Rione laughed again.

"What about the other one?" Geary asked.

"Sakai?" Rione stopped laughing. "He's thinking and keeping his eyes open. He's here representing the part of the grand council that distrusts Black Jack the most. Never forget that. You were busy watching the reactions of your officers, I know, so you didn't see how closely Sakai watched your captain. He knows if worse comes to worst that he'd have to get through her to get to you, and I believe Sakai is only now understanding just how hard a task that would be."

Desjani stood up, her face professionally rigid. "I should be going."

But Rione waved one hand. "No need to hurry on my account. I was just departing." Then her image vanished as well.

"Can we leave her at Kalixa?" Desjani asked.

"No. Has Senator Sakai talked to you?"

"A courtesy call, and occasional drop-ins for leading conversations," Desjani responded dryly. "You know, politics, the war, your ambitions. That sort of thing."

"I hope you reassured him," Geary replied with a smile.

"He didn't believe me, I'm certain." She blew out a long breath. "Sir, I know Captain Duellos talked to you—"

"And I know he told you what I said."

Desjani shook her head at him. "If I actually told Senator Sakai what your ambitions were, he'd think you were crazy."

"So do you."

"And now I'm agreeing with a politician. You do work miracles, Admiral."

He waited until she left, then called Tulev. "I'm sorry for getting you back here so soon, but I wanted to ask you something."

Tulev, stolid, outwardly unemotional as usual, inclined his head slightly. "Nothing too serious, I hope, Admiral."

"I don't know. I understand you served with Captain Kattnig."

"Kattnig?" Tulev's puzzlement briefly showed. "A long time ago, when we were both still enlisted sailors."

"He's mentioned a couple of times that you two were commissioned together."

"Yes, that is so," Tulev agreed. "The fleet was in serious need of new officers after the battles around Hattera. But I have rarely encountered him since then." Tulev eyed Geary. "Is there some concern about Kattnig?"

"I don't know." Geary pounded the table softly with one fist. "He's got a good record."

"Captain Kattnig has spoken with me a few times since *Adroit* joined the fleet. He wished to know more about our return to Alliance space under your command."

Geary nodded, noting that even Tulev never referred to that return voyage as a "retreat." No one in the fleet did, and more than once Geary had barely stopped himself from inadvertently using the word "retreat." But whereas he had to work to avoid employing the term, Geary had slowly come to the conclusion that the rest of the fleet truly didn't think of the return as a retreat. The Alliance fleet didn't retreat, it "withdrew," it "reorganized," it "repositioned," it "departed," or it "altered the axis of attack." Therefore, the return to Alliance space couldn't have been a retreat. "Pardon me for saying this bluntly, but Kattnig seems to think that he has something to prove, maybe because he wasn't with the fleet during the return to Alliance space. He talked about the new battle cruisers proving themselves, but I have a feeling he's actually most concerned about proving himself, and I don't know why."

Tulev thought about that, then nodded in turn. "I believe that is a fair assessment, yes. Many fleet officers and sailors who were not with us feel the same way. But Kattnig's record is, as you say, a good one. I will speak with him again, just the two of us, and try to reassure him. He, like the other new officers, is learning to deal with your different way of fighting. Perhaps that is a factor. The new tactics can appear to leave less room for individual valor."

"Those new tactics are a century old, and Kattnig has already proven his valor. I'd appreciate your talking to him and driving home that the officers whose experiences he admires gained those experiences fighting with those tactics."

"Certainly, Admiral." Tulev gave him a searching look. "Do you worry about his actions?"

"I'm worried about all of the new officers," Geary admitted. "I hope they learned from what happened to *Dungeon*."

"Even though the damage to *Dungeon* made it necessary for her to return home, no harsher punishment for disobedience could have been possible," Tulev agreed.

"They could have died if their commanding officer hadn't pulled up in time."

"They would have preferred death to the dishonor of missing the attack on the Syndic home star system. It would have been a lesser penalty in their eyes."

Geary sighed. "I keep forgetting. To me, death is still something to fear."

"We fear death, Admiral, but there are other things we fear more." Tulev nodded to him. "There are other things you fear more as well. I know this. You could not be a good commander otherwise." Standing again, Tulev saluted, and his image vanished.

The jump for Kalixa felt routine, though the fleet was once again in combat formation and ready to fight. Geary felt the usual discomfort from being in jump space, a strange, formless, gray universe lit by no stars, but also suffered from a restlessness that drove him to frequent walks around *Dauntless*. The crew was happy and confident, certain that Black Jack could do anything.

When Geary got back to his stateroom, he would sit for a while, watching the mysterious lights that flared and faded in jump space.

Finally, they reached Kalixa.

5

The drop out of jump space felt curiously abrupt, as if the jump point itself had somehow been disrupted. Since jump points were created by the mass of the star near them, Geary knew the problem was likely related to the star Kalixa. Then the gray nothingness vanished, and the Alliance fleet arrived in Kalixa.

Nobody spoke for a while, everyone staring at what had been Kalixa Star System. After a few minutes, Geary tore his eyes from his display to check the story there against the Syndic star-system guides the fleet had seized at Sancere.

There didn't seem to be much in common between the old guide and current reality. Not anymore. The guide displayed a fairly well-off star system, one planet comfortably fit for human habitation, other planets and moons with bustling colonies in buried cities, a system-wide population of more than one hundred million, and hanging nearby the hypernet gate, which had helped funnel wealth to Kalixa.

Until that gate collapsed and released a pulse of energy equal to a significant fraction of a typical nova. Despite the anguished account of a Syndic eyewitness Geary had spoken to, the pulse hadn't actually destroyed everything. It would have been easier to handle the result if it had. Instead, it left behind plenty of traces of what had once been there.

"Every planet appears lifeless," the operations watch-stander reported in a hushed voice. "There's tattered wreckage on the fringes of the areas that faced the pulse when it hit. Even the places shielded by being on the other sides of their planets from where the pulse hit have been torn up, probably by earthquakes and other shock effects. There's only a very thin atmosphere left on the main habitable world. Apparently that's the only reason why everything on the planet stopped burning."

Geary had his display fixed on a magnified image of what had been a city on that planet. A few stunted ruins poking up amid the fields of debris, the landscape reduced to rock and rubble, the whole scene having the unnatural clarity of something viewed without much intervening atmosphere. "Can we tell how many ships were here?"

"No, sir. The fleet's sensors have picked up debris floating in orbit, but it's all mangled and dispersed. That Syndic heavy-cruiser officer reported they were the only larger warship present. Based on the damage to that cruiser, any light cruisers or HuKs wouldn't have survived. Ships without armor and military-grade shields wouldn't have stood any chance at all here."

Desjani pointed to the image of Kalixa. "What shape is the star in?"

"Highly unstable, but with so much solar mass blown away, it didn't go nova itself. Nothing is going to be able to live in this star system for a long time, Captain."

She looked at Geary, her face hard. "One hundred million. Those bastards killed one hundred million people here in a single stroke. I don't care that they were Syndics. This can't happen again."

Had the aliens known what was at Kalixa? Had they cared? "At least they can't do it again in any star system that installed the safe-fail systems."

"Until they find another way to do it." Desjani, aware that the watch-standers on *Dauntless*'s bridge were watching curiously, trying to figure out her meaning, leaned closer to the privacy field around Geary. "The aliens can't be permitted to think they can get away with something like this. Lakota was bad enough, but at least other humans pulled the trigger there. The aliens did *this*."

"Agreed. We have to stop it." He took a long, deep breath, knowing that the images of this star system would stay with him forever. "Madam Co-President, please ensure that Senators Costa and Sakai get a good, long look at this star system. I want them to be absolutely clear on what war using hypernet gates as weapons would have involved."

"Yes, Admiral Geary," Rione agreed in an unusually subdued voice.

"Captain Desjani, let's set a course for the jump point for Indras. I don't want to spend a second longer here than we have to."

"I'd rather be around a black hole," Desjani agreed.

Aside from serving as an object lesson of what humanity had narrowly avoided having happen in countless other star systems,

Kalixa also dampened any excessively high spirits in the fleet, reminding everyone of the risks still to be faced and the potential stakes if they failed. Watching the reactions of *Dauntless*'s crew, Geary wondered how they would respond if they learned that Kalixa had not been an accident or a Syndic mistake, but a deliberate act. As revolted as he was by the loss of life and destruction in Kalixa, he also wondered if his biggest challenge might involve fending off the aliens without triggering a vengeful war by humanity. His gut reaction, that the aliens had to pay for this, would be a common one. But a price that produced more human star systems devastated like this would only pitch humanity into another endless cycle of retaliation and revenge. And until they learned more about how powerful the aliens were, whether or not, as Desjani speculated, they might have other star-system-killing weapons to employ, an attempt at retaliation could easily risk many more star systems annihilated like Kalixa had been and uncounted billions more dead. *As badly as I'd like someone, or some thing, to pay for this, all we can really do right now is what we can to keep it from happening again and find out more about the ones who did it.*

Maybe there's something else our resident Syndic can contribute to learning more.

He had the Syndic CEO Boyens brought from the brig to the interrogation room again. "We know the Syndic reserve flotilla attacked Varandal in response to the gate collapse at Kalixa," Geary said. "You must have known the Alliance didn't do that."

"No," Boyens denied, "we didn't. Who else could have done it?"

"You'd been facing the aliens all those years."

The CEO gazed back at Geary for a while as if trying to link the statement to the collapse of Kalixa's gate. "They've never penetrated that deeply into Syndicate Worlds' space. In any case, we reviewed the recording of the collapse that Cruiser C-875 brought to Heradao. There wasn't any trace of alien attack on the gate. They couldn't have done it. But we knew you'd already collapsed at least one hypernet gate in a Syndicate Worlds' star system."

"Are you talking about Sancere?" Geary demanded. "Where we had to prevent a gate collapse started by Syndic warships from producing the sort of devastation that happened here at Kalixa? Or do you mean Lakota, where Syndic warships took down the hypernet gate completely while this fleet was light-hours distant?"

Boyens set his jaw stubbornly. "I've seen records of your ships firing on the hypernet gate at Sancere."

"To cause a safe collapse. But if you've seen the records that heavy cruiser brought from Kalixa, you know that there weren't any Alliance warships at Kalixa when the gate here failed."

"That seems to be true." Boyens furrowed his brow in thought, staring at the deck. "The Alliance was close enough to do it. That was our reasoning. You mention the aliens, but they never collapsed a hypernet gate in the border region facing them. If they were going to attack us, why attack us so far from their border with us?"

There was something critical going on, Geary thought after the interview was over, something far more important than the Syndics blaming the Alliance for the collapse of the hypernet gates at Kalixa and Sancere as well. Something about how the Syndics thought about the aliens. Unable to figure out what it was, he filed the half-formed idea away in the back of his mind.

It took three and a half days to reach the jump point for Parnosa. As the haunted ruins of Kalixa vanished and the gray nothingness of jump space surrounded the ships, Geary could almost feel the sense of relief sweeping through *Dauntless*. He relaxed, too, knowing that the fleet had a long jump ahead. Eight and a half days, almost the limit for normal jump-drive range. By the end of the next week, the strange pressures of jump space would be making people nervous and irritable, but he didn't expect any real problems from that.

Seven days later, as Geary sat watching the lights of jump space and trying not to let the strange itching sensation that grew the longer people were in jump space get to him, his hatch alert sounded with what seemed particular urgency.

A moment later, Tanya Desjani stomped into the stateroom, looking ready to tear a hole in the hull with her bare hands. "I will not tolerate that woman on my ship any longer!"

"Which woman?" Geary asked, already knowing the answer. "And what did she do?"

"The politician! You know how she's been acting! You've been there when she said nice things to me!"

Geary stared for a moment. "Uh, yes, I have."

"Haven't you wondered *why*?" Without waiting for his answer, Desjani rushed on. "I finally asked her straight out, and do you know what she said? Do you?"

"No." Monosyllabic replies seemed safest at the moment.

"Because I'm *important* to you. That's what she said. I'm important to *you*, so she is trying to make sure I stay in á good mood."

Obviously, Rione's efforts had backfired. Geary just nodded silently, not even trusting a single word for a response.

Desjani raised an angry fist, her face flushing with emotion. "It's just like those ugly suggestions that I should offer myself to you as a prize if you agreed to become dictator! I am not a toy or a pawn to be used or controlled by your enemies or your friends! I am a captain in the Alliance fleet, a position I earned by my own sweat and blood and honorable service! I will not accept anyone trying to manipulate me or use me or toy with me just because they want to influence *you*!"

He met her enraged gaze. "I understand."

She glared back at him. "Do you? Can you? Would you like to live in *my* shadow?"

"I would never—"

"It's not about you! It's about everyone else in this damned universe who would look at us and see only you! I did not spend my life to get to this point so that I could become an insignificant sidekick to anyone!"

That image had never occurred to him before, and that fact bothered him. He should have realized how Black Jack would affect Tanya's own image. "You could never be insignificant."

"Tell it to the universe!" Desjani waved one hand as if indicating all of creation.

"I will. I'm sorry. I come with a lot of baggage."

"I told you that this isn't you! It's everyone else, and how they would see me. Or *not* see me." She clenched both fists. "Why did all of this have to happen? Why couldn't my heart listen to my head? When that witch told me her motives, I had to find someone to vent to or I would've blown out every seal on this ship! And you're the only one I can— But you're also the one person I can't— Oh, hell!" Desjani stepped back and ran both hands through her hair. "We're very perilously close to discussing something that you and I cannot talk about."

"Not now, no."

"Not until... Have you rethought it at all? Your giving up fleet admiral? Giving up command of the fleet? Have you decided not to do those things?"

"No," Geary said quietly.

"Do I have to be the sane one here?"

"That depends on how you define sanity."

She gave him a frustrated and angry look. "I truly did not realize... I need to have another talk with my ancestors." Desjani straightened herself to attention, her voice becoming calmer and more reserved. "Is there anything else, Admiral Geary?"

He refrained from pointing out that she had come to his stateroom of her own accord and not been summoned by him. "No, there's nothing else."

She saluted with careful formality, then left.

Half an hour later, Rione came by. "There's something I should probably let you know about," she began.

"I already know. Can't you see the scorch marks that Desjani left in here?"

"You seem to have come through in one piece." Rione shrugged. "I was just trying to be nice. I don't know why that bothered her."

"It was out of character," Geary suggested.

"I suppose that must have seemed suspicious." Instead of being angered by his remark, Rione seemed amused. "She came here for comfort, did she?"

"It's not funny."

"No. I imagine for her it's a bit of a torment. I really was trying to make things a little easier on her." Rione paused. "When she cools down enough, you might find a way to tell her that I have said nothing I did not believe. Too bad she's incapable of accepting that."

"I'll see if I can find a way to tell her the first thing." So much for any idea of defusing the bad feelings between Rione and Desjani. Different though they were, they were like elements that, when combined, could form a critical mass. The only way to avoid detonations was to keep them far enough apart. "She has every right to be angry at fate."

"So do you." Rione breathed out slowly. "I'll try not to make things harder for you both."

"Why? Just because it's important to me? I know you have no love for Tanya Desjani."

"No, on both counts." For a long moment he wondered if she was going to say more, then Rione spoke in a low voice. "Because the woman that I once was wouldn't have confined herself to worrying about how well others could serve her needs and purposes. For a long time I thought I'd bartered my soul for what I believed to be important, but I've learned that my soul is still with me. And if you repeat a word of that to anyone, I will deny saying it, and no one will believe you."

"Your secret is safe."

Rione gave him an ironic look. "It wouldn't do to have people knowing that politicians have souls, would it? By the way, speaking of soulless politicians, Senator Costa has been digging for information on you and your captain, trying to find leverage to use against you if necessary. She's getting increasingly frustrated, probably because your fleet's personnel won't share any dirt with her."

"There isn't any dirt to share." He wondered what lurid gossip might have been flowing to Costa if the likes of Captains Kila, Faresa, or Numos had still been in command of ships.

"Absolutely true. From what I hear, your sailors and officers have been boasting about how honorable the two of you are. Not exactly the stuff of blackmail."

That was gratifying, but also discomforting. Granted that the rumors he was involved with Desjani had started long before they really had any basis in fact, it was nonetheless embarrassing to think of the fleet talking about the two of them even if those conversations were about how honorably they were dealing with it. "Sakai isn't doing the same?"

"Sakai doesn't work that way. His main leverage was supposed to be the fact that he's from Kosatka. No one told you that?"

"No." Desjani and most of the rest of the crew of *Dauntless* were also from Kosatka.

"Sakai has already discovered that won't help much if he wants them to act against you. He's been trying to work on your captain's loyalties to her home world and getting absolutely nowhere."

Geary leaned back, letting his unhappiness show. He had hoped against all reason that the two other senators would just trust him until he gave them reason to feel otherwise. "But you're on our side."

"I'm on the 'side' of the Alliance, Admiral Geary," Rione replied sharply. "Act against that, and I'll do what I must. I no longer expect that to happen, but don't take my loyalty for granted. *I'm* not infatuated with you." She turned and left.

Parnosa. Geary couldn't suppress a sense of anxiety as the fleet flashed into existence on the fringes of Parnosa Star System. Six light-hours away from where the fleet had arrived, around the curve of the star system, Parnosa's hypernet gate loomed. "Get me an assessment of that gate as soon as possible. Before this fleet gets too far from the jump point, I want to know if the hypernet gate has a safe-collapse system installed."

To the optical sensors of the Alliance fleet, six light-hours' distance was child's play. Within seconds Geary's display was updating with assessments of everything within the star system. He waited with barely controlled impatience for the one piece of information he absolutely had to have.

"There's a safe-fail system on the gate," one of the watch-standers announced as the sensors relayed their analysis. "It appears to be basically the same as ours."

Geary let out a breath he hadn't realized he was holding. The major potential threat accounted for, he took a long look at the rest of the Syndic defenses.

"One light cruiser and a half dozen HuKs," Desjani commented. "None of them within four light-hours of us."

"Plus the usual array of fixed defenses." Geary realized something else wasn't there. "They don't have any HuKs on picket duty near the jump points."

"They have one at the hypernet gate," she pointed out. "They know where we want to go from here, or think they know that, anyway. Once that HuK sees us in about six hours, it'll enter the gate, headed for the Syndic home star system." Desjani grimaced. "Two to one they don't try to drop the gate."

Geary gave her a questioning look. "That's been one of the things I was worried about. Why not? They've been willing to do that before to try to stop us, and with a safe-collapse system installed, they don't have to worry about the results to their own star system."

"Syndic government is about corporate profits," Desjani pointed out. "Dropping the gate here would really hit the local economy even though the gate wouldn't fry stuff directly. That's the incentive for the locals not to do it. But the Syndic Executive Council is certain to be ready for us at the Syndic home star system, like you said. That means they want us there, not rampaging around the rest of Syndicate space. And they want us coming through the hypernet gate, overconfident again, so their ambush can chew us up."

"Good points. Let's not keep the Executive Council waiting any longer than we have to."

He held off launching a bombardment of the fixed defenses in the star system, waiting to see what the Syndics did. As the Alliance fleet raced across the outer curve of the star system en route to the hypernet gate, the HuK entered the gate just as Desjani had predicted, but neither attacks nor surrender offers came from the Syndic authorities in Parnosa, and the remaining Syndic warships stayed very distant. "We should still take out those defenses," Desjani finally argued.

Geary shook his head. "Rocks are cheap, but our supply isn't infinite. I have a feeling the Syndic home star system is going to be crawling with so many targets we're going to be glad for every rock we have to throw at them."

One day out from the hypernet gate, the Syndic authorities finally called Geary. He saw only one Syndic CEO, an older man who spoke bluntly. "I am calling on behalf of the innocent civilians in this star system."

Desjani made a rude noise.

"We are aware that you have the ability to destroy our hypernet gate and unleash horrible destruction on everyone here," the Syndic CEO continued. "In the name of humanity, we ask that you avoid doing so. Should Captain Geary be in command of this fleet, I address my appeal directly to him and promise not to engage in hostile acts against your ships if you will promise to refrain from destroying the gate."

"Interesting," Rione commented after the message ended. "He sent it on a tight beam. The Syndic warships in Parnosa wouldn't have been aware of it."

"Typical Syndics. Double-crossing their own defenders," Desjani grumbled.

"Who might bombard them if they knew the locals were going against Syndic central-authority orders," Geary reminded her, then looked back at Rione. "Why are they so concerned about us destroying their gate? When they've got a safe-fail system on it?" He turned to Desjani. "Could it be a fake safe-fail system? A mock-up?"

Rione answered before Desjani could. "The inhabitants of this star system have surely seen the records this fleet broadcast of what happened at Lakota, and they've likely heard about Kalixa, so they know what can happen when a gate collapses. Their government no doubt has assured them that the safe-fail system will prevent disaster from happening here if the gate collapses or is destroyed, but I doubt the Syndics here fully trust the safe-fail system."

Geary nodded. "They're assuming their government might be lying to them."

"Is that so foreign a concept?" Rione asked sarcastically.

He avoided looking at Desjani. The fleet's officers distrusted their political leaders. He wondered how many of them would have believed in the effectiveness of the safe-fail system if one of their own hadn't produced the initial design. "All right, then. Do you think Senator Costa or Sakai would be upset if I handle this myself, or would they regard that as negotiating?"

"You're in a combat situation," Rione replied. "This is fully a matter for your action, Fleet Admiral Geary."

"Captain Desjani, please have your communications watch give me a tight beam to reply to that Syndic CEO."

After the circuit was set up, Geary put on his fleet commander face as he activated the circuit. "This is Admiral Geary for the Syndicate Worlds' CEOs and people in the Parnosa Star System. The Alliance was not responsible for the collapse of the hypernet gates in any Syndicate Worlds' star systems. In fact, some warships from this fleet placed themselves in serious peril to ensure that the gate at Sancere caused minimal damage when it collapsed. We have no intention of causing the collapse of the gate here." Get that off the table first. He didn't want even to imply a willingness to employ such a weapon. "Refrain from attacking this fleet, and we will refrain from any defensive response against the people and installations of this star system." He paused, then added something he still found it hard to have to say, because it reflected a threat that in his eyes the Alliance should never have posed. "This fleet does not war on civilians." Not anymore, anyway, not while he was in command, and he was certain most of the other fleet officers agreed. "We engage military targets only. I know you must be aware of that from our activities in other star systems in recent months. Keep your forces clear of this fleet, do not attack us, and we will not retaliate. To the honor of our ancestors."

Desjani shook her head. "We're in a fairly wealthy Syndic star system, and the fleet probably won't fire a shot." She gave Geary a sardonic look. "In the old days, we would have had a lot of fun blowing up stuff here."

"You mean a few months back?"

"It's been longer than a 'few' months, Admiral." Her expression changed. "But a year ago I wouldn't have believed it if someone had told me how things would change by now."

He almost replied, then thought about where he had been a year ago. Still frozen in survival sleep, his damaged pod lost amid the debris littering Grendel Star System. Not aware that the last remnants of the power on the pod were being slowly drained and that if he wasn't found within a few more months, the systems keeping him alive would fail.

"What's the matter?" Desjani appeared worried as she watched him.

"I just felt cold for a minute," he muttered in reply, wondering if the memory of the ice that had filled his body would ever completely leave him.

She kept her eyes on him a minute longer, then leaned into Geary's privacy field once more. "Whatever I have said or done in the last few weeks, never doubt that I thank the living stars that you survived, that you came to my ship, and that I came to know you."

He nodded, not having to try hard to force a smile in return. "Thanks."

Then Desjani was leaning back again, all business once more. "One more day, then we'll see if this key still works." She smiled like a wolf. "I can't wait to get back to the Syndic home star system. This fleet has some debts to pay there."

Two hours before they reached the hypernet gate, Geary was pretending to rest. *Dauntless*'s bridge was tense enough without him hovering there, too. He would go up in one more hour, to watch the final approach to Parnosa's hypernet gate and make only the second hypernet journey in his experience. He had hardly noticed the first one, still sunk in post-traumatic stress, both mental and physical.

An incoming call promised a welcome diversion. "Geary here."

"You have an incoming conference request, Admiral," *Dauntless*'s communications watch officer reported. "From *Dreadnaught*."

Geary stood up hastily, straightening his uniform. "Accept it."

A moment later, the image of Captain Jane Geary appeared in his stateroom, standing before him as if she were physically present. Her expression was unrevealing, her voice controlled. "Captain Geary, requesting a personal counseling session with Admiral Geary."

"Granted." He couldn't tell how she felt, what she intended

saying. "Please take a seat."

On *Dreadnaught*, Jane Geary sat stiffly in a chair in her own stateroom, the image before him acting the same way. She gazed at him steadily, and he looked back, still startled even now to see the signs of age on her, to realize that his grandniece had aged a few years more than he had. He'd studied her picture before, but only seeing her in person did Geary spot some resemblances to his brother. "May I inquire as to the reason for the counseling session?" he finally asked.

"Yes, sir. First off, I'd like to know why you assigned *Dreadnaught* and *Dependable* to the Third Battleship Division and placed me in command of that division."

That question was easy enough to answer. "The Third Battleship Division had a lot of problems. Leadership, morale, and effectiveness problems. The surviving ships in that division needed good examples and a good leader. Based on what I saw during the fighting at Varandal, I believe that *Dreadnaught* and *Dependable* fill the first requirement, and you fill the second."

Jane Geary took a moment to think about his answer before speaking again. "I understand that you have a message from my brother, Captain Michael Geary." The words still held no apparent emotion.

"Yes. I offered to send you a copy of the transmission containing them."

"Can you just tell me what he said?"

"Certainly." He'd both dreaded and looked forward to this meeting, and neither feeling had yet altered. "He told me to tell you that he didn't hate me anymore."

Jane Geary kept her eyes on him for a long moment, then looked away, breathing deeply. "That's all?"

"We didn't have much time. How much do you know about what happened?"

"I've seen the official reports and spoken to a number of officers in the fleet, Admiral."

Geary sat back, exhaling in exasperation. "What am I supposed to be doing here, Jane? Are you here as my grandniece or as one of my subordinate commanders? Dammit, you're the closest family I have left."

"A lot of us have died in the war." She looked back at him. "Tell me the truth. Michael volunteered for the forlorn hope? You didn't suggest it first?"

"He volunteered. I was still getting my balance as commander, still trying to adjust to what had happened. I wasn't ready to order... to order someone to do that."

Jane Geary seemed to slump a bit, closing her eyes. "He was all I had. You left him in the Syndic home star system."

"Yes, I did." He wouldn't plead the pressures of command, his obligation to the rest of the fleet. The simple fact wouldn't be changed by either of those things. "I still hope he survived, that we'll get him back."

"You know the odds against that."

"Yeah." A bitter taste filled his mouth. "A lot of people didn't make it home. I'm sorry."

She leaned forward, eyes wide, suddenly intense again. "We both hated you. Our lives were never our own. Sometimes as children we'd play a game. One of us would be Black Jack, the boogeyman chasing the other one, trying to catch him or her and drag them off to the war. You finally caught Michael, then me, didn't you?"

"I'm not Black Jack. I want to end this war. I'm sorry for what happened to you and Michael, for what happened to all of the Gearys forced to follow in my alleged footsteps and fight. But I swear on the honor of our ancestors that I would never have agreed to what happened, to the creation of this outsize legend about who I supposedly was. I didn't do it, but I'm still very sorry for what it did to people like you and Michael."

Once again, Jane Geary sat quiet for a while. "Have you told anyone else about that message from Michael?"

He started to say no one, then realized he couldn't. "Just one."

"Let me guess who that could be." She looked around as if expecting to see Tanya Desjani. "What am I supposed to do, Admiral?"

"Are you asking me as my niece or as Captain Jane Geary?"

"Your niece. Captain Jane Geary can maintain a totally professional relationship. I know how to do that."

He frowned, sensing a not-so-subtle slam at Desjani. "You're not the only one who knows how to do that."

She unbent slightly, then. "My apologies. I didn't mean that the way it sounded. I've heard nothing offering proof of improper actions by you or anyone else. But in a short time we'll enter the Syndic hypernet, where communications between ships can't occur. After that we may well face hard fighting. I needed to speak with you before then, because one or both of us may not be around afterward."

"Thank you." Geary let himself relax. "Please be my niece for a short time. I can only imagine what it was like growing up in the shadow of Black Jack and the shadow of this war. I can't change that, I can't change anything that happened while I was in survival sleep. But I want to fix whatever I can. You have to understand, I—" He couldn't speak for a moment, seeing once again the traces of his brother in her. Most of the time he could pretend things at home hadn't really changed, that even though so much in the fleet had changed, that back at Glenlyon his brother still worked and his parents still lived. But he couldn't pretend that while facing Jane Geary.

She watched him, then seemed to change the subject. "I served with Captain Kila for a while when we were both lieutenants."

The memories that name brought up crowded out Geary's grief for a moment. "My condolences. That must have been unpleasant."

"It was," Jane Geary agreed. "Would you have shot her?"

"Hell, yes. She had Alliance blood on her hands."

"I knew Captain Falco, too," Jane Geary said.

Geary grimaced. "He... died with honor."

Something in his answers had satisfied her. Jane Geary nodded again. "There's something I have to tell you. I also have a message, for you. I hope you can forgive me for not delivering it until now."

That had been the last thing he had expected to hear. "A message?"

"When I was a young girl, one night when we were visiting my grandfather, your brother, I found him standing outside, looking up at the stars. I asked him what he was doing, and he said he was looking for something. I asked what it was, and he said. 'My brother. I miss him. If you ever meet him somewhere up there, tell him I missed him.'"

He stared at her, for a moment too overwhelmed to give in to grief again. "He told you that?"

"Yes. I never forgot a word of it even though I never expected to deliver it." She sighed. "I should have given that message to you long before this. He always told us you were everything the legend said, you know. Absolutely perfect and the greatest hero ever."

"Mike said that? My brother said I was perfect?"

"Yes."

He couldn't help a brief laugh. "He certainly never told me that when—when he was alive. Damn. He's dead. He's been dead for a long time. Everybody's dead." Months of denial crumbled and Geary slumped, burying his face in his hands.

Jane Geary finally broke the silence. "I'm sorry. I have to tell you one other thing. We never really believed in you, Michael and me. Black Jack was a myth. But we were wrong."

That jarred him out of his grief. "No, you weren't. Black Jack is a myth. I'm just me."

"I've reviewed the records since you assumed command, and I've spoken to the officers in this fleet! I couldn't have done what you did. No one else could have done it, either." She paused, then blurted out a question. "You've talked to our ancestors since coming back, haven't you? Do you feel Michael is still alive?"

Geary made a fist and hit his chair arm. "I don't know. My ancestors have never given me a clear feeling either way."

She nodded, seeming relieved. "Me, too. You know what that can mean."

"No, I don't."

"Seriously? It can mean that a life hangs in the balance. It can mean that your decisions, your actions can make a difference, decide whether that person has died or is still alive."

"I've never heard that." Beliefs had changed a bit in a century, it seemed. Easy enough to understand, with so many prisoners of war held and no exchanges of information about them. Families would have to grasp at any straw that offered hope or information about the fates of loved ones.

Jane Geary nodded firmly. "Everyone in the family agreed about you. We'd speak with our ancestors, but no one ever felt like you were among them. I swear. That's why Grandfather told me to give you a message if I saw you. If you were dead, he would have expected to see you first, when he died and joined our ancestors, but none of us thought you were there." Her expression turned fierce. "We never told anyone outside the family. That legend grew up, that you'd come back someday to save the Alliance, but it wasn't because the family told anyone that you weren't dead. I don't know where that legend came from. But it was true. It took me a long time to accept that."

"Jane, please don't. I have enough expectations put on me as it is by people I'm not related to." He spread his hands. "It's nice to have people who believe I'm human. It's important for me to have that."

She thought, then nodded. "I think I understand. But I must ask, as family, for the truth. Were you there, during all those years? Among the lights in jump space? Among the living stars themselves?"

The question was obviously a serious one, so Geary managed to avoid a laugh, which might have stung his grandniece. "Not that I remember. I can't remember anything, really. I fell asleep, then I awoke on *Dauntless*."

"Not even any dreams?" Jane asked, her disappointment clear.

"I don't— Not that I can be sure of," Geary corrected himself. "Every once in a while I think I remember a fragment of something. But the doctors all tell me that in survival sleep everything in the body is stopped or slowed down as far as it possibly can be slowed. Thought processes, too. I wasn't thinking, so I couldn't have been dreaming. That's what they say. If anything did happen, I can't remember it." Geary glanced at his grandniece, uncomfortable with this line of questions and wanting to change the subject. "What would you have done if you hadn't gone into the fleet?"

Jane Geary smiled. "Something to do with structures. Architecture. People have drawn on living models for millennia, but I think there's more we can learn when designing things." Her smile faded. "Michael has a daughter and two sons. The daughter will be eligible to enter fleet-officer training in six months."

He had known that but hadn't wanted to bring it up, wondering how those children would feel about Black Jack, the Black Jack who had left their father in the Syndic home star system. "Is that what she wants to do?"

"Maybe you'll get a chance to ask her."

"As long as she really has a choice."

Jane Geary nodded. "Maybe you'll give her that choice, at long last. Please forgive me for not speaking with you earlier. I should go now and let you prepare for operations."

He checked the time and nodded reluctantly. "Thank you. I can't tell you how much this meant to me."

"Perhaps we'll both be able to speak with Michael again." Jane Geary stood up, then saluted in the manner of someone to whom the gesture was recently learned. "By your leave, Admiral."

"Granted." He returned the salute, then stood for a moment, gazing at the place where her image had been before leaving for the bridge.

On Geary's display on the bridge, the Syndic hypernet gate loomed. The actual gate was a bound-energy matrix invisible to human senses, but the hundreds of devices called tethers, which held that matrix stable and in place, were visible in a huge ring *Dauntless* seemed about to thread. He hadn't been so close to a gate since Sancere, and that gate had been collapsing as a result of having too many of its tethers destroyed by Syndic warships trying to deny use of the gate to the Alliance fleet. Remembering the way space itself had seemed to fluctuate as the gate collapsed, Geary took a deep breath to calm himself.

"No problems," Desjani advised him with a reassuring smile.

"Captain Desjani, I only remember approaching a hypernet gate once, and you'll recall that wasn't a pleasant experience."

"We survived."

After a century of war, Geary had to admit that was a reasonable standard for success.

Desjani gave Geary a speculative look. "This is where we find out if it all works right."

He nodded, knowing that she was referring to things they shouldn't discuss on the bridge. All of the probability-based worms they could find had been scrubbed out of the hypernet, maneuvering, and communications systems on every ship in the fleet. Hopefully that would mean the aliens couldn't redirect the fleet while it was in the hypernet as they had a Syndic flotilla. But the Alliance fleet wouldn't know for certain it was safe until they tried it. "How does this hypernet gate and key work again?"

"When we enter the hypernet gate's field, the Syndic hypernet key aboard *Dauntless* will activate. We set the parameters for the transport field to be large enough to include the entire fleet, make sure the destination displayed on the key is what we want, then we order the key to transmit the execute command to the gate. It's simple."

He nodded. "Too simple. What human engineer ever designed something that easy to operate?"

"You're right. We should have suspected that nonhumans were involved right from the start when the activation process didn't involve a lot of arcane commands that had to be done in just the right order, and the destination was displayed as a name rather than using some counter intuitive code. No human software engineer would produce a device that easy to use." Desjani grinned and indicated the fleet. "You're happy with the formation?"

"Yeah. This formation can deal with anything we encounter if the Syndics are waiting at the hypernet gate at Zevos. But that's really unlikely."

Desjani looked over at another part of her display. "The key has activated. Do you want to punch in the data?"

"No. Go ahead, please."

Her hands danced across controls, then she frowned at the display. "Operations watch-stander. Confirm transport field size is correctly entered."

After a moment, that officer nodded. "Confirmed, Captain. The field will include the entire fleet."

"Confirm destination set as Zevos."

"Destination confirmed as Zevos."

Desjani looked at Geary. "Request permission to activate hypernet key for transport to Zevos."

"Permission granted."

Desjani tapped a couple of more times, then the stars vanished.

Geary had barely remembered what the view looked like within a hypernet channel. "There really is nothing to see."

"No." Desjani spread her hands. "The scientists say we're in some sort of bubble where light as we know it doesn't penetrate. So it's just dark."

Just dark. No sensation of speed or any movement at all. "How long again?"

"Eight days, fourteen hours, and six minutes for this trip. The farther you're going, the faster the speed relative to the outside universe. It's sort of weird, but this is a long haul, so we're going faster than if it were a short haul on the hypernet."

"A shorter trip can take the same amount of time as a longer trip?"

"Yes. Or more time." Desjani waved at the darkness filling the display of outside conditions. "Like I said, it's sort of weird. You'd have to ask a scientist to explain why, though I've never been sure they really understand it. They have some impressive names for what they think is happening, though."

Even if a straight-shot journey had been possible, covering that distance by jump drives would have taken at least a couple of months. Yet at the moment, with a battle that might finally end the war looming, those eight days, fourteen hours, and six minutes seemed far too long a time. "I want this over."

"Yes, sir. Me, too. Just remember how long it's been coming for the rest of us."

The war had begun a hundred years ago. Desjani and the rest of *Dauntless*'s crew, everyone in the fleet except Geary, had been waiting for this as long as they'd been alive.

Looked at that way, he could wait another eight days.

If the aliens could still divert the fleet, they didn't do it. Zevos boasted a star system with two marginally inhabitable worlds, a very large population, and a lot of colonies and outposts elsewhere on moons, asteroids, and near gas giants. Not a single Syndic warship was visible to the fleet's sensors as the Alliance warships popped out of the hypernet gate. "They've pulled any mobile defenses into the home system," Desjani suggested. "Probably a lot of the fixed defenses were pulled up and shipped there, too."

"Probably." A Syndic traffic-control buoy near the gate was squawking at the Alliance warships, trying to direct them into proper, approved traffic lanes for progress in-system. "*Diamond*, kill that buoy."

"*Diamond*, aye," the heavy cruiser acknowledged. "Buoy will be destroyed in approximately thirty-five seconds."

The jump point they wanted was only a light-hour and a half distant from the hypernet gate. Geary got the fleet on a course for that point, taking some glee in knowing that the Syndic authorities in Zevos Star System would only see the Alliance warships in several hours, just before the Alliance ships jumped out of Zevos. Since the Syndics had forgotten how to use extended-jump-range capability, they'd think the Alliance fleet was bound for another star named Marchen, which was more distant from the Syndic home star system than Zevos.

"What do you want to do about those merchant ships approaching the hypernet gate?" Desjani asked.

Despite his deception maneuvers, Geary didn't want word of his arrival at Zevos spreading through Syndic space too quickly. He used the maneuvering display to check some solutions as fast as he could tag some Alliance units and ask for an intercept. "Twentieth Destroyer Squadron, you are to intercept and destroy the designated Syndic merchant ships. Do not pursue or engage other targets without orders. Rejoin the fleet prior to jump."

"Twentieth Destroyer Squadron, aye!" Gleeful at getting to hammer the Syndics while the rest of the fleet just transited to the jump point, the destroyers in the Twentieth Squadron leaped forward after their prey.

Geary watched the destroyers charging off in pursuit, then went over his formation choices again. He figured the Syndics wouldn't be anywhere near where the fleet came out of jump space at the Syndic home star system, but he wanted to be ready in case he was wrong. "Captain Smyth, I want your auxiliaries to top off the fuel-cell reserves on every ship as well as their expendable armaments. Let me know if you'll have any trouble getting that done before we jump."

Fifteen hours to the jump point. Ten days in jump space. All to get back to where his command of the fleet had started.

6

A collective sound like that of a pride of lions sighting prey came from the watch-standers on *Dauntless*'s bridge as the Alliance fleet arrived in the Syndic home star system. The fleet had fled this star system six months earlier, running for its life in the face of terrible losses and overwhelming enemy superiority in warships. Now it was back, and the wreckage of those Syndic warships littered space along the path the fleet had taken home. "We've got them," Desjani whispered, her eyes gleaming with anticipation.

Geary paused to savor the moment despite his own resolve not to be distracted. The Alliance fleet had arrived at an angle relative to where it had been when Geary first assumed command, about a quarter of the way around the outer extent of the star system from the jump point the fleet had once used to flee to Corvus. Three light-hours away, the hypernet gate for the star system hung in space. Even from this distance the fleet's sensors could pick out the thick walls of minefields hanging just outside the gate, their numbers and the density with which the mines were laid going a long way toward negating the stealth characteristics of individual mines. Just outside the minefields, another mass of merchant ships waited, hundreds of FACs visible attached to them, ready to launch and strike as an attacking force staggered clear of the minefields. Behind the merchant ships, only fifteen light-minutes from the hypernet gate, the main body of the Syndic defenders waited, a mere twelve battleships and sixteen battle cruisers, but accompanied by sixty-one heavy cruisers, fifty light cruisers, and one hundred ninety-seven HuKs.

Most importantly, the Alliance fleet's sensors confirmed that the hypernet gate had a safe-fail system installed. Not that anyone on the Alliance side had doubted that protection would be in place, but actually seeing a safe-fail system present relieved any lingering concerns.

Elsewhere in the system, there were a few light cruisers and HuKs transiting between planets, and far off, almost opposite the position of the Alliance fleet on the other side of the star system, a single battleship and three heavy cruisers hovered in a small group.

"I know many of those battleships and battle cruisers are new construction, but where did the Syndics get that many escorts?" Geary wondered.

"They must have stripped system-defense forces from a lot of star systems," Desjani suggested. "If we'd run head-on into that trap, it would have been a repeat of the fleet's last visit here. By the time we cleared the ambush, we would have lost so many ships that the Syndics could have won." Her gaze wandered across her display. "Everything in fixed orbit in this star system has rail guns or particle-beam batteries on it. Good thing you saved our rocks."

The Syndic home star system certainly constituted a target-rich environment. In addition to the fixed defenses, the planets in the star system boasted many cities and colonies, though the primary inhabited world also had vast stretches of what looked like parklands, with grand lodges set within them at such wide intervals that nobody in one of the lodges could have seen another lodge. "Nice place," Geary commented.

"The main inhabited world eight light-minutes from the star is almost perfect," Desjani agreed. "The planet four and a half light-minutes from the star is way too hot, but the one at fifteen light-minutes must be nice enough since there are a lot of enclosed cities on it, and that gas giant only thirty-two light-minutes from the star is really convenient for mining. It is a good star system. Can we break it?"

"Yeah. Let's start with the fixed defenses. We'll save industrial and transportation targets as leverage and take them out as necessary to goad the Syndics into negotiating seriously." Geary entered commands into the combat systems, tagging as targets the enemy defenses mounted on planets, moons, asteroids, and artificial satellites in fixed orbits, as well as the command and control locations and sensor systems associated with those defenses, then asked the automated systems for a bombardment plan. The number of targets was so great that the fleet combat systems actually required a noticeable blink of time before they produced a solution. Geary didn't quite suppress a whistle as he looked at it. "I'll have to make certain the auxiliaries are manufacturing more rocks for us. This will seriously dent our inventories."

He moved to confirm the command, then changed a setting and looked at Desjani. "You do it."

"What?"

"I passed approval authority to you. Go ahead and launch the bombardment."

She slowly smiled at him. "You do know how to make a woman happy. This woman, anyway." The smile changed, taking on a feral cast as Desjani looked over the bombardment plan. "Thank you, Admiral. This is for the comrades we lost here last time," she announced, then tapped the approval command.

All over the Alliance fleet, warships began hurling out kinetic projectiles. They would take hours and days to reach their targets, but the intricate network of Syndic defensive batteries would be junk once they had all struck.

Throughout the hundred years of this war, the Syndic home star system hadn't directly felt the impact of the war. Now it would, and Geary felt some satisfaction in that. "Let's go hit that Syndic flotilla. All units in the Alliance fleet, come port four two degrees, down zero one degrees at time three zero." He would hold this formation for a while, until he saw what the Syndics were doing. Despite how well things seemed to have turned out, he had a nagging worry that the Syndics had placed some other traps within this star system that hadn't been spotted yet. "Maintain an alert watch for any signs of other minefields within the star system."

Now that immediate actions had been dealt with, it was time to address the reason the fleet had come here. He called the intelligence section aboard *Dauntless*. "Lieutenant Iger, how precisely can you tell me where the Syndic Executive Council is located within this star system?"

Iger had the look of a subordinate who knew that his answer wouldn't satisfy a superior. "It's very unlikely that we'll be able to give you an exact location. We're scanning all unencrypted Syndic communications right now for any information, and we'll break out what segments of encrypted comms we can, but it's likely that our only indications will be transmission priorities on the star-system comm web."

"You can read message priorities?"

"No, sir, not exactly, but we can tell which transmissions are being given priority by routers throughout the star system. By tracking those transmissions to their origin, we can identify the general location of whoever has the authority to issue the highest number of high-priority transmissions."

That sounded good. "How general is a 'general location'?"

The intelligence officer's discomfort grew. "Once messages get within a closed transmission system, we can't track them anymore. That would be, say, an orbital installation. Or a planet."

"A planet?" Geary stared at Iger. "You could only narrow it down to somewhere on a planet?"

"Possibly, sir," Iger explained. "Once on a planet, there are all kinds of transmission methods we can't monitor from out here. Buried cables, for example. Command nodes on planets tend to use remote sites for actual wireless transmissions to help hide their location. But we should definitely be able to tell you which planet the Syndic Executive Council is on."

It was obviously an explanation, not an excuse, so Geary nodded.

"All right. How long will it take you to get me that?"

"It depends on how tight the Syndic net is, sir. A few hours to less than a day on the outside. Admiral, if some Syndic source provides better information, we can localize the Executive Council better. We just can't count on that happening soon."

"Understood. Have you identified any POW camps, yet?"

Iger shook his head. "No, sir. Nothing that looks like a POW or labor camp, and no comm traffic obviously associated with such a thing. But we'll keep looking."

"Good, but the priority task is finding the Syndic leadership's location. Let me know when you've got that, and get it as soon as you can." He had enough experience with Iger to know the wording he used would be all that was needed to get the intelligence section working at full speed.

Less than a day, or at least a few hours. That seemed far too long to wait, to allow the Syndics to plan more attacks, before offering to open negotiations. Long experience had taught Geary that it was easier to stop a plan from being formed than it was to stop a plan in the process of being carried out.

He couldn't yet target his message on one location, so he would have to broadcast it. Geary sat straighter before transmitting this time. "To the members of the Executive Council of the Syndicate Worlds, this is Admiral Geary, commanding officer of the Alliance Fleet. We are here to end this war on terms both sides can accept. We will end it by negotiation if possible, or by force if necessary. Attached to this transmission is a list of proposed points to form the basis for a peace treaty. I urge you to review that list and respond positively as soon as possible. Alliance forces within this star system will continue offensive operations until a treaty is agreed upon." Rione had suggested that as a way of ensuring that the Syndics wouldn't try drawing out negotiations as long as possible. "To the honor of our ancestors."

As he finished, Geary heard a noise at the back of the bridge and turned, annoyed. Besides Rione, the other two senators stood there as well, crowding that particular area. All three politicians seemed to be arguing, and Desjani appeared to be trying to decide whether she could get away with arresting them all. "Excuse me," Geary said, a little louder than usual. "But we are still facing strong Syndic military forces in this star system and anticipate combat. We'd prefer not to have distractions on the bridge."

"Even though we've had to live with them for some time," Desjani muttered too low for any of the politicians to hear.

Senator Costa frowned importantly. "Admiral Geary, we're simply working out a fair rotation for occupying the observer position on the bridge."

Out of sight of Costa and Sakai, Rione made a defeated gesture to Geary before speaking. "Perhaps this discussion should be held elsewhere," she suggested to the other two politicians. "Someplace quiet, where we won't disturb the crew."

"The brig is nice and quiet," Desjani grumbled under her breath.

"Tanya," Geary warned softly before raising his voice again. "That's a good suggestion, Madam Co-President. Work it out among yourselves, please." He didn't want to get involved in this because he was afraid if he did, he would eventually lose patience with the politicians and order them to follow a certain arrangement. Ordering politicians around could very easily become too comfortable a way of handling them. He couldn't afford to become comfortable with that, not when the fleet and the people of the Alliance would be all too happy to urge him on.

Sakai's feelings were hard to determine, but he nodded. "All right, Admiral. We trust that we will be notified as soon as the enemy combat forces are eliminated?"

The senator made the elimination of the Syndic flotilla sound like a mere formality, Geary thought. Outwardly, all he did was nod. "Certainly."

"I am very proud," Sakai added, "to see so many brave citizens of Kosatka here, playing such a critical role in this fleet. We could not be here without their courageous sacrifices."

Unseen by Sakai, Desjani rolled her eyes, but her voice sounded respectful. "Thank you, Senator." The watch-standers on the bridge from Kosatka all uttered brief but polite responses as well before the three senators left the bridge.

Geary wasn't surprised when Senator Costa showed up a short time later to somewhat smugly take a seat in the observer's chair. He had expected Rione to agree to let another senator sit there for a while, since Rione already knew from her own experience that nothing would be happening for hours. It would still be over two hours before the Syndic flotilla guarding the hypernet gate even saw the Alliance fleet, and close to three hours after that before the Syndic reaction would be seen.

After the first hour had gone by, with the Alliance fleet steadily heading toward the Syndics but little else occurring except for kinetic bombardment rounds hitting a couple of the closest Syndic defensive installations, Costa had grown a little fidgety. Another hour, and not much else had changed. Point one light speed sounded fast, and it was. At that velocity, the Alliance warships were covering about thirty thousand kilometers per second. But given the immense distances in space, even that could feel like a crawl. With ten hours required to cover a single light-hour of distance, and the enemy close to three light-hours away, it would be well over a day before any prospect of battle arose.

"They should have seen us by now," Desjani finally commented to Geary loud enough for Costa to hear. "Only three more hours until we see them react."

Costa, already looking bored, twisted her mouth.

Geary stood up. "I need to walk around and think. Let me know if anything happens before three hours is out."

"I'll do that, sir."

Two hours later he was back on the bridge. Rione sat in the observer's seat again, but she didn't seem self satisfied at having tricked the other senators into a rotation that favored her. Instead, Geary thought he saw worry in Rione. "What's the matter?"

"I don't know."

She said nothing more, so Geary sat down, nodding to Desjani, who also appeared bothered. "How's everything look?" he asked.

"Good." But Desjani didn't seem entirely happy about that.

"What's bothering you?" Geary asked.

"I can't tell, Admiral. What's bothering you?"

"I can't tell, either."

The minutes crawled by, but eventually alerts appeared on the maneuvering display as movement by the Syndic flotilla was finally seen.

"They're avoiding combat," Desjani noted with a scowl.

The Syndic warships had pivoted and were accelerating away from their positions near the hypernet gate, but not on any vector that would bring them to the oncoming Alliance forces. "I wonder where they're going," Geary said. If the enemy flotilla chose to hang around just out of reach of the Alliance forces, it would be an annoying and constant threat. Humans could play games with physics in normal space with such things as the inertial dampers, which made it possible to accelerate and decelerate at rates that would normally have torn apart ships and humans, but no one had figured out how to triumph completely over the simple factors of distance and time. The Syndics were too far distant for the Alliance fleet to have any chance of catching them. The Syndics would have to come a lot closer for combat to happen, but they didn't seem interested in doing that at the moment.

"Wherever they're going, it's nowhere near us," Desjani muttered, as the projected vectors for the Syndic ships shrank from cones to thinner and thinner lines as the Syndics reached their intended course and speed, and the fleet's sensors analyzed the resulting track. "Looks like they're cutting through one segment of the star system, not directly away from us but not coming all that close, either."

Had the Syndics chosen to negotiate without fighting a hopeless battle? But Geary had yet to receive a reply to the demands he had broadcast. "They'll remain a threat in being. Fine. We'll disregard them and head for the primary inhabited world. That will give that flotilla a little over two days to decide whether it will just stand by while we put guns to the heads of their leaders. Either they fight, or we win." It didn't feel very satisfying, but it seemed the best option.

"We can't catch them, so we have to make them come to us," Desjani agreed with evident frustration.

The fleet swung around again, heading toward the star and the planet orbiting only eight light-minutes distant from that star.

Ten more hours crawled by, the Syndic defenses in fixed orbits vanishing in an expanding arc of destruction as the Alliance bombardment reached them. A barrage of kinetic projectiles was fired at the fleet at extremely long range by some of the Syndic fixed defenses, which were so distant that the Alliance bombardment hadn't gotten to them yet, but with literally hours and days to dodge slightly to avoid the oncoming projectiles, the Alliance warships didn't spend any time worrying about them.

When a message finally arrived at the Alliance fleet from the Syndics, it wasn't from any of the planets. "We have a transmission from the flagship of the Syndic flotilla," the communications watch reported.

Geary felt a sense of déjà vu as the image appeared before him. He had sat in this chair before, in this star system, and seen this same Syndic CEO. "Him?"

"The one who commanded the Syndic forces here before and ordered the murders of Admiral Bloch and the other senior officers in the fleet," Desjani confirmed, each word coming out harder than the one before. She hadn't had any personal admiration for Admiral Bloch, but that didn't mean she wasn't mad as hell about his being killed under the guise of negotiations.

"Yeah. That guy." Geary's memories flashed back to when that same CEO had arrogantly demanded the unconditional surrender of the Alliance fleet warships that had survived the initial ambush. He could, if he wanted to, call up the record of the transmission sent to the fleet of Bloch and the others being shot inside the shuttle dock of the Syndic flagship. A surge of old anger filled Geary as he looked at that face again.

The Syndic CEO on the screen smiled as if he knew he would be recognized and wanted to let them know he would enjoy their reactions. "The Syndicate Worlds send their greetings to Admiral Geary. I am CEO First Rank Shalin."

"He's wearing more medals than before," Desjani breathed with barely controlled fury. "Awards for what he did here last time."

CEO Shalin continued speaking. "We're prepared to offer a cease-fire within this star system, in the interests of humanity. We are willing to engage in negotiations with your fleet."

Geary stared at the image, wondering if his mouth was literally hanging open. To have this man speak of negotiating after the atrocity committed during the last "negotiations" with him labeled him as either unbelievably tone-deaf or viciously insulting.

"We have a number of Alliance prisoners of war within this star system" the CEO went on in an almost negligent tone of voice. "They were acquired during your fleet's last visit here. Those prisoners are dispersed in a wide number of locations. It would be a pity if any were harmed by bombardments. I await your reply and trust that you will exercise discretion in your actions to avoid escalating tensions and casualties."

The image blanked, and Geary shook his head in disbelief. "What was the purpose of that? Are they just trying to make us angry?"

"They're succeeding," Desjani growled.

"Would they actually place our prisoners of war at their defensive sites?" He already knew the answer but needed it confirmed. Intelligence still hadn't found any POW camps, which meant any Alliance prisoners in this star system would have to be dispersed and confined in relatively small groups.

"They would." Desjani shook her head. "But it's stupid to make that threat after our barrage was launched. We can't stop it any more than they can, so claiming our POWs are at those locations has no result except to make us madder."

His and Desjani's reactions to the Syndic transmission had been the same. "That's the idea, isn't it? Make us mad, enraged, in the hope that it causes us to do the wrong thing, We've used that tactic against them, and I can't imagine any other reason for the tone and wording of that transmission." He thought for a moment. Senator Sakai was occupying the observer's chair on the bridge just then and, while watching intently, hadn't offered any comments. "Senator, do you have any thoughts on this?"

Sakai, his face impassive, slowly shook his head. "Nothing beyond what you and Captain Desjani have speculated, Admiral. I agree with you that the enemy commander's message seemed designed to provoke us into heedless actions. However, I am accustomed to the tricks employed in political combat, not those used in actual fighting. I don't know what actions the Syndics hope to goad us into taking, and since you are aware that they are attempting to provoke us, I can think of nothing further to add at this time."

"Thank you, Senator." At least Sakai was intelligent enough to recognize his limits and candid enough to admit to them. "Captain Desjani, please forward a copy of that transmission to Co-President

Rione. I'd like her assessment of what the Syndics are up to."

Desjani gestured to a watch-stander to carry out the task, her expression still furious. "If I get within weapons range of that man, and I pray to the living stars that I do, I'll blow his everlasting soul into enough tiny pieces that even his ancestors won't be able to put it back together."

A muted alert sounded, drawing Geary's eyes to his display. "The Syndic flotilla is turning toward us."

Her eyes lighting with eagerness, Desjani focused on her own display. But as the minutes went by and the course of the flotilla steadied out, she scowled. "They've come starboard, but that flotilla's track still has a closest point of approach to us of about a light-hour. If we come onto an intercept, they can still easily evade us."

"What's their game?" Geary wondered. "Make us mad, then hang out of reach. What is it they expect us to do?"

Desjani took a long, slow breath, clearly mastering her own anger enough to think, then glanced at him. "Do you remember Sutrah? As well as Corvus?"

He didn't like to dwell on those engagements early in his command of the fleet, but it wasn't hard to see her point. "This fleet, back then, would have charged that flotilla even knowing they had no chance of intercepting it."

"Because going on the attack was always right, and they would have expected the Syndics to countercharge." Desjani's brow furrowed in thought. "That CEO is the one we most want revenge against, he says things designed to make us want to go after him, and their flotilla cruises along just out of reach."

"They want us angry enough to chase them even though we have no chance of catching them." Geary leaned back, searching his display for something they might have missed earlier. "Why? What's the point? Surely we'd spot any minefields in our path, and in any case, our possible courses cover too much space for this to be an attempt to lure us into prepositioned mines. A delaying action? At best such a tactic would buy them a few days before this fleet got tired of a futile chase."

"If our formation dissolved, and the fleet was strung out, they might be able to hit portions of it that couldn't be supported by the rest of the fleet," Desjani suggested.

"Maybe. I suppose that would give them a chance to hit our battle cruisers if they had charged too far out in front. But we would still have a strong advantage in numbers." Another possibility came to mind. "Do you think they're delaying because they expect help from... anyone?"

Desjani frowned. "External help?" she asked, avoiding speaking directly about the aliens. "Why would the Syndics trust them again?"

"Because it's their only chance? But why try to draw us into a chase instead of just delaying through negotiations?" Too many questions, not enough answers. "Let's hold course for a while and see what they do once it becomes obvious we're not playing their game."

"Are you going to answer that motherless scum?" Desjani asked.

"Not yet." Partly because he didn't trust himself to speak calmly to the man, and partly because he wanted to learn more before deciding what to say.

Half an hour later, long before it could have seen the Alliance fleet's reaction to its previous maneuver, the Syndic flotilla veered to starboard again, coming onto a vector that would intercept the Alliance fleet in about three days. "Now we don't even have to maneuver," Desjani observed, scowling. "I want to blow away those bastards, but if they really wanted to fight, they'd be coming toward us on a much faster intercept. They're just going to run again once we get a bit closer."

"So even though we're not chasing them, for the time being they're happy if we just keep doing what we're doing." Geary squinted at his display as if that would make him see hidden objects there. "There's nothing on our track that could be a threat, right?"

"Not a thing, not unless their stealth mine technology has suddenly improved by several orders of magnitude."

That wasn't impossible if the aliens had rendered more direct assistance to the Syndics, Geary realized. But there had been no way for the Syndics to predict that the Alliance fleet would be on this particular path through space, no way for the Syndics to have laid minefields along that path, so why were the Syndics content to keep luring the Alliance fleet down that path?

Rione came back onto the bridge as he was still considering the question. "We think they used that CEO to goad us into attacking. What do you think?" Geary asked.

"That's as good a guess as any," Rione replied, sitting down herself, as Senator Sakai rose but stayed standing beside the observer's seat. "Yet the odds as we know them offer no reason why that tactic would succeed. I expected the Syndic leaders to stall for time, but this is different, an attempt to ensure we remain focused on that flotilla. Is there anything else in this star system to which they wouldn't want us paying attention?"

He studied his display with that in mind, then pointed. "I expected that battleship and those three heavy cruisers to head for the flotilla and join forces. Instead, they're just waiting there, and the flotilla has gotten steadily closer to them."

"They're near a jump point," Desjani said. "For Mandalon. I don't know why the Syndics would waste a battleship and three heavy cruisers guarding a jump point, though. Maybe they do expect reinforcements to come through that jump point, and the flotilla is moving to join up with them when the reinforcements get here."

"That's possible." Geary rubbed his neck, trying to figure out what the Syndics might be up to. "They must be thinking of fighting us eventually, and waiting for reinforcements would explain what they've been doing. If the Syndic flotilla just wanted to run, they could have used their own hypernet gate or headed straight for the jump point."

"Correct me if I'm wrong," Rione said, "but one more battleship and three more heavy cruisers won't make any significant change to the odds against the Syndics. Nor can they have significant numbers of reinforcements still coming unless our intelligence is far from the mark. There's still something missing, something the Syndics don't want us to see." Rione shook her head, gazing at the display before her. "The Syndic leadership has stayed in control because they are willing to do whatever it takes to maintain that power. They know you have defeated their flotillas time and again. They know their fixed defenses in this star system couldn't defeat a fleet. We've seen the ambush they prepared if this fleet had come through the hypernet gate here. It was thorough and deadly, but the fleet under the command of Admiral Geary has escaped certain doom more than once. What is their hidden card, the one the Syndic leaders planned to play if all else failed to stop a man whom they have failed to stop time and again?"

Desjani spoke with exaggerated patience. "Madam Co-President, the fleet's sensors aren't infallible, but they have scanned this system repeatedly. It is not overconfidence to say that we know everything the Syndics have here. They planned on the ambush at the hypernet gate destroying this fleet."

"I'm aware of what the sensors report." Her tone remaining almost distant, Rione stared at her display. "There's something missing," she repeated. "Every instinct I have tells me that the Syndics would have insurance, something else in the all-too-likely event that Black Jack Geary produced another miracle."

Geary looked from Rione to Desjani, his own misgivings springing back to life. "The Syndic flotilla's actions imply there's something else going on here, but if there is another threat big enough to imperil this fleet, we haven't found it. What could it be?"

Sakai spoke for the first time. "As I said, I have little direct experience with military matters, but I do have some knowledge of dealing with opponents in ways they do not expect. If what you seek is here, and you are confident that we have seen all that is here, then we must have seen it and not known what it means."

"Maybe intelligence has spotted something. It's their job to figure out what things mean." Geary called Lieutenant Iger again. This time, Lieutenant Iger had the unhappy look of an intelligence officer who was about to impart something that wasn't going to make his superior happy. "Lieutenant, do you have anything regarding any threats in this star system that wouldn't have been apparent before now?"

Iger appeared startled by the question. "No, sir. Nothing we haven't reported. We've fed everything we've found regarding threats into the fleet combat systems. But, sir, I was going to call you after we ran a triple check on our analysis of the Syndic net. We do apparently have something odd going on."

Naturally. Something *else* odd. "And what would that be?"

"Sir, regarding the location of the Syndic Executive Council." Lieutenant Iger frowned down at something on his own display, then made a helpless gesture. "We have identified a location that has firm priority within the Syndic net."

"Which planet is it?" Geary pressed.

"It's not a planet, sir. It's in the small group of Syndic warships at the jump point for Mandalon."

Geary's eyes went to his display. "They're on that battleship?"

"That is our assessment, yes, sir. As I said, we were rerunning our analysis—"

"Why? Why would they be on that battleship?"

"We have to assume that they're preparing to run, sir."

"But if the Syndic leaders are on that battleship so they can escape, why haven't they already run? It would have made more sense to leave this star system before we arrived so it wouldn't so obviously be running. And how can they hope to maintain their authority if they flee this star system?"

Iger looked apologetic. "Sir, we don't know the answers to that.

We have to assume that there is a reason the Syndic leaders haven't yet fled and that they have some grounds for thinking they can politically survive such a flight."

"Thank you, Lieutenant." Geary looked to Desjani, Rione, and Sakai. "Intelligence says the Syndic Executive Council is on that battleship at the jump point for Mandalon. Intelligence doesn't know why they haven't already run if that's their intention."

"They're planning on doing something before they run," Desjani replied.

"That's what intel thought. But what?"

"I don't know. I can only think of one reason why as a military officer I'd want to get away fast after performing an action."

Memories flashed into Geary's mind. The last moments of his heavy cruiser *Merlon* in Grendel star system. "If you've activated a power-core overload on your ship. A self-destruct command. You need to be able to get off the ship fast after you give that order."

"Right. But what could the Syndic Executive Council want to do that's anything like that?"

Rione answered Desjani, though her reply sounded more like a prayer. "May the living stars preserve us." She stood up, her face growing pale as an expression of horror flitted across it. "Senator Sakai was correct. We're looking at it. Ancestors save us, it's right there, and we didn't see it."

Desjani frowned, searching her own display. "What are you talking about?"

"I'm talking about what we expect to see and what really is there! How did this fleet defeat that Syndic flotilla at Lakota? It used a large number of ships as an improvised minefield, and the Syndics didn't realize what it was because it didn't *look* like a minefield." Rione's hand came up, pointing. "The hypernet gate."

Geary felt a hard knot tighten in his guts. "It has a safe-fail system installed. We confirmed that."

"Yes, we did." Rione turned a burning gaze on him, then stepped forward quickly, leaning over close so only Geary and Desjani could hear her. "But systems can be reprogrammed, Admiral Geary. The collapse of a hypernet gate can be scaled down to minimize the energy release, or scaled *up* to make it a deadlier weapon."

He got it then. When Captain Cresida had first worked up the necessary algorithms to scale down the energy release from a collapsing hypernet gate, she had also had to work up the reverse, the ways to increase the energy release. He had given that set of algorithms to Rione, not trusting himself with such a weapon.

But the Syndics would have done the same calculations, eventually reached the same conclusions, discovered how to reliably turn their own hypernet gates into weapons that could kill fleets and star systems at a single blow. A self-destruct command encompassing an entire star system, aimed at taking down this fleet.

Desjani's face had gone rigid, and she spoke with extreme care. "Can a safe-fail system be reversed? Made to trigger a powerful blast? Worse than at Kalixa?"

"I don't know," Geary replied, marveling at the steadiness of his own voice. "I can find out." Like Desjani, he didn't question that the Syndic leadership might annihilate even this star system if that price bought the destruction of the Alliance fleet. He had seen far too many incidents where star-system CEOs had ordered actions with a similar callous disregard for their own people living in those star systems.

Rione pointed again, this time to the battleship and heavy cruisers at the jump point for Mandalon. "They had it all set up. They're ready to escape. If the ambush failed, they send the collapse command, then jump to safety."

"And afterward blame us," Desjani finished. "We'd all be dead. Damn. Sir, she's right. The Syndics have the biggest bomb in the galaxy staring us in the face, and we didn't even realize it."

"That's because we'd stopped thinking of the gates as weapons after the safe-fail devices were installed. If Cresida hadn't died at Varandal, she would have warned us, I'm certain." Geary tapped his controls. "Commander Neeson, I need an analysis from you, and I need it five minutes ago." The commanding officer of *Implacable* was one of the best hypernet experts remaining in the fleet since Cresida had died. "Can a safe-fail system be reprogrammed to increase rather than decrease the output of a hypernet gate's collapse? And, if it can, how long would that take?"

Implacable was several light-seconds distant, but Neeson's image stared at Geary longer than that time delay alone could account for. Finally, he nodded. "Yes, Admiral. I don't have to run any analysis. The equipment could be used that way even though that option had never occurred to me." Neeson paused, swallowing, before speaking again. "How long? Once the necessary algorithms were calculated, they could be added as an option to the controlling software. Toggling between options would be essentially instantaneous."

Geary had to pause to ensure his voice remained steady before replying. "Thank you, Commander. Please keep that assessment to yourself for the time being. We're considering possible enemy options over here, not dealing with certainties."

"Yes, sir." Neeson rubbed one hand across the lower half of his face. "Sir, if the Syndics here do that..."

"We know." Geary broke the connection, facing Desjani and Rione again, Sakai standing back deferentially but listening intently. "It can be done. If the Syndics have worked up the calculations, then they could switch the safe-fail system into a catastrophic-fail system in an instant."

"There'd still be time delays for the signal to reach the gate," Desjani said.

Rione had her eyes closed, obviously trying to regain her composure. "Would we have any warning?"

"We'd see the gate starting to collapse, but unless we were very close to a jump point, that wouldn't help," Geary admitted. "But if that was the Syndics' backup plan, why haven't they done it already?"

Desjani, studying her display again, nodded sharply. "They need those ships." She looked at Geary. "The Syndic leaders need the warships in that flotilla. That's their last major force. Without those warships, their ability to keep the Syndicate Worlds together by coercion disappears. They won't want that flotilla destroyed here with us."

"That's why the flotilla didn't head for the hypernet gate to leave after the ambush failed," Geary realized. "Cresida told me no one knew for sure what would happen to ships in transit if a gate anchoring one end of a hypernet path is destroyed. One possibility was that they'd be destroyed as well, but she said the most likely probability was that the ships would drop back into normal space somewhere along their route."

"Light-years away from any star?" Desjani asked. "They'd get somewhere they could use jump drives eventually, but it would be decades, and until they got somewhere, those ships would be of no use to anybody. So the Syndics wouldn't try to use the gate to get their flotilla clear of this star system. We could have intercepted that flotilla if it headed for the jump point for Tremandir. They could have easily reached the jump point for Corvus before we got to them, but instead they bypassed that jump point. Now they're positioned where they can safely reach the jump point for Mandalon before we could catch them."

"But why did the flotilla bypass the jump point for Corvus? What makes Mandalon a better objective than Corvus? Is it just because the Syndic Executive Council is forted up on the battleship there? And why isn't the flotilla headed straight for the Mandalon jump point instead of cutting closer to our path like they are doing?"

"They want us to chase that flotilla. That would draw us deeper into the star system." Desjani's expression grew thoughtful. "Time lags. Look at the geometry. When we arrived in this star system, we were a little more than ten light-hours from the jump point for Mandalon, and about three light-hours from the hypernet gate. The Syndic leaders on that battleship could only see what we were doing as of ten hours before. Any signal they transmitted to the hypernet gate would have taken... about seven hours to reach it. Then the shock wave would have taken three hours to reach our location near the jump point from Zevos. Their information about us would be ten hours old, and it would take ten more hours for their surprise attack to reach us."

"We could go a long ways in twenty hours," Geary agreed. "The fleet could turn around and jump out of this star system while the

Syndic signal was on its way to the gate. So they're trying to get the time lag down and get us deeper into the star system, farther from any jump points we could use. That's why the flotilla and that damned CEO are luring us onward. They want us chasing after the Syndic flotilla with no thought for other possible threats and too far from any jump point to leave the star system between the time the collapse order is given and the shock wave hits."

Sakai shook his head. "Surely even the Syndic leaders realize the effect it would have on their people once it was learned that those leaders had deliberately wiped out one of their own star systems and murdered every Syndic citizen within it? Fear of retaliation from their own government has helped keep the Syndicate Worlds together, but if the Syndic people know they could be sacrificed en masse anyway, they might indeed finally revolt."

"The Syndic leaders would blame us," Rione replied. "They'd tell their people that the Alliance had collapsed another hypernet gate, after practicing at Sancere and Kalixa, but had been caught by our own weapon this time. Enough Syndic people would probably accept that to avoid revolt."

Desjani's own response was stiff and formal. "Even the Syndics know that this fleet under the command of Admiral Geary does not commit atrocities."

"That is true," Rione conceded. "But it would be a cold comfort to us if the Syndic leaders' cover story wasn't accepted after this fleet was destroyed. Can we still get out?" she asked Geary. "Turn about and make it back to the jump point from which we arrived before the Syndics could react?"

"Probably not," Geary replied, trying to decide how long the

Syndics might hesitate before ordering the gate to collapse. "We're already more than fourteen hours travel time at point one light speed from the jump point we came in on, and that much closer to the Syndics at the Mandalon jump point. If they ordered a gate collapse as soon as they saw us turn, we'd have to be very lucky to avoid getting hit."

"Go faster! If they know you're leaving anyway—"

"I can't turn the fleet on a dime, and I can't accelerate every ship like I can a destroyer or a battle cruiser. It might work if we tried it right now, but I doubt it." He paused, wondering if that was, nonetheless, exactly what he needed to do, if that was the only chance the fleet would have.

"But you can't just turn this fleet around and run for the jump point!" Desjani shook her head, keeping her voice low but intense. "This wouldn't be like Lakota, where we could say we were heading to attack another part of the Syndic forces. It would be running with no apparent reason, fleeing this star system. Our fleet believes in you, Admiral Geary, but please do *not* test their faith this way. It would go against *everything* they believe in besides you." Her eyes went to Rione. "And because they wouldn't accept that you would choose to do such a thing, they would instead believe that the retreat had been ordered by the politicians, and that you had either been coerced or had caved in to their demands. Do I need to spell out what might happen then?"

Rione gazed back at Desjani dispassionately, then nodded to Geary. "She is absolutely right. It would be assumed within the fleet that we, the politicians, had sold out the Alliance either because of bribery or simple treachery and ordered you to retreat."

Geary blew out an exasperated breath. "Why is it whenever you two are in agreement, it's about something that's going to make my life harder?"

"Good advice tends to do that," Rione said. "If you haven't figured it out already, bad advice usually makes you feel better in the short run."

Desjani was eyeing her display. "Every second that passes means we're traveling deeper into a Syndic trap, but if we turn around and head for the jump point to escape, the Syndics will trigger the trap as soon as they see us running and before we can reach safety, and our own fleet will mutiny. I don't have any good ideas at the moment."

Geary drummed his fingers on his seat's arm, trying to think of alternatives. "Is there any chance we could get to the hypernet gate before the Syndic flotilla reaches the jump point for Mandalon? Head that way instead so we could take it down safely?"

"Let's see." Desjani's fingers danced across her controls as she ran the maneuvers, then she made a tired gesture. "Yes and no. We could charge the gate with just our battle cruisers, accelerating, then decelerating at maximum, and in theory get there in time, but in order to get close enough to the gate to counter the Syndic collapse we'd have to get through the minefields first. We'd lose every ship trying to ram our way through them. We could blow a path through the mines using null fields, but in order to do that we'd have to slow down a lot."

"Meaning we wouldn't get there in time."

"No, not even if the Syndics held off blowing the gate that long."

"You could fire those bombardment projectiles," Rione urged.

"No. Rocks could take down the gate, but the Syndics would see them en route in plenty of time to order the gate to collapse destructively before the rocks got there. It might cost them that flotilla they want to save, but if we launched rocks at the gate, it would guarantee this fleet's destruction. As much as the Syndic leaders must want that flotilla to get out of this star system intact, I think they'll sacrifice it to get us."

Desjani nodded. "What's one more flotilla or star system to them? Just numbers on a balance sheet as long as they can avoid taking the blame for the losses."

Going back wasn't an option. Going ahead just pulled them deeper into the Syndic trap. "You warned me," he muttered to Rione. "Don't start believing that you're really Black Jack. I did. I thought I was being so damned clever. But the Syndics expected that I might well do something they hadn't anticipated, so they planned for that, too."

"You're not the only person who missed it," Rione corrected, her voice harsh. "But you may be the only one who can get us out of this."

"She's right," Desjani said.

"Stop agreeing with each other!" Geary snapped. He knew they were both correct, but at the moment hearing them in agreement was a little too weird given all of the other pressures on him. "We're too far from the jump point to ensure that the fleet could make it out in time even if we turned this instant. Retreating won't work if the Syndics have laid the sort of trap we think they have, and we can't just hang around this part of the star system, which means we continue to close on the primary world and the Syndic flotilla while we try to figure out another option. As long as the Syndics think we're diving deeper into their trap, and they still have a chance to get their flotilla out intact, they'll hold off collapsing the hypernet gate. Do you both agree with that?"

Desjani shrugged. "I expected to die the last time I was in this star system. If it happens this time, I'd prefer to go down fighting, or at least heading toward the enemy."

It took Rione a moment to reply. "I can't think of any other course of action, Admiral Geary, but I hope one of us manages to do so before too much longer."

"Then let's show the Syndics what they expect to see." He took a moment to work up a maneuver to shorten the time to intercept of the Syndic flotilla, then transmitted it to the fleet. "Should I send an answer to that CEO?"

"What would you say to him?" Rione asked.

"Nothing my mother would approve of."

"Then leave him hanging for now. We need to know what we want to say before we speak to that CEO."

What they wanted to say would, of course, depend on what they were going to do. He wished he had some idea what that was. "I need to walk around and think." Nothing would happen now for a while, if their guesses were right, and just sitting would drive him crazy. Walking at least created an illusion of purposeful movement so that his mind could focus better on finding an answer.

Rione stepped back. "You've always found a solution."

"That's because there have always been solutions to choose from in the past. I don't know of even one at the moment."

To Geary's surprise, Desjani gave him a tight-lipped smile. "Sir, have you ever read *Dauntless*'s commissioning emblem?"

"I've seen it." The information deeply engraved on a bulkhead near the heart of the ship told when *Dauntless* had been launched, when she had been commissioned, and included very brief notations about distinguished other ships of the same name stretching back to the days when every human warship rode only the waters of Earth.

"Including the ship's motto?" Desjani asked.

"It's in some old language." Geary couldn't count how many times he had resolved to ask someone or look up what it meant, but with all of the distractions and other tasks at hand, he had never gotten around to either.

"A very old language, passed down like the name *Dauntless* from far in the past, but every commanding officer is told what it means. 'Nil Desperandum.' It means 'Never Despair.'" She shook her head. "There was a time when I thought that motto mocked us, on the last occasion we faced the Syndic fleet here in their home star system, with destruction certain, with no way to escape any of us could see. Then you assumed command of the fleet, and I have not despaired since."

He gazed back at her wordlessly for a moment. If Desjani had just said she was certain he would find an answer, it would have felt like an added and unwelcome pressure. But instead she had expressed her confidence in him indirectly, invoking ancient words whose meaning held the same force they must have always had. So Geary returned her smile with a grim one of his own, nodded to Rione, then left to walk the passageways of *Dauntless* as if they held the solution he needed.

An hour later, tired but uninspired, he strode into his stateroom and more flopped than sat down in one of the chairs, glaring at the star display over the table. The star itself seemed to be gazing back with a gloating gleam, so Geary moved to block its light.

Then stopped in midmotion, staring at the star.

They had been looking at the danger posed by the Syndic hypernet gate without realizing what it was. Maybe they had also been looking right at the way to save themselves and not knowing it, either.

He began asking the maneuvering systems for solutions, trying out options as fast as he could request them and see the responses.

The fleet conference room was filled with the usual images, only Commander Neeson among them revealing tension rather than simple curiosity about Geary's next battle plan. Desjani appeared as quietly confident as usual, and Rione had schooled her expression into a mask showing nothing of her thoughts.

Geary stood up, deciding only at that moment how to begin. "We face an unexpected and serious threat." He paused a moment to let the other officers absorb that before continuing. "It seems certain that the Syndics had a backup plan." He explained the menace from the hypernet gate while the confident looks on the faces of most of his ship captains were replaced by growing shock and worry.

"Those fatherless, motherless scum," Captain Badaya muttered, his face shading red with fury. "We always make the mistake of thinking we know how low they can go, then they find a new level of hell beneath the last one."

"They'd actually do that? To one of their own star systems?" Captain Vitali of the *Daring* asked. "I have no trouble believing that they'd do it to one of ours, but this is their capital system!"

"The leaders of the Syndicate Worlds already have done it to one of theirs, at Lakota," Tulev answered. "They knew what might happen and gave orders that the gate there be destroyed anyway. On that occasion they could salve whatever passes for their consciences by pretending that the worst case was only a possibility, but they were certainly willing to accept that worst case. It never occurred to us that they would take an action *guaranteed* to wipe out one of their own star systems when they had a safe alternative to collapsing a gate."

"That's because we would never destroy one of our own star systems like that," Neeson said.

Tulev shrugged, contempt showing. "The Syndic leadership refuses to lose this war, no matter the cost to their own planets or people."

"Politicians," Captain Armus grumbled, using the word like an obscenity.

"Some politicians," Geary corrected. "You will note that three of our own politicians are here to share the risks with us." None of the three appeared to be particularly happy to be sharing those risks, but he didn't see any need to point that out. "We've also met some Syndic leaders who don't share the same callousness toward their own people, but the very top ranks of the Syndic CEOs seem to be isolated from that. They'll do anything to win, or rather anything to avoid losing and paying a personal price for their mistakes. But they won't succeed, and when we eventually make it clear to everyone else in this star system what their plans are, it may well change the situation."

"That's your plan?" Armus asked. "To hope the Syndics finally make their own leaders act civilized?"

"No. That's what happens after we execute my plan." The anxiety in the room cleared in a flash, and Geary could see in almost all of the other officers here the same faith in him as Desjani's. "The Syndics missed something. The sort of energy discharge that gate would produce would be too huge for ships to hope to ride out. But, there's one thing in this star system that's big enough to not be destroyed by the energy wave and big enough for this fleet to hide behind." He pointed at the representation of the star on the display. "There's one place in this star system that should offer safety to the fleet if we can reach there." The view on the display pivoted around the star. "Here, in the lee of the star itself."

Silence fell as everyone studied the display. Duellos was the first to speak. "It should work, but it doesn't guarantee safety. The shock wave will consist of particles colliding with each other, being knocked to the sides, so it will spread back some into the area blocked by the star."

"It offers a solid chance," Badaya corrected, "if we get in the lee close enough to the star itself."

"I didn't say otherwise. We also have little choice, it appears."

Captain Armus was shaking his head. "The Syndics are scum, but they're not stupid. They'll see us heading there."

Armus wasn't the brightest officer in the fleet, but he was shrewd enough to spot that. Geary nodded. "That's why we have to conceal our intentions until we've got the star between us and that gate.

Fortunately, the Syndics' own behaviors give us a plausible cover for our movements." He tapped in a command, and projected paths for the fleet arced across the display. "The Syndic flotilla is pretending to be heading for an encounter with us. Given what we've figured out of their plans, we expect them to veer off in about six more hours and head straight for the jump point for Mandalon. They'll expect us to do one of two things, either chase after the Syndic flotilla for at least a while, or try to force it to face us in battle by threatening other Syndic assets in the star system."

Bright arcs appeared on the display. "We'll head onto these vectors, swinging past the frozen, inhabited planet fifteen light-minutes out from the star and flattening every military and industrial target on it at close range, then head for the primary inhabited world, not on a straight trajectory but by swinging around the star to intercept the planet in its orbit."

Duellos grinned. "A more lengthy approach, which will appear to be a transparent attempt to draw the Syndic warships into battle. Will they believe that Black Jack is being so obvious?"

"They're pleased with themselves right now," Desjani replied. "They think they've got us trapped and that we don't even realize it. Overconfidence is exactly what they'd expect from us, and because the Syndic leaders are positioned on the battleship at the jump point of Mandalon, they will still be close to five light-hours from our fleet when we turn to take shelter in the lee of the star and seven light-hours from that gate itself."

Badaya nodded. "Five hours to see us veer onto a new track, then, even if they immediately figure out what we're doing, seven hours for their destruct order to reach the gate, and five more hours for the shock wave to reach us. Seventeen hours, and we'll only be about ten light-minutes from the star when we begin our maneuver. They won't be able to hit us in time."

"If they wait," Armus grumbled. "Why should they wait that long?"

Rione answered. "Because it is certain that the Syndics want no living witnesses to what happens here. They want that flotilla to be in position to jump before any signal they send to the gate can be received and the initial results seen. Then the Syndic leaders can jump their entire flotilla out, everyone except themselves in ignorance of what has been done. Anyone arriving back in the star system after the shock wave has passed will find nothing and no one able to tell them what happened."

Badaya narrowed his eyes at her, then nodded again. "They can say we caused it somehow, just like they're trying to claim about Kalixa."

Commander Landis also agreed with a nod, but he still looked troubled. "What if they do figure out what we're doing before then, though? What if they decide to sacrifice their own flotilla and blow the gate before we get in the lee of the star?"

Geary had already forced himself to face that possibility. He tapped another control and a formation appeared. "We'll form up like this if there is time available once we spot the gate collapsing. The battleships will be as close together as possible, forming as strong a wall as they can, bow on to the gate. The rest of the fleet will array in successive walls behind the battleships. That offers the best chance we have that some of the fleet's ships will survive."

Everyone nodded somberly, including the captains of the

battleships. The armor and shields on the massive battleships served offensively, but were often called upon as a last line of defense when the rest of the fleet needed that. As Captain Mosko had said at Lakota, shielding the rest of the fleet was something that battleships did. They had left Mosko at Lakota, along with the three battleships in his division, holding off the enemy. Facing death was something everyone in the fleet was accustomed to, and dying for their comrades in battle was as good a way to die as any.

Not that anyone expected that to matter this time. They had seen what a hypernet gate collapse could do to a star system. The battleships and everything behind them would surely be blown to fragments if something stronger than Kalixa hit them here. But it was still necessary to do something.

Captain Armus shrugged. "All right, then. If our ancestors smile upon us, we'll beat this Syndic trick, too."

Captain Tulev nodded. "And if they do not, they will know we died facing the enemy."

Jane Geary spoke up. "Admiral, what will we do once we reach the lee of the star?"

"That's going to depend on what else is happening," Geary replied. "We won't just sit there. We'll drop sensor buoys behind the fleet so we can watch the gate even after every ship is behind the star. Assuming the Syndic leaders haven't blown the gate and jumped out of the system by then, we'll take a number of measures to make their lives miserable. From the lee of the star, we can still wipe out the Syndics here if we have to do that. Are there further questions?"

"Admiral," Captain Kattnig said quickly, "may I suggest an action that would discomfort the Syndics? They need this fleet destroyed, but if the entire fleet takes shelter behind the star, our ability to directly pressure the Syndic leaders will be lost. If, however, we send a group of fast ships out directly at the jump point for Mandalon, the Syndic leaders will either have to destroy their entire star system knowing that they will not get most of our fleet in the bargain, or they will have to flee the jump point, or fight."

A lot of officers nodded approvingly to Kattnig. Geary thought about the proposal, realizing that it might well make sense despite his reluctance to send ships out on what could be a suicide mission.

"It would have to be battle cruisers," Desjani said.

"Yes," Kattnig agreed. "I volunteer the Fifth Battle Cruiser Division." Some of the other commanding officers in that division appeared startled, but none of them objected. In this fleet, with its concepts of honor, none of them could object.

But Duellos spoke up, his tone carefully neutral. "The offer is in the finest traditions of the fleet, but I have been reviewing the capabilities of the *Adroit*-class battle cruisers. Because of sensor limitations in the design of your ships, you would require other capital ships to accompany you."

"Certainly," Kattnig agreed. "The First Battle Cruiser Division?" he asked, naming Duellos's own unit. "We would be proud to have them with us."

Geary looked down to think and noticed Desjani glaring at the table's surface. She wanted to volunteer *Dauntless*. He knew that. But she knew that if the enemy realized the fleet flagship with

Admiral Geary aboard was part of the small force, it might well make that a sufficiently worthwhile target.

He hesitated to send Duellos as well. But Kattnig's eagerness to be at the enemy, while not exceptional in the fleet, still concerned Geary. If Kattnig needed to be held back, Duellos was senior enough and wise enough to do the job. Tulev could do it as well. But right now Duellos was on the spot, and he was clearly waiting for Geary to weigh in before replying to Kattnig.

Turn down Duellos and order Tulev's division to go instead? Or just tell everyone that I want to think about the composition of the force and put off deciding which ships go? No, my hand is being forced by the way this happened. Unless I say now that I want the First Division to go, it will sound like I don't want the First Division to go, and while fleet regulations might declare that I don't have any obligation to explain that decision, in practice I would have to justify it somehow. How do I justify that without the crews and officers in the First Division feeling that they had been slighted?

I'm stuck. Duellos isn't a bad choice, but I don't know whether he would have been my choice. Now I have to go with him or create the impression that I don't trust him or his ships.

So Geary nodded to Duellos. "Does the First Battle Cruiser Division wish to be part of the force?"

Duellos read the nod correctly. "Certainly, Admiral. My ships are ready."

That was it, then. Kattnig looked very pleased. Duellos projected calm and confidence. Tulev's feelings couldn't be read. Badaya seemed happy. Desjani was apparently trying not to beat her fists bloody against the table in frustration.

Geary managed to keep his own voice even despite being annoyed at having his hand forced. "I need to determine the mission and full composition for the strike force. The battle cruisers will be accompanied by enough fast escorts to ensure they can handle any threat the Syndics might develop. I will let you know of further plans after we reach the lee of the star."

The images of most of the other fleet officers vanished. Duellos lingered long enough to give Geary a resigned look. "We both walked into that one."

"Yeah, we did. I'll talk to you about it later, one-on-one."

As Duellos's image disappeared, Badaya, who had also remained, nodded again to Rione, then to Geary. "It's useful having someone along who understands how the Syndic leaders think."

"Yes," Geary said, and nothing else, knowing that as far as Badaya was concerned, Rione understood the Syndic leaders because she thought the same way.

"Are the others giving you any trouble?"

Behind Badaya, Rione raised her eyes upward with a weary expression.

Choosing his words carefully, Geary also kept his tone even. "The senators are not causing any problems."

"Good. As long as they remain aware of who's in charge." Badaya smiled, saluted, and vanished.

Rione gave Geary a questioning look. "What are you going to do if he ever finds out that you're not really giving orders to the government?"

"Damned if I know."

With Badaya gone, Desjani stood up. "I'm sorry," Geary told her. "I know you wanted to volunteer *Dauntless* for that strike force."

Desjani shrugged. "Being the flagship usually has advantages. I'd be foolish not to realize that in this case, sending *Dauntless* along with that strike force would be offering the Syndics far too attractive a target."

She wasn't doing too good a job of acting resigned to the situation. "I'm afraid so."

"You need to watch Kattnig," Desjani added.

Geary eyed her. "What about him worries you?"

"The same thing that worries you. I could see it in you. He's too eager. He's not an overaggressive idiot like Captain Midea, but he's too eager."

"Yes." Geary shook his head. "Duellos should keep him in check."

"Tulev would have been better, but you couldn't publicly shoot down Duellos. Appearances matter. And speaking of appearances, Admiral, if we see the gate collapsing, and the fleet is ordered into that defensive formation, where will *Dauntless* be?"

He looked away for a moment. "Tanya, if it comes to that—"

"If it comes to that, the odds of survival for any ship in this fleet are so small as to be effectively zero. I respectfully request that if *Dauntless* and her crew are to die, we die with honor, in the place the flagship should occupy within the fleet." Her voice was calm, firm, and steady.

There didn't seem to be any good arguments against that. "Where do you consider that place to be? In the front rank, with the battleships?"

"No, sir. That would create a weak spot within the wall of battleships. But *Dauntless* should be directly behind those battleships."

Geary closed his eyes, not wanting to look at her as he pronounced what could be Desjani's death sentence. His own, too, but in a sense he had been living on borrowed time ever since being awakened from survival sleep. "Very well, Captain. *Dauntless* will be in her rightful place should the fleet face that situation."

"Thank you, sir."

He opened his eyes to see her saluting him, her own eyes on his, Desjani's expression grateful. "I owe *Dauntless*, and you, at least that much," Geary added as he returned the salute. "But I hope it won't come to that. If it does..."

"*Nil Desperandum*," she reminded him with a half smile, then Desjani left with a quick but relaxed stride.

Rione watched Desjani leave, then shook her head. "Do any of us deserve to have people like that fighting for us?" she asked.

"I thought you didn't like her."

"I don't. She can be almost as big a bitch as I am. But I thank the living stars that she's commanding this ship and not someone like Badaya."

Geary sat down again, his eyes on Rione. The virtual images of Senators Costa and Sakai had vanished earlier, neither of them realizing in time that Rione might hang around to speak privately with Geary. "Badaya is a competent enough officer. If we can rebuild his faith in the Alliance government, he'll be a credit to the fleet."

Rione smiled, but in a sad way. "I think that as long as nothing disastrous happens, Captain Badaya will convince himself that you are really still in charge but pulling the strings in secrecy. He won't be the only one believing that."

He didn't want to go there, didn't want to deal with the aftermath of the war when he hadn't yet managed to end it. "Madam Co-President, have you thought of anything we can say or do that will convince the Syndics that we are ignorant of any peril from that hypernet gate? We need to keep them fooled until we're close enough to being in the lee of the star."

Rione twisted her mouth as she thought. "I think we need to continue on as we have, expressing confidence by our actions and our words. You should resend the demand for negotiations, using a bit more arrogance this time and displaying an appropriate level of contempt for that CEO in charge of the flotilla. Perhaps a few taunts about how much smaller it is than the last Syndic force we faced here would be proper."

"Perhaps one of our governmental representatives could give our demands and taunts a suitable amount of arrogance and contempt," Geary suggested.

"Meaning me? I am better at the arrogant thing than you are." Rione leaned back. "But Costa is even better. I'll tell her you thought she should issue the next demand. It'll make Costa think you've been impressed by her."

"Will she give away our concerns about a trap?"

"Costa? She protects secrets tighter than celibates protect their virginity. That's the last thing you have to worry about with her." Rione smiled. "I'll be up front with her about this being aimed at keeping the Syndics fooled. She'll love that, as well as a chance to mock a Syndic CEO to his face. How long do we have to keep the Syndics fooled, anyway?"

Geary waved toward the star-system display. "As you saw, we can't just charge straight for a lee position without giving away our intent, so we're going roundabout. A bit more than two more days, then we head directly for the lee of the star."

"The Syndics will give us that much time?"

"If their own flotilla continues on its own roundabout transit, it will take three more days to reach the jump point for Mandalon."

"We should have the time, then. Would you like to hear what Sakai said about you?"

He pondered that question for a moment, then nodded.

"Senator Sakai said, 'He listened to us.'"

Geary waited, but nothing more was forthcoming. "That's all?"

"*That* is a great deal, Admiral Geary." Rione studied him again, shaking her head. "I don't know when it happened. Maybe it's always there and just got a lot worse. But at some point the senior officers and the senior politicians in the Alliance stopped listening to each other. We all pretend we're listening, but all we hear and see is what we expect."

"Like Badaya."

"Or Costa." Rione stood, heading for the hatch, then paused and looked back at him. "Maybe there was another reason that I came along with the fleet when Admiral Bloch was in command, a reason that I didn't know of. Healing the Alliance will take officers who trust politicians, and politicians who trust officers."

He made a crooked smile. "Don't you get all mystical on me."

"I wouldn't dream of it, Admiral. If the living stars were depending on the likes of me to carry out their missions, they'd really be scraping the bottom of the barrel."

hoping that we'll get as angry as they would and head for them, trying to force a proper battle."

He had never thought in terms of proper and improper ways to fight, just of smart ways and dumb ways. In peacetime training there had been some dumb things demanded by doctrine or whoever the current senior commander happened to be, but those had always come with an implied or open message that in actual combat things would be done differently. Maybe in peacetime it was easier to figure out what was smart, or maybe it just seemed easier because real battles and real lives weren't on the line. "I've still got a lot to learn, I guess." Desjani managed to look skeptical in a mostly respectful way as Geary continued. "In any case, it shouldn't make much difference now whether we chase after them or not. We're too far from any jump point to reach any of them before that flotilla would be able to jump for Mandalon."

This time Desjani rubbed her neck, then ran some more maneuvers through the system. "The Syndic flotilla is just shy of two light-hours away from us. In theory, it's just possible that we could head for the Tremandir jump point like bats out of hell starting about now and, factoring in all of the time delays for the Syndic leaders at the Mandalon jump point to see us start that way and send orders to the Syndic flotilla to accelerate at maximum for the Mandalon jump point, to get there as fast as possible, and the time required for the flotilla to reach the jump point, and the time needed for the Syndic leaders' signal to reach the hypernet gate after that, and then for the shock wave to get to us, for this fleet to be able to jump for Tremandir in time. I wouldn't want to bet my life on it, but the Syndic leaders may be trying to make absolutely, positively certain that they can get their flotilla out while leaving us no way we could escape when they collapse that hypernet gate."

He traced some paths through the star system and saw what Desjani meant. "If we did chase that flotilla, we'd be heading back toward the Syndic leaders, reducing the time lag in which they can see what we're doing, and we'll be angling closer to the hypernet gate as well, slightly reducing the time before the shock wave hits. Less uncertainty for them, even if every minute wasn't bringing their own flotilla closer to safety." Another thought came to him then. "They're politicians, mostly, but they're making a military decision on when to collapse the gate."

That brought a grin from Desjani. "They'll probably screw it up, then." Her smile faded. "Which could be bad for us if they screw it up in the wrong direction."

"Yeah." Costa was sitting in the observer's seat at the moment but seemed to have dozed off. Instead of disturbing the senator, Geary tapped a comm control. "Madam Co-President, I'd appreciate a politician's perspective on an issue."

Rione listened, then shrugged. "It could go either way, Admiral. A politician deciding when to spring this trap might hesitate too long in the hope of the situation growing more and more perfect for ensuring success. I would tend to favor that option as being most likely because they must feel very safe in their battleship, able to jump to another star system whenever they want to. But it's still possible that they might panic and launch the attack too early. It might depend in great part on whatever their military advisers are telling them."

"What's that likely to be?"

"Whatever they believe their superiors want to hear, and whatever they think will make their superiors do what they want them to do." Rione's image made a gesture in the general direction of the brig. "Look at how the Syndic CEO we're hauling with us has tried to handle you. He tells you what he thinks will dispose you to act in certain ways and tries to avoid telling you anything else. I guarantee you that our guest CEO is acting out of habit as well as calculation."

Geary rubbed his chin as he thought about that. "We have no way of knowing what the commander of the Syndic battleship carrying the Syndic leaders wants them to do. Any guesses as to what the CEO in charge of the flotilla might be telling them?"

It was Rione's turn to think, twisting her mouth and frowning. "My guess, for whatever it is worth, is that he is playing it as straight as he can in an attempt to prove his continued loyalty and make up for allowing this fleet to escape the last time he encountered it."

"Do you think he knows about the plan to collapse the gate?"

She made a derisive sound. "Would you give that information to him? If nothing else, that knowledge would be something he could try to trade to us or to some other Syndic CEOs in order to sell out his current leaders. Even if he did either of those things, we couldn't trust him."

"Because he murdered Admiral Bloch and the other Alliance negotiators."

Rione shook her head, annoyed. "Because he desperately wants to defeat you. Black Jack Geary, the man who snatched away his perfect victory. If not for you, he might be one of the Syndic leaders right now."

That brought up a new idea. "Maybe I should taunt him, personally. If we can get that Syndic flotilla to turn around and come for us, it will mess up the plans of the Syndic leaders."

"That wouldn't—" Rione paused, her expression thoughtful. "It might work. From the perspective of that CEO, defeating you might seem like the perfect solution. He doesn't know that he'll be messing up his superiors' plan, and he'll be thinking that if he defeats this fleet, he'll be the hero he planned on being several months ago. Yes. Stick a knife into his ego and twist it."

"I'll try." Geary leaned back, thinking. Taunting the Syndic CEO might fit in well with the plan to break off the battle-cruiser strike force. "Captain Desjani, aside from the fact that this fleet escaped him once before, what sort of things would torque off that Syndic CEO the most?"

Desjani gleefully offered some suggestions.

Geary activated a transmission aimed at the Syndic flotilla, knowing that every ship in the Syndic force would be capable of picking up his message. That would make it sting the CEO's ego even worse. "To Shalin, the current commanding officer of the Syndicate Worlds' flotilla in this star system. I regret that you are unwilling to face this fleet in combat, perhaps due to your failure to defeat it some months ago in this same star system. Your reluctance to fight is understandable, but the Alliance fleet is willing to give you another opportunity to engage in battle if you will cease avoiding action. The people of this star system must be wondering why a CEO with so many decorations for valor is abandoning them to their fate, but for my part I understand your unwillingness to face me again. It's refreshing to meet a Syndic leader who cares more for the welfare of his personnel than he does for his own honor and prerogatives. If you would simply agree to surrender, I could guarantee the safety of your personnel, while you personally came to my flagship to discuss the conditions for your submission to my terms.

"Think it over, Shalin. A commander with *your* reputation shouldn't have any trouble deciding what to do.

"To the honor of our ancestors. This is Fleet Admiral Geary out."

Desjani laughed. "It might make him want to kill you, but he wants to do that already. Too bad we have to wait four hours for him to get that and see any response, but we can kill time blowing the hell out of the third planet."

"What are you going to do for fun if you can't devastate planets anymore?"

"I'll have to find another hobby, I guess."

Worlds habitable by humans that had only one climate were very rare, but the planet fifteen light-minutes out from the star was literally an ice world. Large enough to retain its atmosphere and with plentiful water, it had boasted vast oceans and seas during the relatively brief period when the planet was no longer molten but hadn't cooled too much. But as the planet grew cooler, and its too-distant star provided too little warmth, the oceans, seas, rivers, and lakes began freezing, and they had been frozen ever since.

Amid the fields of snow and ice were cities and estates serving a population probably numbering less than half a million, but while numerous sport and recreational sites could be seen, very little in the way of industrial locations was apparent. "I guess if you like winter sports, that would be a great place to live," Geary commented.

Desjani tapped part of the planet's image. "Look how they've smoothed large sections of the ice. They've got huge ice plains for racing. Imagine sailing an iceboat across a perfectly smooth field of ice a thousand kilometers long. See right there? An ice yacht. A really big one." She snorted disdainfully. "It's a resort planet. The damned Syndic leaders have actually maintained a resort planet next door to their primary world here."

He tried to imagine how much money it would cost to sustain a planet dedicated to vacationing Very Important People. "We should be grateful that they spent the money on perks for themselves and not on the Syndic war effort. What kind of targets do we have?"

"Spaceports, communications hubs, a few security installations." Desjani's derision shaded into disgust. "I guess any industry other than luxury tourism would have spoiled the views."

"We haven't seen any labor camps," Rione commented, "but it would suit the arrogance of the Syndic leaders to have Alliance POWs working at the difficult and unpleasant tasks of keeping that planet neat and pretty. We can't assume that the Syndic CEO was just playing mind games when he claimed our captured personnel were located at important sites. I would suggest choosing targets with care. Forced laborers could be kept in single buildings, or even portions of buildings."

"Good point." There was no telling how many crew members from the Alliance warships once destroyed here might have been kept around as living war trophies. "How badly did Senator Costa threaten that slime on that issue?"

"I am not myself easily intimidated, but her words and their delivery would have made me reconsider my own actions," Rione responded dryly.

"Thanks." Suppressing renewed thoughts about the possible fate of his grandnephew Michael Geary, Geary ordered the combat systems to screen out targets that might be barracks or living areas for workers or were too close to such places. Despite Desjani's unhappiness, that still left a small but decent batch of targets. Geary paused, then added a few spots scattered through the wide, smooth sailing areas. "Let's also mess up their recreation a little."

"There's actually some liquid water in the deeper parts of the oceans, under kilometers of ice," Desjani said. "Why don't we punch down that deep somewhere? Just for fun?"

A hole that deep in their sailing area would seriously annoy the Syndic leaders and be a very long-lived monument to the capability of the Alliance to strike here. "Sure. Why not?" The hours spent discreetly heading for the lee of the star had been tense, wondering if the Syndic politicians might decide to trigger the hypernet gate before their own flotilla was clear just to ensure that the Alliance fleet was destroyed as well. Slamming a hole a few kilometers deep in a frozen ocean might help relieve a little of that tension. The combat systems worked up a solution for that quickly enough, using a series of kinetic rounds dropped onto the exact same spot one after the other. "Give me a double check on this firing plan, please. I want to be sure we don't hit any spot likely to have POW forced laborers present."

Desjani checked it over, then had one of her watch-standers do a check as well. "It looks as good as we can get, sir. We're not that far from the planet, but they'll still see the kinetic rounds inbound in time to evacuate targets."

He approved the bombardment, and once again a wave of kinetic rounds burst from the ships of the Alliance fleet. Geary pulled out the scale on his display for a moment, seeing where some of the projectiles from the first bombardment launched over two days ago were still heading for their targets in more distant parts of the star system. "All right, so much for the Syndic winter wonderland. Let's pretend we're heading to deal the same treatment to the main inhabited world."

Desjani's mood seemed to have been improved by firing the latest bombardment. "They're trying to get us to chase them, and we're trying to get them to chase us, but we're both actually doing something else."

"I asked... someone else about that, and her opinion was that CEO Shalin doesn't know the plans of the Syndic leaders."

His weak attempt to avoid mentioning Rione by name failed to deceive Desjani. She made another face. "It takes a politician to understand a politician," she muttered.

Costa had come onto the bridge, her expression impassive, and had caught Geary's statement but apparently not Desjani's. "I agree with your informant, Admiral. I doubt if CEO Shalin has been told. He's being punished," she stated bluntly. "I've spent some time reviewing his transmission to us, getting past my own anger at his words and attitude to evaluate what he's trying to hide about himself. Take a close look at the way he comes across. Despite the awards and the surface arrogance, it's clear that he hasn't been living a comfortable life lately, mentally or physically. He let you get away the last time the fleet was here. He *knows* he's expendable."

Rione raised an eyebrow at Costa. "Do you think we can cut a deal with him?"

Desjani spun in her seat, her expression controlled but her tension easy enough for Geary to read. He felt the same way. Reach an agreement with *that* CEO? It wasn't just the Alliance fleet's losses in that long-ago ambush, but rather the murder of the officers who had gone to negotiate with him. But Rione had already told him that she couldn't see any basis for trusting Shalin, so why had she raised the possibility with Costa?

"A deal?" Costa grimaced. "I doubt it. Even if we could trust him. If I read him right, he's the sort who when in disfavor will go to any lengths to regain favor. He'd double-cross us in a heartbeat."

"I agree with your assessment," Rione said.

Geary saw the other senator's flash of pleasure at that, then realized that Rione had only asked the question so that she could publicly state agreement with Costa and thereby earn some measure of gratitude from Costa. *I'll never be a politician. I just can't play those games.* But the conversation brought up another question. "Why does he have new awards if he's being punished? Why did the Syndics give him more medals if they're mad at him for us getting away?"

"Consistency." Costa waved in the general direction of Alliance space. "While the fleet was still missing, the Syndics were broadcasting propaganda that it had been completely destroyed here. If they hadn't presented awards to the CEO in charge of their forces in that battle, it would have looked odd and called into question the claimed victory. Believe me, we were grasping at straws and would have keyed on that."

"If that's the reason he got those medals, it's hard to believe that he's actually wearing them." Geary turned back to Desjani, who had relaxed as it became apparent that no one was going to suggest dealing with the flotilla's CEO. "Two more hours. Then it will be too late for the Syndics to blow the gate in time to hit us."

"It should be an interesting experience in time dilation," Desjani replied. Her eyes went to her display again, and he knew what she was looking at, the same thing that kept drawing his gaze on his own display. The Syndic hypernet gate hung like a huge eye, watching them, playing with them, ready to unleash awesome forces like some cyclopean god out of a primitive myth. "Those hours will probably seem to take days to go by," Desjani continued. "When are you cutting loose the strike force?"

"When we make our move for the lee of the star." He had been putting off giving Duellos detailed orders, but that had to be done.

She nodded, and he realized that Desjani had once again subtly prodded him to get going on something he was avoiding. "The rest of the fleet can bombard more targets in fixed orbit once we're behind the star," Desjani observed, "but if the Syndic leaders decide to run, the strike force won't have a chance of catching them. Even a battleship can keep out of reach of battle cruisers if it has that big a lead on them."

"I know. That's one of the primary issues I'm trying to resolve in my orders to Duellos. I wish we had another way to get at the Syndic leadership. I'd hoped to trap them on the second planet, but with them sitting on that battleship at the jump point, I have no personal danger leverage against them at all." Rione had spoken before about how those most senior Syndic leaders were focused on their own self-interests, so as long as he couldn't threaten them directly, his ability to force a decision was limited. His eyes went to the portion of his display showing the Syndic battleship, which held the members of the Syndic Executive Council. Much too distant to possibly catch unless those ships cooperated. If only there were some levers that would influence the ships they were on...

"Admiral, I—" Desjani began.

"Wait." Geary tried to block out all distractions, seeking the idea that hovered just out reach. The battleship and the heavy cruisers. Something about them. And something about the Syndics, and the captured Syndic CEO aboard *Dauntless*, something Boyens had said... "Senator Costa, there are defensive forces assigned to Unity Star System, aren't there?"

Costa nodded, frowning. "Of course."

"Do you rotate them? Do new units come in periodically, while older ones go out to other assignments?"

A deeper frown. "No. We prefer to have units on hand whose—" Costa looked around, realizing that she had been about to remark openly on fears about the loyalty of some Alliance warships to their own government. "Units which are a known factor," she said instead.

Geary fumbled at his controls, trying to bring up an old situation display. "Captain Desjani, I need the picture from when I assumed command of the fleet. Not the Alliance ships. The Syndics in this star system back then."

Desjani gestured to a watch-stander, and a moment later the historical display popped up to one side of Geary. He swung the image away from the massive Syndic warship formation that had been here then, facing the Alliance fleet, ready to destroy it, and which had always occupied his attention before now. Instead, Geary zoomed in on a small part of the display distant from where the Alliance fleet had been. "Look. Orbiting the primary inhabited world."

"A battleship and three heavy cruisers," Desjani murmured. "That's an interesting coincidence."

"Isn't it? Can we tell if that battleship and those three cruisers are the same warships now stationed near the jump point for Mandalon?"

"We can try. The hulls of supposedly identical ships tend to have small variations. Lieutenant Yuon, have the sensors do their finest-grain analysis on those Syndic warships at the jump point for Mandalon and see if they can match them to the ones orbiting the planet in this record." Desjani was clearly curious but held her questions as the fleet sensors mulled the question for several seconds.

"Captain," Lieutenant Yuon reported, "sensors evaluate the probability of hull matches on the three heavy cruisers of ninety-five percent, eighty-two percent, and ninety-eight percent. Hull match probability on the battleship is ninety-nine point seven percent. There's a very high probability that those are all the same warships that were orbiting the primary inhabited world the last time we were in this star system."

"A palace guard," Geary said. "That battleship and those cruisers might well have been in this star system for years, then."

Senator Costa's frown was still present. "That would match our own policies for the defense of our highest level of government,

Admiral. Why is this important?"

"Because the Syndic CEO we're holding as a prisoner aboard *Dauntless* told me that the Syndics don't like any of their warships developing personal ties to particular star systems."

"Of course not! Not when they might be ordered to enforce order in any Syndic star system by bombarding it! But why—"

"They've been here for years," Desjani interrupted. "Girlfriends, boyfriends, families, personal ties of all kinds."

"Exactly," Geary agreed. "Those crews were kept here because the Syndic leadership wanted ships on hand whose loyalty couldn't be questioned. But by keeping them here so long, the Syndics broke their own policies. Those crews *must* care about the people in this star system. These planets aren't targets to them, they're the homes of individuals the Syndics on those warships are concerned about."

Desjani smiled wickedly. "Somebody ought to tell them what the Syndic leaders are planning to do to this star system and everyone in it."

"Yeah, somebody ought to do that. When this fleet is safe from the hypernet gate, I believe I'll make a broadcast to every Syndic in this star system and let all of them know what their leaders planned to do before those leaders ran for safety."

Rione leaned forward. "Do you think that battleship and those heavy cruisers might mutiny?"

"I think there's a chance they may help us bring about a change of government in the Syndicate Worlds, yes, Madam Co-President. It's going to depend on what the other Syndic CEOs in this star system do. They'll learn that they are expendable, too."

"The CEO in charge of the flotilla will not support a coup,"

Costa insisted. "He knows that he will be thrown to us as a sacrifice by whoever takes over."

That sounded very plausible. "Then he was given the job of commanding that flotilla because the Syndic leaders can be sure he will support them even though those same leaders regard him as an expendable failure."

"Damned if he does and damned if he doesn't," Desjani commented with another smile. "It couldn't happen to a nicer guy." Her eyes narrowed, and her expression grew calculating as she looked at her display. "But if the battleship and heavy cruisers mutiny, or declare allegiance to Syndic CEOs setting up an alternative government, that means Shalin will likely go after them. He'll have to. The current Syndic leaders are his only hope."

Rione nodded. "Yes. We need to be prepared to go to the protection of that battleship and those cruisers."

Desjani's expression changed to disbelief, then revulsion. "*Protect* Syndic warships?"

Geary blew out an exasperated breath. The orders he would have to give Duellos were getting more complicated by the minute.

Hard as it had been to leave the bridge, Geary had gone down to his stateroom to brief Duellos, not wanting to risk anyone else hearing his conversation or spotting expressions through the privacy fields around his command seat.

Duellos sat back, apparently relaxed, but his eyes were alert and tense. "A three-way fight? That would be... interesting."

"A mess," Geary agreed. "Would your battle cruisers protect Syndic warships?"

"Not if I phrased it that way. However, protecting the Syndic battleship would require attacking the Syndic flotilla. That I can order my battle cruisers to do and not worry about their following orders." Duellos sighed. "Part of me just wants to destroy every Syndic warship in the star system and let the Syndics sort out whatever remains afterward."

"We need someone to negotiate with." Geary hesitated, not wanting to say the next thing, but knowing he had to. "If it comes down to a choice between destroying that Syndic battleship or letting it be retaken by the Syndic flotilla, we need to ensure that those Syndic leaders don't get away." No, that wasn't good enough. He had to state his orders clearly, not leave any ambiguities that might protect his own butt and leave Duellos uncertain what was expected of him. "That means destroy the battleship."

Duellos nodded calmly. "Who decides if we've reached the point where the battleship must be destroyed?"

"You'll probably be light-hours distant from me. It'll be your call, based on what's happening. Whatever you decide, I will back you."

"The last time an admiral told me that, I had my doubts as to his sincerity," Duellos observed. "But he wasn't you. I'll try to ensure that your trust in me isn't misplaced."

"Same here." Geary glanced at the depiction of the strike force floating over the table between him and Duellos's image. "I've given you three squadrons of light cruisers and five squadrons of destroyers to back up your nine battle cruisers. I don't want to send so many that your strike force seems too attractive a target, but do you think that's enough?"

"It'll depend on what happens, but it will certainly be enough to at least deal with anything even if we can't outright defeat whatever we run into." Duellos paused. "Depending on what Captain Kattnig does."

"Try to keep him on a tight leash. He's way too eager to fight."

"There's no such thing in this fleet, Admiral." Duellos shrugged. "I'll do my best. The *Adroit*-class ships won't do well if they're thrown into a frontal assault."

"The last scout battleship was destroyed in action, but now I've got the *Adroit* and her sister ships to worry about. When is the government going to figure out that saving money by building ships that aren't big enough and carry too little capability isn't really smart when it comes to survival and effectiveness?"

"If you become dictator, that's one of the things you'll have to put a stop to." Duellos grinned to show he wasn't serious. "Kattnig has fought well in the past. I don't think he'll do anything stupid."

"He shouldn't. Did you get a chance to review his last action?"

Another nod from Duellos. "At Beowulf? Nasty business, but Kattnig distinguished himself."

"Nasty" was a mild word for a battle in which the two sides had been pretty evenly matched and had slugged it out until the Alliance slowly gained an advantage that eventually produced the sort of victory that was as painful as many defeats in terms of lost ships and personnel. "His ship got beat into scrap metal but kept fighting," Geary agreed. Afterward, Kattnig had been focused on the welfare of his surviving crew to such an extent that medical sedation had been ordered. Again, nothing to be ashamed of after such a fight, the fleet medical staff had cleared Kattnig for further service, and in Geary's eyes, being concerned about casualties wasn't exactly a black mark.

There was an inconsistency between that record and Kattnig's apparent eagerness for battle that bothered Geary. "Just keep an eye on him. I'm going to cut loose the strike force in less than two hours, when the rest of the fleet heads for the lee of the star. I don't know what's going to happen, but we're all going to have to react to whatever it is. Good luck."

"If the hypernet gate collapses while my ships are out there, I won't have much time to worry about deciding what to do," Duellos pointed out. "Otherwise, I'll try not to disappoint you."

"There's no chance of your disappointing me, Roberto."

Duellos grinned, stood up, and saluted, then his image disappeared, and Geary returned to the bridge of *Dauntless*.

The impacts of the bombardment hitting the ice world were a pleasant diversion from waiting for any sign of impending collapse by the hypernet gate. The multiple rocks striking in succession at a single point near the middle of one of the frozen oceans made for the most spectacular sight, the fountain of vaporized water rising higher and higher in the atmosphere as each impact drove deeper, the immense heat generated by each rock falling from space turning ice directly to steam, which vented upward through the kilometer-wide hole being drilled by the bombardment. After the steam dissipated in the dry air of the frigid planet, a multispectrum surveillance satellite the fleet had left near the planet managed to get a look down the hole, but the result disappointed Desjani. "There's liquid water at the bottom, but most of it probably came from the walls of the hole melting from the residual heat of the impacts. There's no way of telling if we actually hit water under the ice."

"Sorry about that." Geary commiserated. "That's still one hell of a hole."

"Can you imagine what it'll be like when the sides finish refreezing? High angle, smooth, almost frictionless drops kilometers high. But I bet you the Syndics don't thank us for creating such an excellent site for extreme sports competitions."

"No, probably not, especially with the ice ocean fractured for hundreds of kilometers around the site." It seemed silly to be joking about such things, but it beat staring obsessively at the hypernet gate.

One hour to go before the maneuver toward the star's lee. If the hypernet gate collapsed now or in the next half hour, it would be a cruel irony with safety so close. Despite an irrational worry that stepping off of *Dauntless*'s bridge would result in something bad happening almost instantly, Geary took a few moments to go to the small rooms near the center of the ship where individuals could worship. At times like that, asking for whatever help and mercy could be granted seemed like a good idea. It certainly didn't hurt. He tried to reach out to Michael Geary, but neither his brother nor his grandnephew seemed to respond. Finally, he reached to snuff out the ceremonial candle, but paused before doing so. "I got your message, Mike, from your granddaughter Jane. I miss you, too."

A few minutes later he was back on the bridge, watching the representation of the fleet on the maneuvering display crawl across the vast distances of the star system, the point at which they could dive for safety behind the star still agonizingly distant.

The last five minutes seemed to last an eternity. *Dauntless*'s bridge was totally silent, with everyone present seeming to muffle even their breathing. Only Desjani seemed unaffected, scrolling through routine paperwork, but when Geary used his fleet-commander viewing authority to take a look at the work Desjani was doing, he saw that she was flipping through pages too fast actually to read them.

The count hit zero, Geary took a very deep breath as he realized that he had not been breathing for at least thirty seconds, then he tapped his comm control as he whispered a quick prayer of thanks. "All units in the Alliance fleet, this is Admiral Geary. At time two five accelerate to point one five light speed, turn down zero four degrees and come port three six degrees. Units designated as part of Strike Force One are to shift to tactical control of Captain Duellos on *Inspire* at time three zero."

Then it was a matter of waiting as the signal crawled outward at the speed of light, taking seconds and even minutes to reach the farthest units in the fleet, then waiting some more as every ship acknowledged the order, their symbols flashing to indicate readiness, then waiting for time two five.

Desjani pointed at her maneuvering watch-stander, who punched the execute command for the velocity and course changes. *Dauntless* yawed slightly over and down, then her main propulsion units kicked in as every other ship in the fleet followed suit.

"In about four hours and twenty-three minutes," Desjani observed, "the Syndic leaders are going to start getting very unhappy."

"We're not in the clear, yet," Geary reminded her. "If the Syndics already blew the gate, we can still get caught by the blast."

"It's not that I have any great respect for their intelligence, but surely even they aren't stupid enough to blow away that flotilla when it doesn't look like they need to." She watched the ships of the strike force turning and accelerating away from the rest of the fleet. "How much longer until you inform this star system of what its noble leaders are planning?"

"Just a little while, yet. I want the Syndic Executive Council to see us heading on our new vector, start trying to figure out what it means, then have my message further confuse and pressure them."

Desjani glanced at the back of the bridge, where Sakai was sitting quietly, but with his eyes watching everything. "Speaking of confusing things and pressuring people, did the politicians try to mess with your statement?"

"Costa suggested I run the wording past them, Sakai was ambivalent, and Rione was strongly against it, saying that I needed to sound like myself, not like some politician."

"Damn. I'm agreeing with that woman again."

"It does take getting used to." Geary sat silently for a little while, trying to get in the right frame of mind, then checked the time. Good enough. His statement wouldn't arrive at the ships carrying the Syndic leaders until after they saw most of the Alliance fleet on its way to safety, and would reach most other occupants of the star system well before that. His taunting of CEO Shalin at the Syndic flotilla hadn't produced any apparent results as of yet. It would be interesting to see what this message did.

Two long, slow breaths to calm himself and prepare for speaking, then Geary triggered the circuit to broadcast to every Syndic receiver within the star system. "People of the Syndicate Worlds, this is Admiral John Geary. It is my sad duty to report that your leaders are planning not only to abandon you, but to annihilate every living thing in this star system in an attempt to destroy my fleet.

"You have a system installed on your hypernet gate that was designed to reduce any energy discharge created by the collapse of the gate. However, that same system can be used in reverse, to increase the level of the energy discharge and ensure that the resulting destruction would be close to that caused by your star going nova. Your own leaders intend taking this action, trading all of your lives for the chance to catch the Alliance fleet in the same destruction, and have only delayed in it because they first wish to have their flotilla of Syndicate Worlds' warships in this star system reach a jump point and jump to another star. Instead of using the flotilla to defend you, they want to save it so they can use it to enforce their rule in other star systems.

"Your own leaders don't fear being caught in the destruction because they are out of harm's way aboard the battleship lingering at the jump point for Mandalon, from which they will jump to safety, leaving you all to die. There would be no witnesses to what happened here, every human dead and every device destroyed, so your leaders could continue pursuing a war with no purpose.

"We have offered to negotiate an end to the war, and the terms the Alliance has offered your Executive Council have already been broadcast throughout this star system. At the conclusion of this message, I will have them repeated, and you will see that they are aimed at ending the war on terms with which both sides can live. But your leaders have refused to negotiate, and instead intend wiping out this star system rather than admit error or accept terms they themselves have not dictated.

"By the time you receive this message, most of the Alliance fleet will be safe from the planned assault, in a location where your own star will protect us. But none of you will be safe, not unless you act in your own interests and those of the Syndicate Worlds. You know me by reputation. You know what your current leaders have done in the past. You have to decide which of us to trust. Your lives and the future of the Syndicate Worlds depend on your decision.

"To the honor of our ancestors."

Desjani smiled reassuringly as Geary slumped backward after the end of his message. "Now all we have to do is hope the Syndics actually use their heads instead of just following orders."

Once again, hours had to pass before anything could happen. Geary couldn't roam the passageways of *Dauntless* without encountering members of her crew who might pick up on his edginess, but he also couldn't stand just sitting on the bridge, so he took breaks down in his stateroom, pacing back and forth like a caged animal. He was there when Lieutenant Iger called. "There's been some unusual activity in the Syndic comm net, Admiral. Another site is now trying to establish priority over the site at the Mandalon jump point."

"Where's this other site located?"

"Somewhere on the primary inhabited world, but they're using lots of relays, so it took us a little while even to get that." Lieutenant Iger flashed a quick smile. "The primary world received your transmission about two hours ago, sir."

Long enough for someone to get moving with a takeover, especially with the Syndic Executive Council about five light-hours distant from the planet and unable directly to monitor events there in real time. "There's been nothing overt that we've picked up?"

"No, sir. No transmissions about revolutions or new leaders or anything like that, and no signs of actual conflict or security forces being deployed. But our political analysis routines estimate that whoever is trying to supplant the Executive Council is probably still lining up support among the various military commanders in the star system and with other important players. They'll try to stay quiet until they have all of those backers in hand rather than tip off the Executive Council too early."

A trap being sprung on the Syndic leaders who had been waiting to spring a trap on the Alliance fleet. "Let me know the instant you get anything else."

But his next message was from Desjani. "The fleet is entering the lee of the star, Admiral," she announced triumphantly. "We're in the clear."

"Except for the strike force."

"Yes, sir, but Duellos can take care of himself. No reactions noted from the Syndic flotilla or the battleship at the jump point yet."

Everything seemed to be going well again. He wondered what he might have missed this time.

8

"The battleship is moving," Desjani reported, interrupting Geary's restless attempts to get some sleep in his stateroom. He wondered if she had left the bridge at all in the last twenty-four hours. "The heavy cruisers are accompanying it."

He tried to shake fatigue out of his brain. "What's their vector?"

"It looks like they're heading for the primary inhabited world."

What did that mean? Had the Syndic warships mutinied, and were they bringing the members of the Executive Council back to face whatever form of justice a new government would demand? Or were the members of the Syndic Executive Council still firmly in control of those warships and heading back to reassert their own authority?

Desjani had come up with another possibility, though. "Maybe they're trying to lure us out from behind the star," she suggested. "Get us moving to intercept them, then dart back to the jump point and escape while the hypernet gate collapses on us."

He rubbed his eyes, then glared at the display over the table in his stateroom. "We don't need to move. The strike force can handle that battleship."

"Not if the flotilla joins it."

As if in response to Desjani's words, alerts flashed on the display as the Syndic flotilla's vectors changed. Geary waited impatiently as the Syndics settled onto a new course and speed, the projected path of the flotilla swinging toward, then merging with the projected path of the battleship. "Did you have to say that?" he asked Desjani.

She smiled humorlessly. "It was easy to predict. Either the Syndic leaders are on their way to the primary world to kick butt and take names, in which case they want the flotilla with them, or the Syndic leaders are under arrest, in which case the flotilla will try to rescue them."

One other path merged with that of the flotilla and the battleship. "The strike force will get to the battleship just before the flotilla intercepts it."

"While we're stuck here."

"Sorry."

"You owe me one."

He smiled with an equal lack of humor. "Noted. I don't think we should move yet. We need to hold here for several more hours, to ensure that we aren't being lured out from this position."

"The fleet won't like it, sir, hiding behind the star while the Syndics move back toward us."

"I don't like it, either. But if the Syndic leaders are trying to lure us out, this time around they won't waste any time sending the collapse order to the hypernet gate once we're far enough from the star." Unfortunately, that logic, and the results if he guessed wrong, could drive him to stay in place indefinitely. "Tanya, if I seem to be hesitating too long on moving this fleet, call me on it."

"I always do, sir."

Another hour, while Geary waited with increasing anxiety and an increasingly bad mood. His comm status was set to rest so no messages would get through unless they came from Desjani, Rione, or Duellos. He didn't feel like getting advice from Badaya or anyone else at the moment.

Though there was CEO Boyens. Would he be able to help? *No. By his own admission, Boyens has been exiled on the far border for more than a decade. Even if we could trust him, and we can't, he still doesn't know the big players here.*

Finally, Geary went back to the bridge and sat glumly in the fleet commander's seat while the watch-standers, with well-honed survival instincts, all tried to avoid drawing his notice.

"Admiral." Lieutenant Iger had a happy expression, which disappeared very quickly as he caught the look in Geary's eyes. "Sir, there's a great deal of communication going on between the battleship and the primary world."

"What's that mean?" Geary demanded. Realizing from Iger's reaction how harsh his voice had been, Geary worked to get his tone back to normal. "Do we have any idea what they're talking about?"

"No, sir. But there is a very interesting clue in the transmissions. The messages from the primary world are being given priority in the Syndic net over the communications from the battleship."

"What about the flotilla? Who are they talking to?"

Lieutenant Iger shook his head. "We've seen some transmissions to the flotilla from the primary world but haven't been able to spot anything from the flotilla in reply. Our ships and collection satellites aren't in the right positions to tell if the flotilla and the battleship are talking directly to each other."

"Thank you." Geary rubbed his eyes, seriously considering asking the fleet medical personnel for the kind of painkiller only dispensed by doctors. "Captain Desjani, my guts are telling me that if nothing else has changed in half an hour, we should head out and aim to intercept that battleship. The battleship will still be about four light-hours distant then. What do you think?"

"I think," she commented, "that if we try to wait until we feel safe, we'll miss any opportunity to resolve this situation in our favor. The Syndic battleship won't see us move for four hours. We'll see the battleship's reaction in another four hours. But the primary inhabited world will see us moving much sooner than that. It's only about ten light-minutes from us now. When they see us heading for that battleship, anyone trying to supplant the Executive Council may well talk to us. They want us on their side, and as disgusting as the idea of allying with any Syndics is to me, we need someone to shut off the threat of that hypernet gate."

"Then why not go now?"

"That sounds like an excellent idea, Admiral. I concur."

Geary gave her a sour look and thought about double-checking with Tulev. It wouldn't hurt to have another perspective on this, especially someone as solid as Tulev. But as he reached for his controls, a thought came to him that paused his movement. "Captain Desjani, have you already discussed this with Captain Tulev?"

"Yes, sir."

"And would Captain Tulev's advice be the same as yours?"

"Yes, sir."

He could stay mad or see the humor in the situation. Staying mad hadn't helped so far, so he might as well try laughing about it. "Thank you, Captain Desjani." Geary took a look toward the back of the bridge, where Senator Sakai sat watching, his posture relaxed but eyes intent. "We're going to try to get the political games going on right now out into the open, Senator."

Sakai nodded. "You mean the Syndic political games, I assume, Admiral?"

"Right." It was nice to know Sakai had a sense of humor. Geary checked the maneuvering system, then called the fleet. "All units in the main formation of the Alliance fleet, this is Admiral Geary. Come starboard zero one three degrees, up zero two degrees, and accelerate to point one light speed at time four one."

Another circuit. "Captain Duellos, the main body of the Alliance fleet will proceed to an intercept with the Syndic battleship coming from the Mandalon jump point."

At time five one, Desjani ordered the course and speed changes for *Dauntless*, then yawned. "At least a day, maybe a day and a half until we meet up with that battleship. I think I'll get some rest."

"Good idea." Now that the decision had been made, the tension level on the bridge had dropped dramatically. It was absurd, considering that he had just ordered the Alliance fleet out of its safe harbor, but Geary felt the same release in stress inside him. "Maybe I can sleep now, too."

"Make it quick," Desjani suggested. "We may hear from

someone on the primary world in about half an hour."

"I can live with that."

As it turned out, something happened within ten minutes. Geary had barely reached his stateroom when an urgent notification arrived from *Dauntless*'s communications watch-stander. "Admiral, we have an incoming message from the Syndic battleship."

The image this time wasn't of a CEO, but of a Syndic military officer, his expression grim but otherwise unrevealing. "To the Alliance fleet, be advised that this warship and its accompanying heavy cruisers are responding to orders from the new Executive Council of the Syndicate Worlds. We are in the process of transporting the members of the old Executive Council back to Prime, the second planet from our star. Those members do not have access to any communications or transmission equipment. We—" The Syndic visibly had to brace himself to continue. "We *request* that you avoid interfering with our transit."

That had to have been a hard message to send, but it must have been transmitted before the rebellious Syndic battleship had seen the Syndic flotilla turn to intercept it. Would there be a follow-up message, with the even-harder-to-make request that the Alliance fleet aid the battleship against the Syndic flotilla?

He was still considering that, and how he could phrase such orders, when the communications watch-stander announced another incoming message, this time from the primary inhabited world.

Geary saw a cluster of Syndic CEOs who appeared to be standing in an open area between low buildings, grass beneath their feet and an appealingly blue sky above their heads. They were wearing the usual flawlessly crafted outfits, but for once the polished, practiced, and insincere smiles weren't present, the CEOs instead looking openly serious. "To Admiral Geary and the representatives of the Alliance grand council," one of the CEOs announced, "we are the members of the new Executive Council of the Syndicate Worlds. We have reviewed your proposals and are willing seriously to negotiate their adoption as a basis for ending hostilities. We have ordered all Syndicate Worlds' mobile and fixed forces within this star system to cease offensive action and ask that you suspend offensive action against any people or units of the Syndicate Worlds who have acknowledged our authority."

The CEO put more earnestness into his words. "The programming for subverting what you call the safe-fail system has been disabled. The hypernet gate cannot now be used to destroy this star system and your fleet. We understand you have cause to doubt declarations from the Syndicate Worlds' leaders. Our own location is on the surface of our world. We will remain here as living hostages to our word that your fleet is safe while we await your reply."

That sounded promising. Getting the fleet moving had indeed provoked a response.

An image of Rione appeared on his screen. "I've seen the message. We can't be certain that they're really on the surface of the planet. They could be in a simulation chamber buried deep under the surface. But an analysis I had run indicated that even a deeply buried location wouldn't stand a high chance of survival if a hypernet gate collapsed with an enhanced energy discharge. The Syndics may be treacherous, but their engineers are as good as ours. They'll know that."

"You're saying we can trust them."

"As much as we can trust any Syndic. There's no reason to believe these CEOs are any more ethical, or any less self-interested than the ones they have replaced. In this case, physical survival and self-interest coincided nicely for us. They needed to disable that catastrophic-collapse routine to save themselves." Rione took on a formal attitude. "Admiral Geary, I request permission for the Alliance grand council representatives accompanying this fleet to begin direct negotiations with the Syndicate Worlds' CEOs of the new Executive Council."

"Permission granted."

"If I read between the lines properly, the Syndic flotilla is not acknowledging the authority of the new Executive Council. I anticipate the new Executive Council will request that we defend their planet against their own flotilla. How do you want me to deal with such a request, Admiral?"

His tension headache threatened to come back. "The Alliance fleet will engage any hostile forces in this star system."

Rione smiled. "Very good. Vague enough yet also firm. That should cover all possibilities. I will gather Sakai and Costa and establish communications with the Syndics."

"And I'm going to continue the fleet on a path to join up with the strike force and intercept the Syndic battleship as well as the flotilla. If everyone remains on their current vectors, that means you have a bit less than twenty-three hours to resolve things. If you haven't by then, that flotilla is either going to run, or it's going to get hammered."

"I'll keep that in mind, Admiral. You should keep in mind that we no longer need the former Syndic Executive Council members on the battleship. As long as they are alive, they pose a threat to the negotiations."

"I'll remember that." Geary wondered if his voice was as cold as it sounded to him. "I won't murder them, though."

"I doubt that you'll have to do that, Admiral. The members of the former Executive Council seem very likely to be caught in a three-way cross fire. If they somehow survive that, the Syndic officers on that battleship are very likely to execute the members of the former Executive Council on the spot rather than risk their return to power, just as those members once ordered CEO Shalin to murder the Alliance officers led by Admiral Bloch." Rione's smile was as icy as Geary's tone had been. "The living stars sometimes act slowly, but they do tend eventually to provide fates appropriate to the deeds of men and women."

The Syndic flotilla must have seen by now that the Alliance fleet was on its way, but the Syndics weren't running, instead still aiming straight for an intercept with the battleship fleeing for the Syndic primary world.

"They want the battleship," Geary told Duellos in a message the captain wouldn't see for over an hour. "They have to chase it, so we want that battleship undamaged and heading as fast as it can toward the inner planets. That will force the Syndic flotilla to engage the rest of the Alliance fleet. Try to slow down the flotilla, hit its edges, and in particular watch for the Syndic battle cruisers breaking off to try to run down the battleship before it can get near us. Once we come to grips with the Syndic flotilla, the welfare of that battleship is no longer an issue for us." Was there something else? "Try to remain out of range of the battleship's weaponry. We have been told that it will not initiate combat with us, but we can't trust in that, and even if it does intend to abide by that promise, if you get too close, the battleship might think it's about to be attacked and open fire anyway. Geary out."

Desjani was sitting in her command seat again, looking rested, relaxed, and cheerful as the fleet and the enemy flotilla closed on each other at a combined velocity of about point two light speed. "A Syndic HuK came out of the hypernet gate a little while ago. It looks like it's going to hang around the gate."

"A courier." The HuK had transmitted its message and would wait at the hypernet gate until a reply was received to carry back. "I wonder what it thinks about all of those mines at the gate, and all of the merchant ships with FACs hanging off them." Geary peered at his display questioningly. "Speaking of which, I wonder why the merchant ships haven't moved yet."

"They're too slow to get anywhere in time to accomplish anything," Desjani pointed out. "All of the Syndics, no matter whom they're backing, know that as well as we do. Once we wipe out the flotilla, we'll have plenty of time to go back and wipe out the FACs and their merchant mother ships."

The Syndic battleship heading in their direction was just off the port bows of the Alliance ships, its relative bearing staying steady as the Alliance ships aimed for an intercept as soon as possible. Farther off to port, the Syndic flotilla was closing on the battleship and the Alliance fleet, its bearing drifting steadily starboard. Almost dead ahead, the battle cruisers and escorts of the Alliance strike force were also heading straight for the battleship. But it would be another six hours before the strike force reached the Syndic battleship and soon after began tangling with the Syndic flotilla, and fifteen hours before the Alliance fleet got close enough to the Syndic flotilla for a battle. "Do we want to take out that battleship even if we don't have to?" Geary murmured to himself.

Desjani heard and gave him an approving look. "Am I rubbing off on you? Yes, let's do it. It will be one less battleship for the Syndics to use against us in the future."

"But we don't want anarchy in Syndic space," Geary reminded her. "We might end up with that if we destroy every means of defense."

"That's still an enemy ship. Our job is to destroy enemy ships."

"The Syndic flotilla may try to destroy it as well."

"That will make it easier for us. We help them destroy it, then we destroy them."

Desjani's suggestion did have the virtue of simplicity. "We'll see what happens," Geary told her. "I admit that I'm tempted, but I won't blow them away if that battleship avoids firing on our warships."

She looked dissatisfied, then nodded. "Hitting them when they were abiding by a truce would be a Syndic thing to do, wouldn't it? Fine. We'll be civilized and only kill them after they provoke us."

"You're an interesting woman, Tanya." Geary rubbed his eyes. "I think I really will try to get some sleep now."

Perhaps it was simple exhaustion, or perhaps it was the relief of knowing a decisive engagement would likely take place, but Geary had no trouble sleeping this time. He only got four hours instead of his hoped-for five, though, before a message came in from the strike force.

Duellos appeared relaxed. It was still hard to recall that he was on the bridge of *Inspire* now, and not *Courageous*, which had been lost at Heradao. "My intent is to bypass the battleship and its three-cruiser escort. The Syndic flotilla is currently arrayed with the battleships on the outer edges and the battle cruisers in the center, making it a very tough nut for my strike force to crack. CEO Shalin may be dishonorable and contemptible, but he's playing this smart. I'll see what I can do to slow him down and hurt him, but we need the fleet's battleships to really hammer that flotilla. Duellos out."

Geary gave up on sleep for the next day or so and headed back to the bridge.

Desjani was still there, apparently ignoring Senator Costa in the observer's seat.

For her part, Costa was concentrating on her display. "Is this right, Admiral? Our strike force will engage the enemy in less than two hours?"

"Not exactly," Geary explained as he took his own seat. "In a little less than two hours our strike force will intercept the Syndic battleship heading toward the primary world. We do not intend engaging that battleship unless it attacks us first."

"There won't be a battle soon, then." Costa seemed disappointed.

"I hope not. I need everything those battle cruisers have got for their fight with the flotilla, and battleships are very tough targets even when one has only three escorts with it."

"I came up here during a break in negotiations in the hope of observing firsthand our brave sailors engaging the enemy," Costa complained.

He glanced at Desjani, who was trying to look like she wasn't aware of the conversation. "Senator, the strike force will be almost a light-hour distant from us when it does encounter the enemy. We won't see what happens until an hour after it happens."

Costa frowned. "Yes... of course... that goes without saying. Please notify me before the strike force encounters the Syndic flotilla. I assume the strike force will attack the center of the enemy, where their own battle cruisers are located."

"No, Senator, we will not do that."

The senator's frown deepened. "You just said that battleships are tough targets. I understand that battle cruisers are not designed for one-on-one fights with battleships. Why wouldn't our battle cruisers engage the Syndic battle cruisers?"

He took a long breath before replying. "Because aside from being outnumbered sixteen to nine in battle cruisers, plowing our strike force through the center of the Syndic flotilla would expose our battle cruisers and their escorts to fire from all sides from the battleships on the corners of the Syndic formation, as well as to fire from the overwhelming number of Syndic escorts. The sixty-one heavy cruisers in that flotilla would by themselves be a difficult challenge for the strike force."

"Why isn't our strike force stronger then?"

Geary took another look at Desjani, who seemed to be enjoying herself. *Rione said that politicians and military officers stopped talking to each other. If this is an example of how the conversations went, I have no trouble understanding that.* Every time he gave Costa any details, she asked for more without applying anything learned from the previous answers. Maybe the answer was to avoid any detail the senator could use for further attempts to question his own judgment.

"That was my decision as fleet commander, Senator."

After a long moment spent thinking that over, Costa stood up. "I'd better get back to the negotiations."

After waiting until she left, Geary turned to Desjani. "You set me up."

"I merely informed the senator that there were certain questions the fleet commander was best equipped to answer, sir."

"Thank you, Captain. I'll be sure to return the favor sometime."

Desjani gave him a measuring look. "Are you worried? Duellos won't go up the middle. A year ago, we would have done that. Not now."

"What about Kattnig? If he sends *Adroit* through the middle of that Syndic flotilla, how many other ships will follow him?"

"Hopefully, not many. When did you last eat?"

"I... can't remember."

She pulled out some ration bars. "You can't give your body sleep, but it needs food, too."

Geary took the bars cautiously, remembering some of the horrible-tasting ones he had been forced to eat during the fleet's return to Alliance space. "Bulgorin?"

"They're pretty good. I'm not sure where they eat bulgorin, but it's not bad."

"What's in it?"

"I have no idea, and no intention of looking. Just eat them. You need to be alert for at least the next twelve hours, so your body needs fuel."

"Yes, ma'am."

Desjani narrowed her eyes at him. "If you're not at your best,

Admiral, the personnel and warships of this fleet will suffer."

He couldn't deny the truth of that, so Geary ate the bars, which did taste pretty good for ration bars. After that he tried to relax as he watched the Alliance and Syndicate Worlds' formations moving on his display. The Syndic flotilla had ramped up its velocity to point one five light speed, or roughly forty-five thousand kilometers per second, yet with the scale pulled far out, the depictions of the ships barely seemed to be moving against the huge distances of a star system. But zooming in close presented images of warships that appeared totally motionless with nothing for the eye to measure their movement against.

The Syndics were coming in from an angle at the battleship, which had managed to plod up to point one two light as it headed toward the primary world. It should have been able to accelerate to a better velocity than that though. *I wonder what modifications the Syndic Executive Council made to that warship over the years to enhance their own comfort, at the cost of important capabilities.*

He must have inadvertently asked that out loud. Desjani answered immediately. "That might explain something. Our sensors estimate the mass of that battleship as significantly higher than comparable Syndic battleships, but the armor doesn't appear to be any more massive. So there's something very heavy inside it."

"A citadel?"

"That's what I'd guess. Something with very thick walls made of the densest material the Syndics could manage without dealing with radioactives. The Syndic leaders wanted someplace where they could fort up in an emergency."

"Idiots," Geary grumbled. "Making a battleship even slower so it can't get away from pursuers, and doing that in the name of protecting themselves."

The encounter of the strike force with the Syndic battleship was something of an anticlimax, the two formations tearing past each other outside weapons range without pause or action. But only two light-minutes beyond the battleship was the Syndic flotilla.

"Damn." Geary clenched his fist in frustration. "The Syndics are holding to point one five light speed."

Desjani made a helpless gesture. "They're overtaking the battleship at an angle, so their speed relative to it is only point zero eight light speed. Plenty good for targeting."

"But Duellos is going to have to brake hard, or he'll cross their path at a combined velocity of point three light speed! What kind of hits could he get at that speed?"

Desjani passed the question to the combat-systems watch-stander, who shook her head. "Compensation for relativistic distortion would be inadequate, Admiral. Hit probabilities would be a maximum of five percent, and most likely lower."

"He's braking," Desjani commented.

On his display, Geary saw the same information. An hour and five minutes ago Duellos had pivoted his ships so the main propulsion units pointed forward, then begun killing velocity as fast as the ships' structures and inertial dampers could handle it.

"Duellos cut it close," Desjani added in admiring tones. "He should get down to a decent combined velocity relative to the Syndics just in time to pivot his ships bow forward again for the firing pass."

Geary had to admit that the familiar Syndic box formation

had been shrewdly put together this time. The Syndic CEO had arrayed his ships in a shallow box, with the broad side facing forward. Each corner was anchored by three battleships. In the center, all sixteen battle cruisers formed a cluster in which their massed firepower would compensate for their lighter armor and shields. The sixty-one heavy cruisers were distributed to reinforce the already formidable battleship groups in the corners as well as the battle cruisers in the center. Spread through the areas between the battleships and the battle cruisers were the swarms of light cruisers and Hunter-Killers. There simply weren't any weak points that could be hammered by the battle cruisers in the Alliance strike force. "It looks like Duellos angled to hit one of the lower corners."

Desjani nodded. "You tend to favor hitting upper corners, so he probably chose a lower one to throw off the Syndics."

"I tend to hit upper corners?" Developing a pattern would be dangerous, since the enemy could exploit knowledge of that to counter his moves.

"Yes. I was going to talk to you about that."

"Thanks. Next time bring something like that up a little earlier." The words were light, but inside Geary's guts were knotted with tension. Whatever Duellos had done had happened an hour ago. He couldn't do anything to influence the events he was seeing. He knew that. But it didn't make watching it any easier. Especially when he saw Duellos's formation start to shred in a way that didn't seem planned. "What's that—*Adroit*. Where is *Adroit* going?" Kattnig was doing what they had feared, changing course to head directly for the Syndic flotilla instead of following the glancing firing run Duellos had set up.

But within moments, Geary's outrage changed to disbelief as *Adroit*'s track became clearer. "What the hell."

From her baffled tones, Desjani felt the same way. "*Adroit* is turning away, opening her distance to the Syndic formation." She turned a shocked expression to Geary. "He's avoiding action."

Agonized, Geary watched helplessly as the other four battle cruisers in *Adroit*'s division made initial moves to follow her track, then wavered onto new vectors as their individual commanding officers tried to compensate for their maneuvers away from an intercept of the Syndics.

In the very little time available to react, some of them overcompensated.

"*Damn*," Desjani whispered through clenched teeth, as the Alliance strike force whipped past the Syndic flotilla, *Assert* and *Agile* curving on paths that brought them closer to the Syndics than the rest of the Alliance warships.

Assert came apart as she caught a concentrated barrage from the three Syndic battleships forming that corner of the enemy formation. *Agile*, frantically trying to live up to her name by bending back upward, nonetheless staggered from dozens of hits and tumbled onward, maneuvering and propulsion lost along with many other systems and surely many members of her crew.

The confusion among the battle cruisers following *Adroit* lessened the Alliance blow against the Syndics. One Syndic battleship shuddered under repeated blows, but despite taking heavy damage to one area, kept going with the formation.

It had all happened in less than the blink of an eye as the formations tore past each other, and now Duellos was bringing his formation around and trying to re-form it while the Syndics raced onward toward the battleship.

"Maybe something went wrong on *Adroit*," Desjani said, her voice still reflecting disbelief. "They're brand-new. Some glitch in the maneuvering controls."

"Maybe. That was Duellos's best chance to slow down that flotilla. The battleship with the former Syndic leaders on it is dead meat unless it surrenders and releases them."

"Which it will," Desjani said bitterly.

"No. Rione didn't think so, and neither do I. As long as the battleship fights, her officers stand a chance of survival. If the Syndic leaders they mutinied against regain power, every officer on that ship will die or wish they had."

The flotilla was closing the remaining distance rapidly, angling slightly so that the single battleship and the three heavy cruisers with it would pass between two corners and the concentration of battle cruisers in the center of the formation. Abruptly, the heavy cruisers with the lone battleship angled away, veering off in different directions as the battleship swung left in an attempt to counter the flotilla's maneuvers.

"They left that too late," Desjani commented, as the flotilla overtook the fleeing warships. Two of the escaping heavy cruisers vanished into clouds of wreckage as their former comrades poured fire into them. The third jerked from dozens of impacts, then broke apart, the pieces rolling away.

Even given the firepower it was facing, the Syndic battleship didn't go easily. It lurched onward as its shields collapsed, and its armor was penetrated repeatedly, firing back with enough effect to knock out one of the battle cruisers and two heavy cruisers.

The Syndic flotilla braked as it went past the battleship, slowing enough to match velocities with the crippled warship. Escape pods began spurting from the battleship, spreading out as they fled the wreck.

The Alliance strike force had re-formed and was approaching again when the Syndic flotilla merged with the battleship once more. "Ancestors preserve us," Desjani said in a shocked whisper. "They're shooting up their own escape pods."

"What the hell is CEO Shalin up to?" Geary asked. "Some of those pods might have members of the former Executive Council on them."

He hadn't noticed Rione coming onto the bridge, but she spoke now. "CEO Shalin is eliminating the competition. He intends taking over since he commands the last significant Syndic mobile military force. I wondered if he would realize the opportunity that provided, and it seems he finally did."

"Then he'll try to take out the new Executive Council as well."

"If he can get through us, yes."

"He won't. Why the hell are his ships following orders to fire on escape pods carrying Syndic personnel?"

Desjani gave a grim laugh. "Some of them aren't. Look at his formation."

The neat box, already in slight disarray because of the rapid braking maneuver, was stretching out of shape as some individual warships veered away from their stations. Geary wished again that his fleet was closer to the action instead of being hours of travel time distant. "We could tear the hell out of them while they're disorganized like that."

"They just have to figure out whose side they're on," Desjani said. "How many sides do the Syndics have now, anyway? Three?"

"Two," Rione replied. "Since Shalin has surely killed all of the members of the original Executive Council, that 'side' no longer exists, and the choice is now between him and the new Executive Council."

"If I can get close enough to him," Geary said, "I'm going to do my best to bring the number of Syndic sides down to one."

"And I will return to the negotiations, to see how the elimination of the former Executive Council affects the attitudes of the new Executive Council."

As Rione left, a window popped into existence beside Geary, showing Lieutenant Iger with a delighted expression. "Admiral, sir, we've got it."

"Got what?"

"The flotilla flagship, sir. It's usually impossible to sort out the flagship because it's hidden in the local net traffic, but the Syndic flotilla communications are flailing about in some sort of internal dispute, and we were able to spot the flagship. It's this battle cruiser, sir." One of the Syndic warships on Geary's display glowed a little brighter.

"Outstanding." Geary felt his teeth draw back in a feral smile. "Let's make sure we keep track of that ship." He checked distances and times again. The running battle between the Syndic flotilla and the now-wrecked battleship had kept closing the distance to the Alliance fleet, and the surviving Syndics were still heading down the same vector as they focused on whose orders to follow. With the Alliance fleet coming on as well, the travel time to encounter the Syndics was down to just over four hours.

Duellos was a lot closer, but the strike force was in a stern chase after the Syndics, who were still barreling through space at just over point one light speed. It would be close to an hour before Duellos could manage another firing run on the flotilla.

But should he do it even then? Geary took another look at the disorganization spreading through the Syndic flotilla's formation. Even if the Syndic warships totally lost their order, though, they would still be too tough for Duellos to break. But an attack by Duellos could have the opposite result. "Captain Duellos, this is Admiral Geary. Reduce your closing rate on the Syndic flotilla. The Syndics are engaging in internal debates, and if you hit them, it may resolve those debates quickly in favor of dealing with a common enemy. I want you to slow down enough to be ready to hit them from one side at the same time as the rest of the fleet approaches on the other side. I emphasize that this order does not indicate any lack of confidence in you or your ships. Monitor the Syndic flotilla closely, and if you see what you believe to be an important opportunity, you are authorized to use your discretion in taking action before the rest of the fleet reaches engagement range. Geary out."

Updates were coming in from Duellos's ships, most of which had sustained only minor damage, and from *Agile*, detailing the much more extensive damage she had taken. Geary bit back a curse as he read the data, then called *Tanuki*. "Captain Smyth, I want one of your auxiliaries ready to head for *Agile* as soon as we eliminate the threat from the Syndic flotilla. I need *Agile* able to maneuver again as soon as possible."

Smyth's reply appeared several seconds later. "I understand you want *Agile* to be sprightly once again. I'll send *Witch*, sir, but I'm not liking what *Agile* is sending about her structural damage. It may be more than any of my auxiliaries can handle."

"Understood." Geary settled down in his seat, glowering at his display. "The people who approve stupid designs for warships should be required to ride those warships into battle."

Desjani twisted her mouth. "*Agile* got shot up that badly because of what a fleet officer did."

"We don't know yet why *Adroit* changed course."

"Aren't we receiving status updates from *Adroit*?"

"Yes, we are."

"Have any of those updates reported problems with the maneuvering systems?" Desjani pressed.

"No. The course change was the result of a helm order being entered. I just don't know why that change was made."

"Does it matter?" She paused before speaking slowly. "I read about Beowulf, about Kattnig's other recent actions, and I thought, why is an officer who has fought such hard and bloody battles acting like a brand-new ensign who is talking big because he's secretly unsure of how he'll do in a real fight?"

"I know. It doesn't sound like the same officer."

"Maybe he's not the same officer," Desjani continued in a very low voice. "Maybe he's seen too much blood, lost too many ships. Maybe Beowulf was one brutal fight too many, and he couldn't stand it anymore. It happens."

Geary stared at her. "I thought the fleet medical teams could spot that."

"Not always. It's just like an interrogation cell, which just tells you what someone believes is true. If someone convinces themselves that they're fine, that's how it shows up." She shook her head. "Maybe Kattnig didn't really know, maybe he just suspected that he'd lost his nerve. But we lost at least one ship because of what he did. Maybe two."

"We still don't—" He looked away.

"Captain Duellos has temporary tactical command over *Adroit*, but he does not have the authority to relieve Kattnig of command and order him placed in protective confinement. You do. You need to do that now."

Geary swung his head to glare at Desjani. "It would take an hour for that order to reach them. Why are you so eager to hammer Kattnig? The man has an outstanding record. The fleet medical staff cleared him."

"He *had* an outstanding record. If he was pushed too far, it was his responsibility to recognize that fact, before it cost lives."

"If he's relieved now, it will be the same in most people's eyes as if I'd declared him guilty of cowardice before the enemy! Why do you want to judge so quickly and destroy a man who has given so much to the Alliance?" His tone grew heated.

Desjani's eyes flared, and she leaned close, inside his privacy field, her face reddening, whispering fiercely. "He's *already* destroyed, Admiral Geary. You *know* what this fleet is like. You *know* how we think. Do you still not understand something so basic? Kattnig is publicly disgraced. He avoided battle. Officers and sailors died because of his actions. But he is not a pompous, oblivious fool like Numos. Kattnig knows what he did. He knows how everyone will look at him. He knows the fate that awaits him. What will an honorable man who faces such a fate do, a man already pushed past his limit?"

Her meaning finally hit him. "He needs to be relieved and arrested to protect him from himself."

"Yes, Admiral Geary. And you had better *never* again even imply that I would ever seek the destruction of a good officer!" She leaned back abruptly, out of the privacy field, staring angrily at her display.

Geary tried to relax himself, then called *Adroit*. "Captain Kattnig is hereby relieved of duty and ordered placed in protective confinement. *Adroit*'s executive officer is to assume temporary command pending further notice." Ending the transmission, he gritted his teeth. "I'm sorry, Captain Desjani. I shouldn't have said that. It was unprofessional of me to accuse you of such a thing and unjustified by everything I know about you."

Desjani just nodded, her eyes still fixed straight ahead.

"One of these days, I'll learn to listen to you the first time you tell me something I need to know."

Her face relaxed a bit. "I'll believe it when I see it."

"Do you think the order will get to *Adroit* in time?"

"No. I hope I'm wrong."

"I don't think you are." They sat silently for a while then, watching the formations of warships slowly converge on their displays.

They were closing on both the Syndic flotilla and the Alliance strike force at a combined velocity of close to point two five light speed. As a result it only took a long hour and a half before they saw Duellos slowing his strike force in response to Geary's orders.

As the strike force settled onto its new vector, Desjani nodded approvingly. "If nothing changes, the strike force will hit the flotilla at almost the same instant we do."

The Syndics hadn't fallen apart, but neither had they tightened up their formation again. They hung on their current vector, heading steadily toward the primary inhabited world and a much earlier rendezvous with the Alliance fleet. "What's he planning?" Desjani wondered. "Blowing past us like he did the strike force and continuing on to wipe out the new Executive Council?"

"The new Executive Council won't be that easy to find and hit since they have an entire planet to hide on." Geary rested his chin on one hand, thinking. "Rione suggested that CEO Shalin personally wants me dead and defeated."

"That's not exactly an impressive insight, sir."

He decided against addressing that comment directly. "The point is, maybe he's planning on trying to beat me."

Desjani considered that, then nodded. "It's possible. The last time he faced this fleet commanded by you, we lost... a battle cruiser."

"We lost *Repulse*," Geary clarified in a steady voice.

"Yes, sir. But Shalin may think he beat us then because we did take very serious losses in the ambush, we did have to reposition to Corvus to regroup, and he hasn't faced you since that time. He may be under the delusion that he's a better commander." She nodded again, half to herself. "Defeat the Alliance fleet, then get rid of the new Executive Council, and he could claim leadership of the Syndicate Worlds. It's crazy, but it might seem doable to him. That would explain why Shalin hasn't had the flotilla run again while it debates following him. He wants to slug it out with us."

It fit very well. Geary remembered Captain Falco lecturing him on how fighting spirit could easily overcome mere numerical inferiority. Falco hadn't been alone in the Alliance fleet in believing that, and the Syndics had shown plenty of signs in earlier battles with this fleet of having the same mind-set. "Maybe it's not even an option for him anymore. He has to keep pushing ahead because if he pauses or hesitates or retreats, his ability to hold that flotilla together will vanish."

Desjani gave an evil laugh. "If he stops running fast enough, the wolves he is leading will instead start chasing him and pull him down."

"Which means he's desperate, too, and he's been smart enough to stay alive up until now." He started plotting out in his mind what Shalin might do, and how to counter it, but was interrupted a short time later by a transmission from *Adroit*.

He recognized the officer staring at him from the bridge of *Adroit*. She was Kattnig's executive officer, second in command on the battle cruiser. During Geary's tour of *Adroit* back at Varandal, she had been quietly competent. Now she appeared stern in the manner of someone maintaining control. "This is Commander Yavina Lakova, acting commanding officer of *Adroit*. Regret to report... Captain Kattnig is dead. He... he had a regulation sidearm. It... discharged. Initial assessment is that he was examining the weapon in his stateroom and it... accidentally... discharged. Death probably instantaneous. This occurred half an hour prior to our receipt of your orders concerning Captain Kattnig, so I was unable to carry out those orders. *Adroit* is otherwise ready for combat. I will remain in acting command until otherwise notified. Lakova out."

The screen blanked. Geary closed his eyes and took a long, slow breath. "You were right," he told Desjani.

"Damn. Damn. Damn. After all his honorable service…"

"They didn't get my order in time to relieve him of command. Doesn't that mean it officially never took effect?"

"It might," Desjani agreed.

"It's my responsibility to judge the fitness to serve of officers under my command. I failed."

She turned a severe look on him. "Don't blame yourself. He passed muster with the fleet medical staff, and none of his fellow officers figured it out in time, either."

"It's still my responsibility."

"Then do what you still can. There'll be an official investigation into the cause of death. You get to approve or disapprove the findings."

Geary stared at nothing as he pondered her words. "*Adroit*'s executive officer described Kattnig's death as an accident. Will the fleet bureaucracy accept that?"

"They won't have any choice but to accept it if the fleet admiral endorses that conclusion. It's also up to the fleet admiral whether or not there is any investigation into *Adroit*'s actions in combat prior to the accident."

"I don't see any purpose in such an investigation now. He deserves that much from us."

"Yes, he does." Desjani spoke sternly again. "You can handle all of that later. We're heading into combat. Get your mind back there."

"Right. Thanks, Tanya."

She was facing her display again, but he heard her muttering. "You actually did listen to me the first time."

The Syndic formation slowly began tightening again. "Our estimate from the comm traffic patterns is that the Syndic CEO in charge of the flotilla initially had about a third of the ships backing him," Lieutenant Iger reported, "but that one-third was pretty hard-core while the other two-thirds were mostly wavering. He seems to have won over everybody now, at least to the extent that no one is challenging his authority."

Only four light-minutes separated the Alliance fleet from the Syndic flotilla. "They're going to regret that," Geary commented. "Thank you, Lieutenant. All ships in the Alliance fleet main body, this is Admiral Geary. Assume stations in modified Formation Fox Five at time two one."

"You're reusing that?" Desjani asked. "Won't the Syndic survivors from Kaliban have provided reports on that battle?"

"They would have," Geary agreed. "I'm not going to do the same thing. But the Syndics here may think I plan on doing the same thing."

At time two one the main body of the fleet began splitting, forming into three flattened ovals. The largest oval, centered on *Dauntless* and facing the enemy, held the other three battle cruisers in her division along with twelve battleships and twenty heavy cruisers. That was fox five one. The oval forming above the main formation held the remaining seven battle cruisers and would be fox five two, while the oval forming beneath the main body contained the remaining thirteen battleships and all of the heavy cruisers in fox five three. The light cruisers and destroyers were divided among fox five one and fox five two, while the five auxiliaries were forming another subformation, which was fox five four, just behind the main body. The oval of the main body faced its flat side to the enemy, while the oval formations not far above and below the main body were at right angles to it, the entire grouping almost resembling a three-sided box open on two sides and the top facing the Syndic flotilla. "No escorts for the auxiliaries?" Desjani asked.

"The entire fleet is escorting them," Geary replied. "This time around I'm confident that the Syndics won't veer off and try to hit the auxiliaries first." He focused back on the strike force, which since the ill-fated pass against the Syndic flotilla was down to the four full-size battle cruisers of Duellos's division and the three remaining *Adroit*-class warships, *Adroit*, *Auspice*, and *Ascendant*. The strike force still represented a significant amount of firepower, but it would have to be employed carefully against the mass of the Syndic flotilla.

As the Alliance fleet settled into its new arrangement, the Syndics were barely two light-minutes distant, about ten minutes from engagement range at current closing rates. The Syndic box formation was back as it had been except for the loss of the one battle cruiser during the fight with the Syndic battleship. Once again, the Syndic battle cruisers were massed in the center, with the battleships in clusters at each corner of the box. *He's coming straight on. He expects me to whittle at the edges of his formation, just as I've usually done and as I did using these formations at Kaliban. There's a countermove if I use that tactic, a countermove that would also set him up to punch straight through the middle of the formation in an attack centered on Dauntless. The fleet flagship, holding the guy who stole Shalin's hoped for glory.*

And you still think you're smarter than me, Shalin, smarter than anybody, and you hate my guts. Arrogance and hate. Bad combination. It's going to cost you.

"All right. Let's get slowed down to targeting speed. All units in formations fox five one, fox five two, fox five three, and fox five four reduce speed to point zero four light speed at time three zero. All units in fox five two, pivot formation down zero nine five degrees at time three nine and accelerate to point zero six light speed. All units in fox five three, pivot formation up zero seven five degrees at time three seven and accelerate to point zero six light speed. All units in fox five four, alter heading up zero nine zero degrees at time four zero." He paused to take a breath. "Captain Duellos, accelerate to contact with the enemy on your current heading. Engage targets of opportunity."

Desjani gave her display a startled look. "You're not aiming for the edges of his formation to wear him down."

"No. He expects that. Upper or lower edges, he thinks that's what I'll do." Geary grinned at Desjani. "I do have a pattern."

She slowly smiled as she thought through the maneuvers. "He's planning to do what you did at the first battle at Lakota, right?"

"Probably. Concentrate and punch through the middle of this formation, where *Dauntless* and I am."

Dauntless had pivoted around and was shuddering now as her propulsion units strove to reduce her velocity. Geary felt the strain, heard the ship's structure complain, and knew that if the inertial dampers failed, the ship would come apart, and every human in it would be smashed to jelly. All around *Dauntless*, the rest of the Alliance fleet's warships were braking as well.

The Syndic commander would expect that, too. Geary had often changed velocity right before contact, and this time he had to slow down, couldn't accelerate without effectively eliminating any chance of scoring hits on the enemy.

Dauntless was pivoting again, bringing her bow around to face the enemy with only a few minutes left to contact, the subformations above and below the main formation pivoting to almost parallel with the main formation as the battle cruiser subformation above dove down just behind the main body, and just in front of the main body, the battleship subformation below climbed up in front of the rest. Behind them all, the auxiliaries were climbing straight "up" and away from the path of the Syndics. "All units, weapons free as soon as the enemy enters your weapons engagement envelopes."

The Syndic formation was altering at the last moments before contact, too, shrinking down to much smaller dimensions, concentrating the ships into a tight block aimed at the center of the main Alliance formation. "If we'd aimed at the edges of his formation," Desjani observed, "we would have found ourselves too far out to score hits as his formation shrank. Good call, Admiral. Weapons," she called that watch-stander, "target the enemy flagship."

"One minute to contact," the maneuvering watch-stander announced.

Missiles leaped from warships, filling the space between the flotilla and the Alliance fleet, followed within moments by barrages of grapeshot and hell-lance fire, then on the Alliance side, the battleships and battle cruisers fired their null-field weapons.

Instead of avoiding the glancing blows from the Alliance subformations and hitting the single thin layer of the main formation, the Syndic flotilla found itself running headlong into three layers of Alliance warships, the first and last layers moving rapidly at almost right angles to the Syndic movement and hard to target, but hurling out their weapons along the vector the Syndic flotilla was coming down.

Space flared bright as weapons clashed, and ships exploded, the Syndics ramming through the first Alliance subformation, which held more battleships than the entire Syndic flotilla, then hitting the main body with almost as many battleships and some battle cruisers, before staggering through the third subformation, with its battle cruisers and numerous escorts tearing at the weakened Syndic warships.

Coming close behind the Syndics, Duellos led the strike force through the Alliance formations in a heart-stopping maneuver that took only fractions of a second, then slammed fire into the rear of the Syndic flotilla.

It had taken less than a second for the two forces to clash, and now as they separated again, Geary felt *Dauntless* still shaking from the impacts of enemy hits. He tried not to focus on the damage to *Dauntless*, concentrating instead on the assessments pouring in from the fleet sensors as they evaluated the results of the clash.

"Have a nice trip to hell," Desjani snarled at her display as she directed damage-control efforts.

He knew what she meant. All fifteen of the remaining Syndic battle cruisers were gone, including the flagship, torn apart or exploded into fragments by the successive layers of Alliance battleships and battle cruisers. CEO Shalin wouldn't be ruling the Syndicate Worlds.

Of the twelve Syndic battleships, six were still lurching forward with heavy damage, but those were being overhauled and knocked out one by one by Duellos's strike force. The rest of the enemy battleships were already out of commission and spitting out swarms of escape pods.

Out of nearly two hundred Hunter-Killers, less than a dozen were left, the small warships annihilated by the amount of firepower concentrated on the space they had traversed. Ten light cruisers had survived, five of them still able to run at full speed, and nearly twenty heavy cruisers were still operational, having been small enough to avoid fire aimed at the battleships and battle cruisers and large enough to survive the weapons that had almost wiped out the smaller warships.

Duellos called in, looking quite pleased with events. "We might need some help on a couple of these battleships, but otherwise things went quite well. You might be interested in knowing that as my formation approached yours, and you exchanged fire with the Syndics, our sensors reported the heaviest recorded density of weapons usage and tried to warn us off."

Inspire was opening the distance once more, but still less than a light-minute away, so something resembling a conversation was possible. "That's another one of those things I don't think I want to do again. I'm going to get the fleet turned around, so if you need any assistance, just call."

He gave the necessary orders, pulling the four subformations back toward each other as they turned through wide swaths of space, then forced himself to face the hard part. *Witch* headed off toward an intercept with the crippled *Agile*, accompanied by the battleship *Guardian*, which should be all the escort needed now that the Syndic flotilla had ceased to exist.

On Geary's display, red symbols and text told the tale of the price the Alliance had paid during the brutal exchange of fire with the Syndics.

The battleships and escorts in the fox five three subformation had been the first in line and taken the brunt of the Syndic fire. It only now registered on Geary that Dreadnaught had been one of those battleships. He had sent his grandniece into danger without even realizing it, caught up in the planning and execution of the battle. *Dreadnaught* had been battered but hadn't sustained critical damage. *Orion*, still a bad-luck ship, had taken the most damage and would need a lot of repair work. Aside from them, the four battleships *Fearless*, *Resolution*, *Redoubtable*, and *Warspite* seemed to have been in the wrong places at the wrong time and received the most damage from the Syndic fire.

In the main body, the Syndics had tried to hit the four battle cruisers, assuming one held Geary. Even though the enemy blows had already been seriously blunted, the four battle cruisers had suffered. *Daring* took the most hits, but *Dauntless* was far from unscathed. "How many dead?" he asked Desjani.

She sighed. "Ten confirmed. Three more might not make it. We can get all the damage repaired within a week and be at full readiness again."

Multiply those losses by how many ships in the fleet, and the price once again seemed far too high.

Amazingly, in the third layer the Syndics had penetrated, the most damage by far had been sustained by the new *Invincible*. *I've heard of threat magnets, but it's like the Invincible literally attracted enemy fire.*

Like the battleships in fox five three, the escorts had caught hell,

271

which was why he hadn't put any destroyers or light cruisers in that formation. Four heavy cruisers, *Menpo*, *Hoplite*, *Bukhtar*, and *Squamata*, were either gone or clearly too badly damaged to repair. Another eleven had been badly shot up. In the other subformations, twenty destroyers had been knocked out or torn apart, along with six light cruisers. That was in addition to the battle cruiser *Assert*, lost earlier.

"It could have been a lot worse," Desjani observed.

"You usually say that."

"Because it's usually true. We've crushed the Syndics here, in their home star system, and for the time being they have nothing left except those heavy cruisers and other surviving escorts running for their lives."

Geary looked around, seeing the watch-standers exchanging grins, knowing that all through the fleet, personnel would be remembering the losses in the ambush before Geary assumed command and celebrating the turnabout in their fortunes as well as the vengeance on the Syndic CEO responsible. He tried to shake off the melancholy he felt over the men and women who had died to bring about the victories here and in other star systems, tried to lift his mood to match that of the rest of the people on *Dauntless*'s bridge.

He hadn't quite succeeded when that mood was abruptly shattered by the stunned voice of the operations watch-stander. "The hypernet gate is collapsing."

9

Geary jerked his attention back to his display, where the hypernet gate depiction was pulsing red in warning. Now? What kind of cruel joke would it be for everything to end that way after defeating every other challenge? "How much time left until it collapses?"

No answer. Geary looked back and saw the watch-stander, along with every other watch-stander, staring aghast at their displays.

Desjani's voice, hard, louder than usual, cut across the bridge. "The admiral asked you for the system estimate of the time until collapse."

The lieutenant jerked back to awareness. "I'm sorry, Captain. Sir, fifteen minutes."

"Fifteen minutes?" Geary asked.

"Yes, sir. That's all. It's going down very fast."

Geary closed his eyes, took a deep breath, then looked back at the display. "That's not enough time to get the fleet into the defensive formation."

"No, sir," Desjani agreed, her voice quieter now.

Geary triggered the appropriate comm circuit. "All units in the Alliance fleet, this is Admiral Geary. As you are aware, the hypernet gate here is collapsing. We have been informed that the catastrophic-fail function has been disabled, but could not confirm that, nor do we know whether or not the safe-fail system is functioning properly. We cannot predict the level of the energy discharge. All ships are to position themselves bow on to the hypernet gate location and maximize forward shields." There had to be something else to say, in what might be his last transmission. "If worse comes to worst, the remnants of central power for the Syndicate Worlds' government and mobile forces will be destroyed along with this fleet. Our sacrifice will not be in vain, and our children will be free of this war."

Rione burst onto the bridge and stood staring at the display before the observer seat, before dropping into it. Her eyes didn't seem to be watching the display, though. Geary wondered what she was looking at in her mind's eye. "How are negotiations going?" he asked, amazed that he could actually ask the question with sarcasm rather than bitterness.

Rione shook her head quickly, then focused on Geary. "The Syndics were as shocked as we were. When I left, they were screaming that they hadn't done it, that no collapse order had been sent, that the catastrophic-fail algorithms could not still be operational."

What to say to that? "Thank you."

"Five minutes to collapse," the operations watch-stander announced in a strained voice.

"Forward shields at maximum," the combat-systems watch-stander reported.

"Very well." Desjani was massaging her forehead lightly with the tips of the fingers of one hand, hiding her expression. She glanced at Geary and just for a moment smiled wistfully. "If worse comes to worst, it's been nice knowing you."

"Same here." Possibly only a few minutes left, but they couldn't even touch hands. They had maintained their honor up to now, and they would end that way if that was what fate decreed.

The hypernet gate had actually collapsed more than seven hours ago. The light from that event was finally reaching them, and any shock wave soon would as well. Geary watched his display, part of him marveling at the fact that everything on it closer to the hypernet gate might already be gone.

"One minute." The watch-stander's voice cracked.

"Very well," Desjani repeated, her voice composed but getting louder again. "We will meet this as *Dauntless* and her crew have met every danger, with honor and courage."

A chorus of assents from the watch-standers followed her words. Desjani gave Geary another smile. He nodded back to her. Rione was staring fixedly into space again.

"Thirty seconds until estimated arrival of shock wave... ten seconds... five seconds... four... three... two... one."

The moment came and passed, just as it had at Lakota. "Get me an updated estimate if you can, Lieutenant," Desjani ordered.

"Yes, Captain, I— Captain?" The operations watch-stander was studying his display intently. "I think it's happened. Yes. One second after the estimate. The energy discharge from the gate was so small that our instruments barely registered it. We've got a clear view of where the gate was and all the intervening space. The gate is gone, but everything is fine."

"I'll be damned." Desjani turned a baffled gaze on Geary. "Those Syndic CEOs told the truth."

He felt light-headed as he nodded in reply. "It looks like they did. We're all still alive."

"A miracle," Desjani said, shaking her head. "I mean, yes, we're alive, but Syndic CEOs told the truth. I never expected that to happen."

"I guess we owe the living stars thanks for that miracle and for the fact that we're still alive." Geary tapped his controls. "All units in the Alliance fleet, this is Admiral Geary. The safe-fail mechanism on the hypernet gate functioned properly. The threat is past. Continue previously assigned operations." He turned back to look at Rione. "I believe you can return to your negotiations, Madam Co-President."

Rione stood up, smiling. "I will do that, Admiral. I'll also light a candle to Captain Cresida tonight."

As Rione left, Geary looked toward Desjani. "Remind me to do the same."

"I shouldn't have to remind you about that," she told him in a voice almost as scolding as the one previously aimed at her watch-standers. "But I will, before I light one for her, too. Now, why did that gate collapse?"

"Someone loyal to the former Syndic leaders, and willing to die themselves, might have sent the order," Geary speculated. "Or..."

"Yes. *Or* our mysterious enemies. Somehow they figured out

we were here and sent the collapse order." Desjani leaned back, her posture still tense. "If they had sent that order earlier, before the Syndics deactivated the catastrophic-collapse routines, they would have decapitated the Syndicate Worlds and wiped out the Alliance fleet."

"Nice for them." Geary rubbed his chin, thinking about unfinished business. "It's not going to end here, is it?"

"Hell, no, sir."

"There's a way the aliens could have found out we were here, and that's through the Syndic ships." Geary drummed his fingers on the arm of his chair. "Some of the Syndic warships, especially the battleships, are crippled but still intact. We need to get some of our ships over to them to 'provide assistance.'" Desjani raised disbelieving eyebrows at him. "We'll get some people aboard them, whether they like it or not. We'll make a humanitarian gesture, assist with wounded and evacuating crew who couldn't get off in escape pods. We'll also examine the Syndic operating systems for the alien worms while we're doing that."

Desjani's expression cleared. "If the worms are there, we'll know the Syndics don't know about them."

"Exactly. And it will tell us how the aliens learned we were here. If the worms aren't there, it could mean the Syndics have also figured out how to neutralize them, or it could mean the aliens chose not to spy on the Syndics."

"If I were you, I wouldn't place any money on that second possibility. Whatever those things are, they seem to have pushed for every advantage they can get." Desjani shook her head. "But the cover story will be that we're helping the Syndics. Even you aren't going to have a lot of sailors volunteering for those boarding teams."

"I know." Geary grinned. "But I've got a lot of Marines."

General Carabali took her orders in stride, only the smallest smile betraying her satisfaction when she learned the real reason for the aid missions. "Admiral, I recommend you send the battleships and battle cruisers carrying my Marines very close to the stricken Syndic warships. With the fleet firepower looming close, it will lessen any chance that the Syndic crews might attempt resistance that could cause further damage to their systems."

Not to mention further damaging the Syndic crews themselves. "Good idea. We're putting the plan together now. I'll notify you as soon as the ships are selected, so you can brief your Marines. If you need any fleet-system expert assistance, just let me know, and I'll round up enough 'volunteers.'"

"Thank you, sir. I have a number of Marine systems personnel who should be able to fill the need, but they might require briefings on the worms they're looking for since you say they're based on an unusual principle."

"Very unusual, General. I'll make sure the systems-security officers on the assigned ships are standing by to provide those briefings."

He once again tried to relax. Unless the star literally went nova without warning, there shouldn't be any other threat capable of endangering his fleet. But as the last Syndic battleship went dark under the fire from Duellos's strike force, Geary called down to the politicians. "You might inform the new Executive Council that if they assure us the surviving warships from the flotilla will not attack, then we will avoid destroying those warships."

Rione smiled humorlessly. "I believe the new Syndic leaders are eager to ensure the continued existence of as many of the remaining warships as they can. Congratulations on your victory, Admiral."

"Thank you. I'm counting on you to turn that victory into peace."

"I'll do what I can."

The next several hours had enough distractions to pass fairly quickly as elements of the Alliance fleet closed on some of the derelict Syndic battleships and began sending over Marine Assistance Teams, which didn't appear to vary all that much in composition, armor, and armament from Marine Assault Squads. "A MAT has a primarily noncombat mission and a MAS has a primary combat mission," General Carabali explained. "Of course, each is configured so that a MAT can switch to carrying out the mission of a MAS, and vice versa."

"Basically, then," Geary said, "they're exactly the same thing with different names."

"No, sir," Carabali replied seriously. "They're different things with exactly the same capabilities. Tactical instructions are very clear on that."

Debating semantics with a Marine who had official definitions on her side didn't seem like a winning way to spend time, so Geary accepted whatever logic was at work and went back to watching the Marines comb through the wrecks of the Syndic battleships. He gave in to temptation a few times and pulled up images from some of the Marines, command and control video that offered the exact view those Marines saw through their helmet visors. But the interior of every Syndic battleship looked about the same, intensive damage having reduced the wrecks to an ugly sameness. Where surviving Syndic sailors were found alive but marooned without working escape pods, the Marines insisted that the Syndics accompany them off the derelicts, which (General Carabali assured Geary) was not at all the same as taking the Syndics prisoner.

"Most systems on the battleships were destroyed, and those that still functioned had been wiped clean when the crew abandoned ship," Carabali eventually reported. "But the fleet-system code monkeys had told us that these unusual worms would not be affected by normal system wipes or sanitizing, and they were right. We found traces of those worms in a number of places."

So Boyens hadn't withheld information about the alien worms. It seemed the Syndics really didn't know about them. "What systems were affected?"

"We can't be certain," Carabali admitted. "The enemy battleships were so shot up that functions had been automatically routed by damage-control routines through any available processor and internal server or network. As a result, we can't isolate which specific subsystems on the Syndic ships were originally infected by the worms."

"Thank you, General. Excellent work."

"Will there be more work for my Marines, sir? Somewhere on a planet's surface?"

"I don't know, General. I'll let you know as soon as I know."

Geary rubbed his eyes again, wishing he could get some real rest. He had retired to his stateroom, but the compartment felt more like a prison than a refuge just then. How long would the politicians talk? The politicians had hauled CEO Boyens out of his confinement to assist them, which might or might not be a good sign.

Calling up a display, he pulled out the scale to see what was happening. Near where the hypernet gate had been, the mass of merchant ships carrying FACs still hung almost motionless, as if waiting for orders even though their mission had been completely overtaken by events and even though there was no longer a hypernet gate through which attackers could arrive to be ambushed. The lone HuK that had arrived via the hypernet gate before its collapse had begun transiting across the edge of the star system toward the jump point for Mandalon, but at a velocity that suggested it didn't expect to receive orders to jump anytime soon.

Captain Smyth on *Tanuki* had been a whirlwind of activity, directing the other auxiliaries to close on the most badly damaged warships and provide extra assistance in fixing the most serious damage.

Geary had spoken to Commander Lavona on *Adroit*, formally appointing her commanding officer until further notice and hinting broadly that he wanted the investigation into Captain Kattnig's death completed very soon and what he expected the results to be. Lavona had seemed more than pleased to follow Geary's lead on the matter. "I don't know why things happened the way they did in the battle, but he was a good officer, Admiral."

"He'll be remembered that way," Geary promised.

Geary watched his fleet move, scanned status reports on casualties and damage and repair status, and waited, feeling oddly impotent for a fleet admiral.

When the summons for his presence in the negotiation room finally came, Geary deliberately paused to check his uniform, then walked with a measured pace through the passageways of *Dauntless* until he reached the secure compartment near the intelligence spaces. Marines stood sentry outside, some of them providing security and some of them the guards who had brought Boyens here and would return him to confinement afterward. Inside the room, the Alliance senators and Syndic CEO Boyens were seated around the table. No virtual presences or active comm screens showed any Syndic leaders or negotiators. Costa appeared belligerent and stubborn, Sakai slightly uncertain, and Rione as usual was masking her true feelings. Syndic CEO Boyens simply seemed depressed.

Rione slid a data unit toward him as Geary took a seat. "We have an agreement. The new leaders of the Syndicate Worlds have signed on to terms essentially matching those the Alliance grand council proposed."

The news was so much at variance with the expressions around the table that Geary had to think through it twice to be sure that he had heard right. "Isn't that good?"

Sakai nodded. "It's very good, Admiral." He frowned a bit, his eyes meeting Geary's. "What you see is in part a sense of disbelief. None of us can quite accept that formal hostilities between the Alliance and the Syndicate Worlds will finally come to an end. War between us has been a fact of life for as long as any of us have lived."

One of the words caught Geary's attention. "*Formal* hostilities?"

"Yes." Costa let the one word drip acid. "The Syndic leaders, the former ones, pushed their planets too hard. The new leaders have confessed that as best they can tell what we saw at Atalia, at Parnosa, and here is happening in pockets all over Syndic space.

Rebellion. Revolution. In some cases anarchy."

"The Syndicate Worlds," Rione continued, "are falling apart. We drove the last nail into the coffin of the Syndicate Worlds when we wrecked the flotilla here. By so doing we eliminated the last major mobile force responding to the orders of central authority."

"It wasn't responding to orders from central authority before you destroyed it," Boyens said in dejected tones.

"Granted. In any event, that flotilla was the last existing means by which central authority might have suppressed the factors tearing apart the bonds that have long held worlds and peoples in check. The process is playing out at varying rates all across Syndic space, but the bottom line is that the new leaders of the Syndicate Worlds no longer control all that used to be the Syndicate Worlds. It will also complicate the return of Alliance prisoners of war, and the fleet may well have to take actions to ensure individual star systems abide by this agreement to return and account for all prisoners."

He finally understood the expressions. "Then the treaty means nothing."

Sakai shook his head. "No, Admiral, it's not that bad. We no longer need fear attack from forces operating under the control of the Syndicate Worlds."

"But the successor powers to the Syndicate Worlds are another matter," Costa spat. "The Syndics here don't have a good handle on what's happening everywhere else in Syndic space, *former* Syndic space, that is, but they do know individual star systems and blocks of star systems are breaking away. They're going to try to maintain the Syndicate Worlds, but the odds of that being anything like the old Syndicate Worlds in terms of size and strength are pretty low."

"None of the successor powers have enough strength to constitute a threat to the Alliance," Sakai said.

"Not yet," Costa replied. "But there are wealthy former Syndic star systems with extensive shipbuilding facilities, the means, in time, to create their own fleets for defense or for conquest."

Geary rubbed his forehead with his palms, thinking it through. "The big war is over, but we have smaller security threats all through Syndic space."

"Which we can't let boil over into bigger threats that might affect the Alliance over time." Costa scowled at the table. "Which isn't to say that a bigger threat isn't still out there." Costa rapped hard on the controls before her. "A Syndic courier ship arrived in this star system not long ago. Its transmission was relayed to us by the new leaders of the Syndicate Worlds, along with a request for assistance. One minute they're trying to kill us, the next they're pleading for help."

An image of a Syndic CEO appeared over the table. Contrary to the outward calm and arrogance that Geary was used to seeing, this CEO appeared to be openly despairing. "We have issued numerous requests for defensive support that have gone unanswered. Now we are in urgent need of assistance. We have received an ultimatum from the enigma race, demanding that humanity totally evacuate this star system."

"Enigma race?" Geary asked. "That's what the Syndics call the aliens?"

Boyens nodded. "It didn't seem to be an important piece of information. If it's any consolation, only three of the new Executive Council members had any knowledge of the aliens before this. The others had never been cleared for the information. That's CEO Gwen Iceni of Midway Star System on the screen, by the way. A decent, good person despite the CEO rank, if you'll accept my judgment of her."

CEO Iceni was still speaking. "The ultimatum doesn't allow any room for negotiation or compromise, and all attempts to contact the enigma race have gone unanswered except for reiteration of the demands. Aside from the fixed defenses within this star system, we have only a few minor mobile combat forces available. The flotilla once maintained in this region is gone, I've been told. Everything else was also stripped from this border and sent to fight the Alliance. Now we have no effective means of defending ourselves, but it's impossible for us to get even half the humans here out of this star system before the enigma race's deadline. We require help, everything you can send. Otherwise, most of the population will still be here and nearly defenseless when the ultimatum expires and the enigma race arrives to seize possession of this star system. We will fight, but we can't hope to win unless we get help." The image vanished, replaced by a plain text document laying out the alien demands along with a deadline, which Geary saw was just over three weeks away.

Rione spoke into the quiet that followed the end of the transmission. "Another thing we feared has come to pass. The aliens are seeking to expand into Syndic space, taking advantage of Syndic weakness."

"Seeking to expand into *human* space," Sakai corrected. "Part of humanity is weakened, but every gain these aliens achieve will come at the expense of all humanity's power to confront them later."

"It's a long way from that border to the Alliance," Costa grumbled.

"That depends how you measure it," Rione said. "In light-years? Yes. In jumps? Still a long distance. But by hypernet? Four weeks' travel time."

"Close enough," Sakai agreed.

Costa frowned some more. "The grand council can consider the situation and decide what to do."

"We don't have time for that," Sakai insisted. "The ultimatum will have expired before we could return from a journey back to Alliance space."

"That's too bad for the Syndics. The grand council—"

"Has already granted Admiral Geary the authority to make decisions regarding confronting the aliens," Rione broke in. "We here can offer him advice, but he has the authority, granted by the full council, to decide on his course of action."

And now everybody was looking at him again. Geary felt a sudden nostalgia for the old days, when he was just another officer, able himself to look toward whoever had gotten stuck with having to deal with whatever mess had arisen. But ever since the Syndic surprise attack at Grendel, ever since the days in Grendel leading up to that attack, everybody had been looking to him. Funny how he hadn't gotten used to it.

He had known that the aliens might move. Now he had a specific situation to deal with, and a fleet that had finally won its war but would soon learn that another enemy needed to be faced.

There was someone else Geary could ask questions of, though, and he turned to face Boyens. "Why there? Why that particular star system? Why do the aliens want it first?"

"Because of where it is." Boyens called up a display of that region of Syndic space, pointing to a star at the border with the aliens. "Midway Star System has that name because it's so well positioned relative to other stars. From Midway, ships can jump directly to eight other star systems. It's an excellent waypoint."

Geary felt his jaw tighten as he studied the display. "Which makes it the defensive hinge for that entire sector, doesn't it? If the aliens control Midway, they can threaten those eight other star systems and force their evacuation. The entire border defense falls apart."

"One of the eight star systems is already under alien control, but that's pretty much right. Too many star systems would be within jump range for us to defend. We'd have to fall back all along the border until we could establish a new line where jump ranges limited the number of star systems directly threatened."

"We?" Costa asked sharply.

Boyens flushed slightly. "I meant the Syndicate Worlds."

"There isn't any Syndicate Worlds now."

"That situation isn't settled yet, especially in places like the border, but if we have to, we'll form a new grouping of star systems along the border. We can't afford to let that area break apart. Individual star systems couldn't muster the resources to defend the region."

"By 'we,'" Rione said, "you mean this time the populations of the star systems in the border area."

"That's right." Boyens glared at the display. "Whatever's left of them after this. Look, I know how you feel about us, and how you feel about me. But we have a common enemy here, a reason to stand together."

"Why are they your enemy?" Sakai asked. "How has the Syndicate Worlds dealt with this enigma race?"

"I don't know everything that's happened," Boyens insisted, "especially in the early years a century ago. I know we've been trying to learn their secrets, but as far as I know, we've never succeeded."

"You provoked them," Costa charged. "And now you want us to save your sorry souls from the fates you brought upon yourselves."

"I don't know everything we've done! But what does it matter? Whatever it was is history, done and gone beyond changing. Now, today, countless innocent humans will suffer if you don't do something."

Rione had been tapping controls softly and finally looked at Boyens. "It appears that if this star system is taken by the aliens, you'll have to abandon more than twenty other star systems in order to reestablish a defensible border."

Boyens stared at the display, then nodded. "Something like that. Several billion people would have to be pulled out."

"Do you have enough shipping to do that?"

"In the border region? No. In all of Syndic space? I don't know. I doubt it. We can't draw on it now anyway."

"What happens to humans left on planets the aliens occupy?"

"I don't know. Nobody knows. There's never been any contact, any evidence, any trace of them. Everything we sent in to try to find out something vanished itself without any trace as well."

No one spoke for a while, then Rione turned her face to Geary. "Do we have a choice?"

"What do you think of that ultimatum?" Geary asked in reply. "Does it match what the other CEO said about it?"

"Yes. Blunt, direct, unequivocal, and not a thing in it that provides any clues to how the aliens think. It could have been drafted by a human."

"Maybe it was, since the Syndics don't know what happened to humans captured by the aliens."

Sakai stared at the text of the ultimatum. "Prisoners? Slaves? Servants? Guests? Pets? If only we knew which of those applied."

"You forgot 'dead,'" Rione said in a quiet voice. "In any number of possible ways. We *need* the answer to that question. Without it, we have no way of knowing if peaceful coexistence is possible."

"Peaceful?" Costa asked scornfully. "Whatever they are, peace seems unlikely. You saw what they did at Kalixa! They're inhuman!"

Rione gazed back at Costa. "I recall some who argued we should use the hypernet gates as weapons despite knowing the devastation they would cause. The former leaders of the Syndics did make such a decision. Were these aliens to turn out to be human, it wouldn't bring me any comfort."

Costa flushed but directed her attention back to Geary. "Well, Admiral, what will you do?"

Give thanks that I never got involved in politics. Outwardly, Geary just gestured toward the ultimatum and the star display. "I want to talk to some of my officers before I make any decisions." He started to get up, then focused on Boyens again. "Is there anything else you can tell us? The more I know, the more likely I am to decide to go to the aid of those people."

"*My* people," Boyens muttered. "I've told you what I know. Except one thing. You've accused us of provoking the enigma race, of causing their hostility toward humanity. I told you that I don't know what the Syndicate Worlds did in the first decades after contact, and that was the truth. But our orders for the last decade at least have been to avoid doing anything that might incite the aliens, anything that might increase tensions or cause problems. I always believed that was because we couldn't afford to fight on two fronts at once. Maybe there was another reason. But we haven't done anything in a long time."

"Perhaps these aliens have long memories," Sakai said.

Boyens stared at him, then nodded. "Maybe. I won't swear nothing happened. But I don't know of anything. Certainly nothing recent."

"There are compartmentalized activities," Rione noted. "Actions kept from the knowledge of even those operating in the same regions. Would you have known of those?"

Geary could see the hesitation in Boyens. He didn't need an interrogation cell to know the Syndic CEO was trying to make up his mind whether or not to lie. But, finally, Boyens shook his head. "No. Not necessarily. But why would anyone have done such a thing?"

"Why did the Syndicate Worlds start the war with the Alliance?" Geary asked.

Boyens met his eyes. "I don't know. I guess they thought they could win. I don't know why they thought that."

"Surely there is speculation among Syndicate Worlds' CEOs as to the reasons?" Rione said.

"Not all that much. It doesn't matter. Didn't matter. It mattered a century ago, when they made the stupid decision to start the war. If we talked about it, that's all we said. It was stupid. But the reasons the war started ceased to matter a long time ago. We were stuck with it, that was all, and nobody knew how to stop it." The Syndic CEO lowered his head, but not before they saw his pained expression. "Believe me, some of us wanted to stop it, but since we didn't know how, we had to keep fighting."

"Thank you. Admiral, will you have your Marines escort CEO Boyens back to his room?" Rione waited until Boyens had left with his escort, then sighed. "My advice is to go to the defense of the former Syndic border. If we let it crumble, and allow these aliens to establish control of numerous former Syndic star systems, the mending may be beyond every capability the Alliance possesses."

Sakai nodded. "This is my advice as well."

"It's not mine. We have bled enough because of the Syndics," Costa declared. "They got themselves into this. They can get themselves out of it."

"And if they fail?" Sakai asked. "Won't the Alliance be forced to deal with the results of that failure sooner or later?"

"The Syndics held us off for a century," Costa said. "If they really want to confront these aliens, they'll do it instead of asking us to clean up their mess. We've lost enough men and women, and plenty of children as well, in this war. We've nearly bankrupted the Alliance. We did that because we had to do it. We *don't* have to get involved in a Syndic dispute with an alien race of unknown motivations and power. We don't have to make a stupid decision to start another war." The reference to the folly of the Syndic leaders a century ago was too obvious to miss.

"If we make the decision now not to go to that star system," Rione said, "then we foreclose other options for dealing with these aliens.

We won't even be able to make direct contact with them unless the Syndics agree to allow that. Going to that star system retains our ability to decide what to do. Not going means leaving events up to whatever the aliens and the Syndics do, and personally, I have no trust regarding either of those parties. The Alliance needs a seat at the table, and that means going to Midway."

"Just our presence may eliminate the alien threat," Sakai agreed. "If they are moving because of Syndic weakness, a show of strength may be all that is required to stop them."

"Read your history!" Costa said. "Countless wars have begun because someone thought a show of strength would be all that was needed!"

"I did not say it was certain to resolve the matter. I suggested that it might deal with the problem. If it doesn't, there will still be alternatives to fighting."

"Do you think an Alliance fleet will back down in the face of a hostile force?"

"That depends," Rione said, "on who is leading that fleet. Admiral Geary has not stated his own thoughts, but he is aware of our own positions now. I suggest that we grant him time to consider our options and consult with his own trusted advisers." She nodded to Geary, as did Sakai, and, after a moment, a clearly reluctant Costa did as well.

Geary nodded back politely, trying to keep his own feelings hidden. He already felt that going to Midway was a necessity but wanted to speak to other fleet officers before deciding, and knew he had to bring up something else. "Did the Syndics provide any clues as to who sent the order to collapse the hypernet gate here?"

Sakai shook his head. "They claimed not to know and said there is no record anywhere within their systems of any such order going out from anywhere, even from the flotilla before it was destroyed."

"Who else would have tried to destroy this fleet?" Costa demanded.

"I think we've just been talking about who else, Senator," Geary said. "A hypernet gate collapses with no sign of a signal sent to it. We've seen it before. It could have happened here, and it could have happened before the catastrophic-fail routines were deactivated. I've confirmed that the Syndic ships have alien worms in their systems. That would have told the aliens we were here, but fortunately not in time for the aliens to collapse the gate before the catastrophic-collapse routine was deactivated."

"Then," Sakai said in a low voice, as Costa stared at Geary, "we are already at war with them, as are the Syndics, even though the great majority of the human race has no idea they even exist."

"Wars can be ended, Senator," Geary replied before he left.

Fifteen minutes later he sat in the fleet conference room, accompanied by the real presence of Tanya Desjani and the virtual presences of Captain Duellos and Captain Tulev. He explained the treaty first, pausing as he saw the reaction sweep through the three other officers.

Duellos closed his eyes for a moment. "I never thought to see this day."

"Too long coming," Tulev murmured. "Far too long coming, but it is here. The witch is singing."

"What?" Geary asked. "The witch?"

"The witch is singing," Desjani repeated, looking as if she were trying to blink away tears. "It means it's over."

"No, the witch is dead means it's over. Or, the fat lady sings means it's over."

Duellos opened his eyes and gave Geary a skeptical look. "The fat lady?"

"Yes."

"What fat lady?"

"I don't know. It's just a saying."

"What witch?" Desjani asked. "Why did she die?"

"I don't know that, either. All I know is a century ago those were separate sayings, and somehow you've combined them."

"Perhaps there was a fat witch who liked to sing," Duellos suggested. He laughed, and so did Desjani. Even Tulev smiled a bit.

Geary understood, then. They were giddy with joy, overwhelmed at hearing that the war would finally end. The Alliance senators had been subdued in their own reactions, concerned by the remaining problems, but then to them the war itself had been a distant thing. Unlike the politicians, the fleet officers had been dealing with the death and destruction firsthand.

But now he had to tell them that while the war might be ending, total peace was still a distant goal.

Something in his expression must have given that away to Desjani, whose smile faded into concern. "What is it? The aliens?"

"Yes, as well as the fact that we're going to have a fragmented region where the enemy used to be. Lots of problems in human space, and the aliens trying to take advantage of that." The levity drained from the other three officers as they listened, replaced by a searching appraisal of the information. "Captain Tulev, I would appreciate your frank feelings on this matter."

Tulev gazed back impassively, giving no outward clue that his entire family, every relation, had died decades ago in a massive Syndic bombardment of his home world. "You ask me if we should aid those who caused so much death and destruction to our own?" He sat for a moment, unspeaking, then sighed. "My ancestors long ago told me to protect others from the Syndics, but to be willing to forgive lest hate destroy my soul as war destroyed all else I once had."

"Tanya?"

"What?" she asked, looking angry now.

"Recommendations. I want to know what you think."

"I think it sucks. Sir." Desjani leaned forward, exhaling in exasperation. "I can't find fault with the analysis. At least twenty star systems. That's a lot, and some of those star systems are prime territory. I wish we knew more about these aliens. How could the Syndics have failed to learn much of anything in a century of contact?"

"It would be nice to know what their weaponry is like," Geary agreed. "Or anything much about their ships."

"I have a bad feeling that we're going to have to find out the hard way, aren't we?" Desjani turned an irate look on him. "The alternative is to allow something we know little about to grab a significant chunk of human territory."

"Yeah." Geary kept his eyes on the representation of Midway Star System floating above the table. "How do you think the fleet will react?"

"It depends what you tell them. Say we're going to help the Syndics? That would go over very poorly."

"Protecting humanity? How would the fleet like that?"

She made a face. "Not as badly, but the humanity in question are Syndics. Same problem. Defend, protect, those are all sort of passive things anyway. This fleet believes in going on the attack."

He nodded. "We're going to kick alien butt?"

Desjani suddenly grinned. "The aliens who messed with humanity. You have to give the fleet reasons to know these enigma whatevers have already threatened the Alliance, that they tried to kill us recently with that hypernet gate." Her smile faded. "But if the fleet thinks this is the prelude to another all-out war, enthusiasm will be very limited."

Duellos had been studying the ultimatum. "Whatever they are, they seem to have a good grasp of human legalese. That document feels like any number of human legal documents I've read."

"That's what the politicians thought, too," Geary said.

"Maybe they've captured some human lawyers," Desjani suggested.

"That might be why they want to destroy us, then," Duellos agreed. "What would we do if alien lawyers descended on us?"

"I think they already have. Maybe all lawyers are aliens."

"I know quite a few who could be."

Desjani snorted, then shook her head. "Admiral, you're asking if we should fight these things. We're already fighting them. They cost us at Lakota, remember?"

"Yeah." He would never forget having to watch as *Indefatigable*, *Defiant*, and *Audacious* sacrificed themselves to save the rest of the fleet. "I guess we owe it to those who died to confront the aliens. One more reason to go."

Duellos nodded. "More than that, this Boyens, you say, is not unredeemable."

"He seems, well, roughly like our own politicians."

"That's not exactly an endorsement," Desjani muttered.

"Nonetheless," Duellos continued, "if we can save the Syndic border region and help the star systems there form their own political coalition to replace the Syndic authorities, we could have a friendly power in that part of space. A minor power, to be sure, but immensely better than the entire border region fracturing into individual star systems."

"Having such a power agree to our assistance would grant us access to the region it controls," Tulev agreed. "This would be vital to the future defense of the Alliance. We must be able to meet with these aliens directly."

"They don't meet with any humans directly," Desjani grumbled.

"Maybe we can change that," Geary said. "You're all in agreement, then?" Duellos and Tulev nodded, then eventually Desjani nodded as well though with a resigned expression. "Thank you. It ought to be interesting when I present all of this at a fleet conference. I really don't know how it will be taken."

"They'll follow you," Tulev stated bluntly. "You led them out of hell. You led them to this moment, when the war will finally end."

"But now I have to tell them that I've withheld critical information from them, information about a serious threat to this fleet and to the Alliance."

Desjani and Duellos hesitated, plainly trying to think of what to say, but Tulev immediately shook his head. "I do not often have the pleasure of telling an admiral he is wrong. What critical information has been withheld? Guesses, suppositions, possibilities. We did not even know for certain that this enigma race existed until the Syndics confirmed it."

"We avoided star systems with hypernet gates because of the threat from them," Geary pointed out.

"We avoided such star systems before we had any idea of aliens, Admiral, because the Syndics could too easily shift forces to them using their hypernet." Tulev waved at the star display. "How would any of your orders to the fleet have been different, how would our path home have been different, if you had never suspected that the aliens existed?"

Geary stared at the display, mentally replaying the long retreat home. "I honestly can't think of anything that would have been done differently. We would even have developed the safe-fail systems to protect Alliance hypernet gates from Syndic attack after we realized the threat a collapsing gate posed to its own star system."

"Exactly. You withheld nothing that would have altered your actions or your orders." Tulev leaned back, smiling thinly for a moment. "You need have nothing on your conscience in that regard."

Duellos raised an eyebrow at Tulev, then nodded. "Captain Tulev is right, Admiral. Even at Lakota we learned of the alien intervention after the initial actions, so that knowledge had no effect on your decisions during the actions."

Geary rubbed one side of his face, thinking. "You've got a good point, but we've scrubbed our warships' systems of those alien worms. Other officers and sailors are rightly going to wonder why we didn't tell them we believed those were of alien origin, and why they were never told that someone suspected that an intelligent alien race existed on the other side of Syndic space."

"No, they won't wonder," Desjani said. "They will assume that our political leaders knew something and never told us. They won't blame you. They'll blame the politicians because that's what they usually do. And how do we know they're wrong to do so? How do we know the Alliance government truly never suspected the existence of these aliens? The Syndics certainly kept it very quiet, keeping most of their own military in ignorance. The fleet won't blame you."

"But—" He paused, thinking that through. Rione had said she had known nothing, and in that he believed her even though Geary was sure she would lie if she thought it necessary to protect the Alliance. But Rione had admitted that the grand council could easily have known things not shared with the rest of the senate. "All right. That's possible." Geary noticed a look on Desjani's face he couldn't decipher. "What?"

She stayed silent, but eventually Duellos sighed. "Captain Desjani stated a truth, that the fleet will not blame you. Not in this. Not in other matters. They believe in you too much. Therefore, someone else must be to blame when something goes wrong. In some matters, that will be the politicians. In other matters, it will be those giving you military advice."

That took a moment to sink in. "You? The three of you?"

"Are you really surprised?" Desjani demanded. "You've heard that clumsy oaf Badaya. As long as I'm doing the right things, you should be happy and aimed in the right direction. Whose fault is it if you're unhappy?" She almost yelled that, then subsided, staring at the table surface, her face red.

"Or if you fail," Duellos added to break the renewed silence. "Nobody expects me to keep you happy, though."

"You are a jovial man, Roberto. Perhaps you should try," Tulev suggested in the closest thing to a joke that Geary had ever heard from him. "Admiral, it is simply the other side of the coin. Many look at us and see those you trust the most. It is a status many envy. But if you fail, everyone will assume we have failed you."

Wonderful. He had tried to avoid showing favoritism, yet his reliance on certain officers for advice had apparently been obvious enough. What else might have been obvious?

Desjani, her gaze still fixed on the table, spoke in hard tones. "I have no fear of being held to account for my professional advice to the admiral."

"Nor should you," Duellos agreed.

Another awkward silence descended, which Geary finally cut short. "Thank you. I'll call the fleet meeting in about an hour and break the news. I'm very fortunate to have had the three of you serving with me."

The images of Duellos and Tulev rendered salutes, that of Duellos almost jaunty, while Tulev's salute was steady and precise, then both men vanished from the room.

Desjani stood up, still not looking at him. "By your leave, sir."

"Of course." There were a million other things he wanted to say, at least several hundred thousand of which would have been catastrophically wrong. He couldn't tell if even one of them would be right.

But she said more, her eyes still on the table's surface. "You haven't mentioned this, but I know you've kept your promise to me. The fleet got home, and the war is over. You made no vow to stick with this, the aliens and the mess that is becoming the former Syndicate Worlds."

"I would not leave now. I know I'm still needed." Geary wondered when it had all changed inside him, when he had realized that fleeing his responsibilities was no longer an action he could regard as honorable or realistic. He couldn't simply carry out one mission and be done with it, because each new mission led into the next missions seamlessly. "I have a duty to the Alliance, and to my comrades in the fleet."

"All of them?"

"All of them. I only wish my being here didn't make it harder on some of those comrades, on one of those comrades in particular, who shouldn't have to endure anything on my account."

"I am not without fault in that. Perhaps what I endure is the price the living stars demand for... things that must remain unspoken." She finally looked directly at him again. "What changed? Why don't you wish to leave?"

He shrugged, uncomfortable with the question. "I'm not sure, but a big part of it was watching people like you, Duellos, and Tulev. None of you had given up, all of you kept doing your duty, even though you'd faced this war since you were born. You are all one hell of a good example of doing the right thing, of sticking to the job no matter what."

Desjani looked away again. "Then... you'll remain in command of the fleet, Admiral."

"Until we return again to Alliance space, then I'll relinquish command of the fleet and my temporary rank of admiral. I'll be available if needed, but for a little while, at least, things will be different."

"You're extremely stubborn. And insane. You know that, don't you?" She moved to leave, then looked back, a small, ironic smile twisting her lips slightly. "Do me a favor and try to look happy."

"Yes, ma'am."

"But not too happy."

It was easy to guess what everyone would think had happened between him and Desjani if he seemed too high-spirited all of a sudden. "Yes, ma'am."

"And stop calling me ma'am. You outrank me."

"Yes, Tanya."

She glowered in exasperation for a moment, then shook her head, apparently couldn't help another smile, and left.

10

There was a sense of relaxation in the fleet conference room, the atmosphere more tranquil than Geary had ever imagined it could be. But why shouldn't the fleet's ship captains feel happy and calm? He knew the rumor mill would have already carried to every ship in the fleet word of the treaty with the Syndics.

Now he had to tell them that the job wasn't done.

Geary stood up, and everyone turned to look at him with smiles, but the smiles grew a little uncertain as they noted his somber attitude. "I expect you've all heard that the new leaders of the Syndicate Worlds have agreed to an end to the war and immediate cessation of hostilities. Verification procedures have been agreed upon. They have also promised to repatriate all prisoners of war and provide a full accounting of those prisoners who died while in Syndic custody."

A wave of joy mixed with melancholy rolled through the men and women facing him. Those who had died in battle could never return, but their numbers would no longer be swelled by new battles. Those thought lost forever to Syndic prisoner-of-war labor camps would be returned, but many others had died of health problems or just old age while awaiting a liberation that came too late for them. Geary heard more references to the witch singing as officers congratulated each other.

"That's the good news," Geary continued, hearing his voice becoming harsher. Well, that reflected how he felt, angry that the end wouldn't end everything it should. "The bad news is that the Syndicate Worlds are disintegrating. We're going to have to deal with long-term problems of successor states, which may need to be dealt with and required to abide by the terms of the treaty."

Commander Landis of *Valiant* spoke as Geary paused. "But we're talking minor actions compared to the war, right, sir?"

"Relatively speaking," Geary agreed. "But a lot of such minor actions, and to someone involved in them, they won't feel minor."

"Policing the decaying corpse of the Syndicate Worlds," Armus grumbled.

Commander Neeson shook his head. "That corpse may spawn some regional powers that are strong enough to worry about. This is a real can of worms, but I guess it was inevitable. The Syndics depended on their warships to keep their individual star systems intimidated, and we needed to destroy those warships to win."

Badaya snorted. "If the Syndics had shown the brains to quit a long time ago, they could have held on to their power. But they pushed it too far, and they're getting what they deserve."

"Scores of star systems like Heradao?" Captain Vitali of *Daring* asked. "The Syndics are certainly going to keep paying a price for this war."

"Regardless," Badaya said, "we have won, and the military threats we face from now on will be comparatively minor."

"Except for one," Geary said. He saw puzzlement, as he adjusted the star display over the table to show the Syndic border region facing the aliens. "The Syndics have admitted to us that an intelligent, nonhuman race exists on the other side of Syndic space from the Alliance, along this border."

The silence was so absolute for a few moments that Geary wondered if he had suddenly gone completely deaf. "What are they?" Captain Duellos asked, in tones as if he, too, had just learned of this.

"The Syndics don't know. These aliens have successfully hidden themselves, maintaining a quarantine so tight that the Syndics have been unable over the course of a hundred years to learn anything significant about the aliens, which they call the enigma race."

General Carabali exhaled loudly. "Let me guess. They're hostile."

"Apparently, though to what extent we don't know."

Badaya finally recovered enough to speak. "What proof did the Syndics provide that this race actually exists?"

"I'll lay it out for you, but one proof has been in our hands. You all recall the discovery in fleet operating systems of worms using quantum probability as their programming. Such worms were beyond our own capabilities to create, and we've now confirmed that the Syndics have no such ability, either. As far as we can tell, they remain ignorant of the existence of such worms, which General Carabali can confirm were recently found in the systems of wrecked Syndic warships here. Those worms must instead have been the work of this race, implanted in our ships so the aliens could track our movements and actions."

"They've been working against us, or just monitoring us?"

"Working against us. They can collapse gates with some kind of remote signal. That's what happened at Kalixa. That's what happened here."

"They tried to wipe us out?" Neeson asked.

"Apparently. Let me lay out everything we've been able to reevaluate in light of our knowledge of these aliens and what the situation is on the Syndic border with the aliens."

He went on, outlining the evidence, showing the Syndic CEO pleading for help, and reporting what little could be said about the aliens' capabilities. When he finished, no one spoke for a long time.

Dragon's captain finally broke the silence. "Are we talking about allying ourselves with the Syndics against these aliens?"

"No." Geary saw some of the tension go out of the men and women before him. "No one has suggested that we agree to defend the Syndicate Worlds. Such an agreement could be too easily twisted." Many nods came in response to that. No one here trusted the Syndics at all. "But stopping an invasion is another matter. We don't know what the goals of the enigma race are, and we don't know where they would stop if the former Syndic border collapsed."

"You're not talking about a threat to the Alliance, are you? That's so distant."

"Four weeks' travel time from the border with the Alliance to the border facing the aliens," Desjani said. "By hypernet."

"Can they use the hypernet?" *Warspite*'s captain asked.

"It's possible," Geary answered. "We have reason to believe that the aliens may in fact have covertly provided the hypernet technology to both the Alliance and the Syndicate Worlds."

Everyone stared again, then Commander Neeson spoke as if to himself. "That would explain... there's so many things about the hypernet we barely understand... and the quantum-probability worms came from hypernet keys, didn't they?"

"Apparently so."

"Why?" Badaya asked, his eyes narrowing dangerously. "Give both sides such technology? What was their game?"

Duellos seemed to be looking into the distance. "The hypernets provided boosts to the economies of the Alliance and the Syndicate Worlds just as the costs of the war were growing too great. They also greatly simplified fighting the war by improving logistics and allowing the rapid transfer and concentration of forces."

"They wanted us to keep fighting?" Badaya leaned back, his face reddening, but his expression thoughtful as well as angry. "Weaken us. Both sides. Set us up for their own takeover."

"That may be what was happening," Geary agreed. "Our intent is to get across to these aliens that such meddling in the affairs of humanity will not be tolerated and that internal conflicts will not prevent part of humanity from striking back at any attempt to invade human space."

"Which may require a battle," Jane Geary said. "A battle against a foe of unknown strength and unknown resources, with unknown weapons and unknown defensive capabilities."

"That's right. But if we don't fight now, we'll have to fight some other time, when we're weaker, and they're stronger. We have a chance to draw a line in the sand at that border, make it clear that they cannot force humanity to retreat."

That went over right. He could see spines stiffen at the idea of being forced to retreat. They believed that they had never retreated from the Syndics. They wouldn't accept the idea of retreating from anyone or anything else.

"You said they've taken Syndic planets before this," Captain Parr of *Incredible* remarked. "Planets with some humans left on them? But we don't know what happened to those humans?"

"No, we don't. Nothing has ever been heard from any humans in areas taken by the aliens." That bothered everyone, he could tell. It wasn't simply fears born of millennia of stories about alien races intent on enslaving or destroying humanity, stories that in recent centuries had come to be regarded more and more as fantasy since no intelligent nonhuman species had been discovered until now. No, Geary thought, it was about leaving people behind. The fleet didn't do that by choice, and if it did, it always vowed to somehow return for those left behind. In practice, those vows had rarely been able to be carried out, but that didn't mean they were any less heartfelt.

Badaya glowered at the star display. "They're Syndics, but they're human. Or maybe they won't be Syndics anymore. They'll hang or shoot the CEOs and set up governments that we can deal with. These star systems that need to be evacuated. The Syndics can't do it, can they?"

"No," Geary agreed. "Not enough ships, not enough time. You know how hard it is to evacuate even one star system, even drawing on all the resources of the Alliance. Millions of people would be abandoned on those worlds."

"Then we need to get there and stop the aliens! They may have been able to mangle the Syndics, but they'll find the Alliance fleet on full attack is a threat beyond their abilities to match!"

A spontaneous roar of approval followed Badaya's words.

After the conference ended, Geary stayed standing, wondering how long the enthusiasm for another offensive action against another foe would last.

Duellos had remained, and shook his head, smiling wryly. "Captain Badaya sees the fleet as a hammer, the greatest hammer humanity has ever fielded. Once he saw the problem as a nail, he was bound to urge the fleet's use."

"Yeah," Geary agreed. "Badaya has given me plenty of headaches in the past, but his direct approaches can be useful." That sounded disturbingly like something Rione would say.

Desjani suddenly laughed. Noticing Geary and Duellos staring at her, she pointed at the star display. "That Syndic CEO at Midway is going to be waiting for help to arrive, expecting the aliens to show up in force at any time, and instead of a Syndic flotilla dashing to the rescue, she's going to see the Alliance fleet come popping out of her hypernet gate. Can you imagine? She's going to bounce so high from shock that she'll clear atmosphere."

It took a few days to get damage repaired as much as possible. In a perfect world, Geary would have sent off the most badly damaged ships on a journey home, but even though the Alliance was manufacturing more Syndic hypernet keys using the data taken from the one on *Dauntless*, none of those keys had been available before the fleet left. Only ships accompanied by *Dauntless* could use the Syndic hypernet, so the damaged ships would have to stay with the fleet, accompanying the auxiliaries. The auxiliaries also distributed replacement fuel cells, missiles, and grapeshot to the fleet, along with the spare parts and repair materials they had been manufacturing.

He could either jump the fleet for Mandalon or back to Zevos, and chose Zevos since that star system had a hypernet gate. Even though the Syndicate Worlds and the Alliance were now formally and technically at peace, Geary still felt like an occupying power as he led the fleet to the jump point, knowing that every man, woman, and child in the star system was watching the Alliance fleet with dread and distrust.

If Desjani was bothered by the scrutiny of distrustful Syndics, she didn't show it. "Back to Zevos through jump space, then by hypernet to Midway. If the Syndic data can be trusted, we'll be cutting it very fine, getting there about a day before the ultimatum expires."

"I don't think the Syndics will complain."

"They'd better not."

He called Carabali. "General, I just want to be sure we've off-loaded every Syndic guest your Marines picked up from wrecked warships."

"Every one of our guests was escorted into repaired escape pods and launched toward safe locations," Carabali confirmed. "The fleet database reported that there is one Syndic still remaining aboard *Dauntless*, but I was informed that he was a special case."

"That's right, General. We're taking CEO Boyens back to his home."

"What about our own POWs here, Admiral?" Carabali asked. "They surely want to go home, too."

"I don't want to load them now," Geary explained. "They'd overcrowd our ships, and there's no sense risking those liberated POWs in combat if we end up fighting the aliens. Once we finish with the aliens at Midway, we'll come back through here to pick up our own POWs from the Syndics and take them home with us. I've talked to the senior POWs to explain that, and the new Syndic leaders know they'd better treat our people very well until we get back." Geary smiled. "I personally told those Syndics that if they didn't take good care of our people, then they'd be getting individual visits from Alliance Marines when we returned."

Carabali laughed for the first time since Geary had known her.

Two and a half weeks later, the Alliance fleet flashed out of the hypernet gate at Midway, farther from Alliance space than any Alliance ship had ever been. They had star charts of that region of space, but none of them had ever expected to sail through it.

The first things that the fleet sensors keyed on were the streams of transports rigged with extra passenger modules, the transports strung along long arcs from the inhabited planets toward the hypernet gate and jump points for other human-occupied star systems. But indications from the planets themselves made it clear that the great majority of the human population remained on them, unable to be evacuated in the time remaining before the alien deadline expired.

There were Syndic warships present, too, but not many. A small Syndic flotilla orbited five light-hours distant from the Alliance fleet. "Six heavy cruisers, four light cruisers, fifteen HuKs," Desjani commented. "That's probably everything they've been able to scrape up in this entire region."

"Captain?" the operations watch-stander called. "Some of those ships show signs of not being fully fitted out. It looks like they were under construction and rushed here before they were finished."

"Their crews won't be worth a damn then. Totally untrained and inexperienced." Desjani turned a yearning look on Geary. "They'd be so easy to blow away."

He raised an eyebrow at her. "I thought you preferred fair fights."

"Well... yes. It doesn't matter anyway. We'd never catch them unless they charged us, and I doubt they're that inexperienced."

"Or that suicidal. In any event, that's not why we're here." As the light revealing the fleet's arrival spread through the star system, panic would spread just as fast through the helpless transports and their human cargoes. Geary composed himself, then tapped his comm controls. "People of Midway Star System, this is Admiral Geary, commanding officer of the Alliance fleet. A peace agreement has been reached between the Alliance and the Syndicate Worlds. The war is over. We are not here to attack. We have come here at the request of the current leaders of the Syndicate Worlds to repel any attempt to enforce demands that this star system be evacuated. I repeat, we are here to repel aggression against this star system. We will undertake no action against any human ship, facility, installation, or person unless we are attacked, and then we will act only in self-defense. To the honor of our ancestors. Geary out."

He ended that transmission, then keyed another, a tight beam aimed at where Boyens said the Syndic main command and control center would be located on the primary inhabited world. "CEO Iceni, this is Admiral Geary, commanding officer of the Alliance fleet. We have come here at the request of your new leaders to assist you in repelling aggression by the enigma race. We request that you immediately send us situation updates and any information regarding the enigma race you have any reason to believe might not have already been made available to us."

Geary gestured to Boyens, and the Syndic CEO stepped into the transmission field. "You know me, Gwen. I was captured when the reserve flotilla was destroyed. It won't be coming back. Everything is gone. The Syndicate Worlds have nothing to send you, but what Admiral Geary says is true. The war is over, and the Alliance has agreed to help defend this star system. Admiral Geary is a man of honor. He can be trusted. Please work with him. It's our only hope to save this star system and the many other star systems that would have to be evacuated if this one falls to the enigma race."

Boyens stepped back, and Geary spoke again. "We request that you order your flotilla and other defensive assets not to take any provocative actions, and ask once again that you provide all information that could be of any assistance to us in defending this star system. To the honor of our ancestors. Geary out."

Desjani was frowning at her display. "We're here. Where do we go?"

"I'd recommend heading over to this region," Boyens suggested, indicating a portion of the star display. "That's on the side of the star system facing the alien territory. If they come in, it will be somewhere around there."

"Thank you," Geary replied. He waited until Boyens had been escorted off the bridge again, then ordered the fleet into a vector toward the region the CEO had suggested.

Then they waited some more, while crews on the damaged warships continued their efforts to repair damage, while the fleet swept onward past Syndic merchant ships crammed with evacuees who were surely watching the Alliance fleet with mixed hope and fear.

The eventual Syndic response came as quickly as transmission times allowed. "CEO Iceni is still here," Rione observed. She was back on the bridge, having once again timed her rotation with Sakai and Costa to try to be present when anything important happened. "I suppose Iceni deserves credit for staying instead of finding a reason to get herself evacuated first."

Desjani mumbled something that sounded like, "Not in my book."

CEO Iceni appeared both confused and shocked. "This is the senior Syndicate Worlds' official in this star system. We were unaware of the signing of a peace agreement, but the documents you transmitted and the authentication with them appear to be valid. Nothing prepared us for your arrival. This is... unprecedented. But... we are... grateful for your assistance. We had no expectations of victory, or of survival. My staff is assembling any information we think could assist you. The primary item we can pass on is that the enigma-race ships are likeliest to appear at the jump point from the star we know as Pele. I have sent instructions to the CEO commanding the Syndicate Worlds' flotilla in this star system to contact you directly and to undertake no actions against your fleet unless attacked themselves. All Syndicate Worlds' defenses have been ordered not to engage your ships.

"I would be grateful if you would grant CEO Boyens the right to transmit communications to me separately."

"Fat chance," Desjani grumbled, then her expression brightened. "We can monitor anything he says and anything she sends."

"Right," Geary said. "Can you set it up, Captain Desjani? Please ensure that Lieutenant Iger is in the loop."

It was almost three hours after that when they finally heard from the small Syndic flotilla. "This is CEO Fourth Rank Kolani, commander of Syndicate Worlds' Flotilla Seven Three Four." Kolani's voice and posture were unusually stiff, lacking the standard false smile and real arrogance of a Syndic CEO. She looked young for her position, but then more experienced Syndic commanders had already been sent to die fighting the Alliance. Her uniform was nicely styled, though, and her hair absolutely perfect. Apparently it took more than this kind of crisis to have an adverse impact on the grooming of even junior Syndic CEOs. "I have been *ordered* to contact you regarding the defense of this star system."

"And isn't she unhappy with those orders," Desjani remarked gleefully.

"I... request," CEO Kolani continued, almost choking on the word "request," "that you provide your... suggestions regarding the deployment of..." She had to pause for a moment. ". . . of both Syndicate Worlds' and Alliance mobile assets within this star system." The Syndic CEO's eyes blazed, and her posture grew more taut. "We are prepared to die in defense of our people. Kolani out."

Desjani's glee had faded into a grudging smile. "That's one tough kid. She'd be fun to trade blows with."

"No doubt," Geary agreed.

"Are you planning on asking them to fight alongside us?"

He glanced at her. "That doesn't strike me as a good idea. What about you?"

"It'd be a horrible idea," Desjani stated firmly. "Going into battle with Syndic warships within weapons range? I don't care what the peace treaty says; I don't care that we're suddenly supposed to be on the same side here. You'd still have a very high chance that any number of Alliance warships would 'accidentally' target those Syndics." She thought, then shrugged. "Actually, in the heat of an engagement they might really target the Syndics just out of force of habit, without deliberate intent to strike at someone we're supposed to be at peace with now. We've spent our whole lives thinking of the Syndics as the enemy, as targets. That won't change overnight."

Desjani held his eyes for a moment, and he saw the message there. *If Dauntless were within range of some of those Syndics, I might do that in the heat of battle, target them because they've always been the enemy. I probably wouldn't do it on purpose, but I probably wouldn't feel bad about it afterward, either.*

So Geary nodded in a way that conveyed he understood both what she had said and what she had not said. "Thank you for your candor. It's very important that I keep hearing things like that. Even aside from the concerns you rightly raised, I don't think having the Syndics operate with us would work. We don't have any procedures in place for that, nothing that would ensure we and the Syndics can follow what each other says and does."

"There's that, too. Are you going to tell her to keep far, far away from us, then?"

"Not in so many words." Geary kept his voice level and expression neutral as he sent his reply to the Syndic flotilla commander. "Thank you for your offer of assistance, but given the recent state of hostilities between our peoples and the lack of mutually agreed-upon operating procedures, the chance of misunderstanding or misinterpretation would be too high. We request that your flotilla assume a position roughly one-third of the distance from this star system's primary inhabited world to the location at which the aliens are expected to appear. This fleet will proceed to an orbit about two-thirds of the distance to the expected alien position. To the honor of our ancestors. Geary out."

Desjani shook her head in apparent disbelief. "I don't know how you can talk to them."

"You mean how I know how to phrase things? I encountered Syndic warships earlier in my career, over a century ago, when we were at peace. I had to learn the wording back then."

"That's not what I mean." Desjani's jaw tightened as her eyes went distant with memories. "I don't know how you can talk to them at all except to threaten or demand. I couldn't. I'm not sure any other officer in the fleet could." She switched her gaze to him, appraising now. "The living stars knew more than we imagined. They knew we'd need you to save the fleet, to win the war, and that we'd also need you now, someone without the bitterness and anger of the rest of us who've been fighting these bastards all of our lives.

Someone who could talk to the Syndics once more."

The mission again. He had hoped with the war over the idea that he had been sent from the past by the living stars would fade quickly. But Desjani had always held fast to her faith, and she wouldn't be the only one who kept seeing the hands of higher powers in events. So Geary tried not to flinch at her words.

But she saw his reaction anyway. "I'm sorry. I know you aren't comfortable with my speaking of it."

"I'm only a man," he reminded her.

"Only?" Desjani grinned. "Yes, sir." He had figured out sometime ago that a simple "yes, sir" from Desjani meant she didn't really agree. But then her grin went away as quickly as it had come. "The point is, you're still needed."

"I can't be the only one who can do certain things, Tanya. Others have to learn because I can't be everywhere, and I won't be around forever."

"Granted." She grimaced. "I'll try."

"You've already done a lot more than try, Captain Desjani, and I appreciate that. All right, another six hours or so, and we'll know what that Syndic flotilla is going to do. We'll be in position before that. If those aliens show up, we'll be ready for them."

"And if they don't?"

"We improvise, Captain Desjani."

She grinned. "Yes, we will."

They were in orbit and waiting when a reply came from the Syndic flotilla. The Syndic CEO in command of the flotilla had the same tight expression as during her last transmission, her words coming out like a prepared script. "The mobile forces of the

Syndicate Worlds in this star system concur with your request. We will proceed to an orbit from which we can react as necessary to events. For the people. Kolani out."

Senator Sakai leaned forward, his expression intrigued. "She used the formal, polite ending to her transmission. The Syndics stopped doing that with us over a generation ago. I only know it from viewing historical records. Perhaps this is a sign that they will be willing to speak to us again in meaningful ways."

Desjani appeared alarmed, then determined. "Not before we do. They will not learn to talk to us again before we learn to talk to them again," she vowed.

And then they waited. The Alliance fleet had taken up an orbit that held it motionless relative to the jump point for Pele. The Syndic flotilla, about a light-hour closer to the main inhabited world, had assumed a similar orbit. The Syndic transports, with their human cargoes of evacuees, kept fleeing, the planets and asteroids of the star system kept in motion around their star as they had for countless years, but the warships waited. The Syndics sent no more messages to the Alliance fleet, and Geary noticed that his own officers seemed to be deliberately ignoring the presence of the Syndics, as if the Alliance personnel preferred defending an empty star system to one occupied by the people they still thought of as enemies.

Restless again, Geary did one of his walk-throughs of *Dauntless*, going down the passageways and exchanging a few words with the officers and crews standing by for whatever might happen. Only one of them, a chief petty officer, asked the question that all of the Alliance sailors must have been thinking. "What are they, Admiral?

These aliens?"

"We don't know," Geary replied. "That's a big part of the reason why we're here, Chief, to find out what they are and what they want."

"Word on the decks, Admiral, is they want a bunch of Syndic star systems."

"It looks like it, Chief. But we don't know where that would stop, or how long it might be before they were knocking on the doors of the Alliance. If they're really hostile, we want to stop them here, before they can strike at our homes."

The chief and the sailors around him nodded. That sort of logic made sense to them. "They had something to do with Kalixa?"

"We think so."

All of the sailors grimaced. "Ugly thing to do," the chief said for them all. "We don't want them trying that with an Alliance star system."

"No," Geary agreed. "We don't want them even thinking they could get away with that."

"Sort of like Grendel, isn't it, sir?" the chief commented. "Only this time it's not the Syndics planning to hit us by surprise. We thank the living stars that you're here, sir, like you were there then." More nods.

"Thank you. I thank the living stars that you all are here with me now." He never knew how to handle things like what the chief had said, but a simple truthful reply seemed best, and the sailors all seemed happy when he walked onward.

Geary thought about the chief's words as he walked, though. In some odd ways, this did resemble Grendel. The Syndic flotilla here was actually fairly close in size to the one that Geary had faced at Grendel along with the officers and crew of his heavy cruiser *Merlon*. But here it had been the Alliance fleet's warships that had arrived in a Syndic star system without warning, proclaiming their peaceful intent, the opposite of what had happened at Grendel. And this time the odds versus the Syndics overwhelmingly favored the Alliance forces; the Alliance actually had been invited here and actually did intend no threat to the owners of this star system. Like Grendel, but very different from Grendel.

The people of today fervently believed that he had won at Grendel even though *Merlon* had been destroyed. He wondered what people a century hence would believe of the coming confrontation, and what price might have to be paid.

Eventually, Geary found himself back on *Dauntless*'s bridge, staring at a display in which nothing important had changed even though the alien deadline had expired hours ago. Desjani, still in her own seat on the bridge, didn't seem to have moved, sitting as intent as a great cat waiting to pounce when her prey appeared. The watch-standers on the bridge reflected the same vigilant tension, their confidence in their commanders and their abilities warring with worries about the unknown. Behind Geary, Senator Costa grudgingly gave up her place in the observer's seat to Rione, who settled silently, apparently unconcerned.

Another hour went by, Geary's thoughts dwelling on the battles he had commanded, on the men and women and ships who had survived and on those who hadn't. His decisions, his responsibility. He remembered the Marine officer Carabali's words. *I'm tired of deciding who lives and who dies.*

Suddenly, they were there, shocking Geary out of his memories. Space that had been empty a moment before was abruptly filled with ships.

Lots and lots of ships.

Geary could feel the tension level on the bridge shoot upward and tried to maintain his own external calm. "Looks like they outnumber us."

"By about two to one," Desjani agreed with an equally composed voice. He wondered if she was feigning her own calm as he was his. Desjani had always seemed to grow more tranquil as the chances for combat grew higher. "They're about two and a half light-hours distant from us, and what looks like an unusual distance from the jump point. Lieutenant Commander Kosti, what do the ship's systems say?"

Kosti, seemingly glad for a chance to focus on something other than the numbers of the alien ships, studied his own displays. "They came in at a much greater distance from the jump point than our ships would. The systems can't tell whether that's because the aliens are using a totally different kind of drive exploiting the jump phenomenon, or if the aliens are using the same sort of drive but getting different results out of it."

Desjani nodded. "Thank you. That means they could have longer jump ranges, too."

"Yes, Captain. Maybe a lot longer. We can't tell, though."

Geary focused back on the aliens, whose armada was arranged in six subformations, each shaped like a disc. The six subformations were combined into two v-groupings, with one subformation slightly ahead of the other two. The two v-groupings were stacked one atop the other, the higher one slightly forward of the lower one. "I can't figure out how they'd fight in that configuration. Is that the best resolution we can get on individual alien ships?" The sensors displayed nothing but vague blobs.

"Yes, Admiral," Lieutenant Commander Kosti replied. "That's all we can see. We can tell a ship is there, but not anything else, not even its size, let alone any details about it. I have no idea how the aliens are managing to conceal something the size of ships that well."

"Get a link to Boyens activated. I want him seeing this but not able to hear us unless we address him directly."

"I told you they have awesome stealth capability," CEO Boyens announced after his virtual presence appeared and took in the information on the displays. He wouldn't actually be allowed on the bridge, not when the prospect of combat loomed. "That's the *best* picture we've ever gotten of the aliens. Sometimes they're completely invisible until they reveal themselves."

"Have you ever seen this many ships before?" Geary asked him.

"No. Nothing close to this." The Syndic CEO's face scrunched up in puzzlement. "Why so many? They couldn't have expected us, the Syndicate Worlds that is, to have very much available to oppose them."

"Do they usually appear to want an overwhelming advantage when dealing with humans?" Rione asked.

"It's really hard to say. There hasn't been that much contact for the last few decades, and no fighting with them that I know of for at least that long."

"We'll see what happens this time," Geary said. Despite the presence of the Alliance politicians aboard *Dauntless*, he felt that he should be the one speaking to the aliens. This looked far more like a military confrontation than it did a diplomatic matter. "This is Admiral Geary, commanding officer of the Alliance fleet, speaking to the unknown spacecraft that have arrived in Midway Star System. You are to identify yourselves and refrain from heading deeper into this star system. We do not desire hostilities, but the Alliance fleet will take whatever action is necessary to repel any attack on this star system."

Rione's face was bleak as she stared at her own display. "So it will be a fight, another war."

"Maybe. I'll try to avoid that."

"I know you will, but they saw us here as soon as they arrived, yet they're still coming in toward the star. I had hoped we could talk to them, but if they outnumber us so much, they may not feel any need for that." On the displays, the alien ships were coming around and heading inward, closing on the Alliance fleet.

"They won't receive my message for another two and a half hours. We'll see how they respond then."

"But they already know we're here, and they've chosen to keep coming."

"Yeah." There wasn't much more he could say about that.

Rione came close to him, almost whispering. "Can you defeat so large an alien armada, Admiral Geary?"

"I don't know. There's too much we don't know about them."

Desjani spoke up, her voice louder than Rione's. "If anyone can beat them, it's Admiral Geary."

Rione kept her eyes on Geary. "I'm in agreement with her again. Sorry."

"Just try not to make a habit of it. It's a little unsettling."

"I don't think you need to worry about that," Rione responded dryly, and Desjani, her own gaze still fixed on her display, nodded.

The alien reply showed up in a little over five hours, revealing that they had taken some time to come up with their response. All three senators were present, hoping to be on the bridge when the historic communication arrived, but since they were behaving themselves, Geary didn't ask any of them to leave.

The alien transmission showed a bridge like that of a Syndic warship, with what seemed to be humans on it wearing totally nondescript outfits. Boyens pointed. "See? It's all fake. Our first transmissions to the enigma race were full video, of course, but they only responded at first in audio, and then only a word or two. Then we started getting images like this from them. We ran some analysis of the bridges we were seeing and were able to identify them as composites of bridges from Syndic ships that had communicated with the aliens. Same thing for the 'humans' we're seeing. They're just digital composites of Syndicate Worlds' personnel."

Geary, studying the depiction of a Syndic bridge, nodded. "It's all old, isn't it? I recognize some of the features of that fake bridge from Syndic warships a century ago. The aliens never updated their images."

"You're right," Boyens agreed. "We've debated whether the fact they didn't change the depiction meant they didn't care whether it gave away their game, or if they somehow didn't realize the old, unchanging bridge image was a giveaway."

The "man" seated in the command chair on the bridge of the alien ship smiled in a perfect re-creation of a Syndic CEO's insincerity. "I wonder if they realize that's an obviously fake smile?" Rione asked in a quiet voice.

"Damned if I know," Boyens replied. "They seem to be better at mimicking false human emotions than they are at mimicking real ones."

"Warships of the Alliance," the human avatar began speaking, his expression now altering slightly in ways not quite matching the tone of his words. The effect was very subtle, just as Boyens had said, but it was definitely there. "Your fleet does not have this star, does not belong to it. Dealings are to be with those who occupied this star but do not have it. Leave this star, and you will have peace. Destruction will be inflicted on any who remain here. By long-ago agreement, this star is ours to have."

Geary glanced at Boyens's image, who shook his head. "Not any agreement the Syndicate Worlds made with them."

"They could be meaning that it's theirs by divine mandate or something," Rione said. "Or that they laid some claim to this area themselves a long time ago, long before they could actually extend control over it." She looked at the other two senators. "A claim they don't want to fight matched by threats of what will happen if we don't do as they say."

Costa looked angry. "They want the sort of peace that comes when we comply with all of their demands."

"I agree," Sakai said. "Though that may be merely a display of aggression to open the discussion."

"Maybe. Do you think they're confused by our presence here?" Geary asked.

The three senators considered that, then Rione nodded. "It

may not be confusion, but they seem to be wanting to deal only with the Syndics."

"Because of the worms in Syndic ship systems, the aliens must have gotten used to being able to track human ships. Maybe they were really surprised to see us here and are trying to bluff us into leaving. It doesn't hurt us to keep talking and see if they back down when we don't back down." Geary thought for a moment, then tapped his controls. "This is Admiral John Geary of the Alliance fleet. The war between the Alliance and the Syndicate Worlds has ended. We have been asked to assist against any threat to this star system. There was never an agreement to turn this star system over to you. We do not recognize the legitimacy of your ultimatum. We do not seek a fight with you, but we will repel attacks against this star system and any other star system occupied by humanity or within the borders of those regions of space occupied by humanity. Pull back your forces, so we can discuss sending emissaries to negotiate with you and establish terms for peaceful coexistence between our peoples. To the honor of our ancestors. Geary out."

"Fat chance they'll withdraw," Desjani muttered.

"Yeah, but I had to give it a shot."

Since the alien armada kept on course toward the Alliance fleet at a steady velocity of point one light speed, the answer took less than four hours. This time, though, the first part of the reply took the form of what seemed to be a demonstration of capabilities.

The alien formations abruptly swung upward, then to the side, then back onto their original vectors, every ship moving in perfect synchronization. The speed of the maneuvers and the rapidity of the changes in direction were impressive and frightening. Geary blinked at his display. "Did they really just do that?"

"Yes," Desjani replied, gazing at her own display, her jaw so tight that Geary could see the muscles standing out.

"Captain," the engineering watch-stander reported in a hushed voice, "the alien spacecraft appear to have propulsion systems with significantly higher mass-to-thrust ratios than our own. They must also have inertial dampers capable of performance an order of magnitude better than ours."

The other watch-standers on the bridge were watching their own displays, sudden unease obvious in their postures and expressions.

Desjani relaxed herself with an effort of will that Geary found as remarkable as the alien maneuvering capability, then turned casually to look at the weapons watch-stander. "Can we hit them?"

"Captain?" The watch-stander took a moment to absorb the question, then ran a hasty check of his systems. "Yes, ma'am. Our fire-control systems can handle targets maneuvering the way the aliens just did."

"How about the specters?" Desjani asked, still relaxed.

"Yes, ma'am. If we fire them within the right envelopes." As the watch-stander answered her, he was visibly calming, too, as were all of the other personnel on the bridge.

"They can't outrun specters or hell lances," Desjani observed.

"No, ma'am," the combat watch-stander agreed, grinning by then.

"They can dance all they want, then," she concluded, then surreptitiously winked at Geary as the watch-standers smiled and turned back determinedly to their displays.

He gave her an admiring look in response and leaned close to speak quietly. "You are one hell of an officer, Captain Desjani. Well done. Do you want to broadcast that observation to the fleet?"

Desjani smiled. "I don't need to. The bridge watch is busy passing it on right now. Sometimes the informal comm channels work to our benefit."

He settled back, willing himself to match Desjani's nonchalance, knowing that every eye was on him. He wondered how well the aliens could evaluate such human emotions. Would they see calm and confidence, or arrogance and obliviousness, or nothing they could understand at all?

"Another transmission," the comm watch reported. "The transmissions are assessed as coming from the leading subformation on the bottom of the alien formation."

The aliens' human avatars seemed stiffer this time, their expressions sterner. "Leave. Leave this star. You do not have this star, Admiral Geary. Dealings only are to be with those of the Syndicate Worlds. Your fleet is to leave. Destruction will be certain if you fight. Negotiations will be allowed when what we have has been left by Syndicate Worlds."

"Admiral?" the communications watch announced. "We have another message from the Syndic CEO in charge of this star system."

CEO Iceni appeared now, obviously trying to project calm. "Admiral Geary, the enigma race has informed us that they will not deal with you and demanded our immediate surrender of this star system. I have chosen not to reply to them. Given their numbers and their communications, it appears the enigma race is resolved to fight to gain control of this star system. I do not know under what terms you agreed to come assist in the defense of this star system, but by confronting the enigma race, you have satisfied your own honor. We will not ask you to fight a hopeless battle on our behalf. If you choose to withdraw now, none can fault you. We ask only that you do what you can during your withdrawal to keep the enigma ships focused on your fleet so that as many of our evacuation ships as possible can escape."

Desjani broke the silence following the message. "She thinks we'd *run*?" Her outrage seemed to match that of the other fleet personnel on the bridge.

But Geary understood. "The aliens must have sent her a message at the same time they sent the first one to us. She has no reason to believe we want to die defending Syndic people in a Syndic star system, but she's not faulting us for that."

"Who does she think we are?" Desjani demanded. "This fleet does not *withdraw*."

Actually, it had, at least under Geary's command, run from the initial trap in the Syndic home star system and many times afterward. But he knew what Desjani meant, and it heartened him that her attitude probably would match that of other fleet personnel when they heard that the Syndics had given the fleet an opportunity to withdraw honorably. They might not be thrilled about defending Syndics, but if the alternative was fleeing battle, they would rather fight.

Rione was frowning at Desjani in surprise and calculation, then speaking quietly to the other senators.

Geary gave Desjani a grim smile. "No. We're not going to run." It didn't make any sense, of course. The aliens grossly outnumbered them, and the alien capabilities were unknown but likely to be superior to those of the humans as just demonstrated with their maneuvers. But it was unlikely that a stand anywhere else would

VICTORIOUS

face different odds. Instead, the odds would get worse as the aliens seized more and more human star systems, gaining strength as they weakened humanity. *Might as well see if we can hurt them bad enough here to make them stop here. How bad will that have to be, though?*

He called the Syndic CEO back first. "Your concerns for the welfare of our personnel are noted and welcome, but we have made a commitment to repel aggression against this star system and will not waver from that commitment. We intend to fight if necessary, and we intend to win. I do have some experience with seemingly hopeless situations, and assure you that they are not always so hopeless as they seem. I repeat, the Alliance fleet will fight here if that is required of us. To the honor of our ancestors. Geary out."

Now the aliens. "The fleet will not leave this star system until your ships have left. You will deal with us, or you will fight us. We will not yield this star system. Your ships will not be allowed to proceed past this fleet. We wish to talk, but we will fight if we must."

Geary paused then, thinking, before tapping his controls again. "All units in the Alliance fleet, our communications with the ships of the alien race have so far produced no results. All units are to prepare for combat. Whatever these beings are, they're going to be sorry if they tangle with the Alliance fleet."

The senators were arguing, speaking in whispers but obviously agitated, as they debated, drawing annoyed glances from Desjani and the bridge watch-standers. "Do you wish to carry out your discussion in another location?" Geary suggested to the politicians.

"It doesn't matter," Rione replied with a sour look at the other two senators. "We have no better ideas of how to deal with this than you do."

"Must we fight?" Sakai asked.

"Senator," Geary answered, "I don't want to fight these beings, not facing these odds. But I don't know what else to do if they keep coming. They have to learn that humanity will fight to prevent further atrocities like that at Kalixa."

"Having our fleet wiped out here won't advance the interests of the Alliance," Sakai said, as Costa nodded in emphatic agreement. "It appears this enigma race won't be deterred."

Geary was searching for the right reply when Desjani lowered her brow in thought. "Reserve flotilla."

He stared at her, trying to figure out Desjani's meaning, then it hit him. "The aliens didn't attack, didn't try to claim this star system, when the Syndics had the reserve flotilla defending this region. The border region was stable for decades while the reserve flotilla was here."

"And," Desjani added, "that reserve flotilla was weaker than this fleet."

Costa and Sakai were glaring at Desjani, but Rione nodded slowly. "They could be deterred, it seems. Why was that if they had this number of ships on hand to attack?"

Alerts sounded, and Geary stared again, this time at his display, as more alien ships suddenly appeared, not at the jump point but with the armada. Three more subformations were abruptly there with the first six, forming another v, this time above and slightly ahead of the first two v's.

Just like that, the odds against the Alliance fleet changed from two to one, to three to one.

11

Geary turned on Boyens's virtual presence. "Explain how the aliens did that."

The Syndic CEO avoided Geary's eyes. "It's happened. Not in my personnel experience, but I reviewed the records of earlier encounters. I told you, sometimes you can't see the alien ships at all until they reveal themselves. Syndic ships didn't even see the alien ships, not even those vague blobs, until they suddenly appeared nearby and opened fire."

"When were you planning on telling us about that alien tactic?" Geary demanded.

Boyens met his gaze. "The records from our destroyed ships were fragmentary and could have been inaccurate. But I wanted you to come here and fight them. If I'd told you they could do that, would you have come?"

"I need to know such things if I'm going to fight them!" Turning his back on the Syndic, Geary looked to Desjani. "Okay. It's worse."

She nodded, outwardly unmoved by the multiplication of the threat. "We can hit those subformations, the ones on the top edges, wear the aliens down."

"We can try." Left unsaid was that the aliens appeared significantly more maneuverable than human warships, which would immensely complicate that tactic. He called up a simulator window and started working on formations to counter the alien numbers and confuse their reactions to him, settling on five subformations of his own. By maneuvering them against the flanks of the aliens, he might be able to—

"Another message from the enigma-race ships."

More time had obviously passed than he had realized. The human avatars of the aliens seemed smug by then as well as stern. "Warning is final. Leave. Dealings will be only with Syndicate Worlds. Destruction awaits Alliance fleet if it remains. You do not have this star. Leave. Warning is final."

Senator Sakai threw up his hands. "How can we negotiate if they just keep repeating their demands?"

"They don't want to negotiate," Costa snapped. "Admiral Geary, the situation clearly calls for this fleet to... to... reposition. Its destruction defending a Syndic star system would be a betrayal of the Alliance people."

Geary could sense that everyone else on the bridge had suddenly held their breath, but he felt only a sense of ironic amusement at Costa's words. "Senator, are you accusing me of treason?"

"I did not say that, but—"

"I have been entrusted by the entire grand council with command of this fleet, and I intend living up to that trust," Geary continued, his voice hardening. "Now, I have an engagement to plan, and I would appreciate no further interruptions unless they are of a constructive nature."

Behind Costa, and out of her sight, Rione twisted her mouth in a half smile.

Sakai just kept staring wordlessly at the displays.

Costa reddened but stayed silent, as neither of the other two senators sprang to her defense.

Everyone else started breathing again, and Geary turned to focus back on the approaching armada. They were down to a single light-hour's distance. "Let's get our speed up." He ordered the fleet to accelerate to point one light speed onto a vector aimed at intercepting the alien armada. "About five hours to contact."

"About that," Desjani agreed cheerfully. Geary's putdown of Costa seemed to have put Desjani into particularly high spirits. "There are a lot of them," she added, as if commenting on the weather.

"Yeah."

"Why are they bothering warning us off?"

Geary looked at her. "What?"

"Why didn't they just attack? They outnumber us three to one, if there aren't more of them hidden, and if the hypernet gates and worms are any indication of their technology, their weapons must be at least as good as ours. They could have kept their numbers hidden until they hit us. But they're trying to get us to leave instead of fighting."

Geary frowned at the question. "We're back to Duellos's riddle. Feathers or lead? The unsolvable riddle where the answer changes whenever the demon wants it to change. How can we come up with the right answer when we don't understand the aliens asking the question and don't even know what the question really means to them?"

She shrugged in reply. "They're giving us a chance to leave without fighting," Desjani repeated. "They're *trying* to get us to leave without fighting. But they proved they can be totally ruthless when they collapsed the hypernet gate at Kalixa. So why are they being nice now? It looks like their ships can be totally undetectable by us. If I was them, I'd be charging in and making sure the other side learned not to mess with me again. I would have kept my numbers hidden, my arrival hidden, until I was in among the enemy ships, then opened fire without any warning, just like they've done in the past to the Syndics."

He leaned forward, frowning more heavily, letting Desjani's statements run through his mind. It was odd. Yes, they were dealing with something that didn't think like humans did, but still seemed to be plenty merciless when it wanted. They didn't know the aliens' motivations, but nothing the aliens had done so far seemed outright irrational to humans even though examples like Kalixa showed that the aliens were definitely not merciful when it came to dealing with humans. The aliens seemed pragmatic, in the most cold-blooded sense of the word. Which didn't make them demonic, it just made them self-interested, and humanity didn't have a lot of room to criticize any other intelligent race in that regard. But Desjani had put her finger on the big question and focused Geary's attention there as well instead of just on the looming threat of the alien armada. Why would a pragmatic race of aliens capable of ruthless acts show mercy to a human fleet they might have to face again someday?

If they were human, and offering the Alliance fleet this kind of escape, he would wonder why. What possible reasons could he consider? "If they want us to leave instead of destroying us, why?"

"I asked first," Desjani replied. "I think we can assume they don't have any moral qualms about destroying this fleet."

"Not after they tricked us into building the hypernet gates, destroyed Kalixa, and tried to destroy the Syndic home star system while we were there, no."

"And, they didn't attack when the Syndics had the reserve flotilla here," Desjani repeated.

True enough. "Meaning that flotilla was probably strong enough to concern them even though an alien fleet of the size we're looking at could have easily overwhelmed the Syndic reserve flotilla. Which means we're strong enough to concern them even if it doesn't look that way to us."

"Then," Desjani concluded, "maybe they're not as strong as they look, maybe they're more concerned about being able to win than the odds indicate."

That made sense, but why would the aliens be concerned when they had that many ships? Fear of casualties? But the aliens had fought the Syndics more than once. Maybe it was like the hypernet gate at the Syndic home star system. They were seeing something but not knowing what it meant. Like a Trojan horse of some kind. For some reason Geary didn't understand, his mind kept fixing on the phrases he and Desjani had been using. *It doesn't look that way... maybe they're not as strong as they look...* "Look." Why was his mind telling him that word was important?

It shouldn't be. No one was actually looking directly at the aliens.

Every observation came through the fleet's sensors, and those sensors were very good, able to see much, much farther and much, much more clearly than any human eye could. Syndic sensors differed in small ways but were basically the same, and the Syndics had been trying to find out more about the aliens for decades, with no success to show for it.

Desjani must have been thinking along the same lines. She was frowning heavily at her display as she raised one hand and pointed her finger at it. "It looks like we're badly outnumbered."

"That's what our sensors are telling us."

"But what our sensors are telling us doesn't make sense given everything else we know, given how the aliens have acted in the past, given how they're acting now. If this picture is right, then everything else we know has to be wrong."

He knew where she was going, toward the same conclusions Geary's mind had been developing. "The Syndics *think* they know some things about the aliens, and what they think they know has driven their conclusions about what the aliens can do." Like Boyens, certain that the aliens couldn't have been responsible for collapsing the hypernet gate at Kalixa. Like the Syndics at the home star system, who had been unaware that their warships carried alien worms. "But we didn't start our analysis of the aliens thinking we knew some things about them. Everything we think we know came from new observations, from learning and watching events, and I'd swear on the honor of my ancestors that our conclusions about the aliens and their actions, what we believe we know, isn't wrong. So if those are all correct..."

"The picture we're seeing has to be wrong," Desjani concluded.

A Trojan horse. An unseen threat hidden within. And his attention, along with that of every other officer, was focused externally, on the alien armada. "We've scrubbed every one of our warships' systems of those alien worms, right?"

Desjani nodded. "It's part of the normal system security routines now."

"Have we scrubbed our systems since we arrived here?"

She gave him a grim smile, then turned. "Lieutenant Castries, find out the last time the ship's systems were scrubbed for quantum-probability worms."

A startled Lieutenant Castries hastily checked. "Two days ago, Captain."

"Before we first saw the aliens," Geary commented.

Desjani nodded, her lips drawing back to expose her teeth in what wasn't really a smile anymore. "Lieutenant, order the ship's security personnel to run another detection routine, in *all* ship's systems."

"*All* ship's systems? Now, Captain?"

"Half an hour ago, Lieutenant."

"Yes, ma'am!"

As the lieutenant raced to notify the systems-security officer and run the system scrub, Desjani gave Geary a sidelong glance. "They activated new worms."

"I'll lay you odds."

"In the sensor systems. And the analysis systems. And the display systems."

"Yup."

"Because we have no idea how they create those worms. They could be somehow dormant and undetectable until an alien ship arrives and sends an activation signal. And if their ability to track the fleet was any clue, that activation signal moves faster than light, so those worms would have been activated before we even knew the aliens had arrived. All we would have ever seen was what they wanted us to see."

Geary nodded. "It's like you said, why aren't they attacking when the odds favor them so much?"

"Because the odds aren't what we think." She looked into his eyes, grinning, and he felt it, too, the unparalleled feeling when someone else is totally in sync with you, filling in some parts of a puzzle while you fill in the rest, two minds working perfectly together. Her smile turned rueful. "We're one hell of a team."

"That we are." He left it at that, and they both waited until a window popped up between them and a startled systems-security officer reported in.

"Captain, Admiral, we found a bunch of quantum probability worms in the systems. Combat, sensors, maneuvering, analysis. Just ugly as all hell. I have no idea where they came from or what they're doing, but we're getting rid of them."

Geary's display flickered, then updated, wavered again, updated once more, each time large numbers of alien ships simply vanishing, the alien fleet dwindling as fast as the worms were wiped from *Dauntless*'s systems. The alien ships that had recently appeared from nowhere vanished completely, while the great majority of the alien ships in the lower two v's also disappeared.

Desjani's fierce grin was now definitely a ferocious snarl. "We can *see* them."

The blurring that had kept even the shapes of the alien spacecraft hidden had vanished, revealing that every alien ship, regardless of size, had roughly the same shape, blunter and more rounded than the human warships. If the human ships were sharklike, the alien craft more closely resembled spiny tortoises. "I'll be damned. No wonder the alien stealth system always fooled the Syndics so well. It wasn't anything on the alien ships. It was alien worms altering the picture the Syndics' own sensors were seeing."

"Good work, Admiral Geary."

"I never would have seen it if you hadn't pointed me in that direction." He grinned back at her. "One hell of a team, Captain Desjani."

Boyens had noticed the changes and was staring at the displays, his mouth hanging open. "What did you do?"

"For now, that's our secret." He imagined they would have to share with the Syndics how to find and neutralize the alien worms, but at the moment enjoyed leaving the Syndic CEO in the dark. "The bottom line is that far from being badly outnumbered, we actually outnumber them two to one."

Desjani was speaking again, still smiling, though now in a somewhat bone-chilling way. "The Syndics said they could hardly ever hit an alien ship, and when they did it had no effect. But if their weapons systems and combat systems and sensor systems all had those worms in them, the worms probably misdirected the Syndic shots to avoid hitting real alien ships, and of course when a shot hit a fake ship, nothing happened. The aliens aren't invincible, and now we can hit them."

"Do we have to?" Rione asked. She had taken in events, figured out what had happened, and by then stood close to Geary. "We can let the aliens know we've discovered their worms, that we can clearly see and shoot at their ships. When they know that, surely the aliens will back off and agree to talk."

"Will they?" Desjani asked the air. "Or will they spring another trick, one we haven't figured out how to counter?"

"That's a real concern," Geary agreed. "Madam Co-President, these aliens caused the collapse of the hypernet gate at Kalixa. They've got a lot of human blood on their hands."

"I'm not disputing that," Rione replied. "But I don't see any virtue in leading them to spill more human blood if we can avoid that. If we spill a lot of their blood, it may trigger a feud between our races, one beyond our ability to put a stop to."

Desjani stayed silent this time, but the fingers on one of her hands lightly drummed the arm of her seat near her weapons-targeting controls. Her advice didn't have to be asked.

But Rione had a good point. Would killing a large number of the aliens deter further aggression or encourage it? They simply knew too little about how the enigma race thought. Or did they? "The aliens didn't seem too worried about how we'd respond to their actions." Rione gave him a questioning look. "Betraying the Syndic leaders at the start of the war, if our guess is right. Tricking humanity into placing the hypernet gates in our most important star systems. Diverting the Syndic flotilla to Lakota so this fleet was almost destroyed. Deliberately collapsing the hypernet gates at Kalixa and the Syndic home star system."

"What's your point?" Rione asked.

"That the aliens haven't acted as if they feared us retaliating for their actions against us, as if they feared giving us grounds for a blood feud. But anyone examining the history of humanity, or the course of the war we just ended, could have easily seen how humans strike back and retaliate for provocations and attacks."

Desjani gave him another sidelong glance. "They don't think in terms of retaliation?"

"They don't seem to have expected it from us, or maybe they didn't fear it."

Rione eyed him, her thoughts hard to read. "You're trying to determine how they think by how they've acted."

"That's all we've got to go on. What do you think?"

She took several seconds to answer. "I want to find a reason to reject your argument, and I can't, unless, as you suggested, they simply don't fear retaliation from us. Even that would imply a level of arrogance that needed to be countered for our own security. But, if you're right, will the aliens even understand our own actions?"

"Maybe if we phrase it differently." Geary turned to CEO Boyens again. "The Syndics keep saying this is their star system. That they 'have' it. Does the enigma race seem to understand the concept of defending its own territory?"

Boyens laughed harshly. "You might say that. Look what they're doing now. They're not saying, 'Give us this star system because we want it.' No. They're saying, 'This star system is ours so you must leave.' They're justifying their actions by saying this star system is theirs, and we're not allowed on their property."

"That's consistent with their past behaviors and statements?" Rione asked.

Boyens paused to think before replying. "As best I can recall, yes. This is ours, you have to leave. This is ours, stay out. That sort of thing."

"They're territorial."

"Yes. Extremely territorial. We, the Syndicate Worlds, that is, have tended to view their actions as focused on security, on keeping us from learning anything, but the same actions could just as easily have been manifestations of an extreme no-trespassing attitude."

"Thank you." Rione faced Geary, her expression uncharacteristically openly discontented. "It all matches. I wish it didn't. The aliens leading this armada don't seem to be able to grasp why we're here, in a Syndic star system, and why we haven't simply left when told to do so. The aliens don't understand our motivation, because this isn't *our* star system. To them, we should have no reason to defend something we don't own. On the other hand, they believe that they can simply assert ownership and force humans to leave star systems we've occupied for some time. In light of your assessment, Admiral, and that of CEO Boyens, it appears the best course of action is to carry out a vigorous defense of this star system, to establish in the minds of the aliens that we consider any human-occupied star system to be our own territory."

Desjani shot a surprised glance at Rione before recovering and appearing to concentrate on her display again.

The other two senators stepped forward and began arguing with Rione again, but she led them toward the back of the bridge, away from Geary.

"All right, then," he said to Desjani. "Let's give those enigmas a bloody nose so they know we can be just as territorial as they can."

"Do we claim this star system, too?"

"Not in so many words. Sorry."

"We could use it," Desjani pointed out. "Nice, convenient access to the border with the aliens. It's not like the Syndics won't owe us if we kick alien butt back to Pele."

"Are you serious or just high on the idea that we're heading into battle with these creatures?"

She seemed to ponder the question before answering. "Half and half. It's a nice star system from a military perspective, Admiral. Very nice."

"Maybe we can work out an agreement with the Syndics here, assuming they're still Syndics once the Syndicate Worlds finishes falling apart." He bent back to his display, thinking. "We have to go in carefully, approaching in such a way that it seems we're still being tricked by the alien worms, then shift at the last moment and hit some of their real ships."

Desjani nodded. "Lieutenant Yuon, can you superimpose the fleet sensor picture over the picture from *Dauntless*'s own sensor analysis?"

"Show both at once, Captain?"

"Yes, but keep them isolated from each other."

"The net isn't set up to do that, just the opposite in fact in terms of integrating data from all sources, but it can be done, ma'am. It'll take a little work, though."

"How long?"

"Five minutes, Captain."

"Do it." Desjani smiled at Geary. "The rest of the fleet's ships have systems clouded by the alien worms. We can use them to get a picture of what the aliens think we're seeing."

He nodded. "Yes, but we can't leave most of our ships with those worms active. The worms will mess up the targeting systems, too. We'll need to have the majority of the fleet's ships sanitize their systems and leave just a few to provide the distorted view."

"The auxiliaries? They don't have much armament, anyway."

"That seems like a nasty trick to play on the engineers, but that's a good idea. None of the alien ships should get close to the auxiliaries, so they'll be safe even with the worms clouding their sensors. Let's set it up."

The tactical problem had changed. Instead of avoiding the mass of alien ships, he had to aim to hit them hard on the first pass, before the aliens realized that their worms were no longer distorting the sensor and combat systems on the Alliance warships.

"We finally got some information from the Syndics," Desjani informed Geary. "There's not much there."

He checked the transmission, finding that Boyens's use of the word "fragmentary" to describe the surviving records from destroyed Syndic ships was, if anything, optimistic. The aliens had apparently taken pains to pound such ships into scrap. But Geary studied what was there. "Tanya, while I'm working on the engagement plan, I want you to analyze these yourself and run them past the combat-systems people. My impression from the records is that the alien weapons are not as superior to ours as their propulsion systems seem to be. I'd like to know whether you agree."

"We're on it, Admiral."

He focused back on planning, surfacing only long enough to hear Desjani report that she and everyone she'd consulted had the same impression of the alien weapons. "Maybe more range, maybe more power, maybe not. Basically particle beams, lasers, and kinetic projectiles."

Alien they might be in thought and form, but the enigma race was bound by the same fundamental rules of how the universe worked. Certain weapons made sense given certain levels of technology. Maybe the aliens also had null-field weapons, but that didn't seem likely since null fields could have been used to totally destroy all traces of knocked-out Syndic ships.

Finally happy with his plans for the engagement, Geary sat back with a heavy exhale of air. "How far off are they?"

"Seventeen light-minutes," Desjani answered.

"That close?"

"I would have interrupted you to tell you when they reached fifteen light-minutes."

"Thanks. I want the aliens to think they know what we're going to do, so we're going into our combat formations early. Take a look at my plan before I send it."

She spent several minutes doing that, then nodded. "You're pretending to be aiming at the actually nonexistent top formations of alien ships. How do you know the second layer of alien formations will turn up like this?"

"If their weapons aren't too much superior to ours, they'll have to. They'll be assuming we're going to strike at the fake ships in the top layer, so they'll want those fake ships to stay within range of our weapons so we waste our shots. But they also want their second-layer ships to be close enough to us to hit us as we pass. That should require them to maneuver like I'm estimating."

"That's a lot of assumptions," Desjani cautioned.

"I know, but I'm basing them on what we know."

She grinned. "They certainly won't expect us to maneuver the way you're planning on. It would be pure suicide if all of those alien ships were real. They're going to be making a lot of assumptions, too. I think it's good. It looks like a plausible approach if every alien ship were real. And they don't have experience with you, so they won't know how atypical it is for you to set up your combat formation this early."

"Good." He hesitated just a moment, knowing how much was riding on his assumptions. There was no way to fight this battle without facing risks, though. "All units in the Alliance fleet, this is Admiral Geary. Maneuvering orders are being sent to you now. Execute Formation Merit at time four zero. Geary out."

At time four zero the Alliance fleet split, forming into four flattened discs with the thin edges facing the oncoming aliens. Three of the discs were even with each other, side by side in a line facing the enemy, and each of those held about one-third of the Alliance fleet, eight battleships and seven battle cruisers in the subformations to either side of the main body, while the main body contained nine battleships and six battle cruisers. That had required splitting up the three *Adroit*-class battle cruisers in the Fifth Division, but Geary had decided that it made more sense to pair the *Adroits* with formations of bigger, more capable battle cruisers rather than keep them in their own division. The heavy cruisers, light cruisers, and destroyers were distributed roughly equally among the three subformations, their own positions bolstering the protection of the more badly damaged but combat-capable Alliance warships in the fighting formations.

Above the three fighting formations and hopefully out of direct danger, a much smaller disc held the five auxiliaries, the battle cruiser *Agile*, and the other warships too badly damaged to be in the front line of battle.

Geary waited until the subformations had settled out, then adjusted the fleet's course slightly to aim the three fighting subformations directly at the three imaginary alien formations on top of their armada. As Desjani had said, it looked plausible, since each Alliance subformation roughly matched the size of the alien subformation it was aimed at, as if the Alliance fleet were trying to engage only a portion of the aliens at a time to negate the apparent huge alien advantage.

He could tell that Costa was burning to ask what he was doing, but Sakai remained impassive, offering no support for that, and Rione had a look of calm confidence that implied that she knew what was happening.

"The enemy is five light-minutes distant. Estimated time to contact is approximately twenty-five minutes."

Sakai shook his head. "The Alliance's first encounter with an intelligent, nonhuman race, and we must refer to them as the enemy."

"It's not by our choice," Rione reminded him. "But if Admiral Geary chooses to offer the aliens one last chance to veer off and avoid battle..."

Desjani flicked a sour look back at the politicians, but Geary shrugged. "It doesn't hurt to say it again." He tapped the broadcast control again. "To the armada of nonhuman ships proceeding through this star system. You will not be allowed to pass this fleet without a fight, you will not be allowed to attack humans or human property within this star system, you will not be allowed to seize control of this star system. Veer off now and return to the vicinity of the jump point from which you arrived if you wish to avoid senseless loss of life. To the honor of our ancestors. Geary out."

"Do we have to keep offering them outs," Desjani muttered too low for the politicians to hear, "or is it okay to kill them now?"

"It's okay to kill them now. Damn shame, though. Think what we could learn from each other if they'd just talk."

"We can talk after they've learned not to mess with us."

At a combined velocity of point two light speed, the two groupings of ships bore onward, neither altering course or speed. "Ten minutes remaining to contact."

Geary nodded, letting his mind feel the right time for the maneuver. He had ordered his ships into their combat formations close to an hour ago, giving the aliens plenty of time to assume they knew what he would do. Now his final maneuver had to be at the last moment, so the aliens wouldn't see the change in targets in time to alter their own plans. If he had guessed wrong about the alien plan, then the pass might be a fiasco, but that was the worst case unless the aliens did have secret wonder weapons they hadn't employed yet. "All units in formations merit one, merit two, and merit three, at time three five alter course down zero one five degrees. Fire as targets enter engagement envelopes. Geary out."

On the display to one side of him, the one relayed from the auxiliaries with systems still contaminated by alien worms, the maneuver he had just ordered looked just as Desjani had described, a suicidal dive by the Alliance fighting subformations between the second and third layers of the alien armada, facing two-to-one odds and fire from top and bottom simultaneously. On his clean display, it showed the Alliance attack forces would be heading downward at the last moment toward the alien ships in the second layer, with the firepower advantage at the point of contact four to one in the Alliance's favor.

He thought about the tragedy that this first alien contact was, as Sakai said, with enemies. But Geary also thought about all of the Syndic ships that had been destroyed by the aliens in the last century, ships whose crews had not known how badly they were handicapped by the alien worms. The aliens had possessed a huge advantage and apparently had not hesitated to use it.

At time three five, the three Alliance subformations tilted downward while the subformation with the auxiliaries maintained course, soaring past safely above the fray. "Turn up, you bastards," Desjani whispered, then whooped with glee. "Here they come!"

Unable to see the last-moment Alliance course change in time, the entire alien formation had tilted upward, swinging up so that the ships in the second layer could have hit the Alliance warships aiming at the alien craft in the illusory third layer.

But the Alliance ships weren't aiming there, instead coming down to meet the rising aliens.

The close encounter came and went, and Geary let out the breath he had been holding. No alien superweapons had compensated for the loss of their worm advantage. *Dauntless* was still intact, though he could hear reports of hits being passed.

The worm-driven picture from the auxiliaries showed no change in the alien armada after the encounter, but the fleet's uncontaminated sensors were rapidly updating their own assessments. The second layer of the alien armada had been devastated, caught unawares by greatly superior firepower, roughly three-quarters of its ships either destroyed outright or reduced to helpless wrecks.

The aliens seemed to have concentrated their own fire on Alliance battle cruisers, ignoring the escorts and battleships, but their barrage had been weakened as their own ships were destroyed. *Invincible*'s curse remained intact, that ship having been hit hardest and left barely maneuverable. *Illustrious* had also been hurt, as had *Ascendant*, *Auspice*, *Formidable*, *Brilliant*, *Daring*, *Dragon*, and *Valiant*. The other battle cruisers, like *Dauntless*, had taken hits but not serious damage.

"This is Admiral Geary, formations merit one and merit four come up one nine zero degrees at time four two, formation merit two come port one nine zero degrees at time four two, and formation merit three come starboard one nine zero degrees at time four two." The four subformations began wide turns, the formation centered on *Dauntless* coming up and over to pursue the aliens, while those formations to either side turned outward and around to face the enemy again as well.

It apparently took the aliens a few minutes to realize just how badly things had gone and see the Alliance maneuvers, but then the surviving alien ships bent down at a jaw-dropping rate, twisting onto a vector that would take them below and past the three Alliance subformations trying to trap them into another firing run.

"We can't catch them, Captain," the maneuvering watch-stander reported with dismay. "They turned too fast. They'll pass under us while we're still coming over."

"We can still chase them out of this star system," Desjani suggested.

Geary considered that, then shook his head. "No. That might just reinforce for them how superior their maneuvering capability is compared to ours. Let's allow them to leave with the fact that we beat them uppermost in their minds. Besides, we've got some hurt alien ships to exploit." The helplessly drifting wrecks of many alien ships would offer a treasure trove of information. Alien bodies certainly, and hopefully living aliens with whom they could conduct real dialogues, and alien equipment that could be copied and learned from. "Have we seen any escape pods from the alien craft?"

"No, sir," the maneuvering watch-stander reported. "Nothing has come off those alien ships."

"They must have some life-raft capability," Desjani objected.

"If they do, they're not using it. Let's get some ships over to those wrecks—" Geary began. His words cut off as alerts flared on his display. "Ancestors save us. They're all blowing up."

Every alien wreck had exploded at the same time, bright lights blossoming to mark the total destruction of the ships and whatever, as well as whoever, had been aboard.

The engineering watch-stander studied his own display closely. "Sir, the characteristics of the detonations roughly match a core overload on our ships, but are significantly more powerful, especially for ships that size."

"That stands to reason," Desjani remarked, her voice and face hard. "For them to maneuver like that, they'd need more powerful energy cores. I guess mass suicide is acceptable to them."

"Captain," the engineer continued, "I don't think it was suicide. The core overloads weren't quite simultaneous. The times of the explosions were staggered milliseconds apart in an expanding wave pattern. Someone sent a signal to cause those detonations, and the wave looks like it propagated from the surviving alien ships."

Desjani's expression shifted into anger. "Those cold-blooded snakes. They blew up their own. Whoever was in charge of the aliens blew them all to hell to make sure we didn't learn anything. Those merciless scum!" The watch-standers on the bridge clearly agreed with their captain's sentiments.

"You're judging them by our standards," Rione said, though the reluctance in her tone made it clear that she, too, agreed with Desjani.

"And I intend continuing to do so," Desjani replied shortly.

Geary looked back toward the engineering watch-stander. "Will there be anything left of those wrecks that we can learn from?"

"Doubtful, sir. All we're seeing is debris so small it registers as dust. Maybe analysis can yield some good ideas about what alloys and other materials they use, though."

"Ruthless and efficient," Geary said to Desjani. "A bad combination."

"What about," Sakai asked, "what they're made of? It would be useful to at least know if they were carbon-based life-forms."

The engineer scrunched up his face in thought. "I don't think so, sir. If you blew this ship to dust, there would be a lot of sources of possible organic material. Our food supplies alone would really contaminate the samples; then there's clothing, parts of furniture, and a lot of other things."

Geary stared at his display, wondering what kind of mind-set would go to such extremes to keep anyone else from learning anything about them. "Madam Co-President, should I send some parting words to our hastily departing alien acquaintances, or should that be a function of the political representatives aboard?"

"I would recommend you do it, Admiral." Rione looked angry, too. "Whatever they are, the extremes they are willing to go to in order to keep us from learning anything more about them means finding out more is not going to be easy. They may be extremely xenophobic, or paranoid. That may feed their territoriality, or spring from it. I fear a strong defense will be necessary while we try to establish the right means for further contact with these aliens."

Geary heard Desjani mumbling something about "more hell lances and grapeshot" under her breath. He had to admit that he shared something of those sentiments after watching the wholesale destruction of any possible alien survivors. How could they ever deal with, ever trust, someone willing to do something like that?

It wouldn't be easy. He wondered to what degree losses in combat would dissuade a race willing to annihilate its own rather than have them either captured or examined. Maybe the aliens didn't care about individuals the way humans did. *Right. We care about individuals. Except when we drop rocks on them from orbit or send them off to die. And yet we do care. I suppose aliens would have a hard time figuring us out, too.*

He thought through his words, then transmitted a final message to the fleeing aliens. "This is Admiral Geary of the Alliance fleet. We have this star. We have all stars occupied by humanity. We do not have stars occupied by you. We do not seek war with you, we will not try to take from you, but we will defend what we have. We seek peace. Come in peace, to talk, and we will talk. This is what we want. But if you come for war, to fight, then we will fight. Any further attacks on humanity will be met with equal force. Aggression in any form and any place will not go unanswered by us. If you attempt to destroy any more of our star systems by collapsing hypernet gates, we will exact a high price from you. To the honor of our ancestors."

Rione sighed heavily. "That was well said. The sword in one hand and the olive branch in the other. Hopefully, they will choose the offer of peace."

Boyens entered the shuttle dock, his Marine guards halting at the hatch. The Syndic CEO walked steadily toward the shuttle, then stopped to face Geary. "I owe you thanks, Admiral Geary. Thanks from me and thanks from every human being in this region of space."

"Your thanks should go to everyone in the Alliance fleet, and we didn't do it for you personally."

"I know. But you didn't have to do it at all." Boyens nodded to Rione, Sakai, and Costa. "There's a lot of very ugly history between our peoples right now, but this is an important start to something different."

"You can save the speeches for later," Costa said.

"I mean it." Boyens gestured around. "The star systems on the border with the aliens need you. We know that. The central authorities now trying to run what's left of the Syndicate Worlds will have their hands full trying to defend and maintain what they still control. We can't expect meaningful help from them for a long time. But there are good shipyards at Taroa. That's one of the star systems we'd have had to abandon if Midway had fallen. Even those shipyards will take time to turn out a decent number of warships, though, especially with supply lines disrupted by the ongoing collapse of the Syndicate Worlds' central authority. We're going to be on our own, and not able to muster a strong defense for quite a while."

Sakai gestured in turn. "Do you speak of your star systems being something still part of the Syndicate Worlds, or of something else?"

"I don't know." Boyens flashed a grin. "I have to watch those candid statements. It's going to depend on what people here want. I can guarantee you that folks in this region are very unhappy at being left high and dry by the Syndicate Worlds while their defensive forces were stripped from them and sent to fight the Alliance. But there's new leadership at Prime, now. So maybe people will be willing to stick with the Syndicate Worlds, but that might mean demanding more autonomy, forming a regional confederation here that isn't tightly tied to whatever remains of the Syndicate Worlds. More like what the Alliance does. I promise to keep you informed."

Boyens looked at each of them, then twisted his lips ruefully as if he had clearly read their reactions to his last statement. "The promise of a Syndic CEO. I know what that's worth. But it's my personal promise. I'm not stupid. We need you. And we owe you for saving us this time. I won't forget that."

"You apparently dealt with us honestly," Rione answered,

"though not always as candidly as you should have. That will be remembered."

"What will happen to you now?" Geary asked.

Boyens gave him a bemused look, and Geary realized that the Syndic hadn't expected any of the Alliance officials to care what happened to him. "I don't know for certain. Standard procedure calls for putting me in an interrogation facility to see if I gave out any information while a prisoner, followed by questions about how I got away or why I was released, usually followed by a public trial for treason, concluded by an execution or maybe a very painful prison exile. But the situation is a little different than usual. Gwen Iceni is a decent person for a CEO, and she's smart enough to see that we need to break with some past practices given what's happening all over Syndic space and given what you did here. So, I don't know. Maybe I'll end up in a cell, maybe I'll be appointed an ambassador to you, maybe I'll be given command of some of our new mobile defensive forces as they get built, maybe I'll be shot. You'll hear sooner or later."

"We could use access to this star system," Geary said.

"I'm not sure anybody can stop you from coming if you really want to," Boyens replied with a wry look.

Rione had her best poker face on, and her voice stayed carefully neutral. "Nonetheless, an agreement granting such access would be of great advantage to the people here as well as to the Alliance. Tell your people that the Alliance would be interested in pursuing such an agreement on the basis of mutual self-interest."

Boyens eyed her with a similarly unrevealing expression. "Even if the people here decide to go their own way from the Syndicate

Worlds, I doubt that they'd be interested in becoming part of the Alliance."

"The Alliance doesn't force or demand association," Sakai answered this time. "There are many levels of cooperation short of that."

"All right. I'll pass that on."

Rione and Sakai nodded to Geary, while Costa scowled but said nothing. Geary held out a data disc to the Syndic. "This contains descriptions of the alien worms. How to find them, how to deactivate them. You'll probably find just about every system on your ships and planets infested with the worms. That's how they stayed invisible to you and how they avoided being hit in battle."

Boyens stared at the disc, then reached slowly to take it as if expecting it to be yanked away at the last moment. "Why are you giving us this?"

"Because you can't conduct an effective defense of the border without it," Geary explained. "And as a sign of goodwill to the people here." He didn't mention that he, Sakai, and Rione had concluded that with what Boyens could tell them, the Syndics here were eventually likely to figure out on their own that the worms existed. This way the Syndics would hopefully feel a debt of gratitude to the Alliance. But he also hadn't wanted to leave Alliance warships behind, isolated far from home and dependent on the goodwill of Syndics, to ensure that the aliens didn't run roughshod over the Syndics in the near future. Far better that the Syndics be given a tool to allow them successfully to face the aliens. "That disc doesn't explain how the worms work, because we don't know. If you figure it out, we'd appreciate your returning the favor and telling us."

"I'll certainly encourage my people to do that." Boyens stared glumly at the data disc. "We've been in contact with them for a century, and we never figured this out. How did you do it?"

"We were looking at the problem from a fresh perspective. Maybe that helped. We didn't have a century of experience and assumptions that pointed us in the wrong direction. It was perfectly plausible that the aliens possessed something on their ships that blocked your ability to see them, and a hundred years ago the means to identify the quantum-probability worms might not have been available. You reached conclusions that drove all of your research from that point onward."

Boyens nodded, his expression rueful. "Like that ancient saying goes, sometimes it's not what you don't know that's dangerous, it's the things you think you know that aren't really true."

"Exactly. But the worms were also found because a brilliant officer in the Alliance fleet looked for something she suspected might be there without limiting herself to where she expected to find it."

"A single brilliant individual can make a big difference," Boyens agreed. "I'd like to thank her, too, sometime."

Geary kept his expression rigid. "I'm afraid that's impossible. She died during the battle with your flotilla at Varandal."

The Syndic CEO met Geary's eyes for a moment. "I'm sorry. For what it's worth, I lost friends in that battle, too. I wish all of them, yours and mine, were still with us."

"Then," Rione said in a firm voice, "do what you can to ensure that our peoples work together in the future rather than meet in battle. We can't bring back those who have died, but we can prevent more deaths."

Boyens closed his hand around the data disc. "Yes. I can't speak for all of Syndicate Worlds' space, just for this region near the border with the aliens, but I will try." His gaze lingered on Geary. "Are you going to remain in command of the Alliance military? People are going to want to know."

Geary phrased his answer carefully. "I serve at the pleasure of the Alliance Senate. I currently command only this fleet, not the entire Alliance military. I don't know what will be asked of me after this."

"Fair enough. I'll be blunt. People here will trust you. I hope the Alliance government keeps that in mind." Boyens nodded to Geary and the three senators, then turned and walked onto the shuttle.

They watched the inner dock seal, then the shuttle depart, and Geary felt some of the tension leave him. Somehow, returning the Syndic CEO here, to where the reserve flotilla had come from, completed a necessary circle.

"It is a shame no Alliance POW camps exist this far from the Alliance," Sakai remarked. "We could have asked for all of those captured personnel now while these Syndics are still grateful."

"They'll be grateful just as long as we've got our guns trained on them," Costa grumbled. "I still think we were foolish to tell them about the worms. We could have studied them, learned how to use them, then employed the worms against the Syndics if necessary."

"We have another enemy now," Rione replied. "A mutual enemy, it seems, whether we desire it or not. And these particular Syndics would be very useful allies."

Costa's glower deepened. "I can't think in terms of Syndics being allies."

"They may not be Syndics much longer, if that makes it any easier."

"A wolf can call itself a dog, but it's still a wolf." Costa gave Geary a sour look. "I hope you're not planning on retiring soon, Admiral. I can guarantee that won't be approved."

Geary kept his own expression unrevealing. "I expected as much. But I do have certain agreements with the council."

Costa didn't quite conceal a flash of sardonic amusement at Geary's words. "Of course," she said, while Sakai avoided showing any reaction. Rione, for her part, managed to flick a warning glance at Geary without either of her fellow senators noticing.

Any lingering doubts he had felt that the grand council was going to play games with their promises to him vanished.

But he could play games, too. He had managed to defeat the tricks played on him by the Syndics and the aliens, and he would do the same with the grand council.

As he left the shuttle dock, Geary couldn't help noticing the irony that just like Badaya, he was now seeing the Alliance government as one more obstacle to overcome. Unlike Badaya, though, his goals were purely personal. The government could make policy, but Geary wanted at least a little control over his own life.

He figured that he had earned that much.

Geary rejoined Desjani on the bridge, watching as the Alliance shuttle mated with the Syndic heavy cruiser, Desjani seeming ready to launch specters in an instant if the heavy cruiser opened fire on the shuttle. But after several minutes the shuttle reported a successful transfer and broke away from the Syndic warship, heading back to *Dauntless*.

As the shuttle reentered the dock on *Dauntless*, Desjani herself finally seemed to relax. "Are we going home now?"

"Yes." He leaned back, gazing at the images of the fleet on the display. "We're going home."

12

It felt odd to be going home with no immediate prospect of combat facing them, to be using the Syndic hypernet, to transit Syndic star systems (or former Syndic star systems) without fear of attack. Some of the Syndic CEOs even offered to sell raw materials to restock the bunkers on the fleet's auxiliaries, but no one in the Alliance fleet was willing to trust in such a transaction yet.

As they crossed the last Syndic star system before jumping for Varandal in Alliance space, Geary held what felt like a last meeting with his most trusted advisers. Desjani appeared pensive, but she had been finding reasons not to talk to him lately, so he didn't know why. Duellos had lost the air of melancholy that had always been mostly hidden behind his jauntiness. Tulev seemed like he was considering relearning how to smile but hadn't yet convinced himself. "Is this what peace feels like?" he asked.

"I don't know," Geary confessed. "To me, with all of the threats that still remain, it's not peace."

"But the Syndicate Worlds will be a shadow of its former self."

"The Alliance may face the same pressures. Rione expects a lot of star systems, and larger groupings like the Rift Federation and her own Callas Republic, to push for more autonomy and fewer commitments to the Alliance."

"Fewer commitments," Desjani said scornfully. "You mean less money. Now that they'll feel safe, they'll still want the Alliance to keep defending them, but they won't want to have to pay to be defended."

"That's pretty much it, yeah. The big common threat is gone, and getting across the need to deal with the successor states to the Syndicate Worlds as well as the unknown size of the alien threat isn't going to be easy with such a war-weary population."

"The price of winning was very high," Duellos said. "Almost too high for the Alliance. But then the price of defeat is far worse for the Syndics."

They toasted victory and survival, then the virtual presences of Duellos and Tulev took their leave.

Desjani stayed sitting at the table, though, her hands clasped before her, head slightly bowed.

Geary waited for a while, but she didn't say anything, so finally he did. "What's up?"

"I don't know." Her voice came out low.

"Is it anything you can talk about?"

"It's the one thing I *can't* talk about."

"Oh." He waited a little longer. "Can we talk about you?"

"About me? No, Admiral. I don't think that would be wise."

That hatch had slammed shut firmly. Geary couldn't help feeling a little annoyed. She seemed to be wanting to talk but wouldn't.

"Let's try this, then. The admiral is concerned about one of his best commanding officers, who appears to be considerably upset about some personal matter. Is there anything about it appropriate to share with him?"

"Maybe there is." Desjani looked away, running one hand through her hair. "I've spent so many years becoming me. The idea of everyone looking at me and seeing someone else is very hard to accept."

"You told me that before. I wish I had an answer."

"I can't expect an answer, let alone an open discussion. All I need to know right now is whether you can really understand how I feel."

"Extremely well," Geary replied. She glanced at him with a frown as he continued. "When I first woke up on *Dauntless*, and you were all standing there and talking about this Black Jack guy, this hero and these legends, and you were all looking at me. I've understood how that feels ever since then."

Her frown vanished, replaced by embarrassment. "You have me there. It took me a while to look at you and see you, not Black Jack."

"But, as you've said, the universe is always going to look at me and see Black Jack."

"Do two wrongs make a right?" Desjani wondered. "Two wrong visions of people. I don't know. I just don't know. And I don't know if you really see me. Who do you see? Who do you think I am? Don't say anything. We can't go there."

"I believe I see the real you," Geary said carefully.

"You've been on *Dauntless* since you awoke. Confined to this ship, for all intents and purposes, while we endured great stresses together because you were required to be in my company."

"So?"

"Think about it." She stood abruptly and walked out.

Geary sat for a while longer, then called his niece on *Dreadnaught*. They talked awhile longer, Jane Geary finally confessing that she couldn't decide what her future held. "As long as I could understand what being a Geary meant, I've always seen the fleet as an inescapable doom. But it's also what I've known as an adult, it's what I know how to do. I know the survivors from *Repulse* that we picked up along with other Alliance POWs when we came back through the Syndic home star system don't think he made it off his ship, but they weren't certain that he died. Maybe, just maybe, Michael is still alive out there. In the fleet, I can help find him."

"It's your choice," Geary told her, and for the first time he saw Jane Geary smile as she realized that really was true.

The next morning they jumped for Varandal, Geary feeling increasingly restless as the last few days passed slowly. He wanted to ensure critical functions could continue without him personally remaining at Varandal, but there were only so many plans you could make for repairs of battle damage and maintenance and rotation of duty among warships so that crews could get some leave and rest.

Three days out, Rione paid one of her now-rare visits to his stateroom. "My conscience is bothering me, believe it or not. Do I have to warn you what's going to happen when we get back?"

"I don't think so, not if you're talking about the grand council's promises to me."

Rione smiled crookedly. "They'll stand by the exact letter of those promises. Don't count on anything more than that."

"So I've heard from others. But I'm going to take some time off, some leave, to get some personal things done."

"Leave?" Rione asked skeptically. "You think they'll grant you leave?"

"As commander of the fleet, I approve my own leave," Geary replied.

"How convenient. Do you intend being gone long?"

"No. Thirty days."

She looked impressed. "If you manage to stay away from the Alliance bureaucracy that long, it'll be quite an achievement. You must have accumulated a great deal of leave in survival sleep, though I imagine the pay you accumulated during that century is a greater comfort to you."

"Pay? Leave?" Geary shook his head. "I didn't accumulate any." He saw Rione's puzzlement. "Sometime while I was asleep there were rulings, 'clarifications' of the pay and leave regulations, because some guys had been picked up after being in survival sleep for a couple of years. The personnel bureaucracy ruled that time spent in survival sleep did not count toward pay, accumulation of leave, or obligated service time."

"I see." Rione also shook her head, smiling ruefully. "The bureaucracy figured out how to avoid paying anyone or giving them credit toward the length of their service contracts. How did they justify that?"

"Because you're not in a 'duty status' while in survival sleep since you are not 'available for duty if called.'" Geary shrugged. "Fortunately, the issue of seniority never came up, so officially my years in survival sleep did count in terms of accumulated seniority in my rank. Otherwise, I might have been the most junior captain in the fleet."

"I shudder to think how events might have differed if that had been the case." Rione sighed. "Even an agnostic would have to admit that some very critical things for the Alliance went right in your case, Admiral Geary."

He laughed briefly. "Too bad the living stars didn't look after my old bank accounts. They were closed out once I was declared dead, so I don't even have the benefit of a century's worth of interest on what I had in them. I have whatever I've earned since being found and awakened. The fleet admiral pay I've earned lately will be a nice bonus, but I'm not coming out of this well-off. I do have some extra leave time available, because what I had already accumulated a hundred years ago didn't go away."

"Ah, well, at least you know that she's not after your money."

Geary shot an irritated glance at Rione. "I never suspected her, or anyone else, of being motivated by that."

Rione feigned a mock spasm of pain. "That hurt." Geary didn't respond to her humor, and she raised an eyebrow at him. "What's the matter? Isn't everything wonderful now? In another few days you can actually talk to her. Believe it or not, I know how hard it must have been to avoid doing or saying anything that might have compromised either of you."

"Thank you." He knew he was frowning as he rubbed the back of his neck. "It's just... I don't know."

"Cold feet?" she asked softly.

"No. Not on my part."

"Oh."

He looked at her quickly. Rione was gazing into a corner of the room, her expression once more unreadable. "What's that mean?"

"It means, Admiral, that you need to deal with this yourself."

"I wasn't—"

"I am *not* the person to discuss your personal relationship problems with. *She* is the one you need to talk to."

"I can't. Not for another week. I just hope I say the right things then."

Rione shook her head again, but before leaving gave Geary a sharp look. "Follow your instincts, Admiral."

After Rione had left, Geary sat for a while, thinking, then left his stateroom, walking through the passageways of *Dauntless*, the passageways filled even at this late hour with excited crew members talking about going home and the end of the war. They looked at him not with hope now but with thanks, and that was much easier for Geary to endure even though he made a point always to tell them that they had won the war and all of the victories leading to its end. He had just been fortunate enough to lead them.

Geary went all the way down to the worship spaces, crowded with those giving thanks to higher powers than mere admirals, and found a room for himself. Inside, he sat for a while in the solitude before lighting the candle and speaking to his long-dead brother. "I still sometimes wonder if it's all real. From commanding officer of a single heavy cruiser to commanding officer of a fleet a lot bigger than anything the Alliance could muster in my own time. Who would have thought that I'd be stuck with trying to save that fleet lost far behind enemy lines, that I'd be expected to save the

Alliance? I know your granddaughter Jane says you always told her I was what the legend said, but you and I both know better. I'm just me. I don't know how I got through this, but I do know I had a lot of help.

"Tell your grandson Michael I'm sorry. He was a fine officer. He was a real hero. We're bringing some of the crew from *Repulse* home with us. They were still being held in the Syndic home star system. They can't confirm he died, but none of them think he could've gotten off the ship alive. I will always regret not being able to save him.

"Your granddaughter Jane is a fine woman. I'll try to look out for her. But she's a Geary. Stubborn and willful. I don't know if she'll stay in the fleet now, or leave it to become an architect.

"Now she has a choice. So do Michael's kids. I thank the living stars that I was able to do that."

"Admiral, the last units of the fleet have assumed their assigned orbits in Varandal Star System."

"Thank you." The comm panel in his stateroom went dark again, and Geary looked toward the display floating over the table. *Dauntless* and a number of other warships had been in position not far from Ambaru station for more than half a day. Shuttles had already taken some personnel from *Dauntless* to the station for official business or to start long-postponed personal leave. But other warships had taken more time to reach their assigned orbits, some of them near different orbital stations. The fleet was large enough that no one wanted to overwhelm one or two facilities with the amount of personnel traffic all of the warships would generate.

That was it, then. The orders and plans he had worked up for the fleet once it got back had been sent and set in motion. He had now satisfied everything, his promises, his sense of duty, his honor, and the conditions to which the grand council had agreed. Even the threat of a military coup had vanished for the moment, with Badaya and his allies convinced that every important decision was covertly being made by Geary and more than satisfied by the formal end of the war. Geary reached up and removed the admiral of the fleet insignia, not without a pang of regret since Tanya had pinned them on. He stood before the mirror for a moment, attaching his captain's insignia.

Geary looked around his stateroom on *Dauntless*, the starscape on one bulkhead, the chairs, the table over which he had worked out countless simulations and battle plans. Except for the couple of weeks before Admiral Bloch died, this had been Geary's home in this time. His only home in this time.

He was going to leave it for a while. Surely the Alliance owed him a few weeks to rest, and things couldn't go awry in such a short time. He wondered where to go in Alliance space and what to do there. Everywhere there would be people wanting to mob him, and all he wanted to do was find someplace to hide for a little while, to not have to worry for a brief period about grand decisions or the fates of warships and the Alliance.

Not alone, hopefully. There was someone to whom he could finally speak his heart. Though Tanya Desjani had definitely been avoiding him the last couple of days. Maybe she had felt the same way he had, fighting off an urge to blurt out feelings just a short while before they could honorably speak of them.

Even though he was leaving the ship, he was certain that he'd be back on *Dauntless*. The Alliance was surely going to be calling on Black Jack again because the universe hadn't been tied up in a neat package. Just how much the Alliance could or should do inside the mess that had once been the Syndicate Worlds was very much open to question, but Geary had no doubt that the fleet would be called upon. If nothing else, there were a lot of Alliance prisoners of war stranded among the wreckage of the Syndicate Worlds, people to be found and brought home.

And the aliens remained, still far too little known about them, a lingering threat on the far side of Syndic space, doubtless watching humanity, doubtless coming up with new tricks to cause humanity to work against itself, perhaps planning new offensives of their own, their feelings about their own recent losses as unknown as just about everything else about them. What lay beyond the aliens remained a mystery as well. Where there was one nonhuman intelligent race, there could be many others.

No. History hadn't come to a happy end. But he'd saved the fleet. He'd stopped the war. He had done more than he had believed possible.

Geary did a final check of his message queue, ignoring the long list of transmissions from fleet headquarters. Whatever they were would wait. He was certain that at least one of the messages would be notifying him of a promotion back to admiral, and at least one other would contain orders for him, but the grand council and fleet headquarters had outwitted themselves by giving the messages all standard priorities and innocuous titles. That had been intended to keep him from guessing what was in those messages before he read them, but it also offered him a perfect excuse not to read them since none of them looked important. *I may be just a fleet officer, but I'm not a dumb fleet officer, especially not after hanging around Rione and watching her at work.*

Geary tapped out a quick message to his chain of command.

> *In accordance with agreements made earlier, I hereby relinquish my temporary war rank, revert to my permanent rank of captain, and yield command of the fleet. In my last acts as Admiral of the Fleet, I have authorized myself thirty days of leave beginning today, and hereby temporarily transfer command of the fleet to Admiral Timbale pending any decisions in that regard by fleet headquarters and the Alliance grand council.*

> *Very respectfully,*
> *John Geary,*
> *Captain,*
> *Alliance Fleet*

Ordering the message actually to be transmitted in ten hours, he headed out to look for Desjani.

But as his hatch opened, Victoria Rione was standing there, eyeing him with an enigmatic look. "Going somewhere?" she asked.

"As a matter of fact, yes. If you don't mind—"

"They haven't promoted you back to admiral yet?"

"The promotion message is probably in my in-box, doubtless along with messages containing orders for me to report somewhere and command something, but I have no intention of reading any of those messages for the next thirty days. As far as I know, I'm a captain, and I have no obligations stopping me from taking leave." Geary gave Rione a half-annoyed, half-apologetic look. "I *have* to go."

"But there's something we *have* to talk about, Captain Geary." She brushed past him into the stateroom, and he followed, trying not to get angry as Rione turned to watch him. "Have I told you how grateful I am, Captain Geary?" she continued. "For what you did for the Alliance. For all of the things you could have done and didn't. I owe you as a senator, I owe you as Co-President of the Callas Republic, and I owe you as an individual."

"That's okay." Geary waved one hand dismissively. "I did my duty."

"You did much more than your duty, Captain Geary, and that is why despite some personal issues I have regarding a certain other captain of our acquaintance, I have nonetheless come here to inform you that you have one message in your in-box you should read before you go wandering around this ship looking for someone."

What was Rione up to this time? "Why?"

"Trust me. Call up your in-box."

Feeling increasingly curious as well as annoyed, Geary reopened his message file. "Which one of these messages is so important?"

"None of those. The one I'm talking about is set for delayed delivery. It's in your file but won't be visible for... oh... another hour or so. Unless you happen to enter this override code." Rione's fingers danced across the controls, and a moment later another message popped into existence. "My, would you look at that."

Frowning, Geary examined the message. Eyes Only, Personal For. It had originated on *Dauntless*. He opened the file and read.

Dear Admiral of the Fleet Geary,

I hope you will forgive this means of communication, but it seemed the best way to avoid putting you in an unpleasant or awkward situation.

You have fulfilled the promises once given, but unspoken promises lie between us. We both know what they are. I do not doubt your sincerity. But you have been confined to Dauntless *since your awakening, con fined to this ship under great stress, forced to associate with certain individuals in order to fulfill your duties as fleet commander. It was only natural that you should develop an emotional attachment under those circum stances. But, given time and freedom, you may well grow to regret unspoken promises made under duress, nor can I blame you for that.*

I will not hold you to promises that were never spoken.

By the time we meet again, you will have had a chance to look around, to see life outside the confines of Dauntless, *and to decide what you truly choose. There are many challenges still facing you. You have many opportunities.*

It was a great honor to fight under your command, and I hope you will consider sailing on Dauntless *again.*

Very respectfully,
Tanya Desjani,
Captain, Alliance Fleet

He stared for what felt like a long time at the message, then finally turned to Rione. "What the hell does this mean?"

"Why do you think I've read it?"

"Because I know you! What's Tanya talking about?"

Rione spread her hands. "She says it all, more or less clearly. She's worried that sooner or later the great hero Black Jack Geary, who could have any woman he wanted, will want someone else." Rione smiled sardonically. "Like me, she won't be any man's second choice."

"How could she think that?" Geary frowned, another question coming to him. "Why did she set this for delivery to me in another hour?"

"I can't imagine," Rione replied with mock bafflement. "Did you set your message to the fleet headquarters announcing your departure for immediate transmission?"

"No, of course not, I wanted to be gone before——" He stared at Rione, suddenly remembering something in the last part of Desjani's message. *By the time we meet again.* "Desjani's going? Where?"

"Do I have to tell you *everything*?"

He stopped to think and immediately realized the answer. "Kosatka. She's going home on leave." Geary took a long breath, trying to calm himself. "Why didn't she talk first? We *finally* would have been able to talk about it."

"You read the message. She doesn't think you're ready to talk about it."

"How could she make that decision on her own?" Geary felt himself getting angry now. "I can't believe she ran away instead of——"

Rione's snort of exasperation was intense enough to stop Geary's words. "Are you planning on telling her you think she 'ran away'?"

He took another deep breath. "No."

"Good. You're not hopeless. But you're not thinking about what's going on inside her. Duty and honor tell her one thing, not to stand in the way of what you need to do for the Alliance in the future. Even I have to respect her concern on those grounds. Her doubts make her wonder how real your feelings are, feelings you've never actually been able to talk with her about, and how long those feelings will last. Is she just an infatuation born of your isolation in this fleet? Is a mere fleet captain going to be a worthy partner for someone as powerful as you? She's probably even wondering if you're going to return to me now, as if I'd have you again."

Geary shook his head, trying to find holes in Rione's argument. "But—"

"And against all of that," Rione continued, her voice sharpening, "your captain has only her own love for you, which she also has never been free to express openly and which has no doubt been a source of considerable private guilt for her when she dared dwell on it. Love needs expression, Captain Geary, or doubts grow amid the silence. Doubts of the other and doubts of yourself."

He took a few breaths this time, then nodded. "You left something out. She's worried about being known as just my partner, not as herself, as Black Jack's companion instead of for what she's accomplished herself."

"Ah, yes. That's a big one. So what will you do, Black Jack?"

He glared at Rione. "What am I *supposed* to do?"

She sighed and relented again. "What would your captain tell you to do if you were facing a very difficult decision?"

He thought about that. "She'd tell me to follow my instincts."

"What did I tell you to do a few days ago concerning your captain?"

Geary tried to recall. "To follow my instincts."

"Hopefully you'll listen to one of us. What do your instincts tell you to do now?"

"To find her and tell her how I feel, to let her know that she won't stand in the way of my duty, that her honor helps give me the strength to do what I must, that I will always stand beside her and she beside me, and that I will never choose another."

"Not bad." Rione pointed toward the hatch. "Then what are you waiting for?"

"I'm still trying to understand why she didn't wait around for us to talk about it. It's the first time we've had a chance, so why not meet me while we're still on the same ship?"

This time Rione rolled her eyes. "You mean catch you in your stateroom? On her ship? The ship you've been confined to for months? Catch you before you can get away?"

"That's not— She did say something like that."

"Of course she did. Your captain is giving you an out, a chance to reset things, to go if you wish, to salvage her own pride and honor without forcing you to tell her that 'things have changed.'"

"But how am I going to catch her if she's already left the ship?" Somehow he knew that Desjani was already gone.

Rione raised one eyebrow. "You've got a chance, John Geary, if you truly want to catch her. That's what she wants to know, and you've got a way to prove it to her. Instead, you're standing here talking to me."

Geary was halfway to the hatch before he remembered to turn back to Rione. "Thank you."

"Thank me?" Rione shrugged. "If my husband still lives, the end of the war and the prisoner-exchange process will return him to me. And you think you owe me thanks?"

"Yes. I'll see you around, Madam Co-President."

"Yes, you will, Captain Geary. There's still much to be done." She gestured toward the hatch. "Your target is getting away."

He headed down the passageway, then veered to the nearest comm panel to call the bridge. "Where is Captain Desjani?"

The duty watch-stander on the bridge stared at Geary, then swallowed nervously before answering. "Uh, sir, Captain Desjani is indisposed. She asked us not to disturb—"

That confirmed his suspicions. "Is she still on the ship?"

The bridge watch-stander hesitated, then obviously made a decision. "No, sir. She departed on leave just two hours ago and took a shuttle to the main passenger terminal." The words came out in a relieved rush.

"You didn't announce her departure from the ship?"

"Sir, Captain Desjani ordered us not to—"

"All right. I need one of *Dauntless*'s shuttles for a lift to the main passenger terminal at Ambaru station, and I need it now."

The bridge watch-stander looked and sounded horrified. "Sir, all of *Dauntless*'s shuttles are down for maintenance. It's very unusual to take them all down at once, but Captain Desjani ordered it. The one she took was put into full maintenance as soon as it got back."

She just has to make it as tough as possible. Geary paused, trying to think of the next best course of action. Getting a shuttle sent to *Dauntless* from another ship would take time, perhaps a lot of time, and might tip off fleet headquarters that he was trying to make his own escape. But he didn't have any other option. Geary was about to order that when the bridge watch spoke again, now appearing startled.

"Sir, a shuttle from *Inspire* just reported that it's on final approach for our shuttle dock. They say they have orders for a high-priority passenger transport. Is that you, sir?"

Thank you, Captain Duellos. I don't know how you figured out what was going on, but I owe you one. "Yes, that's me. I need that shuttle ready to go as soon as I reach the dock."

He ended up having to wait a couple of minutes, though, before *Inspire*'s shuttle tore away from *Dauntless*. "Any particular dock in the passenger terminal area, sir?" the shuttle pilot asked. "It's really big."

"I need a dock as close as possible to wherever a passenger ship bound for Kosatka and due to leave soon would be loading."

"Civilian passenger traffic?" the pilot asked doubtfully. "I can find out that dock assignment easily enough, sir, but I'm supposed to use only military docks, so I may still have to dock a long ways away."

"There's no way you can use the civilian docks?"

"No, sir. Well, there's one way. If there's an in-flight emergency on approach, and I need to get to the nearest dock."

Geary tried to keep his voice casual. "An in-flight emergency?"

"Yes, sir, like... uh... the cabin-depressurization alarm."

"I see. What do you suppose the chances are of that alarm going off while we're close to the dock I need?"

He could hear the pilot's grin. "For you, sir? I can feel it getting ready to pop right now. I assume we need the least-time-highest-velocity transit to the terminal that I can manage?"

"You got it."

"Consider it done, sir."

About twenty-five minutes later, Geary staggered off the shuttle, whose pilot had indeed done an enthusiastic job of hurling his bird through space. At the dock exit, he walked past some annoyed-looking civilians wearing outfits he didn't recognize. One tried to halt him, but Geary held up a hand. "I'm in a hurry."

"You still need to—" The civilian's eyes locked on Geary's face, and his jaw dropped. "I... I..."

"Sorry. I'm in a hurry," Geary repeated, rushing past him.

There were plenty of uniforms among the crowds there, but the civilian clothing everywhere still felt jarring, not simply because of all the time he had spent aboard warships but also because the styles had changed so much in the century since he had been among civilians. The senators he had dealt with had all worn formal clothes, the sort of styles that changed very slowly and so had been close to what he had known a century ago, but these civilians were in casual clothing that looked odd to his eyes. He knew those styles were just the tip of the iceberg, a small part of the changes he'd have to deal with.

But that could wait until he reached the right dock. If he could get there in time. He kept running into bottlenecks and knots of stopped people that slowed him down. Geary kept his head lowered and plowed toward the dock whose number the shuttle pilot had provided, trying not to notice the curious glances turned his way. But then a cluster of sailors turned, saw him, and with broad smiles saluted, while some of the other military nearby watched, puzzled by a gesture still unfamiliar to them.

He couldn't ignore the salutes. Geary returned them, then looked for the dock numbers nearby. One of the sailors, whose patch indicated he was off *Daring*, stepped forward. "Sir? Do you need something?"

"Dock one twenty-four bravo," Geary replied. "I need to get there fast."

"We'll get you there, sir! Follow us!" The sailors from *Daring* locked arms, forming a flying wedge, and began charging through the crowd clearing a path for Geary despite angry and surprised cries of protests from those they shouldered aside.

Grinning despite his worry, Geary followed, hearing in his wake startled voices saying his name and hoping he could stay ahead of any gathering crowd.

Moments later, the sailors came to a halt, and their leader gestured. "Here you are, sir. Courtesy of the Alliance battle cruiser *Daring*. Are you going to be leading us again, sir?"

Geary paused and smiled back at them. "If I'm lucky. Thanks." Another quick salute, then he was in the waiting area just outside the dock.

Tanya Desjani turned as he entered. She had on a dress uniform, standing out even among the other military personnel waiting to board the passenger ship. He stumbled to a halt at the sight of her, momentarily unable to both move and take in the fact that he had caught up to her, that Desjani was standing there, finally no barriers of honor or duty between them and their feelings, her face lighting with recognition, her eyes widening in what he thought and hoped was sudden joy as she realized that he was there.

Then she was controlling her expression, adopting the formal, professional posture that he had come to know so well. "Sir?" Desjani asked. "What brings you here?" She noticed his captain's insignia, and new emotions rippled across her face too fast for him to read.

"I think you know the answer to that, Tanya. And I'm not sir to you anymore. I'm not in command of the fleet, we're both captains, and you're not my subordinate now. Just how the hell did you expect me to get here in that little time?"

That flash of happiness showed again in her eyes. "You've done more difficult things when you really wanted to do them. Are you happy you got here so quickly?"

"Happy?" Geary sighed. "Tanya, when I walked in here and saw you, I swear for a moment there was no one else and nothing else in the universe. Just you. Are you happy to see me?"

"I—" Desjani bit off her words and started again. "If you read my message—"

"I already read it."

"You already... It wasn't supposed to..." Desjani looked annoyed now. "All right, then. Wasn't I clear?"

"Not entirely, no, but I figured it out." Even he knew that mentioning Rione's role in the whole thing would be a very serious mistake. "I don't need time to think it over. I know what I want. I just hope you still want it, too."

Annoyance shaded into exasperation. "I am giving you every opportunity to rethink things."

"Thank you. I have no need for those opportunities."

Desjani leaned close, speaking in a whisper as Geary became aware of all of the eyes turning their way. "You're not being fair to either of us. You haven't had any time to really see the Alliance today. In a few months, things will have changed."

"My mind and my heart won't have changed." Geary shook his head. "Tanya, I had a life before Grendel knocked me on a new course. I saw a lot of people then. And I've seen a lot of people now, even though almost all of them were in the fleet. There was no one like you a century ago, and there's no one else like you now."

"Do not patronize me, Captain Geary! I know how badly losing everything in your past hurt you!"

He spent a moment looking at her, vaguely aware that an increasing number of sailors had gathered facing away to form a protective wall between him and Desjani and the rest of the occupants of the waiting area, as well as the growing crowd outside. "It did hurt. I lost everything. But eventually I realized that I'd gained something, too. If I hadn't come to this time, I wouldn't have met you. Maybe that was always what was intended. It just took me a while to get here."

Desjani stared at him. "You actually believe the living stars sent you to this time because I was here?"

"Why not? Oh, I was able to do a few things, important things, but I couldn't have done them without the people I met here. And you have been and are by far the most important of those people to me. You give me the strength to do what I have to do. I told you that before, sort of, as best I could at the time. I can't face this future without you, Tanya."

She shook her head. "I think you are greatly overstating my

importance to you, Captain Geary."

"It is impossible to overstate your importance to me," he replied in a low but forceful tone. "You don't stand between me and my duty, you stand beside me, a strong and remarkable individual, and I swear everyone will know that."

"You're hopeless. Do you actually think anyone will listen?"

"I'll keep saying it until everyone does. I'm sort of stubborn when I have to be, you know."

"You don't have to tell me that." Desjani almost smiled, then turned serious again. "But there was much we couldn't say, much we couldn't tell each other."

"I know. We can say it now. With honor. We can say the truth to each other."

"And what is that, Captain Geary?"

"That I love you. I am certain of that."

"You sought comfort during a difficult time," she said.

"If all I'd wanted was comfort, there were easier ways of finding it."

"I'm well aware of that. For a while, you *did* find it, in another woman's arms." Desjani's eyes flashed with anger this time as she brought up Geary's brief physical relationship with Rione.

He couldn't very well deny it. "Yes, I did. It was a mistake. I never loved her. She never loved me."

"And that's supposed to make it all right that she shared your bed?"

"No. It doesn't excuse it at all. I'm sorry I did that. The only excuse I can offer is that I had not yet realized how I felt about you. When I did so, it ended. I swear it."

She gave him another aggravated look. "It would be easier to stay angry with you if you were less repentant and less honest. I'm not perfect, either. But it hurt me."

"I know. I will never hurt you again."

"Don't make promises that no man, or woman, can hope to keep, Captain Geary." Desjani shook her head. "I know who I am, and I have a pretty good idea of who you are. Even if we resolve every other issue, a relationship of you with me would be... Let's just say it would be challenging."

"I know it will be difficult at times," Geary replied. "It already has been. Being in love with you, and unable to do or say a thing about it, was very hard. You may not believe this, but I don't go seeking out ways to make my life miserable."

Desjani's gaze on him sharpened, her mouth set in tight lines. "Loving me makes you miserable?"

"It did when I couldn't do anything or say anything." Geary waved his hands in frustration. "I can't say this right. I'm bad at this sort of thing. I'm pretty good at commanding a fleet, I guess, but I'm not nearly as good with women."

"Really?"

"Yes, really." Was she still angry, or was she actually making fun of him?

"Have you thought it through?" she demanded. "Believe me, I have. For the moment, we are both captains, but only for the moment. You know the Alliance will promote you back to admiral immediately. The message alerting you to your promotion has probably already been sent."

"Probably. I haven't read it though."

"How long do you think you can go without reading your message traffic? Captains can date each other. Captains can be involved with each other, as long as they're not in the same chain of command. Admirals and captains *cannot* engage in personal relationships." Desjani closed her eyes, her expression hardening. "I will not be your secret, or not-so-secret, mistress."

"I would never ask that of you. I didn't and I won't."

"But what alternative is there?" she demanded, fixing her eyes on Geary again. "You're probably already an admiral again."

He couldn't argue with that. "I guess that means we'll have to work quickly, before I have to read any messages or talk to anyone who knows. There's one way I can prove that I want to be with you and only you, and one way an admiral and a captain can have a personal relationship, and that's if we're married before I'm promoted. Before I know I've been promoted."

Desjani seemed to stiffen, then spoke slowly. "Married?"

"Yes. Will you? I mean it. I swear I've never meant anything as much as I do this."

"You're proposing to me? On a public passenger dock?"

"Um... yes. I'm sorry I couldn't arrange a better location."

Desjani looked away, uncharacteristically flustered, her expression once again very hard for Geary to read. "And if I say no? If I tell you firmly, captain to captain, woman to man, that I do not want that, and I do not want you that way, what will you do?"

It was Geary's turn to just look at her for a long moment. Had he misread every emotion he had thought he had seen in her? "Then I will ask you to reconsider, I will ask you to listen to how I feel, but if you are indeed firm in those feelings, then I must respect them. I'll treat you from then on as a fellow professional and never raise the subject again."

"I'm about to leave on that ship. We have only minutes left. You wouldn't order me to stay? Order me to listen?"

He felt a vacant sensation inside, as if a tiny black hole had appeared at the core of his being and was devouring everything, but he shook his head. It might cost him the most important thing he had left in this universe, but he had to say the truth, had to answer the question without any pretense or shadings. He could not lie to her. "No, Tanya. If you truly wish to go, then go. I have no authority over your person, over your choices, nor would I ever have such authority. If you don't believe that I've given you back your honor yet, I do so now, with no strings attached. You're the captain of your soul as much as you are captain of *Dauntless*, but they're different things. I can give orders to one but never to the other. I know that."

One corner of her mouth twitched, then Desjani smiled, then she crossed the space between them in one step. Her arms went about him, and her lips sought his in a hard and hungry kiss.

When she finally broke the kiss, Desjani paused to breathe, then smiled. "I've been waiting a long time to do that. That was the right answer, by the way."

Geary, feeling slightly dazed from that kiss, stared at her. "Is that your answer to me?"

"Wasn't it clear enough? Yes. Yes to everything. Your behavior toward me, your refusal to take advantage of my feelings, gave me my honor back a long time ago. How are we going to get married before that promotion catches up to you? Even if we get out of this star system without the authorities finding you, the promotion will probably be sent by a fast courier ship and will be waiting by the time we get to Kosatka. That means we'll have to get married on the passenger ship as quickly as we can arrange it."

"On the ship?"

Something in his tone must have sounded like hesitation, because Desjani narrowed her eyes at him. "Yes. Are you getting cold feet already? You don't get to back out of this now. I already gave you every opportunity."

He briefly imagined trying to run away from a vengeful Tanya Desjani. It would probably be an eventful and a short existence. "No. I mean, yes. That is, getting married on the ship is a great idea. Appropriate, I guess."

"She's not a warship," Desjani noted wistfully, "but she'll do. You do realize that current fleet regulations discourage assigning married couples to the same ship?"

Actually, he'd forgotten to look up that particular thing. "If I'm an admiral again, I won't actually be assigned to your ship as part of the crew."

"Space lawyer," Desjani snorted. "But you're right. If we're to work together, though, we can't be a married couple aboard ship. We have to have the same kind of working relationship we did before."

"I have to be miserable?"

"If you say that again—"

"Yes, ma'am." Geary smiled. "I agree. We can do that. We *have* done that. I was sort of hoping to get married on Kosatka, though."

Desjani grinned. "We can honeymoon there, until your orders catch up with you. Which means it might be a very brief honeymoon. Our ship is leaving soon. Where's your baggage?"

"Baggage?" Only then did it occur to Geary that he had rushed off *Dauntless* with nothing but the uniform he was wearing.

Desjani's smile grew. "Just like when we pulled you out of that escape pod. You're not very good at packing, are you? We'll pick up a few things for you in the ship's store. I don't suppose on the way here you bothered trying to get a ticket for this ship to Kosatka?"

"Uh... I was actually just focused on getting to you and, uh... what to say, and..."

Desjani laughed. "That's okay. I've got a private cabin. I hoped against all reason and against all of my own doubts that I'd need it, that *we'd* need it, and it seems we do. We just have to add your fare on to it." She laughed again. "I think my parents are going to be a little startled. They thought I was married to *Dauntless*. Instead I'll be bringing you home as a son-in-law. Oh, that reminds me. There's one other nonnegotiable condition on our marriage. If someday we're blessed with a daughter, she must be named after Jaylen Cresida."

Geary smiled and nodded. "Of course. Did you think I'd have a problem with that?"

"No, but unlike you, I don't spring surprises on people. Except my parents in this case." She paused and gave him a serious look. "What about after Kosatka? If we have the time, do you want to go to your home world, to Glenlyon? The people there will want to see you."

Geary shook his head. "Someday I'll have to go back there, but right now it scares the hell out of me. Glenlyon was my home world a century ago. Now my home is the fleet, and wherever you are."

"Lucky you. Since my home is also the fleet, you won't be torn between two places." Desjani looked up as a commander came forward through the ranks of sailors. "Yes?"

The commander saluted, his face a formal mask, and held out a standard fleet duffel bag. "Captain Geary, sir, with compliments from Captain Tulev."

"Thank you, Commander." Geary took the duffel and looked inside, seeing it neatly packed with spare uniform items and other travel necessities. "Am I the only person in the fleet who didn't realize what was going to happen today?"

"No," Desjani replied. "You and I seem to be the only *two* people who didn't know. But then we've been the only two people in the fleet who couldn't talk about it." A flight attendant was standing at the boarding hatch, vainly trying to get people moving. "Shall we lead the way or wait for someone else to show up with a minister and a marriage certificate?"

"I think we can handle that part ourselves."

"Yes, we can." Desjani linked her arm in his and started them both toward the hatch. "Even if the living stars aren't done with you, and the Alliance certainly isn't done with you, for now you've earned a short respite. Welcome to the rest of your life, Black Jack."

"I'm not Black Jack," Geary protested. "I could never be him."

"You're wrong, John Geary. You've been him every time it counted."

The sailors broke their wall as Desjani and he, arms still linked, walked toward the flight attendant. Then the sailors and the officers among them began cheering. Desjani flushed slightly but kept smiling, raised her chin with pride, and winked at Geary. Geary brought up his free hand to wave to the sailors, feeling pretty damned proud himself of the woman who'd chosen to link her arm with his.

The past would never be gone, but it no longer hurt, and no matter what challenges tomorrow held, today it was good to be Black Jack.

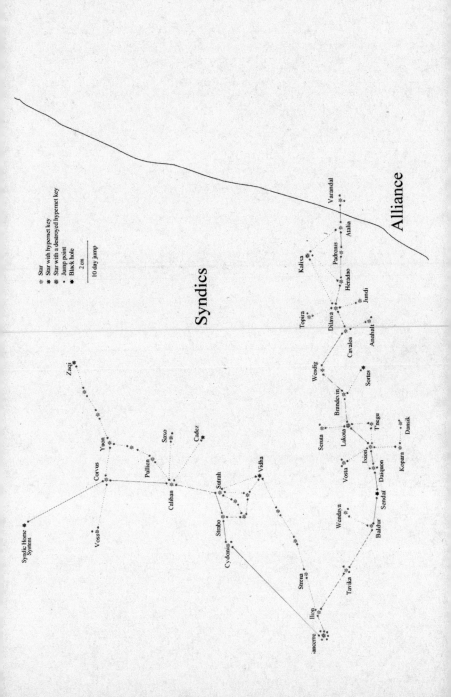

Star
Star with hypernet key
Star with a destroyed hypernet key
Jump point
Black hole

2 cm

10 day jump

Syndics

Alliance

Zagi
Yoon
Corvus
Pullien
Saxo
Cadez
Caliban
Sutrah
Vidha
Strabo
Cydonis
Voss
Wendya
Strina
Taviika
Baldur
Sendai
Daiqpon
Kopara
Dansk
Tnega
Ixion
Vesta
Senta
Lakota
Brandevin
Sortes
Wendig
Cavalos
Anahalt
Dilava
Topira
Jundi
Heradao
Kaliva
Padrons
Atalia
Varandal
Iboji
Sancerre
Syndic Home System

ACKNOWLEDGMENTS

I remain indebted to my agent, Joshua Bilmes, for his ever- inspired suggestions and assistance, and to my editor, Anne Sowards, for her support and editing. Thanks also to Catherine Asaro, Robert Chase, Chuck Gannon, J. G. (Huck) Huckenpohler, Simcha Kuritzky, Michael LaViolette, Aly Parsons, Bud Sparhawk, and Constance A. Warner for their suggestions, comments, and recommendations. Thanks also to Charles Petit for his suggestions about space engagements.

ABOUT THE AUTHOR

John G. Hemry is a retired US Navy officer and the author, under the pen name Jack Campbell, of the *New York Times* national bestselling *The Lost Fleet* series (*Dauntless, Fearless, Courageous, Valiant, Relentless,* and *Victorious*). Next up are two new follow-on series. *The Lost Fleet: Beyond the Frontier* continues to follow Geary and his companions. The other series, *The Phoenix Stars*, is set on a former enemy world in that universe. Under his own name, John is also the author of the *JAG in Space* series and the *Stark's War* series. His short fiction has appeared in places as varied as the last Chicks in Chainmail anthology (*Turn the*

Other Chick) and *Analog* magazine (which published his Nebula Award-nominated story 'Small Moments in Time' as well as most recently 'The Rift' in the October 2010 issue). His humorous short story 'As You Know Bob' was selected for *Year's Best SF 13*. John's nonfiction has appeared in *Analog* and *Artemis* magazines as well as BenBella books on *Charmed*, *Star Wars*, and *Superman*, and in the *Legion of Superheroes* anthology *Teenagers from the Future*.

John had the opportunity to live on Midway Island for a while during the 1960s, graduated from high school in Lyons, Kansas, then later attended the US Naval Academy. He served in a variety of jobs including gunnery officer and navigator on a destroyer, with an amphibious squadron, and at the Navy's anti-terrorism centre. After retiring from the US Navy and settling in Maryland, John began writing. He lives with his long-suffering wife (the incomparable S) and three great kids. His daughter and two sons are diagnosed on the autistic spectrum.

Read on for the sixth extract of our exclusive interview with Jack Campbell (John G. Hemry), in which he talks candidly about writing, space travel, his influences and inspirations and much more.

1. How did you achieve your first writing success?

In short fiction, I had been sending out stories and getting no success. It had me feeling a bit cynical. Well, you give up or you double-down. I knew that Marion Zimmer Bradley, who had her own magazine, didn't like to get dragon stories. So I wrote a dragon story for her ('Agent Problems'), about how hard it was to be a successful writer. And it was different enough that she bought it. That was my first sale.

In novel length, the first success grew out of having sold some short stories. That qualified me for membership in the Science Fiction and Fantasy Writers of America (SFWA, which despite the name also has many non-American members) just before the annual World SF and Fantasy convention was due to take place in Baltimore, Maryland, not too far from where I live. I went to the convention as a newly "professional" writer, and there found that other SF and fantasy writers were for the most part a very welcoming and supportive bunch who were happy to offer advice and assistance. One of them introduced me to an editor from a publisher, and eventually I figured out that I should ask what she was looking for. "Oh, I have something like that. Would you like to see it?" That gave me my first connection to an editor, and after she had looked at what I had and made some suggestions, her publisher offered me a book deal. At the same convention I had also met an agent who had impressed me (Joshua Bilmes of JABberwocky Literary Agency), so I called him up and said "they want to buy my book, will you represent me?" and Joshua was happy to take me on.

That didn't lead to a literary happily-ever-after, of course. Every book takes work, success of any book is far from guaranteed, I've had ups and downs on sales, and all in all the life of an author calls to mind the advice of the Red Queen in the Alice story *Through the Looking Glass* ("It takes all the running you can do, to keep in the same place. If you want to get somewhere else, you must run at least twice as fast as that").

2. What can you tell us about what's coming next for John Geary?

He will have more "opportunities to excel." What does a democracy do with an incredibly popular war hero when the war is over? What dangers and opportunities lie beyond Syndicate Worlds space? Is there more than one other intelligent race out there? Those questions need to be answered. The Syndicate Empire is coming apart, creating numerous immediate and long-term problems. There are also Alliance prisoners of war still to be recovered. What will hold the Alliance together when no great enemy looms at the door, who will control the government, and how much military is now needed? Geary still lives in interesting times, and he will have to make numerous decisions that influence the fate of many. Fortunately, he won't be alone.

3. Would you ever consider going back and telling the story of John Geary's life up to the point of his first 'death'? Do you think he would be a very different person?

I have done a short story about his battle at Grendel, but that offers only a glimpse of who he was then. I have thought about doing more, but how to focus it and keep the tale interesting would be a challenge. Readers are used to a story about Geary involving constant danger, major decisions, and so on, whereas a story before the war would show him with relatively little power and influence, and dealing with relatively minor problems. It would be different, though not impossible since my *JAG in Space* series dealt with "routine" operations by an officer in a situation always short of war. Would Geary be a different

"WHAT DOES A DEMOCRACY DO WITH AN INCREDIBLY POPULAR WAR HERO WHEN THE WAR IS OVER? WHAT DANGERS AND OPPORTUNITIES LIE BEYOND SYNDICATE WORLDS SPACE? IS THERE MORE THAN ONE OTHER INTELLIGENT RACE OUT THERE? THOSE QUESTIONS NEED TO BE ANSWERED."

person? I think fundamentally he wouldn't be totally different. Who he is would always be there, though perhaps much less obvious, less on display. He would be a bit happier, though, and his burdens would be significantly less, even though he would probably worry about them just as if they matched what he would find a century in the future. Like anyone else, Geary would take for granted much of what he had until he lost it. I imagine such stories would have some foreshadowing, small events and conversations that hint at what was to come for him but which he could not possibly imagine happening.

4. Do you listen to music when you write? Do you recall what you listened to when writing *The Lost Fleet*?

I do sometimes, especially when I'm trying not to actually write but to think up ideas and scenes. Letting the front of my mind listen to the sounds frees up the back of my mind to run free and discover things. What I listen to varies wildly, because I like a lot of different kinds of music. Rock from the sixties, eighties and nineties, classical, swing (or classical swing, Benny Goodman's version of Ravel's *Bolero* being a real favourite), Pink Martini, Rodrigo y Gabriela, the Mariachi Divas, the *Streets of Fire* movie soundtrack, soundtracks from good anime like *Haibain Renmei* and *The Girl Who Leapt Through Time* or anything from a Studio Ghibli movie, the latest top ten hits. Some music won't work for me when writing because it tells too strong a story itself. Pink writes those kinds of songs. I get so wrapped up in how well she's telling her story that it distracts me from the story I'm trying to write.

As best I recall when I was working on *Dauntless* I was listening to Martin Denny (1960s lounge exotica), and the soundtracks from *Haibain Renmei*, *Princess Mononoke* and *Spirited Away*. That was what worked then.

5. What book are you reading now?

I've usually got several going at once. I'm reading my eldest son the latest in L A. Meyer's *Bloody Jack* series (*The Wake of the Lorelei Lee*). I'm personally alternating between Seth Lerer's *Inventing English*, Kat Richardson's *Labyrinth*, the latest volume of the *Girl Genius* graphic novels by Phil and Kaja Foglio, and David Sherman's *The Junkyard Dogs*.

Check out the other books in *The Lost Fleet* series for more exclusive interview extracts!

"WHEN I WAS WORKING ON *DAUNTLESS* I WAS LISTENING TO MARTIN DENNY (1960S LOUNGE EXOTICA), AND THE SOUNDTRACKS FROM *HAIBAIN RENMEI*, PRINCESS MONONOKE AND *SPIRITED AWAY*."

TOP TEN TV SHOWS

(1) *Star Trek The Original Series (TOS)*

There's a lot to mock about *Star Trek TOS* ("It's love, Shana!"). But there's also a lot to admire. The characters were unforgettable, even those without names (you know, the ones wearing the red shirts, who became an archetype). Captain Kirk remains *the* starship captain to this day, the strength of the character only emphasized by comparison with later captains both inside and outside the *Star Trek* universe. The triumvirate of Kirk, Spock and McCoy still stands out for the stories built around it. *Star Trek TOS* was grounded in reality. Everybody wasn't an expert on everything. If somebody was hurt, you needed McCoy. If it was a science or technology issue, you needed Spock. And if you needed someone to act so irrational that it melted a computer's circuits, you called on Kirk. *Star Trek TOS* featured a tough but hopeful universe, in which hard decisions have to be made but also one in which Kirk is going to do what's right no matter what that pesky Prime Directive says. Many of the episodes were penned by good SF writers, and it shows. (On a side note, I was one of a lucky few to be able to see *Star Trek TOS* originally on the big screen. Living on Midway Island at the time, we didn't receive television from the States, but on weekends the base theatre would show episodes of *Star Trek TOS*. For the teenage me, Kirk really was bigger than life on a movie screen. In *TOS*, that is. The movies based on the series are best described as varying in quality.)

(2) *The Prisoner*

With the exception of the so-very-sixties, so-very-weird and so-very-meaningless final episode, this was a brilliant series that brought Orwellian concepts to the secret agent genre. *The Prisoner* would never tell his captors why he resigned, and he found ways to thwart their every plan to get the answer. He couldn't win, he couldn't escape, but he wouldn't surrender. A hymn to individuality and freedom wrapped in the prison of the Village. The 2009 movie/mini-series redo of *The Prisoner* is best forgotten.

(3) *The Avengers*

Emma Peel. Best. SF. Female. Character. Ever. John Steed wasn't bad, either. The writing was great, the ideas inventive, the atmosphere wonderful, and the bad guys always trounced before tea. For anyone wondering why Americans are enamoured of Great Britain, this series contains everything that explains the attraction. The movie was terrible, naturally, leading me to wonder why so many movies based on SF TV turn out to be awful (see also *Wild, Wild West*).

(4) *Quantum Leap*

Scott Bakula did not make the best starship captain, but he was at his best in this ingenious series, occupying a different body in a different time every episode. As if that weren't problem enough, his character always faced some challenge in that body, something that required him to change history for the better. It made you think about history and about people, and what you would do in each case. The series finale, surprisingly, actually held up and left the viewer satisfied, a relative rarity.

(5) Mystery Science Theatre 3000 (MST3K)

Sturgeon's Law (named for the great SF writer Theodore Sturgeon) says that ninety percent of everything is junk. *MST3K* did its best to pay back-handed tribute to that ninety percent of movies that could induce anything from sleep to nausea. The set-up involved a man and two robots imprisoned on a satellite and forced to watch bad movies by an evil scientist. They didn't hesitate to take on big names either, as when they skewered the movie version of *2001 A Space Odyssey*. (Some time after a long discussion in the movie about how HAL 9000 series computers never malfunction (and as an aside computers that never malfunction was one of Arthur C. Clark's less successful predictions) we see a big red button labelled "Computer Malfunction" light up. At which point the *MST3K* crew cry "If the computers never malfunction, why did they install that button?")

(6) Futurama

At its best when it didn't take itself seriously, *Futurama* regarded absurdity as simply another state of mind. None of the characters were the sort you would actually want to know (except Lela, who was nonetheless a highly strung control freak), but it was fun to watch them mess up a fictional future. Even though the episodes could include such themes as the players from planet Globetrotter coming to our jive planet to beat us at basketball, they could also sometimes end on powerfully poignant notes, as in the one where Fry learns what his long-dead older brother really thought of him.

(7) Stargate SG-1

Richard Dean Anderson's Colonel Jack O'Neill, Amanda Tapping's Major Sam Carter, Christopher Judge's Teal'c, and Michael Shank's Dr. Daniel Jackson. A great team. The episodes might be pure adventure or they might involve crises for the individual characters. When the series was at its peak it was fun and exciting as well as thought-provoking. It did drag on too long, and made the mistake of trying to continue after Anderson left, which only emphasized how much his Jack O'Neill character contributed to the series. But the series redeemed itself with an outstanding finale that mocked SF TV and TV in general while also paying serious tribute to the grand visions that SF can evoke.

(8) The Twilight Zone

Does this need an explanation? It has become a cultural icon. Everyone knows the concept behind at least a couple of the episodes, which ranged from totally weird fantasy to hard SF. The only thing you could count on was an ending that in one way or another freaked you out.

(9) Phineas and Ferb

How can you not like an animated series when one episode features a musical number about reverse engineering? Where every episode features kids using their imaginations to come up with new gadgets? Where their pet platypus is actually a secret agent for the OWCA (Organization Without a Cool Acronym)? This is a "kids' show" which adults can get a big kick out of, and one which celebrates thinking and building. What's not to like?

(10) *Doctor Who*

You didn't think I'd forget this, did you? My own favourite Doctor remains Tom Baker, complete with scarf and jelly babies. The special effects were... primitive, but something about the stories and the actors held your attention. Despite their clunkiness, the Daleks were properly menacing as they screeched "exterminate!" On our honeymoon trip to the UK, my wife and I went by the London Film Museum, where I startled her by pointing and crying out, "It's K-9!" There he sat, faithfully waiting for the Doctor to pop in.

Check out the other books in the series to discover Jack Campbell's Top Ten Sci Fi books and movies!

STARK'S WAR
BY JACK CAMPBELL
(WRITING AS JOHN G. HEMRY)

The USA reigns over Earth as the last surviving
superpower. To build a society free of American influence,
foreign countries have inhabited the moon, where Sergeant
Ethan Stark and his squadron must fight a desperate enemy
in an airless atmosphere.

STARK'S WAR
STARK'S COMMAND
STARK'S CRUSADE

"A gripping tale of military science fiction, in the tradition
of Heinlein's Starship Troopers and Haldeman's Forever
War... The characterization is right on... the plot is sharp
and crisp...Give this one a try." *Absolute Magnitude*

"The *Stark's War* trilogy has great action scenes, interesting
characters and an original concept." The British Fantasy
Society

"Solidly written, action-packed mil-SF... a good page-
turner that will amply satisfy fans of John Scalzi's *Old
Man's War* series, Jack McDevitt, David Weber or John
Ringo." SFF World

JAG IN SPACE

BY JACK CAMPBELL

(WRITING AS JOHN G. HEMRY)

Equipped with the latest weaponry, and carrying more
than two hundred sailors, the orbiting warship, USS
Michaelson, is armored against the hazards of space and
the threats posed in the vast nothing between planets. But
who will protect her from the threats within?

A JUST DETERMINATION

BURDEN OF PROOF

RULE OF EVIDENCE

AGAINST ALL ENEMIES

"Superior military sf… The last third of the book recalls
nothing so much as *The Caine Mutiny Court-Martial*
in an sf setting, and it attains the same high level of
achievement." *Booklist*

"Fascinating and addictive… Young Paul Sinclair is exactly
the kind of guy you want to serve with, and exactly the
kind of reluctant hero that great series are made from." SF
Revu

"Intelligent and engrossing legal drama… something of a
tour de force." SF Reviews

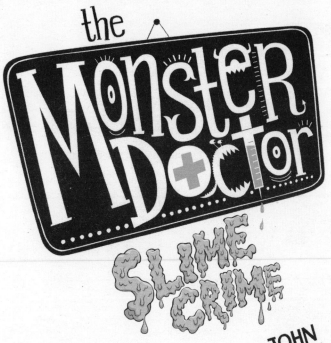

the MONSTER DOCTOR

SLIME CRIME

JOHN KELLY

First published 2021 by Macmillan Children's Books
an imprint of Pan Macmillan
The Smithson, 6 Briset Street, London EC1M 5NR
EU representative: Macmillan Publishers Ireland Limited,
Mallard Lodge, Lansdowne Village, Dublin 4
Associated companies throughout the world
www.panmacmillan.com

ISBN 978-1-5290-2131-8

Text and illustrations copyright © John Kelly 2021

The right of John Kelly to be identified as the author and
illustrator of this work has been asserted by him in accordance
with the Copyright, Designs and Patents Act 1988.

1 3 5 7 9 8 6 4 2

A CIP catalogue record for this book is available
from the British Library.

Printed and bound by CPI Group (UK) Ltd, Croydon CR0 4YY

MIX
Paper from
responsible sources
FSC® C016486

Dear reader,
I wrote this especially for you.

CONTENTS:

Look out for words with the doctor's symbol
after them and look them up in the glossary.

'IS IT A LEAFY GREEN?'

Chapter 1

The monster doctor's voice crackled from the heavy *walkie-talkie* radio dangling on my belt.

'What is the exact colour of the boil, Nurse Ozzy? Over!'

I didn't reply because at that precise moment both of my hands were terribly busy preventing me from falling off the top of a hundred-foot-tall ladder. To distract myself from the **dreadful drop** below, I examined the huge boil that was six inches from my face. It was roughly the size of an over-inflated **space hopper** and looked very angry indeed.

The boil was attached to the end of an enormous nose, and that nose was attached to an equally enormous giant called Little Lionel. (Lionel is small for a giant. Hence his name. Most **giants** are about two-hundred-feet tall, so at almost half that height Lionel is probably borderline ogre, to be honest.)

'Come in, Nurse Ozzy!' said the doctor's insistent voice. *'I repeat: what colour is—'*

'I CAN'T REACH THE RADIO!' I bellowed down towards where the doctor stood holding the bottom of the wobbly ladder. The animated **blob** of messy hair, tweed and industrial-framed glasses that is Annie von Sichertall – a.k.a. the monster doctor, a.k.a. my boss – looked up at me. And, not for the first time, I wondered why it was me perched dangerously on top of this ladder examining **a giant's boil,** instead of the monster doctor herself.

When we arrived, we had extended the roof ladder from Lance, the ambulance.

I'd assumed (wrongly, of course) that the doctor would climb it. After all, it was her turn.

Instead, she just stood there, looking at me expectantly.

'No!' I'd said firmly. 'I did the last suicidally dangerous thing. It's your turn!'

The doctor had responded with a very convincing reason as to why she couldn't climb up. Well, it had seemed very **convincing** at the time, but now I couldn't remember what it was. It was something about her **dodgy left knee,** or an insurance policy having lapsed. I forget which.

'Nurse Ozzy!' her voice gently chided me from the radio. *'A monster doctor never shouts in front of a patient – unless they insist on lecturing you about a silly treatment they've found on the monsterweb. Then you can really let rip at—'*

'THE BOIL IS BRIGHT GREEN!' I shouted in order to cut off her rambling.

'Ah! Now that's rather interesting,' she said. *'Would you say it was a leafy green? Or closer to the lovely bright green of freshly exuded troll pus?'*

I thought about that for a moment. After three weeks as the monster doctor's assistant, I was now well acquainted with all the wondrous shades of troll pus.

'NEITHER,' I shouted down. 'IT'S MORE LIKE THE CHUNKY BITS IN DELORES'S *PISTACHIO* AND **PHLEGM** BISCUITS.' Delores is our surgery's grumpy receptionist. I can't decide which is more scary: Delores or the contents of her special biscuit tin.

Somewhere around my ankles I felt Lionel's mouth begin to open. Oh no! He was going to speak again. I grabbed on tightly to the ladder.

'SPOT...NOT...THERE...AT... BREAKFAST!' he said in a voice as slow and as loud as a passing car stereo.

Giants aren't stupid, by the way. The reason they speak like that is because their **brains** are so MASSIVE that it can take a while for information to travel from point A to point B. (Like when you're trying to show your mum and dad how a new TV works.)

'EXTRAORDINARY!' exclaimed the doctor.

'So this boil is almost as fast-growing as a human teenager's acne!' She went silent for a moment.

This was worrying. When the monster doctor goes quiet, it usually means one of three things:

1. She has run away.
2. She is stuck in the pharmacy cupboard again. (We should really get that door fixed.)
3. She's about to ask me to do something very **dangerous** and is thinking of a nice way to put it.

'**Ozzy,**' she continued in a suspiciously innocent voice, '**I wonder if you might just give the boil a gentle tap and measure how much it wobbles.**'

'I'VE ALREADY DONE THAT,' I shouted smugly. I happened to have read about Diagnostic **Jellification** the previous night in my wonderful *Monster Maladies* book. It contains tons of information about the most common monster illnesses out there and it has a lot of really useful stuff that **every trainee monster doctor** needs to know – it is especially helpful for trainees who are human, like me. For instance, there's a very useful section at the beginning about running very fast.

Diagnostic Jellification

Diagnostic Jellification is how monster doctors are able to measure exactly how **rubbery** a patient – or part of a patient – is. This can be an extremely useful thing for a medical professional to know. Especially if they are about to try to stick something **sharp** into the patient, like a **needle**. Some monsters' skin is so soft that it can be pierced with a **breadstick**, while others may require the use of a rocket-propelled armour-piercing syringe.

The DJ scale begins with extremely **sloppy** and **gloopy** substances like fresh dog drool (0.0 DJs), custard (1.8 DJs) and jellified creatures like blobs (3.5ish DJs).

At the opposite end of the scale you will find much harder materials like steel (8.8 DJs), **Collososaur armour-plating** (9.6 DJs) and even dried-on breakfast cereal (10.0 DJs).

'IT'S NOT VERY WOBBLY!' I shouted. 'I'D RATE IT AT ABOUT 4.5 DJs.' (Well-inflated space hopper.)

'*That's not right,*' mused the doctor. '*A boil that size should have a squishy consistency somewhere between Bob the Blob and human brains or blancmange. You'd better take a sample, Nurse Ozzy. There's a medium monster needle in your kit.*'

I shifted very carefully on the rickety ladder and rooted around in the emergency medical kit dangling from my right shoulder. My fingers closed on a needle that would have made a pretty useful **spear point for a Spartan warrior.**

'I'm very sorry,' I said, holding the huge syringe up in front of Lionel's giant crossed eyes. 'But I need to use this.'

9

Fortunately, monsters aren't as *squeamish* about needles as humans are.

'NO ... PROBLEM ...' he boomed. 'ONLY ... A ... TEENY ... WEENY ... LITTLE ... NEEDLE.'

He laughed gently, almost knocking me off the ladder. But I held on grimly until the ladder – and my teeth – stopped rattling.

'Remember, Ozzy!' the doctor's voice fuzzed once again through the radio. *'Giants are as thick-skinned as reality TV talent show candidates. You'll have to give it a bit of welly.'*

So I gripped the syringe, took a deep breath and imagined that I was trying to cut a piece of my gran's pastry.

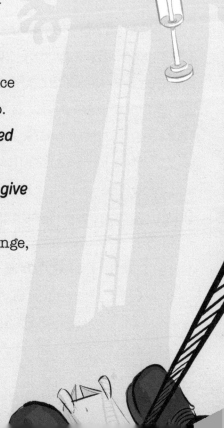

I swung the needle down with as much force as I could and, as the sharp point **PUNCTURED** the tough skin of the boil, there was a noise that reminded me of mealtimes at home.

It was a louder version of the noise my baby sister makes when she suddenly decides that the food she has been *chewing* would be better back on the plate. Or on the nearby wall. Or my face.

It was a

SPLAT!

But much, much, **louder.**

And all of a sudden I was very wet and the same colour as the chunky bits in one of Delores's biscuits.

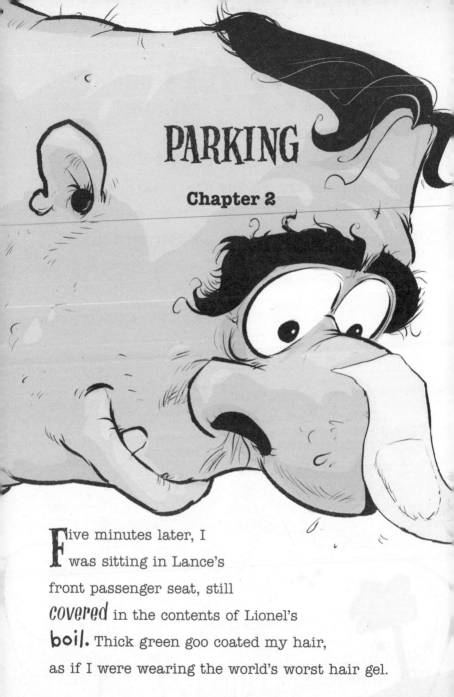

PARKING

Chapter 2

F ive minutes later, I was sitting in Lance's front passenger seat, still *covered* in the contents of Lionel's boil. Thick green goo coated my hair, as if I were wearing the world's worst hair gel.

And my sweatshirt was so **contaminated** that it would probably have to be burned, then the ashes disposed of somewhere in the middle of the Atlantic Ocean.

I sat scooping handfuls of the **ghastly goo** from my jeans pockets and watched *grumpily* through the windscreen as the monster doctor applied a plaster the size of a small duvet to Lionel's nose.

She waved goodbye to the giant and jumped into Lance's* driving seat.

* Lance is the monster doctor's ambulance. He is just like any other ambulance apart from the fact that:

A. He is alive.
B. He can travel almost instantly through any of the six known dimensions.
C. He has absolutely no sense of direction.

The monster doctor smiled broadly and clapped me on the shoulder.

'**A boil exploding** in the face is so refreshing, isn't it?' she said. I obviously didn't look refreshed because she added, 'Of course! How thoughtless of me. I always forget that you ordinaries have this **weird aversion to bodily fluids**. Never mind. You can have a nice shower when we get back to the surgery, now that the leak in the *swamp-spa treatment room* has finally been mended.'

She switched on Bruce, the BAT-NAV. This involved **whacking** the side of his jar to wake him up.

16

Bruce's* screen lit up.

> ## OH, IT'S YOU.
> ## I WAS HAVING A LOVELY DREAM
> ## ABOUT A DARK DANK CAVE –

His eyes suddenly alighted on me and he gave an evil little smile.

> ## OOOH! I LIKE OZZY'S NEW HAIRSTYLE!

Did I mention that Bruce is very *rude* to everyone?

But he likes to be especially rude to me.

'Now, Bruce,' chided the doctor. 'Do please try and be *nice* to Ozzy. He's had a difficult morning. And be so kind as to take us back to the surgery via a nice quiet route this time. I do NOT want to travel through the **"very hairy"** dimension today, please.'

YOU'RE SO BORING.
WE NEVER GET TO DO ANYTHING DANGEROUS
SINCE YOU HIRED THE HUMAN.

But he did as he was told and we were immediately transported into inter-dimensional space.*

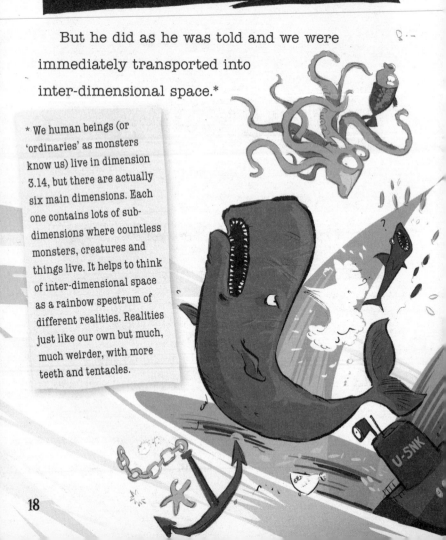

* We human beings (or 'ordinaries' as monsters know us) live in dimension 3.14, but there are actually six main dimensions. Each one contains lots of sub-dimensions where countless monsters, creatures and things live. It helps to think of inter-dimensional space as a rainbow spectrum of different realities. Realities just like our own but much, much weirder, with more teeth and tentacles.

19

Thankfully, this time, we had a nice quiet trip home.

The bottom of the Pacific Ocean was peaceful (as rush hour had just finished) and aisle fourteen (barbecues and lawn furniture) at the North Pole branch of B&Q was as *deserted* as usual.

Finally, we emerged on to Lovecraft Avenue and trundled down the road towards the surgery.

As we drew closer, Lance began to rev his engine **aggressively.** Which was very odd, as Lance is usually such a gentle monster.

The doctor patted his steering wheel. **'Steady on, Lance,'** she soothed. 'Calm down, boy! I'm sure it's not a deliberate insult. Yes, I know it's very clearly marked as your bay.'

'What's the matter?' I asked.

Bruce's screen pinged.

ISN'T IT OBVIOUS?
SOME IDIOT HAS PARKED IN LANCE'S SPOT!

The doctor pointed to where a large, shiny black car was parked in Lance's **EMERGENCY WAITING BAY.**

Its bonnet was turned up, in what somehow looked like a rather smug, self-satisfied air. And I could have SWORN there was a sneer on the overly shiny bumper.

'Lance gets upset if someone parks in his spot?' I laughed.

NO PARKING!
BY ORDER OF LANCE

But that was a *mistake.* Lance growled angrily at me, like my dog Piglet does when I touch his squeaky squirrel without permission.

'Ozzy!' hissed the doctor. 'PLEASE be careful what you say about parking! YOU might not think it's a big deal, but Lance is an Inter-dimensional Vehicle and they have very – very – **strict rules about parking.'**

'Can't we just give it a ticket or something?' I asked.

'Oh, dear me, no!' said the doctor. 'It's much too serious an **offence** for that. As you know, IDVs can travel anywhere in any dimension at will, but, sadly, as you also know, **the poor things have a dreadful sense of direction.** Just try and imagine what it feels like to take decades getting back home from the shops, only to discover that another IDV has nicked your precious parking spot!

I can assure you, Ozzy, wars
have been fought
over less!'

I supposed that did explain an awful lot about
the tense conversations my dad sometimes
has with Mr Woffell at number 37.

'Anyway, I can't trust Lance to park himself
now,' added the doctor. 'He might "accidentally
on purpose" smash that car into tiny pieces. And
then smash those pieces into even smaller ones.
And then drive back and forth over them a few
times. **Be a dear and pop inside and tell the
idiot owner to move it?'**

I ran into the surgery as the doctor chaperoned
a growling Lance off towards the garage.
Despite her best efforts, Lance still managed to
'accidentally on purpose' swipe off the other car's
shiny wing mirror. He disappeared round the
corner, his engine revving in a happy little laugh.

The surgery was
packed with patients.
Simon Salamander,
the owner of
**The Battered
Squid chippy,**
was there with his front
legs covered in dozens
of sticky plasters.
(He'd obviously been
wrestling with the
lunchtime specials again.)

My old zombie pal Morty Mort called out, 'Wotcha, Ozzy!' and waved with his right arm. This arm, his torso and his left leg were poking out from a **BRAINSBURY'S carrier bag,** while his head, left arm, feet and nose were distributed between two other *MESSCO carrier bags.*

He'd clearly gone to pieces again – and there was no sign of his right leg anywhere.

'That'll teach me to enrol in mixed **martial arts** classes!' he said, laughing. In fact, he laughed so hard his head rolled off the chair.

Vlad the vampire, who was sitting next to him, leaned forward. He caught Morty's head neatly and popped it safely back on the chair.

'Morty, my very good friend,' he said seriously in his thick **Transylvanian accent,** 'you muzt learn to treat being dead viz more respect!'

Vlad ran the all-night garage and convenience store down the road, and we were treating him for a very nasty case of sunburn. **His wife, Vladness, elbowed him in the ribs and laughed.**

'Muzt you always be zo gloomy, Vlad?' she said. 'Let Morty live a little! After all, ze poor fellow will only be dead vonce!'

I coughed loudly and said, 'Excuse me, everyone!' But the various monsters, things and assorted **un-classified creatures** were all too busy chatting to notice me. So I picked up the *bell-bug* ⍦ the doctor uses to signal the surgery is open and rang it. *It CLANGED loudly* and they all turned to look. 'Does anyone here drive a shiny black IDV with the number plate I1YR CA5H ?'

Nobody answered me. I looked around with a frown, and noticed that there was a monster I didn't recognize talking to Delores the receptionist. The monster looked an awful lot like a **T. Rex** – apart from the fact that it was wearing high heels and a very expensive pinstripe business suit, and was no larger than a well-fed Great Dane. (The dog, obviously. Not the nationality.)

'Excuse me,' I said. 'Is that your car outsi—?'

Delores held up a single tentacle in that annoying **talk-to-the-tentacle-thing** she does when she's extremely 'busy'. She normally does this when she's reading a magazine, painting her tentacle tips or eating a chocolate-covered beetle.

'As I was saying,' she continued, turning back to the miniature dinosaur, 'before I was so RUDELY interrupted –' she scowled at me – 'will this supposed "wonder drug" of yours cure the dreadful pain in my sixth, seventh and eighth tentacles? I mean it's EXCRUCIATING when I have to do something strenuous, like lift a piece of paper or stick a stamp on an envelope.

But the doctor doesn't listen to me. **Oh, dear me, no!** She just goes on and on about psycho-something-or-other. If you want to know what I think—'

I was about to engage my 'tune-Delores-out filter' when the newcomer began to speak.

'Would you hold that fascinating thought for a second, Delores dear?' she said. And then, turning to me, she **smiled broadly** and added, 'I'm sorry, did you mention something about an IDV being parked badly?'

I didn't reply immediately. And when I finally did all I could manage to say was, 'Teeth.'

Which may sound a bit stupid. But in my defence I was completely **transfixed** by her smile. It was very, very wide and seemed to contain about as many teeth as **a very large dental museum.**

MON-MED

Chapter 3

'**O**h dear!' said the toothy monster with a laugh. 'Has my naughty IVAN parked in the wrong place again?' She held out her hand. *Her nails were beautifully manicured,* but looked sharp enough to open a can of beans.

I shook it very, very carefully.

'I'm so sorry – how rude of me,' she added. 'My name is—'

'Ms Diagnosiz!' the doctor's loud voice boomed across the surgery as she emerged from the door to the basement garage. 'As I live and – occasionally – breathe! How on earth are you? **I haven't seen you since that food poisoning conference on Mushroom Island.** Do come straight through to my office. You too, Ozzy.'

I sighed. I had been hoping that I could go up to the swamp-spa treatment room and wash Lionel's boil goo out of my trousers. As we walked away a disgruntled Delores called out, 'Oh, I see! Just ignore me and my tentacle pain, then. And I suppose you'll be wanting some *tea and biscuits!*'

'**BISCUITS!**' cried the doctor. '**Marvellous idea!** And none of those cheap ones with nails in them. Break out the special biscuit tin.' She quickly closed the door on any further moaning and turned to me. 'Ozzy, allow me to introduce Ms Diagnosiz. **She is a sales rep from FANG-PHARMA Medical Supplies Inc.** They make—'

'Wunda-Wipes, Claw-Rotnot and No-Fungontung!' I interrupted proudly. I'd been brushing up on my monster medicines recently and remembered FANG-PHARMA because of their reassuring corporate motto:

FANG-PHARMA Medical Supplies
MUCH SAFER THAN LAST YEAR

The doctor sat down behind her desk and I took a chair, letting out an embarrassing squelch as I did so. But no one commented, as embarrassing **squelches** are pretty common in the surgery.

'Oh, I'm not working for them any more,' Ms Diagnosiz trilled. 'I'm at **MON-MED** pharmaceuticals now.'

She placed her shiny briefcase on the doctor's desk. Then, after a quick struggle with the locks (due to her tiny arms and big nails), she offered me a business card.

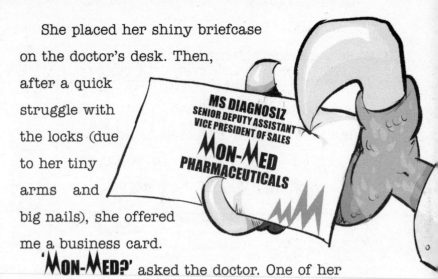

'**MON-MED?**' asked the doctor. One of her ears wiggled in suspicion. (FYI: One ear wiggling = mild suspicion. Two = total disbelief.) 'Didn't they have an **enormous scandal with their tentacle ointment** causing that—?'

'Oh, that's all in the past now,' said Ms Diagnosiz waving one tiny arm dismissively. 'They had a complete shake-up after the previous management team were convicted and dropped into a volcano.'

Ms Diagnosiz gave a tinkling laugh as she took out a very expensive-looking shiny packet from the case. It was embossed with a snazzy letter 'F' on it. She opened it, tossed the packet into a nearby waste bin and pulled out a small bottle.

'Now, Annie, the reason I'm here is this little wonder.' She held the bottle up to the light. It contained a thin, green, slimy liquid that glowed ever so slightly in a way that liquids probably shouldn't. *'It's called* **FIXITALL** *and it will instantly cure any of over three hundred major and minor monster illnesses!'*

Ms Diagnosiz smiled brightly, before adding, 'And associated Thing complaints.'

I looked at the bottle dubiously. 'Can it heal giant-squid bites?' I was thinking about poor Simon Salamander in the waiting room.

'Of course!' answered the toothy sales rep smoothly. 'It's also available as a *handy tube of* **extra-gloopy slime** *ointment.*' She pulled a sample from her briefcase and tossed it to me.

'What about **severe sunburn?**' asked the doctor excitedly. 'We always have dreadful problems with vampires who forget to put on their factor one thousand sun cream on a nice day.'

'Oh yes, indeed!' Ms Diagnosiz went on. '**FIXITALL** will cure all major monster skin conditions including – but not limited to – **crustacea-irritata, scratchy-scab, arachnid-acne and werewolf silver blisters.**'

'But surely that's impossible?' I protested. 'How can a single drug cure so many different illnesses? It doesn't make any—'

Ms Diagnosiz reached for another box, and happened to knock me off my chair and into a **potted carnivorous shrub** in the process.

As I tried to extract myself without being bitten, she handed a glossy promotional leaflet to the doctor.

The doctor looked at it eagerly and asked, 'So how does it work, then?'

'Now, now, you know I can't possibly tell you that, Annie!' cried Ms Diagnosiz. 'It's all very hush-hush.' But then she leaned in conspiratorially and whispered, 'What I can tell you, though, is that **MON-MED**'s top scientist has made an *incredible breakthrough in Spaghetto-Genetics.* I don't want to say too much, but it may well be that soon **MON-MED** will be able to cure almost every monster illness!'

I looked between the two of them in confusion. 'Spaghetto-Genetics? What's that?'

'It's the monster genetic code.' The doctor sighed in exasperation and looked at me with **eyes full of disappointment.** 'It was in your reading *homework* for last week – along with some of the complications caused by head transplants and treatment for **babble-jaw syndrome.** You'll have to catch up later, in your own time,' she added crossly. 'Right now, I want to see this universal cure in action!'

I was just about to explain that I'd been helping babysit my monstrous little sister last week, and homework had been tricky because I had been busy dodging objects thrown by her and **cleaning up the various bodily fluids she deposited without warning** around the house. But at that moment Delores barged through the door. She was carrying a tray filled with cups of steaming, **fizzing bile tea** and a plate of scary-looking biscuits. She plonked it noisily down on the table right beside Ms Diagnosiz's open briefcase.

'Is this it, then?' she asked, snatching the bottle of **FIXITALL** from the T. Rex. 'This is the universal cure that'll fix my aching tentacle cramps?'

And before Ms Diagnosiz could stop her, the receptionist had opened the bottle of **FIXITALL** and 𝓰𝓵𝓾𝓰𝓰𝓮𝓭 the slimy gloop down as if it were a mug of cold bile tea.

Now this may sound like a **shockingly dangerous** thing to do, but then you've never seen the contents of Delores's side of the office fridge.

'I don't feel any different,' she said after a pause. 'How long does it take this stuff to—'

But she was unable to finish the sentence. An annoying *whine* had suddenly filled the room and for a moment I thought a bee was trapped in her hair. But then I realized the sound was actually coming from somewhere **inside Delores's left nostril.**

'Is this sort of thing normal with **FIXITALL?**' the doctor asked Ms Diagnosiz with interest.

The saleswoman smiled and nodded. 'Oh yes,' she said. 'Always the left nostril. *Quite normal.* And, as you can see, it's quickly followed by the smoke.'

'The smoke?' asked Delores, concern creeping into her voice. I noticed there were *indeed wisps of blue and green smoke* starting to pulse from her ears. It looked as if her brain had taken up pipe-smoking.

I started to back away, just in case the receptionist was actually about to explode. Because even though **I hadn't yet seen an entire monster explode,** much weirder things have happened to me in the last three weeks.

I took cover behind the swamp-water dispenser, which is nice and heavy, so I figured it might offer some protection in the event of Delores suddenly going **BOOM!**

A FEW TINY SIDE-EFFECTS

Chapter 4

Ms Diagnosiz, however, seemed unconcerned about the possibility of an explosion.

'Patients may be alarmed at first,' she explained, 'by the **nasal whining** and *ear smoke*. But they're a vital indicator to the medical professional that **FIXITALL** slime is **working.**'

'Jolly useful,' agreed the doctor. 'And is the right eyeball revolving clockwise normal too?'

'Yes,' said Ms Diagnosiz. 'And you'll notice that the left one is moving anti-clockwise at the same time. She is entering the final treatment phase now. But don't worry. **It'll all be over any second** . . .' She looked down at her very expensive bejewelled watch. 'In fact, right about . . . **now!**'

Exactly on cue, both eyes stopped spinning. (Which was just as well as I was starting to feel **a bit dizzy.**)

'Are you all right, Delores?' I asked the grumpy receptionist nervously, getting ready to dodge her nearest tentacles or suffer some particularly cutting remark about my hair.

To my **astonishment**, she smiled pleasantly back at me.*

I shuddered.

'Are you all right?' I repeated, cautiously emerging from behind the crusty water dispenser.

'All right?' She beamed.

* The words 'Delores', 'smiled' and 'pleasant' are an unnatural combination to find in any one sentence. In fact, I'd only ever seen the receptionist smile once before. And that had been as unsettling an experience as my grandma's 'special' vegetarian chilli.

'Oh yes, Ozzy! I'm as right as rain, sweetie! **My dreadful tentacle cramp is completely gone!** And I feel simply . . .' She stretched her sixth, seventh and eighth tentacles out and twined them around each other as if they were newborn puppies wriggling in a basket. 'OOOOOOOH! What's the word . . .? *Lovely! I haven't felt this flexible since I was young and starring in Madam Squidling's dancing-tentacle troupe.'*

Then, to my utter horror, she laughed girlishly and actually tossed her hair like a pony.

UGH!

'What an extraordinary achievement!' cried the monster doctor. 'A universal cure? Why, this could be even more **significant** than the discovery of Head Massage Therapy.'

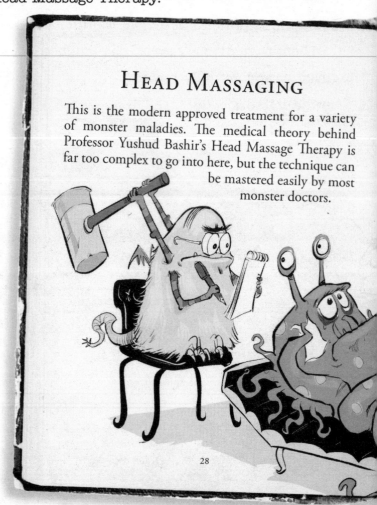

HEAD MASSAGING

This is the modern approved treatment for a variety of monster maladies. The medical theory behind Professor Yushud Bashir's Head Massage Therapy is far too complex to go into here, but the technique can be mastered easily by most monster doctors.

28

In short, the patient is seated in a comfortable chair while the therapist approaches them from behind with a large massage hammer.

The patient is then struck repeatedly on the head.

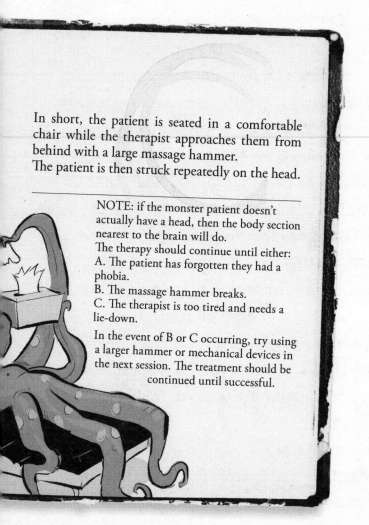

NOTE: if the monster patient doesn't actually have a head, then the body section nearest to the brain will do.

The therapy should continue until either:

A. The patient has forgotten they had a phobia.

B. The massage hammer breaks.

C. The therapist is too tired and needs a lie-down.

In the event of B or C occurring, try using a larger hammer or mechanical devices in the next session. The treatment should be continued until successful.

I still wasn't sure. A **universal cure** sounded a bit like **a shortcut** to me. And in my experience shortcuts didn't work – especially when Dad was driving, as they always seemed to end up with us in the *wrong country,* or having to be pulled out of the canal. But the doctor didn't seem to be worried at all.

'A universal cure for monster illness . . .' she said dreamily. 'That might mean I can start thinking about taking it a bit easier. What with Ozzy's studies coming along so nicely, perhaps I could finally go part-time. *Spend more time on my hobbies.* It's been decades since I did any still-life boil painting. And the campaign to reintroduce mammoth racing has stalled recently . . .'

'Well, now's your chance to try it,' said Ms Diagnosiz quickly. '**MON-MED** is giving *an exclusive* list of monster doctors and celebrities a chance to try **FIXITALL** before it goes on general release.'

The doctor positively beamed. 'Well, you can count us in!'

'Excellent!' said Ms Diagnosiz, once again showing off all her teeth as she rummaged around in her briefcase. 'There are just a couple of tiny things I need from you. Firstly, there's the small **administration fee** of eight hundred Karloffs.'

'Eight hundred Karloffs!' I blurted. You can buy a three-course dinner for two at **The Battered Squid chippy** – including a large plate of dread and butter – for less than one Karloff.

'Oh, it's only money, Ozzy!' chided the monster doctor. 'What's the other thing, Ms Diagnosiz?'

The saleswoman produced a legal form.

'I just need your signature here –' she pointed with one extremely sharp claw – **'here, and ... here!** It's just the standard **legal stuff** about **side-effects,** patients' legs **falling off,** et cetera.'

'Er . . . should **MON-MED** really be selling medicine that makes patients' limbs fall off?' I asked. But for some reason the doctor, Ms Diagnosiz and even Delores all began to laugh.

'BAN a medicine because of a few side-effects?' exclaimed the doctor, wiping the tears from her eyes. 'Oh dear. Whatever next? There's **nothing wrong** with a few side-effects, Ozzy. All the really useful monster medicines have side-effects. Even No-Fungontung causes **large horns to suddenly sprout from inappropriate parts of the body.** But a few dozen extra horns is a price worth paying to have a nice slimy tongue, isn't it?'

I wasn't sure.

The doctor turned to the very eager-looking Ms Diagnosiz. 'I'll take the lot!' she said enthusiastically.

Ten minutes later Ms Diagnosiz was driving away in her shiny black car. There was a **large pile** of **FIXITALL** packets on Delores's counter and an even larger hole in the doctor's wallet.

'Hand these out to **any patient** that wants them, Ozzy,' said the doctor. 'And then please get yourself cleaned up. **You're trailing boil pus all around the surgery.'** She was right. The contents of Lionel's nasal boil had been slowly sliding down all morning and was now starting to congeal unpleasantly in the **underpants region.**

As I dispensed the **FIXITALL** slime, not a
single monster seemed to share my worries about
potential side-effects. Simon Salamander, both the
Vlads, Mrs Graves, Oswalt Sadbottom and every
other **sickly patient** gratefully took a bottle of
the slimy 'universal cure' and scurried off home.

In a few minutes the **FIXITALL** was all gone
and the surgery was empty, save for the doctor,
me, an **unnaturally happy Delores** and an
unnaturally grumpy Morty. (Even a wonder
drug couldn't stitch a zombie back together.)

'Do you need my help stitching Morty back together before I get cleaned up?' I asked the doctor.

Delores laughed and said, 'Don't you worry yourself, Ozzy. I'll help the doctor.' The idea of Delores actually volunteering to help is about as unlikely as hearing that a **giant asteroid,** which was about to wipe out all life on Earth, has just bounced harmlessly off **Milton Keynes.**

I excused myself from the weirdness and **squelched** out of the room. It was going to take some time to get used to 'nice' Delores. (And even longer to get the disturbing mental image of her dancing out of my brain.)

But luckily I had something wonderful to look forward to. I was about to have the *finest shower in the known universe.*

SPURTIE

Chapter 5

The swamp-spa treatment room on the third floor of the surgery is not really safe for humans. And by 'not really safe for' I mean 'extremely dangerous for'.

It was built to treat monsters whose natural environment can best be described as damp and **fetid.** For instance, there is a swamp-gas *sauna booth* that is best avoided if you are stubbornly attached to human ideals like breathing. And there's a brand-new quicksand jacuzzi that is very useful for treating **serious troll skin conditions** – as long as you're not bothered about the possibility of suddenly **bursting** into flames.

Still, despite this, the spa contains two things that are very *special to me.*

The first is my locker. This is where I keep changes of **clean clothing**. (As you may have noticed being a trainee monster doctor can be an extremely messy, slimy business.)

The second is Spurtie.

Spurtie is the **shower snake.**

I mean, electric showers, power showers and even those fancy home spas with the **nozzles** that squirt water into places you weren't really expecting are all fine, but for the ultimate shower experience you really, really, REALLY need to have a shower snake.

Extract from Archibald Flim's *THE ODDER PLACE: A Traveller's Guide to the Stranger Bits of Dimension 3.71*:

The inhabitants of dimension 3.71 are the shower snakes of Fountane Lake. Their bodies comprise of a long wriggly tube with a hole at each end. They spend their days sucking filthy swamp water in (via the end without eyes) and then spraying it out (via the end with eyes). Amazingly, the water exits their body sparklingly clean, nicely warm and with a natural soapy additive that smells of vanilla.

No one knows why they do this.

But we should be eternally grateful that they do.

I opened the door to the spa – remembering to step over the **hydrochloric acid footbath** – and began to undress. One by one, I dropped the soiled clothes into the open and eager mouth of the laundry monster.

The hungry creature burped, said, **'Fank yoo vewy much!'** and began to greedily suck all the dirt and boil pus off my clothes. **They'd be nice and clean-ish sometime tomorrow.** Though it would probably hang on to one of my socks as payment.

I opened the door to the shower cubicle.

'Good morning, Spurtie,' I said to the shower snake as he uncoiled from his perch. **Spurtie was about six feet long,** as thick as a vacuum cleaner cord and was striped bright blue and orange.

'GOOOD MOORNING, OOZEEE!' he replied. **'YOO WONNN A WOSHHHH?'** Shower snakes find it very hard to make anything other than vowel sounds because their mouths are shaped like a nozzle.

'Yes, please!' I replied eagerly as Spurtie dipped his tail (the end without eyes) into the **sewage outlet.** 'And is there any chance you could make it a little bit more gentle this ti—' But before I could finish speaking the shower snake was enthusiastically *blasting* me with its fire-hose jet of warm, sweet-smelling soapy water.

It was bliss!

Ten minutes later I was towelled off, wearing clean clothes and back downstairs in the deserted surgery. Since no one was about and all my chores for the day were done — **bile leeches fed, nasal worms safely locked up, toe and horn clippers sharpened** — I decided to have a quick read about Spaghetto-Genetics.

I made myself a nice cup of *hot sluggaccino*, grabbed a plate of mostly human-safe biscuits and settled down in the waiting room with a copy of *TANGLED UP IN YOU – A Basic Primer on Monster Spaghetto-Genetics.*

Introduction

What is Spaghetto-Genetics?

We monsters come in an extraordinary variety of shapes and sizes. From the two-inch long nasal worm to the fifteen-thousand ton maxocolossosaurapod. From the slippery lagoon lizard to the dry and dusty Saharan sponge worm.

Nasal worm   **Maxocolossosaurapod**

Over the centuries many theories have been put forward to try to explain this extraordinary diversity – which is especially extraordinary when compared to other creatures like human beings and monkeys, who only come in one rather boring shape.

Lagoon lizard   **Saharan sponge worm**   **Human being**
(Tail optional)

Could this brilliantly diverse range be something to do with the colour of underwear your monster ancestors wore? Could it be caused by eating too much rusty metal, or maybe the wrong kind of people?

Tentaclio Spaghetti

There was no answer. That is, until monster doctor Tentaclio Spaghetti discovered that every single cell in a monster's body contains hundreds of intertwined strands of genetic code. We now call this code DNA (Dexy-Noodleclaic-Acid) or, more commonly, Spaghetto-Genetics. And it's the very complexity of this DNA that allows for the amazing physical diversity of monsters. Tentaclio was awarded the Trollsmell Prize for monster cleverness in 1921.

I was just about to read the first chapter when I was disturbed by the sound of raised voices coming from the street outside. Then someone began **hammering on the front door.**

Whoever it was did not sound happy.

'DOCTOR!' I yelled.

She instantly appeared with her shirt sleeves rolled up, carrying something wriggling. 'What's going on?' she said, handing me a large needle, some thread and Morty's still-wriggling left hand. She grabbed the door handle and **flung the door open** to reveal an angry mob of the surgery's patients.

MUSTARD CREAMS

Chapter 6

'**SIDE-EFFECTS!**' slobbered Simon Salamander. '**Is that what you call this?**' He held up three of his arms for the doctor to inspect. I was amazed – the bite marks were gone! He was completely healed.

Unfortunately, his **healed skin** was now a rather **unpleasant combination** of yellow, pink and mauve vertical stripes. 'It's been like this since I took that **stupid slime** you prescribed!' he complained. 'And it's not just me that's been affected. **Look at that poor monster!**' He pointed across Lovecraft Avenue at Oswalt Sadbottom, a very shy ogre the doctor was treating for his nerves. Oswalt seemed to be unable to reach the surgery because his right leg had shrunk to **half the length of the left.** The poor ogre was finding it almost impossible to walk in anything other than a circle.

Vlad and Vladness the vampires appeared suddenly from behind us, making the doctor and I jump. (How did they do that?) I noticed they were both carrying shopping bags full of *fresh salad.* And Vlad was gnawing like a beaver on a stick of celery.

'**Help us, doktor!**' pleaded
Vlad. 'Ever since ve drank **zat
disguzting zlime of yours,**
ze sight of blood makes my vife
and I feel very queasy.'

'Now all ve can do,' added Vladness, tossing
radishes into her mouth as if they were *chocolate
bonbons,* 'iz eat zis awful salad. But ve cannot
live like zis. What kind of monster eats just
vegetables?'

As they spoke, other monsters pressed in on the
doctor, also demanding answers. And even more
were heading up Lovecraft Avenue towards us.

'I don't understand,' said the doctor. 'It must be
the **FIXITALL. But surely no single medicine
can have so many bizarre side-effects?**'

'We didn't actually read the side-effects
leaflet, though, did we?' I said.

The doctor gave me the same blank look my **grandpa** does when I try to explain a **really modern invention, like the internet or the indoor toilet**.

'What side-effects leaflet?' she asked.

I ran to the doctor's office and retrieved the **FIXITALL** packet from the waste bin. On the way back outside, I extracted the **thick folded paper leaflet** and passed it to the doctor. I got the distinct impression that it was the first time in her long life that she had ever seen such a leaflet.

'Are you seriously telling me there's a complete list of side-effects inside every packet of monster medicine ever produced?'

I nodded.

'Well, I'll be blowed!' the doctor said. 'I always thought that bit of paper was in there for padding! What will they think of next, eh?

I suppose we'd better read it.'

So we read it.

It was a very long list.

Here is a short extract.

MM MON-MED PHARMACEUTICALS

FIXITALL SIDE-EFFECTS (MILD)

Dry eyes.

Watery eyes.

Extra eyes.

Stiffness.

Floppiness.

Extreme dizziness leading to extreme falling over.

Skin rashes consisting of spots, stripes, tweed, plaid, herringbone, leopard, tiger, ocelot and, in some severe cases, obscure Scottish tartans.

Individual leg lengths may differ from one day to the next.

Putting on weight – including skin.

Unnatural niceness.

Unexplained, rapidly growing boils.

Unexpected and unwanted air in undesirable places.

Strange appetites. (Manure, corrugated steel, pilchards (including canned), sliced white supermarket bread, radioactive isotopes and, in some severe cases, salad.)

Sudden unexplained fluency in Classical Japanese.

And it went on and on. There were **seventeen** more pages of symptoms. And these were only the mild ones!

I looked up and spotted Gordon the ghoul
approaching, shouting something incompre-
hensible in what I assumed was *Classical
Japanese.* Melisssa Medusa was slithering up
the pavement, a furious look on her face and her
snake hair all **stiff and erect like a reptilian
pincushion.** Even the normally polite and very
neat skeleton, Mrs Graves, was heading for us,

dragging her bony little dog, Tibia, behind her. She looked as if she'd put on some skin, and she didn't look very happy about it.

It was turning into an **ugly crowd.** (Well, uglier than usual, anyway.) And if we didn't do something quickly we might end up with another **patient riot** on our hands. But luckily one thing living with my family has taught me is that there is a **sure-fire way of nipping any potential riot in the bud.**

Tea and biscuits.

'Delores!' I called out cheerily. 'I think it's time to make a nice pot of bile tea for everyone and –' I paused dramatically – 'perhaps break out the special biscuit tin.'

The monster crowd instantly went very still.

Delores's special biscuit tin was **legendary** among the doctor's patients. Many had heard of it, but few had ever been lucky enough to be granted a glimpse of its contents.

'What a lovely idea!' Delores beamed. (Which was **REALLY** weird, as she would normally have removed a limb from anyone who touched her special biscuit tin.) 'Everyone follow me!' She slithered happily off towards the kitchen while *gaily whistling a creepy monster music-hall tune.*

But it worked.

Vladness said, 'Zat vud be lovely! I vunder if she has any of thoze *hairy baldis* you like, Vlad?' And before long the monsters were following Delores inside to the waiting room, arguing about which biscuits were the best: mustard creams, chocolate indigestives or whinger snaps.

Biscuits – as always – had averted a **riot**.

The doctor smiled reassuringly at the patients as she dragged me towards her office.

She closed the door and hissed, 'This is terrible! I've never seen so many different side-effects before! We've got to find out what is going on before someone gets really annoyed and **eats us.**'

'Can you call someone at **MON-MED?**' I asked.

'Another brilliant idea, Nurse Ozzy!' she exclaimed. **'There's bound to be a perfectly natural explanation as to why a pharmaceutical sales rep would sell me a patently dangerous medicine.'**

I didn't say anything.

She pulled out her monster mobile and began dialling. Someone answered, and the doctor put it on speaker.

But it was only the answerphone.

A smug voice began to recite,

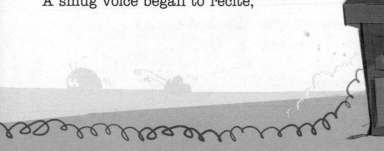

'You have reached **MON-MED** pharmaceuticals. Unfortunately we have ceased trading due to ongoing legal action. If you experience any unusual or dangerous medical issues we suggest you contact ***a fully qualified monster*** doctor. Failing that, you could lie down in a nice dark box. Or, if you don't have a box handy, you could just hang up now. We would also like to take this opportunity to thank you for being a customer of **MON-MED** pharmaceuticals and please remember, your sickness was always very important to us.'

And with that the line went dead.

MALPRACTICE

Chapter 7

'**A**h,' said the doctor as she replaced the phone receiver. '**This is bad. Very bad.**'

'I thought you said a few side-effects were OK in monster medicine,' I said.

'Oh, Ozzy!' she exclaimed. 'This isn't the same thing at all. It's not like giving monster aspirin to a Thing,* or giving a mother a baby with the wrong number of heads! No, this is SERIOUS! **This is a FOUR M EMERGENCY!**'

Now, by an amazing coincidence, I knew exactly what the doctor was referring to. You see, my **homework** the previous evening had been to read Dr Yuri Tooblaym's popular book:

* Monsters and things are very different. Monsters are born weird. Things are made weird by events.

OOPS! THAT WASN'T SUPPOSED TO HAPPEN!
A Beginner's Guide to Monster Medical Malpractice.

MULTIPLE MONSTER MEDICINE MALPRACTICES

Giving a patient the wrong (or dangerous) medicine is quite normal and not actually that serious if you have good enough malpractice insurance. Unfortunately, even this won't protect a doctor who has dosed multiple patients. If this happens, there are three main options available to the monster doctor:

FLEE.
Dimension 2.6 has a no-extradition policy with the 'civilized' monster universe – and it has some lovely red-hot swampside resorts.

BLAME YOUR ASSISTANT.
This is why I personally recommend hiring one or more stupid assistants. It is at times like these that they really come into their own.

TRY TO FIX THE PROBLEM.
This will give you the rosy glow of having done the right thing. But it has some obvious downsides: expensive court cases, prison, being eaten, etc.

'But what are we supposed to do?' I asked. 'If **MON-MED** pharmaceuticals has *gone bust*, then where are we going to find a *cure* for **FIXITALL?** It's not as if we can just break into their top-**secret research lab**, find out how **FIXITALL** works and then try to make a cure oursel—'

I stopped talking, realizing that the doctor was staring at me very oddly. Was she considering Dr Yuri Tooblaym's tempting option number two? But before I could make a break for the surgery's exit the doctor had seized me in her **orangutan arms.** She was laughing like a hyena who's had eight double espressos.

'YEEGHR CRUSHING ME!' I gasped.

She let me go. 'I'm sorry. I forget how delicate you are.' She was still beaming at me, though. 'You're such a little marvel, Ozzy! One moment I'm staring at your strange dorsal nasal appendage and thinking, **Annie, why did you hire this human assistant? The poor thing is less intelligent than a recently revived zombie slug.**'

That was nice to know.

'But then the next moment you come out with a **completely brilliant** plan like that!' She opened a drawer in her desk and flung the glossy **MON-MED** pharmaceuticals brochure at me. 'See if you can find the address for the **MON-MED** head office in there.'

It was on the inside back page. Right beside one of those inter-dimensional 'WE ARE HERE' maps that are about as easy to understand as one of my little sister's drawings on the fridge door. Still, Bruce would understand it.

'But how are we going to get in?' I asked.

'Don't fret,' she replied, rummaging around in the bottomless drawer of her desk. **'THIS** will get us inside.' She produced *a tube that was roughly the size of a rolled-up boy-band poster.* One end was painted green and the other was red. The red end was labelled very clearly with a large arrow and the words:

THIS END TOWARDS PATIENT

'Therapy bazooka,' she explained, seeing my confused look. 'Incredibly useful for advanced *head-massaging therapies,* un-blocking the surgery's drains and opening stubborn doors.'

'But surely breaking into the **MON-MED top-secret research lab** must be dangerous,' I said in a feeble attempt to avoid the embarrassment of having my parents come and bail me out of monster jail. 'Won't they have security guards with **large teeth or fiery breath?'**

The doctor dismissed my concerns. 'We mustn't let little things like –' she made air quotes – 'being **"badly bitten"** or **"burned to a crisp"** get in the way of helping poorly monsters, Ozzy!'

'Can't we?' I said with some concern. 'Why ever not?'

She drew herself **up to her full height** – which, even counting those extra storeys of hair, isn't as tall as me.

'CURA OMNIA, Ozzy!' she insisted, quoting the monster doctor's motto to me. **'HEAL ANYTHING!** We are **highly trained** monster doctors and it is our **duty** to help any monsters who are ill – especially if we caused that illness! Come!'

She jabbed a button on the **intercom** marked GARAGE.

'We have sick patients to cure.'

Swamp Spa Treatment

NO.

GARAGE
lance + Bruce

toxic sludge store

GUEST SUITE

PANIC

Twinky Horn- Screamer

OUT of ORDER

There was an answer from the garage. The
speaker emitted a subsonic **grumble** that made
all the ornaments fall off the doctor's
desk.

'Hello, Lance –' the doctor paused as the desk
began to shake again. Then she said, 'Oh dear! I'm
sorry! **I didn't realize you were in the bath.
But this is an emergency.** Would you mind
terribly putting Bruce on, please?'

There was the sound of loud **revving** as
Lance shouted for Bruce to pick up the phone.

81

Bruce replied with a high-pitched screech that would have made my dog Piglet feel an inexplicable urge to go and round up some sheep. Then the **small monitor** beside the **phone** lit up with Bruce's familiarly unfriendly font.

WHAT DO YOU WANT? IT'S MY AFTERNOON OFF.

'I know, I know,' said the doctor. 'And I'll make it up to you later. But right now we have an emergency and I thought you might *appreciate*

the chance to do something exciting for a change? Something like *breaking* into **MON-MED** pharmaceuticals' top-secret research lab.'

There was a second – even higher-pitched – screech from the phone.

The doctor winced and held the receiver a safe distance from her pointy ears. And I knew that *somewhere out in the real world* Piglet was running round and round in circles looking for sheep.

'I assume that's a "yes",' said the doctor.

OFF THE TELLY

Chapter 8

Five minutes later, after another dizzyingly terrifying journey through inter-dimensional space, we were back in reality and *rolling along a long, smooth driveway.* It wound through an

enormous spread of manicured lawn towards a strange structure that I assumed was MON-MED headquarters. I assumed this because it seemed highly unlikely that anyone else would have had the money (or the bad taste) to **build a seven hundred and fifty foot tall tower out of glass and gleaming chrome,** in the shape of an **enormous** hypodermic syringe.

Lance screeched up to the lobby and **reverse-parked** (rather showily) in the spot reserved for the **VICE PRESIDENT WITH THE SECOND-LARGEST HEAD.**

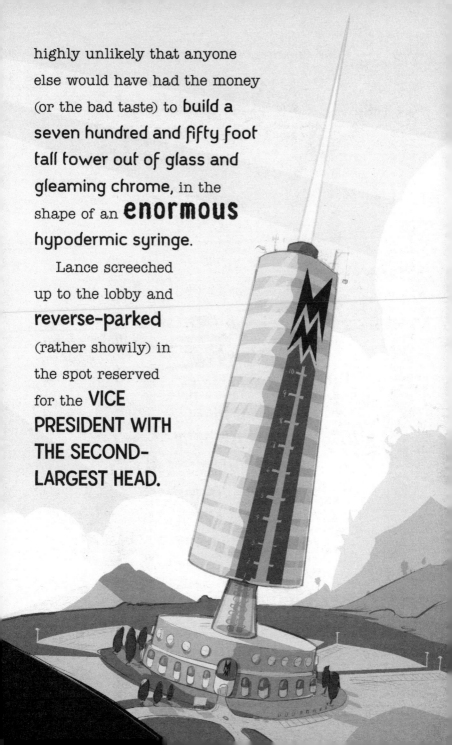

The doctor and I eagerly leaped out, to find – as expected – that the whole place was completely **boarded** up.

Posters with large red type announced:

MON-MED REGRETS TO INFORM VISITORS THAT OUR OFFICES ARE CLOSED UNTIL FURTHER NOTICE.
PLEASE FEEL FREE TO LEAVE IMMEDIATELY. OR STAY TO BE SAVAGED AND BURNED BY OUR SECURITY CONTRACTOR.
THANK YOU.

I didn't like the sound of being 'savaged and burned', and mentioned my worry to the doctor.

'**PAH!**' she scoffed, retrieving the therapy bazooka from Lance's back seat. 'We'll be inside before any **sluggish five-tonne grottviler** can catch us.' She raised the bazooka to her shoulder and took aim at the entrance.

Her finger tightened on the **trigger.**

I closed my eyes, stuck my fingers in my ears and waited for the explosion.

BOOOOOOOMMMMM!

The earth shook.

This was a bit odd. Did a *therapeutic* **rocket-launcher** really need to be that strong? But when I opened my eyes the door was still intact. The doctor hadn't even fired the **bazooka.**

'Did you hear that?' she asked.

'You mean the—' I began, but was interrupted by another earth-shaking tremor.

BOOOOOOOMMMMM!

But this time it was louder and closer.

'Is it an—?'

BOOOOOOOMMMMM!

My teeth rattled.

'. . . earthquake?' I asked.

BOOOOOOOMMMMM!

My fillings rattled.

BOOOOOOOMMMMM!

'Doctor?'

But she wasn't listening. Instead, she was staring rather rudely up past the top of my head. She had dropped the therapy bazooka and her hands were **clutched together** – almost in *prayer*. She wore an expression I had seen many times before on the faces of my friends. It's the one they get when they see someone *famous off the telly or the internet*. Someone who's incredibly good at applying lipstick or running around after various-sized balls.

'By the extremely **damp** dining rooms of Atlantis!' she cried. 'It's HIM! It's actually HIM!'

There was another

BOOOOOOOMMMM!

that was so close it felt as if someone had dropped an aircraft carrier right behind me. So I turned round, and my eyes immediately fell upon a hill that hadn't been there a minute ago.

Of course it wasn't actually a hill. Hills can't walk (most of the time) and aren't usually covered in **armour-plated scales.**

It was the **biggest monster** I had ever seen. 'Gorgonzilla!' whispered the doctor. She was gazing up adoringly at two colossal legs, each as  tall and thick as the Leaning Tower of Pisa. They supported a colossal body, an equally colossal neck and a head *the size of a five-bedroom detached house.* The creature must have weighed five thousand tonnes and was built as **solidly** as an office block. Which made it slightly worrying that it appeared to be swaying, as if it didn't quite have its balance.

'MR GORGONZILLA, SIR!' bellowed the doctor. 'I'M A HUGE FAN! THOUGH NOT AS HUGE AS YOU, OF COURSE!' She gave an embarrassed laugh. 'CAN I JUST SAY HOW MUCH I LOVED YOU IN *FRIGHT OF THE BUMBLE-BOMBS?* I WAS THERE IN TOKYO BACK IN '68.

THAT HEART-BREAKING DUET WITH CATERPILLEROID LITERALLY BROUGHT THE HOUSE DOWN.'

And most of the city too, I suspected.

Gorgonzilla looked ponderously down towards the source of the noise. Buzzing around his head was a small cloud of media camera drones (which is quite normal for such a **huge monster celebrity**).⸙ One of them seemed to cause him to momentarily **lose his balance,** and he put an arm out to steady himself. Unfortunately, the nearest support was the hypodermic spire of the **MON-MED** building, which snapped off in his **scaly claw** like a breadstick. The media drones darted excitedly in for a closer look.

'He doesn't seem very steady on his feet,' I observed.

'Steady on his feet?' snorted the doctor. 'Have you never heard of Gorgonzilla? He's one of the most graceful dancers in *modern monster ballet!*'

'That's a *dancer?*' I asked disbelievingly.

'Oh, don't let that **crusty exterior** fool you,' the doctor gushed. 'Beneath his ten-foot-thick *armour plating beats the heart* of a *true artist.* I've been his biggest fan ever since – ugh, don't look now.' She scowled. 'But one of those **ghastly media parasites** has spotted us.' And, sure enough, one of the buzzing things had swooped down from the sky.

Up close, it looked like a cross between a small helicopter and a very large, fanged mosquito. It hovered a few feet away, wielding an impressive selection of **long-lensed TV cameras** and several **mobile phones**. It was wearing a bright orange vest with the words 'COLOSSAL-GOSSIP TV' emblazoned across it.

'No pictures!' buzzed the drone as it pointed to the therapy bazooka on the ground. '*COLLOSAL-GOSSIP* has an **exclusive contract** with Mr G's management team.

We're shooting a true-life behind-the-scenes all-access exposé of Mr G's comeback tour. No outside press allowed.'

'We're not press,' I explained. 'We're doctors – or at least the doctor is.'

'And this isn't a camera,' added the monster doctor. 'It's a therapy bazooka. Would you like me to **demonstrate** on you?'

The drone quickly backed off to a safe distance. 'My apologies!' it buzzed. 'Bizzi Fartangle at your service. Senior video correspondent for *COLOSSAL-GOSSIP TV.'*

Far above our heads, Gorgonzilla swayed alarmingly again, and Bizzi zoomed *several lenses* up at him.

'Ooops-a-daisy!' he said. 'He's been like this all morning. Ever since he drank that **slimy wonder** drug. Now, what was it called? FEXITALL . . .? FOXITALL . . .?'

The doctor and I exchanged a glance. **'FIXITALL,'** we said simultaneously.

'Oh! You know about that?' asked Bizzi. 'Then you must know that *lovely* Ms . . . whatshername.'

'Diagnosiz,' I said with a sinking heart.

'That's her,' said Bizzi, nodding. 'Well, she signed a contract with Mr G's management team to try out this *hush-hush* new wonder cure for his RSI.'

REPETITIVE STOMPING INJURY (RSI)

RSI is a painful condition that affects very large monsters, and even some giants who are unfortunate enough to have both large feet and anger-management issues.

It is caused by repeatedly standing on otherwise harmless objects like buses, houses, railway trains, office blocks and Lego. Over time, the crushing impact can damage the delicate bones of a large monster's feet.

TREATMENT:

- Rest.
- No stomping.
- Sensible shoes.
- Avoid stepping on military vehicles like tanks, or Lego.

'Anyway,' continued the drone, 'Mr G has been as dizzy as a *helicopter-harpy* ever since he drank a **tankerful** of **FIXITALL** this morning. We were on our way here to shoot a totally spontaneous confrontation scene between him and the **MON-MED** management team. But he seems to have taken a turn for the worse.'

The drone was right. The **gigantic colossosaur** was now swaying as badly as the final terrifying moments of a game of *Mega-Jenga.* ⸙

'Doctor!' I exclaimed, thinking back to the list of **FIXITALL** side-effects. 'The leaflet said "extreme dizziness leading to extreme falling over"! We need to get Gorgonzilla safely lying down before he **falls over** and **injures** himself – or takes out a nearby town.'

The doctor instantly took charge. She cupped her hands and bellowed up at the colossosaur, **'MR GORGONZILLA, SIR? YOU'RE HAVING A FUNNY TURN. I REALLY THINK YOU SHOULD HAVE A NICE SIT-DOWN.'**

I could see the dizzy monster trying ever so hard to focus on her. But the effort made him sway even more **alarmingly** than before.

'PERHAPS YOU COULD TAKE A SEAT ON THAT HILL OVER THER—'

She never got to finish her sentence. Because at that very moment Gorgonzilla lost his **balance** completely. Five thousand tonnes of monster began to topple over like a *chimney demolition* gone badly wrong.

Bizzi Fartangle buzzed away to safety, his cameras **whirring** as he **barked** orders into his multiple phones. 'CAMERA SEVEN, close-up on the face! CAMERAS THREE TO FIVE, **don't miss any collateral devastation!** CAMERA SIX, switch to slow-mo!'

But I just stood there, frozen to the spot. My **brain** was completely occupied with the fact that I was about to become **very, very flat.**

Luckily, the doctor's lifetime experience of certain-death situations has left her **immune to panic.** She simply tutted, picked me up by the back of my trousers and scurried towards Lance. Her tiny legs were *moving so quickly* that they were as ᗷᒪᑌᖇᖇᖿ as a bad holiday photo.

'LANCE! OPEN YOUR DOORS!' she yelled.

The ambulance's passenger side door obediently flapped open and the doctor flung me through it like a **bowling ball.**

She managed to grab hold of Lance's wing mirror and, just as I hit the driver's side door, she yelled, **'DRIIIIVVVVE!'**

The ambulance immediately tore off across the parking lot as if someone had announced there was a *free oil bath* at the local garage.

But, unfortunately, he went in completely the wrong direction.

A DROPPED SAUSAGE

Chapter 9

Have you ever seen one of those **films** where an enormous building or *crashing* spaceship is collapsing and the hero idiot tries to get away by running *TOWARDS* the thing that is falling?

Well, that's **exactly** what Lance did.

(I told you he has no sense of direction.)

I grabbed his steering wheel and desperately turned it to the left.

Nothing happened.

'LANCE!' I shouted. **'GO LEFT!'**

Nothing happened.

'LANCE!' the doctor yelled from where she hung from the wing mirror. **'GO RIGHT!'**

The ambulance kept going straight ahead.

We were **racing** across the car park, but it was
no good. Gorgonzilla's five-thousand-tonne body
was now so close that it was **blotting** out the sun.
We were moments away from being completely
squished when something from the IDV **manual**

I had recently been reading popped into my head.

Extract from **YOU MAY FEEL SICK AT FIRST: IDV driving for beginners:**

> The novice driver must always remember that IDVs cannot understand ordinary dimensional commands like LEFT, RIGHT, UP or DOWN. When issuing directions to your IDV, you should always use correct IDV terminology like 'Reverse-Wibble', 'Liftish' and 'Shim-wards'. And PLEASE take the time to learn the life-saving difference between a Wibble, a Wobble, a Wubble and a Wirbble.
>
> Failing that, just buy a BAT-NAV.

In the instant before we were crushed, I screamed a stream of complete nonsense.

'LANCE! DO A LIFTISH REVERSE-WIBBLE SHIM-WARDS!' The little ambulance's engine revved and my **stomach flipped** as if I'd just been ordered to perform a dance during school **assembly** in my most embarrassing underwear.

A second later, I realized with relief that Lance was a hundred yards away from the *collapsing* Gorgonzilla, and we were travelling in a safe direction.

Phew.

There was a PING! from Bruce. He was annoyed.

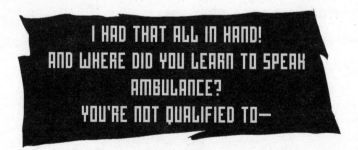

I HAD THAT ALL IN HAND! AND WHERE DID YOU LEARN TO SPEAK AMBULANCE? YOU'RE NOT QUALIFIED TO—

Fortunately, he was drowned out by a two-hundred-decibel

CRASSSSHHHH!

Five thousand tonnes of Gorgonzilla collapsed on top of the **MON-MED** headquarters. The *gleaming* chrome-and-glass building was completely squished as clouds of dust, invoices, purchase orders and **customer complaints billowed** into the air.

They slowly floated back to earth, settling to reveal poor Gorgonzilla lying in the wreckage. He was sprawled on his back, colossal legs and arms **wriggling** in the air like a super-tanker-sized beetle. Bizzi Fartangle and her monster drones **swarmed** around, filming the whole incident.

The **MON-MED** headquarters was now as flat as my hair after ten minutes under Spurtie's shower.

The doctor jumped off Lance, *raced* over and **scrambled** up a small slope of **crushed executive**  desks. I followed a bit more cautiously.

Finally, she reached the monster's **enormous** right eye. Gorgonzilla saw her and gave a sad little roar. And by 'little' I mean about as **loud** as a volcano erupting.

But the doctor seemed to understand what the colossosaur was saying. She pulled out her mobile phone and shouted, **'DO YOU HAVE THE NUMBER?'**

Gorgonzilla roared out what I assumed was a telephone number. Each roar made the **pile of debris** on which the doctor and I were perched tremble.

'Hello!' the doctor said into the phone. 'Is that COLOSSO-RECOVERY pick-up services?'

The doctor finished her

call and put the phone away.

'THE DESPATCHER SAID THEY'LL BE HERE WITHIN THE HOUR, MR GORGONZILLA, SIR! SO YOU'D BEST STAY LYING DOWN TILL THEN. DON'T WORRY, THOUGH. MY ASSISTANT AND I ARE WORKING ON A CURE FOR **FIXITALL** AND WE EXPECT GREAT RESULTS VERY SOON!'

'Do we?' I whispered as the doctor and I **clambered** back through the ruins of the **MON-MED** building. 'I'm relieved you've got a plan B!'

'Of course I don't have a plan B!' the doctor snapped. 'We must work on your medicinal lying, Ozzy. It's very useful for keeping a

109

patient's spirits up.' She *manoeuvred* around a pile of motivational posters. 'Somehow, we have to find a cure for that cursed slime medicine, and any answers that were in here –' she peevishly kicked the award for 'LEAST TOXIC LAXATIVE 1983–7' out of her way – 'are now as flat as sliced **wholemeal head.**'

'Surely you mean "wholemeal bread", I asked as we climbed back into Lance.

'What's "wholemeal bread"?' said the doctor **absent-mindedly** before adding, 'Home, please, Bruce.'

As Lance *rolled off across the car* park, I heard her mutter, 'Perhaps if Delores is still in a good mood she might let me run some experiments on her . . .'

But her musings were interrupted. For some reason, Lance began *madly swerving* back and forth. 'Oh! What on earth are you doing now, you **silly ambulance?**' cried the doctor. 'We don't have time for any more of your nonsense today!'

Lance screeched to a halt.

Then he *shot off again* in a completely different direction, changed his mind once more and began to spiral *round and round and round* in ever tighter and tighter handbrake turns. The doctor and I were thrown around like the ball bearing in a **vigorously** shaken can of spray paint.

'**BRUCE!**' snapped the doctor from somewhere in the footwell. 'Tell Lance to stop this nonsense right now and take us straight home!'

'I know what he's doing!' I cried excitedly as I tried to extract my left foot from the glovebox. 'He's behaving like **PIGLET!**'

'Are you delirious again, Ozzy?' asked the doctor. '**I did warn you against having one of Delores's toadstool vol-au-vents.**'

'No! It's not that. I just recognize Lance's behaviour.' I said this in as **un-smug** a way as I could manage (which was not very). 'He's searching for a smell. My dog Piglet goes back and forth across the kitchen floor looking for the EXACT spot where someone dropped a **sausage** two weeks before.'

I didn't add that when he finds the spot he spends the next three hours **licking the colour off the tiles.**

Lance came to a screeching, **tyre-burning** halt. The little ambulance's bonnet was pointing at a **nondescript patch of tarmac**. His engine purred proudly.

'What have you found, then, boy?' asked the doctor.

There was a loud **PING!** and Bruce's screen lit up.

> ## HE SAYS HE KNOWS WHERE IT WENT.

'It?' I said.

> ## THAT FANCY-PANTS CAR OF MS DIAGNOSIZ. OH, AND A LOAD OF FIXITALL TOO.

'She must have helped herself to all the remaining **FIXITALL** before the building was locked,' I exclaimed.

The doctor looked outraged. 'Come on, Ozzy!' she said. **'We have to find her before she can injure any more harmless monsters** like Gorgonzilla. Where is she, Bruce?'

ASTHMATIC PARROT

Chapter 10

Ａnd it literally was just round the corner.

Lance didn't even need to go inter-dimensional. He just drove for about a minute before turning into a **decrepit-looking trading** estate. A **totem sign** displayed the businesses unfortunate enough to have premises at such a **seedy** spot.

MELTING screams TRADING ESTATE

101 NIBBLES DESIGNER WEASEL CAGES

102 FLEA-BAG INC.

103 THIS UNIT CLOSED DUE TO SEVERE INSECT CONTAMINATION

104 SCALPINGTON'S SECOND-HAND SKINS

105 KRASSH BROS. FRIGHT-SIMULATOR TRAINING

106 THE CREAKY DOOR & SQUEAKY HINGE COMPANY

107 MEDICAL STORAGE FACILITY (NO CALLERS!)

'Medical storage?' scoffed the doctor as Lance parked round the back by the *lock-up* garages and dumpsters. 'The cheek of that woman!'

She **strode round to the front of Unit 107** and took aim at the closed doorway with her therapy bazooka.

'WAIT!' I shouted.

The monster doctor does have this *regrettable* habit of trying to solve problems by hitting things with a **blunt object** or, failing that, the use of medicinal explosives.

'Let me guess,' said the doctor, giving me a disgusted look. 'You have a **revolutionary** way to find out what's going on inside without resorting to **explosives**.'

'Well, we could try looking through here first,'
I suggested. There was a small window further
along the wall that was mostly covered from the
inside with *old newspapers.* Luckily, one corner
(the **Daily Fang** sports page) had peeled away,
allowing just enough **space** for me to **peer** inside.

'Can you see Ms Diagnosiz?'
hissed the doctor.

'Yes,' I said.

She was sitting on a
chair at the side of the room, flicking
through holiday brochures for dimension 2.6.

'But there's something else . . .' I said
slowly. 'There's some kind of lab in there.'

'WHAT?' cried the doctor as she
squeezed in beside me. Together,
we took in the scene inside
Unit 107.

There was a **tall** glass **tank** surrounded by a maze of clear **tubes** and **glass chambers**. The tank reminded me of the home-made *aquarium* my grandad built in his first-floor flat at the nursing home. But instead of a collection of constantly **terrified fish**, this contraption contained a sort of bubbling, glowing, *gloopy green slime* that looked an awful lot like **FIXITALL**.

'By my auntie's fatally flammable flatulence!'  exclaimed the doctor. 'She seems to be manufacturing **FIXITALL** in there!'

No sooner had she spoken than **two nimble little monsters** in spotless white lab coats appeared. They scurried across the complex assembly of glass and plastic, pausing only to **jot** down notes in a **tiny** notebook, tweak a valve or pull a lever.

Suddenly an automated voice began to count.
'TEN!'

Next to the tank, a hospital gurney I hadn't previously noticed was hoisted into an upright position.
'NINE!'

On the gurney was some kind of lizardy-fishy monster strapped (very tightly) on to it. The tiny lab-coated creatures began filling a very fearsome-looking syringe with the glowing slime from the tank. They pointed it straight at the strapped-down monster's arm.

'EIGHT!'

'What on earth are they doing?' asked the doctor.

'SEVEN!'

'Some kind of an experiment?' I suggested.

The doctor gasped. 'By **Frankenstein's** fatal folly!' cried the doctor. 'We have to save that poor monster!'

'SIX!'

A second later she was back on her feet by the doorway to Unit 107. Her face was bright blue with anger and the therapy bazooka was once again aimed right at the front door.

'FIVE!'

I just had time to stick my fingers in my ears before **she pulled the trigger.** There was a muffled **BANG** and the door turned into a thousand-piece jigsaw puzzle. As the shattered pieces hit the floor, the doctor charged inside.

'THREE!'

'STOP THIS!' she cried. 'WHATEVER "THIS" IS – AT ONCE!' The two tiny monsters were frozen in shock at the sight of her, so the doctor waved the therapy bazooka to emphasize the point.
'TWO!'

One of them sneezed in alarm, *yanked* open a valve and threw its hands in the air.
'ON—'

The countdown stopped. There was a loud gurgle and the contents of the syringe drained back into the *main tank*. A stunned Ms Diagnosiz hurriedly hid her holiday brochure and sprang to her feet. Her huge mouth opened in her **automatic** toothy smile.

'I can explain everything,' she began, but
any 'explanation' was cut short by a **furious
squawk** of anger behind us.

There was another monster in the room.

'Who are you?' a voice croaked. The doctor
and I turned to find ourselves confronted by what
looked like a five-thousand-year-old parrot. It was
wearing a **'white'** lab coat. (I say 'white' but it
had seen more action than one of my baby sister's
reusable eco-nappies.)

'What is the meaning of using a therapy
bazooka on my front door?' the monster
demanded, glaring angrily at us from beneath a
rather obvious wig. 'And where on earth is Ms
Diagnosiz going?'

We turned at the sound of running footsteps just in time to see Ms Diagnosiz's **tail** slipping out of the back door.

'Stop her!' cried the doctor.

I was about to give *chase* when the elderly avian croaked, **'Hold on a moment!'** His voice was as dry as that of an asthmatic parrot, and he was squinting up at the doctor through a pair of spectacles with glass thick enough for **submarine portholes.** 'I know you!' Then his gnarly old beak opened in what could have – in more sympathetic lighting – been considered a smile. 'Von Sichertall, isn't it? Why, I haven't seen you since you were nearly expelled from Sorebones College for **that incident with the blue whale and the bicycle rack!'**

The doctor lowered the therapy bazooka as recognition suddenly dawned.

'By my grandfather's aerodynamic bingo wings,' cried the doctor. **'Professor Peckham,** from the department of Spaghetto-Genetics! I'm sorry I didn't recognize you, sir. It's just you've grown so horribly old and horrendously wrinkly!'

'Ha ha!' cackled the elderly avian, before dissolving into a fit of coughing.

'Can we leave the college *reunion* till later?' I said with some frustration.

'Ms Diagnosiz is getting clean away!'

'Calm down, Ozzy,' said the doctor. 'Sometimes the villain does get away. After all, this isn't some **silly made-up story** – this is the real world of monster medicine.'

I was about to protest, but at that moment the professor finally regained his breath. 'It's charming of you to *drop in* to see your old lecturer, Von Sichertall. And perhaps we can *reminisce* later. But right now I am in the middle of a vital – I say **VITAL** – experiment.' He gestured to his two tiny assistants. 'Ms Tenement! Mr Nimby! We shall begin again!'

One of the tiny creatures picked up a clipboard, while the other *refilled the large syringe.*

The professor flicked a switch and Mr Nimby (or Ms Tenement) positioned the syringe over the monster in the gurney.

'Professor!' exclaimed the doctor. 'Surely you can't mean to keep **experimenting** with **FIXITALL?** You realize there are terrible side-effects?'

'I know all about the side-effects,' replied Professor Peckham, **absent-mindedly** twiddling a knob.

'So why do it, then?' asked the doctor.

'Because I asked him to,' interrupted the patient.

The professor waved to where the monster lay strapped on the gurney. 'Dr Von Sichertall,' he announced. '*Allow me to introduce* my former assistant, Mr Gillman. Mr Gillman, this is Dr Von Sichertall and her nurse-monkey-thing.'

'*Charmed,*' said Mr Gillman, offering his webbed hand to us.

It was covered in maroon **tartan.**

'That's not right,' I said, studying the pattern. 'If I'm not mistaken, you're a *Swampus noir lagoonis* and should be covered in mucus-coated scales.' (I'd recently watched an old black-and-white documentary about his species on MonTube.)

'Quite!' snapped the professor irritably. 'As you can clearly see, Mr Gillman is suffering from very severe **FIXITALL** side-effects. Now, if we are **quite finished** with the formal introductions, perhaps the old fool that invented **FIXITALL** –' he **pushed a button on the control console** – 'can be allowed to get on with trying to CURE **FIXITALL!**'

There was a **loud clunk,** which was either the syringe *plunging* into Mr Gillman's tartan arm or the doctor and my jaws hitting the floor.

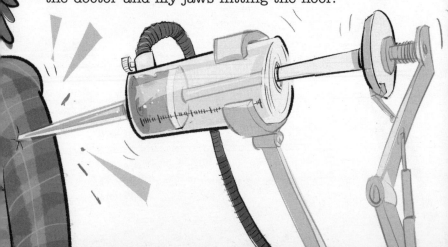

SUCH PROMISING RESULTS . . .

Chapter 11

'**Y**ou invented **FIXITALLL?**' asked the amazed doctor.

'In a manner of speaking,' replied the beaky professor. '**My research team** at **MON-MED** created it when things got out of hand at last year's **XXXmas party.**'

The two tiny assistants looked embarrassed.

'They thought it would be funny to make a chemical that could grab hold of a monster's DNA and jiggle it about a bit. Caused all sorts of **hilarity.** Smoke pouring out of ears. Eyes revolving. But imagine our surprise the next day when we discovered that the **jiggling** also happened to cure an amazing number of monster **MALADIES!'**

'How on earth can jiggling a monster's DNA do that?' scoffed the doctor.

'Well,' said the professor, 'the actual process is far too complex to go into here. But in principle it is as simple as **untangling a headphone cable.'**

I didn't think that sounded very simple at all. In fact, I once spent an entire double maths lesson trying to **untangle** my headphone cable and somehow ended up lashed to my chair.

'We refined it and had SUCH promising results at first,' said the professor wistfully. 'Quite astonishing, really. A single dose of **FIXITALL** could completely cure previously untreatable monster conditions like **compulsive lurkivitus** or jargonese. **MON-MED** management were VERY excited . . .'

'But then you noticed the side-effects,' prompted the doctor.

'Yes,' admitted Professor Peckham, looking crestfallen. 'We found that if you try to untangle monster DNA **it often ends up even more tangled than before.** It's a bit like trying to untangle a headphone cable and ending up lashed to your chair.'

I said nothing.

'Of course, I immediately told the CEO of **MON-MED** that **FIXITALL** was **far too dangerous** to ever sell,' said the professor.

'Then why did they sell it?' I asked.

The professor sighed. 'It had something to do with all the expensive packaging that had already been printed. I forget the details . . . Ah!

Look at our patient! The **serum** is taking *effect.*
How are you feeling, Philip?'

Mr Gillman's eyeballs had begun rotating
in opposite directions. 'A little dizzy, Prof,' he
replied. 'But no worse than being **trapped** in
some of the whirlpools in the Amazon.'

'That's a little odd,' said the monster doctor.
'Surely the **nasal whining** and ear smoke come
before *eyeball-rotating?*'

'Not with my serum,' explained Professor
Peckham. 'It is deliberately designed to reverse
the effects of **FIXITALL.** The nasal whining, ear
smoke and *rotating eyeballs* all now happen in
the reverse order. Which is why Mr Nimby
rather amusingly calls it **ЯEVERSITALL.'**
The professor's laughter was cut off by another
violent coughing fit. Copious amounts of smoke
were now pouring out from Mr Gillman's ears. Ms
Tenement switched on an extractor fan.

'That's better,' the professor continued, once
the **air** had cleared a little. 'Where was I?'

'You were selling dangerous **FIXITALL** to
monsters,' I reminded him.

'Ah, yes, indeed,' said the professor. 'And before we knew it there were hundreds of poor monsters with **wonky walks, strange diets** and *unfashionable skin patterns* turning up at HQ and threatening to eat the CEO and senior management team. So they took fright and fled to dimension 2.6.'

Mr Gillman's nasal areas began to whine.
'So I determined to find a cure! I
borrowed –' the professor looked a bit
shifty – 'a few hundred gallons of
FIXITALL and set up this lab. And
by a marvellous stroke of luck,
the lovely Ms Diagnosiz from
sales offered to help me in any
way she could.'

How clever of her. With access
to a **stash** of **FIXITALL** and
a *potential cure*, she could make
money however the professor's
experiments worked out.

The doctor pointed to where Mr
Gillman's skin remained stubbornly tartan.
'It doesn't look like you've had much luck.'

'Nonsense!' sniffed the professor. 'Look.' And,
as if on cue, Mr Gillman's maroon tartan pattern
began to fade. It was being replaced by something
else.

'Incredible!' exclaimed the doctor. 'What is that
pattern? I don't recognize it.'

'Looks like **tabby cat** to me,' I said.

But Ms Tenement was flipping quickly through a large ring **binder of pattern swatches.** She held it up for the professor to see.

His beaky face fell.

'**Mongolian snow leopard,**' he sighed, slumping back into his chair. 'A thirty-seven point five per cent improvement on **maroon** tartan, but nowhere near a cure. Blast!'

'Can't you just tweak the serum a little bit and try again?' I asked.

'You don't understand,' he said frustratedly. '**ЯEVERSITALL** works by using **simpler DNA** to "smooth-out" the patient's tangled DNA. It's a bit like taking a hopelessly tangled headphone cable, throwing it away and just buying a nice new one. And that batch of **ЯEVERSITALL** was based on a **monster amoeba.** There is no living creature anywhere with a simpler DNA structure than that blob of gloopy slime.' He broke off, looking utterly despaired.

'Hmm . . .' the doctor said, considering for a moment. Then she turned to me and said, in a rather **smug** voice, 'Oh, there is . . . I know of one creature that only has two strands of DNA.'

'This is a poor moment for jokes, Von Sichertall!' chided the professor, and he shook his shaggy head dismissively. 'A creature with only two strands of DNA wouldn't be capable of any behaviour more **complex** than **slithering back and forth** between the TV, the fridge and the toilet. Nothing could possibly live like that.'

The doctor pushed me forward.

'Allow me to introduce my assistant,' she said. 'His name is Ozzy, and he is a human.'

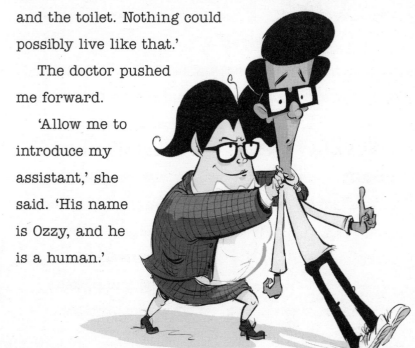

HE CAN EVEN READ AND WRITE!

Chapter 12

The words were *barely* out of her mouth before my legs were **seized** by tiny (but surprisingly strong) hands. I looked down to find Ms Tenement and Mr Nimby had grabbed one each.

I couldn't move.

'Er . . . what are they doing?' I asked Professor Peckham. But he ignored me and picked up another

enormous

hypodermic syringe.
Then – rather
worryingly – he
began to
advance
towards
me.

'Don't panic,' he
tried (and failed) to reassure me. 'If
what my **illustrious former student** says is
true, then, in the name of progress, I must have a
teensy tiny sample of your blood. There is no need
to worry, though – I don't need more than sixteen –
maybe seventeen – pints. Dr Von Sichertall,' he
added, **'would you please tell your student to
stop shaking so much?** My hands aren't as
steady as they once were.'

The huge needle headed towards me, as
menacing as a **stray javelin** on sports day.

'Professor!' I protested loudly. 'As an expert on
human anatomy, I can say with some confidence
that I don't actually contain sixteen or seventeen
pints of blood.'

'Really?' said the professor. He looked disappointed. 'Well, I suppose I could use a slightly smaller needle. Would that work for you?'

I managed to breathe again. 'Nothing larger than a **monster-size extra extra extra small**, please.'

And so a few minutes later I was sticking a monster plaster on my arm and watching as Professor Peckham's machine analysed my **blood.** There was a soft CHIME and the **twisting double spiral** of human DNA appeared on one of the screens.

'*WOW!*' I said in amazement. 'So that's actually MY very own DNA.' The doctor and professor were also staring at it with a sense of complete wonder that was very flattering.

'I would never have believed it possible – if I wasn't looking at it with my own eyes,' said an awed Professor Peckham.

'I know. Incredible, isn't it?' agreed the doctor. 'I remember Professor Twinky telling us back in medical school that humans had only two strands of DNA. **I'd always assumed he was pulling everyone's tentacles.** But here –' she squeezed my arm affectionately – 'is the living proof! A creature that can walk upright, speak – albeit with an **amusing accent** – read, write and is even learning to drive a monster ambulance! The universe is clearly far stranger than any monster can imagine!'

There was another soft **CHIME** and the automated voice announced:

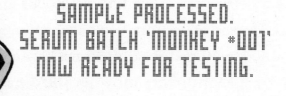

SAMPLE PROCESSED.
SERUM BATCH 'MONKEY #001'
NOW READY FOR TESTING.

The professor extracted a small vial of gloopy liquid from the machine. 'Mr Gillman,' he said. 'I realize it is an awful lot to ask of a monster, but are you prepared be tested with a serum derived from –' he paused dramatically – **'a human being?'**

The lizardy monster's head crest *twitched* with disgust. 'It's a pretty revolting thought,' Mr Gillman said. 'But, if it's a **choice** between that and wearing tartan for the rest of my life, I'm prepared to take the risk.'

'That's the spirit!' said the professor. Then, without warning, he plunged the huge needle into Mr Gillman's arm.

The swamp creature's eyes began to revolve again, and for the next few minutes the workshop was almost silent. We all waited on *tenterhooks.* The only sounds were the whirr of the extractor fan sucking Mr Gillman's ear smoke away, the **furious scratching** of Mr Nimby making observations in his tiny notebooks and – eventually – the all-too-familiar nasal whining.

Finally, Mr Gillman's skin pattern began to change from **Mongolian snow leopard** into something else. Ms Tenement stood poised by her **ring binder** full of pattern swatches. But it wasn't needed.

'**IT WORKED!**' we all cried together.

Mr Gillman's healthy, slimy scales had been restored.

The two tiny assistants embraced each other, kissed (surprisingly passionately) and began a charming little **dance of celebration.** Even Mr Gillman's head crest jiggled in the universal swamp signal for happiness.

'Oh, how marvellous!' cried the monster doctor. 'And well done, Ozzy, for being so – 'she hunted around for the right word – '**uncomplicated!**' She turned to Professor Peckham. 'How quickly can you make this slimy brilliance? Five gallons should be enough to treat all my patients.'

It only took Professor Peckham half an hour to produce a **five gallon** bottle of ЯEVERSITALL. While we waited, he also made a few *calls* to old friends at monster pharmaceutical companies. ЯEVERSITALL would soon be produced in **quantities large enough** for even a dizzy colossosaur.

We walked happily out of Unit 107 and looked around for Lance.

'LAAAANNNNNNCE!' shouted the doctor. 'HERE, BOY! WE'RE GOING HOME!'

'Shouldn't we call the monster police about Ms Diagnosiz?' I asked as we waited.

'**There's no point,**' replied the doctor. 'She'll be well on her way to dimension 2.6 by now. Sitting on *lovely* red-hot swamp sand, drinking freshly squeezed bile juice and counting her ill-gotten gains – now where is that silly ambulance? Probably rooting through the bins for spare parts, if I know him. LAAAAANNNNCE!' she screeched.

There was a loud revving, followed by the sounds of banging and clanging coming from behind a **row of garages**.

'I knew it!' cried the doctor as we ran towards the noise. 'What are you up to back there, you naughty ambulance?'

We rounded the corner into the alleyway and came face to face with Lance's rear end. His *wheels* were *spinning* like a **bull pawing the ground** and he kept lunging at something trapped further down the alleyway.

'Oh, what have you got hold of now?' groaned the doctor. 'I swear, one day you'll try on some garish bumper that *doesn't even suit you* and catch a horrid disease like **fender rot.** And then where will you be? DROP IT! I said, DROP IT!'

The excited ambulance obeyed the doctor and reversed out of the alley to reveal the shiny black car of Ms Diagnosiz.

And there, with her tiny hands on the **steering wheel**, was the glum-looking saleswoman herself.

'GOOD BOY!' praised the doctor as she patted Lance. 'Who's a clever boy? You are! Yes, you are!' She tickled his *wing mirror* and the ambulance revved happily.

Ms Diagnosiz wound down the limo's window and *hitched* on her toothy smile. 'Hello, Dr Sichertall,' she said as innocently as someone with two hundred and forty-seven huge teeth can. 'I can explain everything—'

'No, you can't,' interrupted the doctor. 'Your greedy, irresponsible behaviour might have **harmed** my patients! And imagine if poor, delicate, defenceless Mr Gorgonzilla had injured himself when he fell over! *What a loss to monster ballet* that would have been.'

I could see Ms Diagnosiz thought the idea of a five-thousand-tonne colossosaur being injured by *falling over* was as **ridiculous** as I did. But she knew to stay quiet in the face of such a serious monster ballet fan.

'Luckily for you,' continued the doctor in a calmer tone, 'my **primitive** assistant, Ozzy, has once again saved the day. So perhaps we should **all** treat this as a **"teaching moment".** Me to put all thoughts of a "universal cure" to one side, and you to go and find yourself a more **ethical career.** Use your **undoubtable sales talents** on something nice and safe, like **volcano time-share villas.'**

The saleswoman nodded gratefully. 'I am very sorry for the mix-up, Doctor. Maybe you're right. My sisters have always wanted me to join the family custom-denture business, Pointy Sisters Prosthetics.'

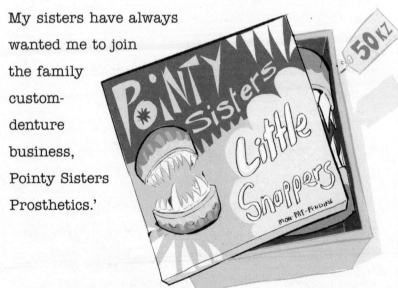

'A fine company,' said the doctor sharply. 'I'm wearing a set from their "Little Snappers" range right now.'

'Perhaps I'll give that a go,' said Ms Diagnosiz. **'I'm dreadfully sorry for all the trouble I've caused.'**

'LANCE! RELEASE HER!' called the doctor, and the ambulance backed away reluctantly. Ms Diagnosiz seized the opportunity and drove away quickly for a career in orthodontics – although not quickly enough to prevent Lance from 'accidentally on purpose' clipping the IDV's one *remaining* wing mirror clean off.

A LOVELY SINGALONG

Chapter 13

So the doctor and I went home.

The journey took a bit *longer* than expected as we got stuck for a while in dimension 3.9.

We were just pulling up in front of the surgery when Delores came *skipping gaily* towards us. Sadly there was still a **HUGE** smile on her face.

'Doctor!' she cried happily. 'How simply marvellous to see you – and the lovely Ozzy – back home so soon. As you can see, everything is going *wonderfully* well here.'

'Excellent. So the patients are all still in the waiting room, then?' the doctor asked.

'Not as such,' said Delores.

'But I specifically told you to keep them in here,' the doctor cried.

'I know,' admitted the horrifically apologetic receptionist. 'But, you see, I ran out of tea and biscuits about an hour ago and there were *ever such a lot* of **grumpy faces.** Still, you know me, Doctor – always trying to cheer everyone up. So I **slithered up** on my desk and started a lovely *community singalong* of old show tunes. You remember **'All the Fun of the Graveyard!',** **'My Old Man's a Dust-Monster'** and, my favourite, *'I Left My Heart in Your Bedside Cabinet.'*

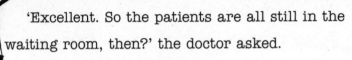

She began to hum a creepy yet somehow surprisingly **catchy** pop song. 'And before too long I had everyone up on their feet and **jumping** around so much they simply had to get outside! And they were enjoying themselves SO MUCH I couldn't get them to come back in.'

As she was talking, I noticed that Oswalt Sadbottom was trying to **conceal himself** in the doorway of Mrs Scabies's Ye Olde Flea Shop.

But he had to keep hopping from one leg to the other to avoid falling over. And there was Simon Salamander, desperately attempting to blend into a **JOIN THE MONSTER MARINES CORPSE** poster on the **opposite side** of the road – but was given away by the violently coloured stripes on his skin.

In fact, a closer look revealed the rest of the doctor's patients all *desperately attempting* to hide from Delores's enforced community fun.

I pointed this out to the doctor while Delores continued humming loudly to herself.

'Blast!' the doctor whispered. 'We'll never get the patients back to the surgery with Delores in this **terrifyingly** *cheerful mood.* And they urgently need the **ЯEVERSITALL!'**

I looked around at the terrified monsters. 'I think I've got an idea . . .' I said. 'Pass me the **ЯEVERSITALL** bottle, please. And, Lance, be a good chap and run your *extendable ladder* up to the third floor.' In seconds I was out through Lance's sunroof, *scampering up* his **ladder** and hopping through the window of the swamp-spa treatment room.

'GOOOD AFTERNOOOON, OZEEEE!' said Spurtie as he spotted me. **'DOOO YOOO WANNN ANOTHHERRR WOSHHHH?'**

'Yes please, Spurtie,' I said eagerly. 'But can you use this *extra-special shampoo*, please?' I unpacked the barrel of **FIXITALL** antidote and unscrewed the cap.

'OOOOH!' said the shower snake as he stuck his tail into it. 'TASTES LOOOVLY!' Then he began to greedily suck up the slimy substance.

I grabbed his nozzle head, pointed it out of the window and shouted, *'HEY, EVERYONE! I'VE FOUND DELORES'S HIDDEN BISCUIT STASH!'*

Immediately, there was a **tremendous rumbling** as all the monsters in the **street** below (including Delores) left their hiding places and *rushed* towards the surgery's entrance.

'HIT IT, SPURTIE!' I yelled, and the shower snake began to rain **ЯEVERSITALL** all over Lovecraft Avenue.

The barrel was barely empty before the eyeballs of every monster in the street started **spinning** in opposite directions. When the ear-smoking phase began, Lovecraft Avenue became **completely engulfed in smoke.** The only things still visible were the tops of **lamp posts** and Oswalt Sadbottom's damp comb-over.

By the time I got down the stairs and back outside, the **smoke** was clearing and even the massed nasal whining was coming to an end.

Simon Salamander was back to his usual healthy pinky-green. Vlad and Vladness were spitting out the remains of **celery from their teeth.** Even Oswalt Sadbottom's legs seemed to be approximately the same length again. From what I could tell, everyone was completely healed of their nasty **FIXITALL** side-effects!

Even Delores.

Her face was back to being as **dark** and **threatening** as the **inside of a troll's ear canal.** She brandished her empty biscuit tin in one tentacle and a large collection of **unwashed mugs** in the other seven. 'All my special biscuits gone! All this washing-up to do! Blooming patients! The doctor should snip off their limbs and *superglue* them back on in completely the wrong places. She should peel off their tentacled tips and dip them in **salt-and-vinegar crisps.** She should . . . Why are you smiling?' she snapped at me.

I patted her on the nearest tentacle. 'Because it's so nice to have you back to normal, Delores,'

I said, and she was so confused that she *slithered*
away without saying anything rude.

The doctor and I watched as the last of the
patients wandered off, heading back to their
houses, caves, graves and **coffins.**

'Well done, Ozzy!' said the doctor. 'And no doubt
they'll all be back tomorrow with their in-growing
eyeballs, scarlet weasel-measles and broken
tongues that need urgent splinting . . .'

She broke off and smiled at me. 'I should have listened to you, Ozzy. There'll never be a cure for all illness. The answer for monster maladies is medicine – not magic!'

We stepped back into the surgery. 'Still, we mustn't grumble.' She laughed. 'I actually got to meet Gorgonzilla! **Now run along and fetch me** a number twenty-seven needle and thread.'

'What for?' I asked.

'Have you forgotten Morty, Nurse Ozzy?' she chided. 'He's still in a collection of *carrier bags* in reception. I'll go and ask him where his missing right leg is, and then together we'll **STITCH** up your **clumsy zombie friend.'**

THE END

GORGONZILLA

PRIVATE BOX FOR TWO MONSTERS (OR ORDINARIES)

KAIJU PRODUCTIONS

INVITES YOU TO THE PREMIERE
OF AN EARTH-SHATTERING NEW WORK

BY AWARD-WINNING COLOSSO-CHOREOGRAPHER

RODANO!

STARRING

GORGONZILLA & MILLICENT MOTH

[Date & Venue To Be Confirmed]

GLOSSARY

Acne: A healthy layer of angry sores covering up the unpleasant face of a young human. One of the few times that monsters don't find humans completely disgusting to look at.

Bell-bug: Small monsters who communicate with each other by clanging their hard metal shells. Bell-bug species come in different musical keys and can therefore be played together as a charming musical instrument. Sadly, as F# & Bb bell-bugs are now extinct, the bell-bug musical repertoire has become somewhat limited.

Celebrity: A term used to describe a human being who is well known for having the amazing ability to be well known.

Compulsive lurkivitus: An affliction that causes monsters to feel an overwhelming desire to conceal themselves in ridiculous spaces and snigger quietly at their friends or family. If your relative is missing, try the loft, the space beneath the bed or the back of the wardrobe behind the outdoor coats. Failing that, just open a large box of chocolates noisily, and wait.

Executive: A highly prized job in the human world. The job title denotes that an employee is so good at their job that they no longer have to do it.

Fender rot (also known as bumper rot): An unpleasant mould that spoils the shiny parts of inter-dimensional vehicles. It can be caught by frequenting unsanitary garages or through the revolting practice of swapping hubcaps with strangers.

Flatulence: One of the most moving musical art forms ever devised.

Grandpa: An elderly human male. Easily identifiable as they have removed most of their head hair and inserted it forcibly into their ear and nasal cavities. No one knows why they do this.

Homework: A particularly cruel and unusual human torture technique involving large amounts of paper and small sharpened sticks.

'I Left My Heart in Your Bedside Cabinet': A slow and tender ballad from the legendary monster singer Awreatha Fangling. She was better known for her more up-tempo hits such as 'Stalking After Midnight' and 'Radio Gaaargh-Gaaargh'.

Manicure: A human process that is quite similar to the monster practice of claw-sharpening. One major difference is that in the human version manicurists are very rarely eaten by their dissatisfied customers.

Mega-Jenga: The rules are the same as the popular human party game Jenga. But a monster Mega-Jenga block is 50 feet long, made of concrete and weighs over 200 tonnes. The game requires any of the following: teamwork, very large muscles or access to heavy construction machinery.

Modern monster ballet: Traditional monster ballet has easily understandable plots full of romance, tragedy and the thrill of stamping large buildings flat. Modern monster ballet, however, claims these are 'cliches' and favours the dancers looking serious while standing on one leg or tentacle and wearing a brightly coloured, ill-fitting leotard. It is not very popular.

Mr Woffell: An unusually talented teacher at Ozzy's School. Mr Woffell has the incredible ability of being able to talk about any subject, for any length of time, without either breathing or communicating any useful information at all.

Patient riot: These are usually caused by long waiting times, extremely rude receptionists and desperate hunger caused by broken vending machines. Fortunately, most patient riots end quite quickly. Especially since sleeping-gas sprinklers became a common feature of doctors' surgeries.

Salad: Vegetables that you can eat. As opposed to vegetables that can eat you. See: Triffids, Razor Radishes and Spring-loaded Onions.

Tartan: Centuries ago, the Scottish people decided that it was far too confusing to have to choose between fabric with a spotted, striped or diagonal pattern. So they replaced all three patterns with a single new one: the Tartan!

Unfortunately, people immediately began to modify the original design. As a consequence, there are now approximately 18,694,290 different tartans.

Daily Fang: The most popular vampire newspaper. It has a winning combination of sharp incisive journalism, biting commentary and an excellent recipe section. A much easier read than its worthy (but rather dull) rival *The Whole Tooth*.

XXXmas party: Once a year, sensible monsters gather together beneath damp bridges, in dark cellars or in their charming Swedish-style open-plan chalets to celebrate *XXX*mas. They drink, eat their least popular relatives and pass the time playing traditional games like Pasta-parcel, Blind Monster's Huff and Table Pong-pong.

Turn the page to read an exclusive extract from

Ozzy and the doctor's next hilarious adventure

the

MONSTER DOCTOR

Foul Play

It will have you laughing your head off!

GHASTLY COLOUR COMBINATION

Chapter 1

I had just turned the corner into Lovecraft Avenue when a head-sized object came *flying* through the air towards me. Without thinking, I caught it. Then I peered down and realised that it wasn't just 'head-sized'.

It actually was a head.

A **scruffy, smelly** and **smiley head** with a friendly face that I recognised at once.

'Hello Morty!' I said. 'Where's the rest of you today?'

My friend Morty is a **Level-1 registered dead person** (or a zombie to you) and therefore his arms, legs, eyeballs and belly buttons are only attached to each other with **MY DODGY STITCHING,** or lashings, of *ICBINS super-glue.*

'Oh! Hello Ozzy!' Morty replied, grinning up at me with his **gap-toothed mouth**. 'Never mind that now. What a lovely catch! **Bravo!** I didn't know you were playing.'

'Playing what?' I asked, confused.

I should note here that one of the reasons Morty's body parts are often in several places at once is because he's always felt that being dead shouldn't get in the way of his sporting hobbies. He plays *mugball* (Monster rugby), **zombie football, mixed monster martial arts**

(MMMA) and – on one memorable but catastrophic occasion – he even went **bungee-jumping.**

'Why, we're playing **Monsterball** of course!' Morty laughed. 'Surely you know that today is the Dimension 3 Monsterball Championship finals?'

I looked at him blankly. As I always do whenever anyone mentions human sports like Kickball, Basket-hoop or Runny-Jump-thing. I forget their names. So, I'm sorry if I've given you the impression that I'm not a big fan of sports.

It shouldn't be an impression.

I'm as fond of human sports as I am of **scraping the cheese out from between a troll's toes.** So monster sports couldn't be

any better.

'Never mind,' continued Morty, 'a few of us thought we'd celebrate *cup final day* by having a nice friendly amateur game here in Lovecraft Avenue.'

'Who is 'we'?' I asked. But the words were barely out of my mouth before there was **a loud roar** and **a mob of hideously ugly monsters** charged out of the alleyway that runs down the side of that new ghoul fashion boutique, **'DIG-IT!'**

I wasn't frightened. You see being **'hideously ugly'** is completely normal for monsters. And after spending the summer working for the monster doctor, the sight of *slobbering jaws,* **razor-sharp horns** and **quivering eye-stalks** isn't any more frightening than my Granny Freda's *sherry & lavender flavoured moustache.*

The mob all sported scarves with the same ghastly colour combination: **Rabid Red and Yahoo Yellow stripes.** I recognised regular patients like **Bob the Blob,** who was slithering rapidly along in a thick slick of his own **snot.** There was Mr Gillman, a swamp creature who'd recently moved into one of the new super-damp basement flats beneath the **snake-grooming parlour.** And at the head of the mob was the **fifteen stone of thrashing tentacles, temper and tasteless knitwear** that was Delores, the charmless receptionist from the monster doctor's surgery.

Before we go any further, I should probably let you know that Delores once scored ⎯⎯ on the **inter-dimensional standardised monster grumpiness test.** Which is pretty amazing since the test only goes up to 10.

So you can imagine exactly how I felt when she pointed a **quivering tentacle** in my direction

and bellowed – in a voice like a T. Rex auditioning for the role of an evil pirate captain in a pantomime –

'AWFUL ALL-STARS! ATTACK!'

The mob of monsters following her roared in response and charged straight at me.

'Morty,' I said, as calmly as I could manage in the circumstances, 'why are Delores and those patients charging at me?'

Morty grinned. 'They're not charging at you, Ozzy.' And before I could check whether his eyes had fallen out again (they often do) he added, **'They're charging at ME!'**

'Ah!' I said. As if that made the slightest difference. I was, after all, currently holding him. 'Is there any particular reason why?' I was hoping that he'd come up with an answer that didn't include us both ending up as **flat as Lucy Liverwort** when she got caught in the *triple-chocolate-toffee cake* **stampede** in the school canteen last year. Tragic.

'Like I said,' my zombie friend replied, 'we decided to play **Monsterball.** But as the ball said she was feeling a bit sick – someone she ate, apparently – I volunteered to take her place!'

As answers go that clearly wasn't a great deal of help.

Luckily, the monster doctor had taught me to always keep an eye out for a *potential escape route* – a vital skill for any trainee monster doctor. You never know when you'll need a quick getaway from an **angry** or **dissatisfied** patient! So as the **fangs, horns, teeth** and *slobber* of the AWFUL ALL-STARS bore down on me I tucked Morty under my arm and began edging towards an alleyway to my right.

Unfortunately, just as I was about to make a break for it, a second (and equally hideously ugly) **mob of monsters** erupted from that alleyway too.

Oh, super.

This new lot were headed by Vlad, the vampire who runs the all-night convenience store on the corner of Lovecraft Lane and Cushing St. It was made up of his regulars like Colin the Ghoul, Simon Salamander from the **Battered Squid Chippie** and Mrs Stunck, a very nice jellified thing who lives in one of the larger bins round the back of the restaurant.

With the depressing inevitability of a **bad mark in a maths test**, the second mob spotted Morty and howled, **'FANGTON FANTOMS NEVER DIE!'** Then they put their heads down (or whatever passed for a head) and charged straight for us.

Two monster mobs. Me in the middle.

I groaned with disappointment.

It wasn't the **imminent danger**, as such. After all, a typical day as an assistant monster doctor isn't complete without **extreme danger**. For instance, so far this month I'd been **eaten, blown-up, covered in foul-smelling bodily fluids** (most days) and last Wednesday was even carried aloft to an impressive height of 17,000ft in the claws of a **SHORT-SIGHTED DRAGON MOTHER** who mistook me for her **BABY DRAGLING**.

No. I was disappointed because I hadn't even had a chance to sit down and prepare myself for the day with a nice cup of Coughee and a chocolate indigestive!

It was so unfair!

And that was when I was suddenly distracted by a wastepaper bin shouting at me.

TO BE CONTINUED . . .

ACKNOWLEDGEMENTS

Huge thanks are owed to the following
people who helped bring you these silly pages.

My wife, Cathy, whose never-ending
weirdness and unacknowledged acting genius
is the inspiration for 48.3% of the monster
characters. (I'm not telling you who the
other 51.7% are based on.)

Jodie, Emily, Molly and everyone at United
Agents for opening up a whole new dimension
for the monster doctor and Ozzy to explore.

And, finally, Cate, Amanda, Sue, Rachel and
all the amazingly hard-working and talented
people at Macmillan. I couldn't have completed
this book without their calm and creative
support – especially in that final exhausted
push to the finish line.

ABOUT THE AUTHOR

John Kelly is the author and
illustrator of picture books such as
The Beastly Pirates and *Fixer*, the
author of picture books *Can I Join
Your Club* and *Hibernation Hotel*, and
the illustrator of fiction series such
as Ivy Pocket and Araminta Spook.
He has twice been shortlisted for the
Kate Greenaway prize, with *Scoop!*
and *Guess Who's Coming for Dinner*.
The Monster Doctor is his first author-
illustrator middle-grade fiction series.